STILL LIFE

THE RESURRECTION

Second Edition

Published by The Nazca Plains Corporation
Las Vegas, Nevada
2013

EBOOK ISBN: 978-1-61098-000-5
ISBN: 978-1-935509-85-1

Published by

The Nazca Plains Corporation ®
4640 Paradise Rd, Suite 141
Las Vegas NV 89109-8000

PUBLISHER'S NOTE
Still Life is a work of fiction created wholly by *Robin Anderson's* imagination. All
characters are fictional and any resemblance to any persons living or deceased is purely by
accident. No portion of this book reflects any real person or events.

Cover Photos
Mannequin, Petar Lazovic
Film, Robyn Mackenzie
Rat, Karen Hoar

Art Director
Blake Stephens

DEDICATION

For Bob Miller
Memories are Made of This

STILL LIFE

THE RESURRECTION

Second Edition

Robin Anderson

CONTENTS

PROLOGUE

'The winner of tonight's prestigious Golden Phallus award is' – here the smirking presenter paused for added impetus – '*Ethelred Jones* for his documentary, *A Day in the Life of a Turd*!'

A beaming Ethelred Jones, graciously acknowledging the thunderous applause, drew himself up to his rangy full six-foot-five and, giving his equally beaming wife a sly wink, slowly made his way between the whistling and clapping audience towards the podium to claim the coveted reward. The presenter, a minor soap star with a penchant for young boys dressed up as meter maids, eyed the tall, lean, wild-eyed, bearded man with some apprehension. The Charles Manson lookalike film maker was well-known for his acerbic tongue, and even more unpredictable behaviour. Ethelred's blatant public urination onto a can of film at the Godiva Film Festival in Bridlington – he had deemed the film, 'My Tongue in Your Cheeks', both as puerile and lacking in imagination – saw him elevated to the heady heights of an overnight celebrity. No doubt this particular evening's success could easily lead to some even more bizarre behaviour. To the presenter's obvious relief – and the audiences' disappointment – no such behaviour was forthcoming. Instead, Ethelred simply accepted the gold-painted wooden phallus and, having duly thanked the judges for their vote, calmly stepped down from the podium and returned to his table.

'Try that for size!' he chortled, thumping the gleaming gold penis onto the littered table top. 'Surely they could have found a better role model?' Cries of laughter greeted his comment, followed by even louder laughter and several hoots of derision at his punch line. 'I mean, had they asked, I would have happily posed without charging a fee!'

'Maybe they would've run out of plaster of Paris for the mould!' screeched a voluptuous blonde, one of the four guests seated at the table.

'Oh yes? And how would *you* know, Melanie Peebles?' quipped Clytemnestra Jones, Ethelred's beautiful artist wife, an evil smile quickly having replaced the earlier beaming version, playing on her heavily carmine-coloured lips.

'Only joking, Clyte dearest, only joking…' snickered Melanie, delighted at Clytemnestra's innuendo. 'Clyte can be quite terrifying at times' she would endlessly confide to her best friend, Mariana Mayhew, 'one never knows if she's serious or not!' 'Darling! You'd better believe it, that bitch is *always* serious' being Mariana's drawled reply.

'Good,' said Clytemnestra. 'As long as you're only joking and haven't been poking' – she nodded towards her husband – 'you've just saved yourself a fate worse than having your cunt stitched!' She leaned across to clasp a grinning Ethelred's long, bony hirsute hand. 'Congratulations, husband, lover, stud!' Giving the gaping Melanie a lewd wink she added. 'Rest assured, Melanie, I'll be sticking to the original model or – to put it in laymans terms – the original can happily keep sticking me!'

More laughter followed the gaily-enunciated comment, while a momentarily panic-stricken Melanie gave vent to several hysterical, relieved shrieks. A smiling, blond, fey and extraordinarily beautiful, sashaying, willowy young waiter suddenly materialised carrying a magnum of Dom Perignon champagne. 'Compliments of the management,' he said in a soft, camp voice, smiling winsomely at Ethelred. 'And may I say, Mr. Jones, I simply *adored* your film.' the compliment being accompanied by a fluttering of dyed eyelashes and a *moue* by a pair of perfect cupid bow-lips.

'Did you now?' said Ethelred giving the blushing young beauty a predatory smile. He glanced at his wife who sat regarding him and the captivating, willowy waiter with amusement; her smile having now switched from evil laser to a whimsical, flirtatious twitching. 'What do you say, Clyte; a possible candidate for a future film?'

'Oh, Mr. *Jones*!' breathed the young man, the magnum wobbling dangerously above the table in his trembling hands. 'Would you?'

'I'm sure he would if he could, but leave *me* your name and number,' smiled Clytemnestra. 'I'll put you on file.' With a 'cat-that's-got-the-cream-look' she couldn't resist adding, 'I always have to warn aspiring young men of your persuasion Mr. Jones is a "proper front bum" guy, so it'll be a bona fide audition and not a *boner* fide one!' She turned to the other guests. 'One finds talent in the most unexpected places,' she added, elegantly putting up a hand to steady the wildly shaking magnum. 'Whoa, steady Neddy! I'm not into golden showers, albeit a champagne one! Help me out here, Ethelred! The glorious, golden sprite is about to splash!'

'Almost a case of *tails* of the unexpected at times!' snickered her husband, stretching out his long arm and clutching both the bottle plus the young man's hands. Nodding in the direction of the now furiously blushing youth's spectacular derriere, he widened his dark eyes as he quickly flicked his long, wet pink tongue in and out lasciviously between his thin, bearded lips.

'I saw that!' screeched Melanie, eyeing the young man's pert, mini melon-like buttocks stretched obscenely against his black serge trousers, 'Typical Ethelred humour! Tails as in arses, ha ha! Did you get that, Clyte?'

'I'm not too keen on it in the tail, Melanie,' replied her hostess acidly, swiveling round to fix the unfortunate woman with a second laser-like stare. 'But, from what we hear, you're somewhat of an expert in *those* quarters!' Diverting her attention from the duly rebuffed woman back to the mesmerised young waiter who, having finished pouring the champagne, was standing by breathlessly hanging onto Clytemnestra's every word, she added with a dazzling smile from her endless repertoire well-versed facial acrobatics, "What is your name, young man?'

'Oswald, ma'am,' stammered the young waiter.

'Oswald?' Ethelred gave a whoop of mirth. He smiled conspiratorially at his wife. 'Do you remember that mad film we shot in South Africa, Clyte? The one on the ostrich farm at that way out place, Oudtshoorn or something like that?'

'Of course I do, stoker of my rapacious fires! "Oswald the Arse-stretch" you called it; such a misleading title. Everyone expected to see a series of poor ostriches being buggered by those well hung, randy black farmhands, whereas it was all about making the biggest possible omelette using an ostrich egg!'

'Yes,' laughed Ethelred. 'The omelette had to be made on a sheet of iron placed over an open fire…'

'And the result?' the question coming from Peter Peebles, Melanie's husband and Ethelred's accountant, a plump, smirking, self-satisfied bald-headed man who referred to himself as Etheldred's 'financial guru.' Someone had once described him as the poor man's Kojak, a comment having gone – literally – to Peter's bald head.

'A three foot overall omelette and the equivalent of twenty plus eggs.'

'That's some arse-stretch,' guffawed Peter.

'And how many sperm eggs can you produce, when asked to fill a plate, Peter?' quipped Clytemnestra giving Melanie a conspiratorial wink.

Melanie choked into her champagne flute.

'I think we should be going, dear,' said Ethelred, glancing at his watch and giving his wife another adoring look. 'Although Trisomy is with the capable Charles, she does become panicky if we're later than usual getting home.'

'How *is* little Trisomy?' shrilled Melanie, her nerves more strung out than usual at the rapidly deteriorating level of the conversation.

'As well as can be expected,' said Clytemnestra, a slight catch in her voice. She smiled bravely at the quickly readjusted, and therefore suitably solemn-faces around the table – Trisomy and her wellbeing were sensitive subjects at any time – 'But, we soldier on, don't we, Ethelred dearest?'

'We do what we have to do,' answered her husband, equally as solemnly. He looked around unwaveringly at the decidedly uncomfortable guests. 'Though it may be difficult for the majority of you to understand, both Clyte and I feel *blessed* with our little girl, our little Trisomy.' He lifted his award from the centre of the table and, giving a sardonic smile, added, 'She'll enjoy playing with this alongside her favourite Ken and Barbie!'

'To Trisomy!' Melanie suddenly cried, grasping for her champagne flute.

'To Trisomy,' echoed Ethelred, waving the golden phallus in the air.

'To Trisomy,' murmured the rest of the guests as Clytemnestra, wiping an imaginary tear from her porcelain-white cheek, clasped her husband's long, muscular raised arm.

'My details,' whispered Oswald sibilantly, choosing the rather inappropriate moment to press a crumpled part from the evening's special menu into Clytemnestra's hand. He watched with added fascination as the lady in question lightly dabbed her eyes with his 'personal details,' prior to stuffing the information down between her shapely breasts. Blinking bravely, Clytemnestra whispered seductively, her mouth taking on the mode of a femme fatale. 'Thank you Arse Stretch. Trisomy and especially our conscientious carer, Charles, along with Ken, Barbie and now her daddy's award, will all *adore* playing with you! Whatever means of intercourse you've written down we'll be in touch on the morrow.' She fluttered her long lashes seductively. 'Ethelred's correct as always. Wonderful, *wonderful* contours... your cheek bones and your cheeks...'

'So noble... so *brave*,' murmured Melanie, her eyes squinting in the direction of the departing couple. 'Such a sad story, a tragedy really,' she hiccupped discreetly.

'That it is, that it is,' agreed her husband unsuccessfully attempting to hide a belch, as opposed to his wife's daintily disguised hiccup.

'What *is* the story?' This from Belinda Bartholomew who, with her husband Freddie, ran the 'Over The Rainbow Dance Studio', a tribute to their golden heyday when known on the professional ballroom dancing circuit as the Bandana Bartholmews. Dressed as gypsies and wearing sequinned bandanas, Belinda and Freddie had stunned the public with their erotically, explicit tango. The Bartholomews had met Clytemnestra when they had been guests of the Peebles at the review opening of Clytemnestra's much lauded and equally derided art exhibition charmingly titled 'Secretions'.

'Melanie, the story, dear?' repeated Belinda, frowning slightly at her embarrassed-looking friend.

Melanie gave her equally uncomfortable-looking husband a questioning look.

'Go ahead, dear,' Peter said encouragingly as he reached for the bottle in the ice bucket; Oswald, his mission accomplished, having quietly disappeared. Handing his wife a replenished flute, he nodded encouragingly. 'We are,' he added softly, 'among friends.'

Melanie took a long sip. 'Clytemnestra and Ethelred, their ambitions as artists of perfection already fulfilled, had another major ambition which, up until about ten years ago, remained unfulfilled. They planned to create a perfect child, a son. A son they planned to call Tristan, as in, 'Tristan and Isolde...' Melanie's voice faltered.

'Go on,' murmured Belinda, touching her friend lightly on the arm.

'To their great delight, Clyte – after a scan – was told she was having twins, a boy and a girl. She and Ethelred were ecstatic, Tristan would have his Isolde and they all would live happily ever after.' She paused for another sip. 'Oh dear,' she whispered, 'this is the part that makes me want to cry. Of course, we only *heard* about Clyte's pregnancy. We were abroad for the whole time, Peter handling that extraordinary financial scandal in Hong Kong involving several banks, one of them...'

'The story dear, the Jones story, not the banks,' interrupted Peter, his bland forehead creasing with irritation and causing a further ripple of wrinkles on his bald pate.

'Excuse me, but as I said, I do get somewhat emotional!' sniped Melanie, giving her husband a reprimanding look. 'To cut a long story short, the twins were born but the boy, Tristan, died a few hours later.'

'Oh my God!' Belinda pressed her hand to her mouth. 'But there was, is, still Trisomy… an extraordinary name if I may say so.'

'You may, indeed,' cut in Peter, who never liked not being the centre of attention for more than a few moments, especially when those moments involved his wife's meanderings. 'Clyte and Ethelred decided that the little girl should still be named Isolde but with the TR of their deceased son's name added to hers in memory.'

'How macabre,' muttered Freddie.

'Obviously Trisolde, after a time – the little girl was a quick learner and speaking by the age of two – became known as Tris.' Melanie gave a sad, slightly drunken smile. 'Little Tris's favourite expression, when addressing her devoted mother, was to chirrup "kiss Tris mommy," so it was only natural this would see her parents, in return, starting to call her Trisomy.'

'But how weird,' Belinda gave a shrug. 'Correct me if I'm wrong, but aren't I missing something here? Isn't trisomy another word for Down's Syndrome?'

'Exactly!' said Melanie triumphantly, 'But it gets worse, if that is humanly possible. No, make that *inhumanly,* given the circumstances. Not only was the poor child given such a cruel and unfortunate name, she also suffers from a hideous affliction: Progeria!'

'Progeria?'

'Yes, dear, Progeria, or in laymans terms, premature ageing. Trisomy may only be ten or thereabouts but she looks sixty!'

'Oh my God!' gasped Belinda and Freddie in unison.

'Clyte and Ethelred and their wonderful nurse, Charles, are so brave with her. Poor little thing is a terrifying sight. She's bald, wizened, hideously wrinkled, lost most of her teeth and has only a few more years to live.'

'Oh my *God*!' this again from Belinda and Freddie who – still seated – were clutching each other as if about to break into a torrid tango.

Peter Peebles, well and truly into his cups and suitably impressed with their friends' reaction, felt compelled to top Melanie's grim disclosures. Leaning forward conspiratorially he couldn't resist the genetic gesture of tapping his large, hooked, Jewish nose. 'For all the emotion, those crocodile tears and the toasting to "Little Trisomy" tonight, the Joneses are no fools. Anticipating the poor child's imminent death, the two are working on a major, combined effort, involving Clytemnestra's skill as a bacterial artist and Ethelred's skill as a film maker. I've heard hints of a cartoon film made up of characters created from Trisomy's bodily functions and items such as hair, nails and the odd tooth.

'Apparently the nurse has been saving clippings and such, knowing the most basic bodily wastes will still be available until the inevitable. Teeth and hair have been saved over the years.'

'That's *grotesque!*' gasped Belinda with a shudder. 'Why, it even makes Tim Burton look saintly!'

'When is this film due to be made?' This from a shocked Freddie; his and Belinda's arm unconsciously stretched out in what appeared to be a combined, Nazi-style salute.

'That is the sixty-thousand-dollar question,' said Peter, his fleshy mouth twitching. 'Put it this way, "Project Progeria"' – he couldn't resist a slight snigger – 'may remain on hold as long as there is *still life!*'

'Oh Peter, *really*!' snorted Melanie, her bonhomie quickly restored by her husband's light-hearted attempt to change the downside mood which had descended on the four. She smiled brightly, 'As Peter says, if there is *still life*' – she gave a nervous titter – 'we may be spared little Trisomy's tribute for another year or two.' She raised her flute. 'To Trisomy, long may she wrinkle!'

'Oh *Mel,* that's so wicked!' squeaked Belinda. Not to be outdone she raised her glass. 'To Trisomy, long may she grow old disgracefully!'

'To Trisomy,' guffawed Freddie. 'Old before her time, bless her!'

'To Trisomy,' toasted Peter. 'Or Project Progeria. Long may that be on hold while there is *still life* left in the old child!' the raucous laughter following his callous remark causing a few curious diners' heads to turn.

'Oh Peter,' trilled Melanie, 'mark my words, you and your humour will be the *death* of me!'

———

'Charles? Ossy! We're on. She's taken my details – stuffed them well down in between her much-touched tits! – still, better there than in her knickers I suppose!' Oswald gave a high-pitched giggle. 'I think they both fell for the arse twitching trick. She was quick to say he wasn't interested but you could tell both *were*! Randy sods! What's that? Yes, she's going to contact me so... oh, I'm sure she will. From what you tell me, I sound right up both their alleys! As you suggested, we'll leave it for a day or two... and then, next step, Operation Trisomy.' He paused, listening to Charles's reply. 'Oh, once we're there together, Charlie boy,' continued Oswald. 'Little Trisomy, plus her mummy and daddy will be putty – or in dear little ailing Tris's case *potty* – in our hands!' He couldn't resist a snigger. 'Yes, I *know* there's a problem with little Tris, you *have* explained all to me. And yes, I'm braced for a bit of a shock, if not a terrible one!' Oswald listened for a few moments longer. 'Yes, Charlie boy, I've got the message loud and clear. See you on the morrow, lover!' Blowing a kiss into his mobile, he clicked off.

'A *very* successful evening, young Os!' said the smirking young man out loud to nobody – and nothing – in particular. Rummaging into his backpack, tossed carelessly down on the threadbare carpeting alongside him, Oswald pulled out a regular-sized bottle of Dom Perignon – courtesy of the reception – and made his way to the kitchenette of his small bedsit. Taking a wine glass – courtesy of his part-time work place, a Balans restaurant – Oswald quickly filled it with the sparkling liquid. 'Here's to a glorious future to you and me, Charlie boy!' he murmured, toasting his fuzzy, devastatingly pretty reflection in the glass of the kitchen cabinet door. 'Rather like Adonis admiring his reflection in the pool of water,' he mused. 'Here's to you, me and Trisomy, the world's most twisted triumvirate!'

CHAPTER 1

Present Day

'Charles? We're back! Charles?'

'Here, Clyte, back in the kitchen with Tris… she demanded an iced lolly!'

'An iced lolly at this time of night? Naughty, *naughty* Tris Tris!'

Charles, a thin angular man, balding and with what could only be described as a permanently bewildered expression, looked up at Clytemnestra as she entered the large, thoroughly modernistic kitchen, an antithesis to the exterior of the Jones mansion, a converted Gothic-style edifice of an almost hideous exquisiteness. He jutted his pointed chin in the direction of the child in question who looked up with a glare, gave a small grunt and went on spooning and noisily swallowing a turgid, yellow-coloured ice cream from a bright red bowl. Reaching forward to wipe a dribble of the yellow goo from the little girl's wrinkled chin, Charles added with a wink, 'It won't be long. I've laced the ice cream with Amitriptyline, a mild sedative… well, not too mild. She should be out in a minute or two… ah, there she goes!' He put out a bony hand to catch Trisomy as her brown, kernel-like eyelids began to flutter and her small bald head fell forward.

'What's she doing up so late and why the ice cream?' this from Ethelred who had followed his wife into the kitchen.

'I caught her doing the usual,' responded Charles, a grimace of distaste accompanied by a bony shrug. 'Unable to sleep; she was down here and had clambered up onto one of the stools in an attempt to reach the cupboard where cook keeps the cooking sherry and brandy! You know her penchant for one or the other; the sherry being her preferred tipple!'

'Shit!' Ethelred gave a grinning Clytemnestra and an equally grinning Charles a glare. 'It's not fucking funny. Since Madam Trisomy discovered the joys of alcohol, it's become a mind game as to where to put the stuff.' He gave a sigh. 'I take it the booze cabinets in the study and drawing room haven't been tampered with?'

'No, Red, they're fine and again, I made doubly sure the doors to both of your studios and the wine cellar is locked.' He gave a light laugh as he lent over and kissed the softly snoring child's wrinkled forehead. 'But we forgot the kitchen cupboards, didn't we, little Tris? Who's a clever, messed-up baba then? Christ!' He looked at the parents in mock alarm, 'The vodka and champagne in the ice cabinet!'

'Oh, lay off it, Charles,' said Clytemnestra irritably, stifling a yawn. 'You know she's been terrified of the ice cabinet ever since she inadvertently crawled in there one Sunday, and Monday didn't pay any attention to her muffled screams for an hour or so before letting her out!' She looked with distaste as Charles stood and swept the tiny, snoring figure into his arms. Trisomy, between a snore, a sniffle and a dribble, let out a loud fart.

'Charming,' said her father, 'she gets more adorable by her final hour.'

'I'll go and put her down,' murmured Charles, making his way towards the main door.

'If only,' muttered Clytemnestra.

'Now now,' remonstrated her husband from where he was standing by the aforesaid ice cabinet, about to reach for a bottle of champagne. 'You know you really *adore* our little treasure!'

'Perhaps, at times, it would be better is she was *buried* treasure, Ethelred dearest!'

'Now mummy dearest, that wasn't very charitable of you.' Ethelred gave a laugh as he opened the champagne and poured three flutes taken from Trisomy's recently assaulted cupboard. 'As the saying goes, charity begins in the home.'

'In our case, Ethelred dear, shouldn't that be *hospice?* Ah, Charles, back again. The Sleeping Beauty well and truly smothered under the duvet?'

'Right up to her precocious, wrinkled, pug-like nose!' replied Charles with a snicker.

'You make her sound more adorable by the minute,' laughed her father. Ethelred looked up at the other man from where he was seated.

Gesturing at the third, brim-full flute, he added, 'Help yourself and sit down, we have a lot to discuss. I just happen to have had a corker of – no, make that a *genius* – of an idea!' He looked around the cavernous kitchen as if searching for someone. 'Is Monday about?'

'Well, he's obviously not here, *dear,*' said Clytemnestra sarcastically. 'I appreciate Monday's black – ha ha – but as opposed to lurking in the shadows, I expect he's in his flat.' She took an appreciative sip from her glass. 'Is it vital for him to be around so as to hear this *genius* of an idea? It's already after two in the morning in case you mayn't have noticed; so why the urgency?'

'Shall we say the heady triumph of this evening has got the gonads going, Clyte dearest? That, plus the determination of one pushy young man; now there's casting couch fodder, if ever.' He turned to Charles. 'Well done Charles, obviously you haven't lost any of your bedside manner skills!' Ethelred gave the smirking man an evil smile. 'See if Monday's still awake, would you Charles? If he is, ask him to join us. If he isn't, wake the bugger!'

'As sire commands,' answered Charles rising to his feet and loping his way from the kitchen.

'My God at last!' Clytemnestra reached across and squeezed Ethelred's long, bony hand. 'Tell me, is this what I think it is?'

Ethelred gave a nod and a sly smile, covering his wife's hand with his other and squeezing it with equal fondness.

'You *divinity!*' Crooned Clytemnestra, 'And before I forget...' Fumbling down the front of her dress, Clytemnestra pulled out the crumpled piece of torn off menu. 'Eager little arse-stretch couldn't wait to give me, us, his peculiars' – she couldn't resist a chortle at her choice of word – 'and I bet you a blow job – or pussy suck – our little eager beaver' – a snigger this time – 'has already been on the blower – get it? – to our Charles. And to answer that question, *both* our comrades in charms are here!'

'I found him sitting on one of Clone Zone's biggest, black vibrators and watching 'Chicken Shed', camped Charles as he came through the door closely followed by a large shadowy figure.

'Bullshit,' rumbled Monday, the Jones's Man Friday, a giant black man who had moved alongside Charles and stood beaming at his employees, a pair of loose white boxer shorts doing little to obscure his own massive, black vibrator. 'If I'd wanted to sit on anything big and black, I'd sit on myself,' he added, his broad smile becoming even broader. 'Who needs a vibrator when you've your own Monday monster?'

'Well, sit yourself and your monster down, and listen.' Ethelred gestured towards the ice cabinet. 'As you're standing Charles, another bottle would not go amiss. Monday? Champagne for you or something else?'

'Rum 'n Coke'll do me!' The big black man smiled at Charles. 'I'll get it and let me get the champagne. You sit, Dr. Charles, after all you've been busily at it playing nursey all night.'

'Too true,' laughed Charles. 'It's heavy work doping a defenceless old crone!'

'That Charles, was quite uncalled for and not worthy of you!' reprimanded Clytemnestra.

'May I suggest Monday gets the fucking drinks and you all sit down, shut the fuck up, and listen to what the fuck I have to say?' cried Ethelred irritably, his handsome forehead creasing into a frown.

'I can't see any *fucking* reason why not!' giggled his wife. 'So, fuck away, Ethelred. We're ready!'

'To quote a certain clansman of Monday's, I too have a dream, a wonderful *wet* dream *mes enfants!* Gather ye round whilst Daddy Ethelred enthrals you!'

'Before you enthral us,' added Charles camply, 'I couldn't help but overhear your last comment about Oswald and yes, the little bugger has been on the phone. It was easier than I thought. The young hopeful is such a star fucker – he fell for my suggestion – hook, line and blinker!'

'Very witty Charles and well done. Even though the response is a bit premature, our little arse-stretch is certainly keen… quite a coincidence really.' Ethelred blinked rapidly and gave the three a bright smile. 'However Clyte dear, it's not so much "Adonis in Reflection" I'm talking about.' Giving his wife an anxious look as her expression darkened, he reached across the black laminated table taking Clytemnestra's hand in his, giving it a reassuring squeeze. 'What I'm about to propose could – no, make that will – *will* include "Adonis in Reflection." In fact, there is no reason for us not going ahead immediately, hand in hand as it were, now we've found your Adonis.'

Ethelred playfully waggled a long, bony admonishing finger at a visibly relaxing Clytemnestra. 'Never let it be said, precious heart, your Ethelred is ever the unready! Instead, let the *ever* ready Ethelred whet *all* our salacious appetites by saying there's much, much more to it.' He gave an even broader smile, a combination of lasciviousness and amusement. 'Think, dearest Clyte, think of your Adonis, his reflection and further adulation. Think Charles and Monday; think of mutual satisfaction, mutual benefit and mutual stimulation! All of which will now be achievable thanks to my brilliant, no, make that positive, *genius* of perception!' Ethelred gave a dry chuckle. 'Shall I go on?'

'As you always do Red darling; my most maddening of darlings! So why change a lifelong habit now?' Clytemnestra gave a throaty laugh. 'Pray continue for – as you can see – we're all agog, gasping and positively *gagging* for the punch line to end *all* punch lines!'

———————

The eye-catching Jones residence, confusingly named 'Bethlem Báthory' by its owners and referred to as 'Castle Dracula' by the neighbours, stood defiantly alone on ten-and-a-half acres of an immaculately tended wooded garden, surrounded by a high, red brick wall in a remote area close to the famous Ascot race-course in Berkshire. A pair of tall, heavy, black painted, electronically controlled wooden gates added further protection – and mystery – to the hidden property from the curious. Built by an eccentric millionaire in the early nineteenth century – Jeremiah Alsop-Jessop, the original owner, had made his fortune out of the manufacture of medical "utility goods" which was another way of saying bedpans, bottles and other necessities for the more intimate bodily functions – the house was a splendid mishmash of towers, parapets and distraught-looking gargoyles. For Clytemnestra and Ethelred, on viewing the derelict property several years back, it had been a case of – to quote Clytemnestra – 'Love at first fright!'

The love had never diminished but had developed into what could only be described as an obscene passion. Visitors to 'Bethlem Báthory' were kept to a select few. When questioned about the strange name for their home, both owners would refer blithely to their eccentric life style. Clytemnestra would smile adoringly at her husband and murmur in her low contralto voice, 'My husband is so gloriously talented and so gloriously insane, so why not 'Bethlem?' – the original fourteenth century name for what was later to become Bedlam – the notorious and brutal mental hospital!' With an added laugh she would deliver her final witticism. 'In the eighteenth century, people could pay a penny to "view the freaks of Bedlam," whereas nowadays they pay slightly more to visit the cinema to view one of my husband's equally as freakish films!'

Ethelred's response to his wife's explanation was equally as compelling. Affectionately stroking his wife's long, thin hand he would add his own dissertation. 'When I first met Clyte, not only was I drawn to her extraordinary beauty, warmth and intelligence, but also to her immense and highly original talent as an artist. Who else had ever before taken the very essentials, the very spirit of the human form and converted it to art? Nobody until Clytemnestra with her genius came onto the scene.' Here he would pause for effect before continuing. 'Who else would take the most basic bodily secretions such as saliva, blood, tears and semen; yes even my semen has been immortalised, not only via our dear child Trisomy, but in Clytemnestra's magnificent paintings, which will endure for centuries to come!'

Ethelred's final disclosure to rival his wife's witticism apropos his films was equally as bizarre. 'Think only of the Countess Elizabeth Báthory, a Fifteenth century Austrian countess otherwise known as "The Bloody Lady of Csejte". Her secret for eternal youth, for *immortality*, was to bathe in the blood of young virgins she ritually killed. Forget your Bradys and Hindleys; forget your Jack the Rippers and your Ted Bundys; Elizabeth Báthory was the greatest serial killer ever. Now it's Clytemnestra's turn! But *her* immortality – her eternal youth – is from the *living*, a turnabout Elizabeth Báthory. Hence "Báthory" being used as a fitting tribute to the birthplace of her geniuses! Welcome therefore to "Bethlem Báthory!"'

The bewildered visitor would then be given the 'Grand Tour' which in itself was equally as confusing. While a frantic confusion of Gothic-style on the exterior, the interior of 'Bethlem Báthory' was pure twenty-first century minimalistic. Ethelred, working hand in hand with a disgraced architect friend Hank Floyd-Blight, who had been blackballed for his notorious disregard on safety regulations for a series of buildings he had designed to house asylum seekers, guaranteed by a regularly stoned Hank to be as safe as 'the houses Jack built.' Dozens of these illegal residents had been subjected to collapsing ceilings and unfortunate electrocutions, curtailing their need for asylum. Ethelred and Hank, with endless time and money at their disposal, had created a sleek masterpiece of the latest materials and electronic devices available. A click of the fingers could control the lighting; a wave of the hand could open and close doors.

Hank, his swan song duly completed, emigrated to Namibia – where it was said he was planning to build the biggest air-conditioned sand castle incorporating several massive inland dunes; the piéce de résistance being a glass-domed swimming pool surrounded by a lush profusion of exotic plants and caged jungle animals – 'My very own Okavango-styled oasis!' according to Hank.

The finished mansion comprised of two massive studios, an editing and filming studio for Ethelred along with a laboratory and paint studio for Clytemnestra. Apart from the studios, there were the main living quarters consisting of a 'penthouse-style sitting room,' a study, the main bedroom suite, Trisomy's nursery suite and three guest suites. A small gymnasium, an indoor pool and cinema, the aforesaid kitchen and a massive wine cellar, completed the owner's private living area.

Charles and Monday resided in their equally splendid quarters, each with their own sitting room, en suite bedroom and kitchenette. Both units, set in one of the several turrets, also boasted a small roof terrace.

The employment of both Charles and Monday was as clandestine as the intrigue surrounding 'Bethlem Báthory.'

Charles Conrad Crosby, M.D., was a former doctor surgeon who, due to an indiscretion too many while under the influence of his house special, a 'Conrad Cocktail' – a snort of cocaine followed by a hefty inhalation of amylnitrate – had led to him being 'struck off,' due to inadvertently removing a patient's testicles instead of performing a simple hernia operation. Needless to say, the hospital in question was still heavily involved in an ongoing and massive lawsuit. In the ensuing drama over the impending lawsuit, Charles' more discreet practice had been overlooked.

Unknown to his associates, the doctor had been running a lucrative sideline in secret organ donations. Many a cadaver was despatched happily from the hospital mortuary missing a kidney, heart or more. Desperate and destitute Charles, his legal and illegal forms of income curtailed, found himself reduced to working in a local charity bookstore to make ends meet. The money he earned, barely covering the rental of a sordid bedsit in London's equally sordid Earl's Court, plus his regular aptitude for 'Conrad Cocktails,' the despairing man – while laconically searching the shop's website for unusual work offerings – had unsuspectingly come across the Jones's questionable advert for a member of medical fraternity to join their household. Reading between the lines of 'Discreet Private Family Doctor Required – Cerebral and Caring – Must be prepared to Travel,' Charles had, with shrewd insight, correctly translated this into, 'Unscrupulous Doctor Who Can Turn a Blind Eye – Is Suitably Devious and Corrupt – Must Be Prepared for a Quick Getaway!' A further three words in Japanese proved to be the ultimate in seduction.

On meeting with his employers-to-be, Charles had found an instant rapport. Having carefully done his research on the couple, he was well aware that 'Bethlem Báthory' was more Munster House than a simple family home. His introduction to his charge – Charles had been told in the response to his application that there was a daughter with 'emotional problems' who required 'round-the-clock attention' – saw him mentally raising a questioning eyebrow. Being no fool, Charles was prepared to literally overlook his proper diagnosis of the daughter's 'condition' and, as he was later to confide to Monday, 'To go with the flow.' A scowling Trisomy's initial response to Charles was a flicked out tongue and a series of indignant grunts. However – due to Charles immediate response in doing the same in return – saw her initial gesture followed by a toothless grin and a high-pitched giggle. Without further ado, the wrinkled child shuffled around the Rabih Hage coffee-table of recycled-floorboards, and grasped Charles's bony hand in her small, gnarled, spotted one. 'I like Charlie!' she croaked. 'Is Charlie mine to play with?' the question resulting in Clytemnestra and Ethelred to cast the doctor an anxious look. Charles, stooping over a still-grinning Trisomy, glanced up at the anxious couple. Giving a matching grin to the child's – Charles seemed to have taken to duplicating Trisomy's gestures with first the tongue and now the grin – the disgraced surgeon gave a sibilant hiss. 'I think it's safe to say to little Trisomy, Nurse Charles is quite happy to be played with!'

Smiling with relief her parents were able to assure the grinning, scrunched up child that Nurse Charles would hopefully be joining the household and yes, they were sure *Nurse* Charles would be more than happy 'to play.'

'Lovely!' gurgled the drooling little girl. 'Can I show *Nurse* Charles my collection of dead beetles?'

'Later dear, later,' said Clytemnestra patiently. 'Now, go off and see if cook has one of her special chocolate cookies for you. Today's Wednesday remember, and Wednesday is always cookie day!'

Giving another toothless grin, Trisomy shuffled out of the taupe, white and black sitting room towards cook and the kitchen.

'She's sweet,' muttered Charles.

'Bullshit!' retorted her father, 'she's a total nightmare!' Ethelred gave a long sigh followed by a thin smile. 'I can immediately suss out you understand our "little girl" more than most. If you're prepared to accept the position, it's yours.'

'I accept,' Charles said with alacrity. 'But reading between the lines I take it there's more…?'

'We're well aware of your history and your fall from grace.' Clytemnestra cut in, 'And yes, of course there is.' She gave an added, tight-lipped laugh. 'You obviously must have gathered...' – she gave her husband a quick look and on receiving a discreet nod, continued – 'or known something untoward would be in the offing?' Charles dipped his head in agreement. 'Good, when the time is right, we'll take it further; you'll certainly be told when this *something* will be!'

'Well done, verbose, eloquent wife of mine, I couldn't have described it in a more roundabout, complicated and totally spastic manner even with all my genius!' added Ethelred with a sardonic smile. 'And definitely time for a welcome drink!'

Charles moved into Bethlem Báthory the following day. To his amusement, he found Trisomy had left one of her special chocolate cookies on the coffee-table in the sitting room of his tower. On thanking the wizened little creature later for her kind gesture, the given response had been a gurgle of delight followed by a toothless grin and a high pitched fart. 'Trisomy *likes* Charles,' she had growled before fluttering off in her loose fitting multi-coloured shift, her pink, plastic 'Croc' sandals making a squeaking noise on the polished wooden floor.

'And that's what worries me,' whispered Charles to the otherwise empty room.

Having settled in – his unpacking of one small suitcase and its meagre contents having taken only a few minutes – Charles decided to go exploring. On making his way down from the staff turret back into the main part of the house, he ended up in the kitchen where he introduced himself to Mrs. Norelle – a large, formidable, middle-aged, Breughel-like woman whose fearsome, almost Neanderthal looks belied a warm-hearted, earth mother-type soul. The kindly cook had gone out of her way to make 'the doctor' feel welcome, offering him more of what were to become known as 'Tris Treats' – chocolate biscuits – and several cups of steaming *cafe au lait*.

'Goodness!' said Charles, 'At this rate I'll be the Michelin Man give or take a few weeks, Mrs. Norelle!'

'Nonsense!' came the brisk reply. 'Why, you're skin an' bone. Like one of 'em skeletons Mr. Red 'as 'anging as a wind chime in his studio. "Shake, Rattle and Roll" is what 'e calls 'im!'

'A skeleton as a wind chime? Now there's a first!'

'Wait 'til you see some of the stuff Mrs. Clyte puts under that microscope of 'ers. "Sin-spirational" she calls it,' grunted Mrs. Norelle, emphasising her observation with a loud, indelicate sniff through her broad, flat nostrils. 'Do you know doctor,' she added, 'the other day she comes in 'ere, bold as brass, and asks me what I'm preparing for dinner. When I tells 'er it's sweetbreads in a white wine sauce followed by roasted leg of lamb, she promptly nicks a few of them raw starters sayin' – as she leaves me gawkin' – "An ideal inspiration for my new work, *Spring Thymus*."' Mimicking her employer's contralto voice and accent with startling accuracy, the cook continued. 'Thank you *so* much for the heavenly insight Mrs. N; I don't know *what* I did before without you as my sinspiration!" An' before you correct me doctor, that's the very word she used; *sin*spiration.' Imitating Clytemnestra once more Mrs. Norelle added haughtily, 'Remember how *sin*spirational that sliver of sheep's brain was a few months ago? Everybody *loved* my rendition of *Brain Dead*. All those *extraordinary* Pollack-like splashes of colour I was able to indulge in. And the feather effects of those purple and red capillaries… *Exquisite!*'

Before Charles could interrupt the woman's enthusiastic flow, another steel and laminated door leading into the kitchen was flung open. Charles did a double take and immediately fell in lust.

"Evening, Nanette,' said the glorious black man standing in the doorway. He gave a dazzling smile. 'And you must be the doctor.' Speaking in a deep, rich 'Christ, have-I-got-mega-balls-and-you'd-better-believe-it,' bass voice, he held out a giant black hand. 'I'm Monday, the Jones's caretaker, gardener, odd job man. You ask it and I do it!'

'A Man Friday called Monday? I like it!' said Charles weakly, for want of something to say, his eyes caressing Monday's muscular frame glowing like polished ebony from within the confines of a stretched tank top, and a grotesquely bulging pair of well worn, tight fitting jeans, 'With quite a lot of – err, days… in between!' the suggestive comment slipping out unintentionally.

'Oh yes,' laughed Monday, not missing a beat. 'A great deal, if you catch my drift!'

'Before you two drift away with all yer fancy talk, what can I get you, Monday? The doctor's 'aving a milky coffee and I'm 'aving a cup of tea,' interrupted Mrs. Norelle; Clytemnestra's former, precise enunciation forgotten.

'It's after six so I'll have a rum and Coke. Doctor, can I twist your arm? Nanette?'

'Oh, what the 'ell!' said the cook, wiping her hands on her apron, 'As long as you don't tell, Monday!'

'As if I would, Nanette!' laughed the handsome giant. Monday gave Charles a broad wink, causing the aroused doctor to almost swoon. 'Nanette's culinary skills are something to be believed,' he said from over his massive shoulder as he reached into one of the cabinets for three highball glasses. 'Wait until you try her Beef Wellington. You'll never have had anything as delicious in your mouth. *Ever!*'

Had Charles been holding the proffered glass he would have dropped it.

'I think I'm going to like living here,' a slightly woozy Charles confided to Monday, several rum and Cokes later. The two returned to Charles's new home to enjoy 'one for the road,' Mrs. Norelle having ushered them out of the kitchen in order to prepare dinner.

'It's great,' Monday agreed. 'But be prepared. Strange things seem to be the call of the day for our lord and lady.'

'Can you clarify that, please?' slurred Charles, his gaze laser-like homing in on to the black man's bull-like crotch.

'You'll find out soon enough,' grinned the big man getting to his feet. He held out a ham-sized hand. 'Nice to meet you, Doc. I've got to run, I've got a little transaction to take care of. See you at breakfast. We all have this in the kitchen at eight o'clock sharp.' With a hearty, warm handshake the handsome O.J. Simpson lookalike made his exit.

'Oh yes, I'm definitely going to like living here,' repeated Charles, pouring himself a refill. 'A mad film director; his equally mad wife; a stage effect, so-called retarded monster, Munster child; a cook with a chocolate cookie fetish; and you, Monday, who would be a catch *any day*; plus heavily dropped hints galore of stranger things to happen – what more could a disgraced doctor ask for?' Taking a large sip he sank back onto the deep, black leather Roche Bobois sofa. 'So all I say,' he added as he raised the glass to the silent room, his voice bouncing spectrally off the rounded walls of the turret, 'Fuck all of you at the clinic! Yes, fuck you and all your fucked up patients. Charles Conrad Crosby has met his Waterloo or' – Charles gave a high-pitched giggle – 'his watermelon!'

––––––––––

Two years on Charles's desire to munch on Monday's much anticipated juiciest of juicy watermelons had not abated, nor had his thirst in any way been quenched. Monday was strictly off bounds, his hidden preferences being firmly taken care of elsewhere. Try as he could, albeit over endless cups of *cafe au lait* and cookies with Nanette – they had soon gone onto first name terms with the cook, however, preferring to use the more respectful 'doctor' as opposed to the more informal Charles – Monday's story remained an enigma.

All Nanette could offer was Monday had been working as a scaffolder on a building site when he had been spotted by Ethelred on the lookout for such a person to play 'a scaffolder' in a short film he was making. The film, titled 'Rigor Mortar', involved the reverse running of a collapsing building, starting with the demolished ruin and showing its slow resurrection. The end symbolism, supposedly conveyed by a dust covered Monday – buck naked except for a hard hat and a massive hard on – standing on the roof of the now pristine edifice, was to quote Ethelred, 'the significance of fallen man "dusting himself down and starting all over again."'

One ecstatic critic had described the brief film as 'a glorious Phoenix rising from the ashes of genius' while another more cynical thespian deemed it 'a wanking waste of celluloid' adding, 'The original building, filmed – for some obscure reason known only to Ethelred Jones himself – at an angle of alarming propensity, ended up looking more like *The Leaning Tower of Penis* than an up-righted building.' Ethelred, needless to say, had not been amused. For Monday, however, his short-lived film career well and truly 'nipped in the bollocks' – Ethelred's comment – saw him coming, hard hat in hand, and seeking the director's advice apropos a career change from that of a scaffolder to something more lucrative. Although the big man did his best to convince Ethelred that he had 'gotten the acting bug' and would be prepared to do anything and everything for another chance to appear on the black-and-white screen, Ethelred was unable to offer any other immediate roles.

On Clytemnestra's suggestion, Monday was offered casual work around the estate. 'He's too glorious to lose,' she admonished Ethelred. 'Think of future films. Something is sure – especially our man Monday – to eventually come up! Meantime, Monday can be our very own Man Friday!' The latter comment accompanied by a throaty chuckle. Ethelred, aware that Clytemnestra's byline would no doubt be put to frequent use, simply groaned out loud.

Monday accepted the position with alacrity, his reactions to the endless requisites under the term 'handy man' being first one of incredulity and then greeted and performed with a voracious enthusiasm.

For the growingly frustrated Charles, Monday's final denouement was to come as a horrendous shock.

CHAPTER 2

Three years earlier

'A small, good luck token for tonight,' said Ethelred, handing a smiling Clytemnestra a brightly coloured 'fun' condom tied at the open end with an even brighter piece of ribbon.

'How very *personal,* darling,' laughed his wife. 'And how very *you!*'

'Oh, it's very me, that I can assure you!' Ethelred gave Clytemnestra a tender kiss on her long, pale neck. 'Open it,' he whispered. 'See if you approve.'

'It feels like a charm or something… on a chain of sorts!' With eager fingers, the laughing woman pulled open the bow and shook out the contents of the condom into the palm of her slender hand. 'Oh Red!' she cried, 'I love it, simply *love* it!'

'Here, let me help you put it on.' Taking the small glass phial attached to a fine platinum chain, Ethelred gently fastened the necklace around Clytemnestra's elegant neck.

'Let me look; let me look!' she said as she glided elegantly over to a mirrored panel framed in faux-black crocodile skin. 'Don't tell me?' Clytemnestra added mischievously, a playful smile on her perfect, purple-glossed lips. 'Is it what I think it is? If it *is,* all I can say is it's not only a brilliant idea but the instigator is simply the most *wankerful* husband a woman could ever wish for!'

'Put it down to an obsession; an obsession to always be *with* you when I cannot be *in* you! Much more personal than a wedding band, don't you think?'

'Oh you wonderful, wankerful, husband, lover you!' cried Clytemnestra as she clasped a beaming Ethelred to her slender frame. 'When?' she whispered.

'When you were in the shower, I felt extremely guilty – rather like an errant schoolboy – but thinking of you soaping yourself, your cunt and your clit had the desired effect!'

'I should be jealous of this lucky little crystal phial, but how could I when it's filled – literally – with your love!' Clytemnestra gave Ethelred another kiss. 'Our carriage and my exhibition awaits!' Picking up a silver and purple-shot silk pashima, she took her husband by his arm. 'A quick goodnight kiss to Trisomy; you know how she adores seeing Mummy and Daddy in their evening finery.' Clytemnestra gave a girlish giggle. 'And I'm sure our little treasure is also going to ask for – no, *demand* – a necklace like Mummy's!'

'But minus the same inspiration and with only the masturbation!' laughed Ethelred. 'Also,' he added with a chuckle as they made their way to the nursery, 'The stimuli regarding you, my love, caused the mighty Ethelred cock to spurt overtime.' He gave a grinning Clytemnestra a sidelong wink. 'And why waste it? I'm not known as Ethelred the Ready for nothing! Two phials were filled and little Trisomy's necklace-to-be is now happily ensconced in the freezer in my studio! And before you question the durability of the content contained in *your* phial, my darling, give it time and it will look as if you're wearing a piece of sandblasted Lalique around your glorious neck. A mysterious piece which is an even more mysterious token between the two of us.' He gave his wife another kiss. 'So you see, both my girls have their very own *Ethel Ready to Wear*!'

Clytemnestra let out a shriek of mirth. 'Red, that was truly *awful!*' Punching him playfully on the arm, she quietly opened the door to the nursery suite. Taking Ethelred's large hand, the two tiptoed towards the extra large cot in which a small figure laid sleeping. Leaning over the protective railing Clytemnestra gently stroked the small wrinkled head covered in fine wisps of sparse, dark, curly, pubic-like hair. 'Sleep well, little Tris,' she whispered. Doing likewise, her husband softly murmured, 'Our very own special piece of magic. Sweet dreams, mystery angel.'

The sleeping figure opened one tiny eye before giving a small yawn and blowing a series of small bubbles resulting in a soft popping sound; a surprisingly loud fart bringing an end to the mini symphony.

'Oh, Red,' said Clytemnestra, biting her lower lip. 'She looks so helpless, so alone...'

'She's not alone, dearest,' said Ethelred quietly. 'We both know she's in her own special world with her special friends.' He tenderly wiped a tear off Clytemnestra's cheek. 'And she's happy here with us, you know that. So...' he gave a smile. 'Let's leave her to her dreams and let's go and bring yours to fruition. Your public awaits you.'

———————

'Secretions,' the latest exhibition of the works by celebrity 'Bacterial Artist', Clytemnestra Jones, was another grand occasion for London's artistic elite to come flocking to the preview being held at one of the most prestigious galleries in the sometimes dubbed 'Art Alley' or – to give its correct name – Mayfair's elegant Cork Street.

The Claudia Cordelle Gallery had achieved a certain notoriety by staging the first 'Penis Profiles' exhibition, a one-off which had led to several exhibitions with copies of the original photographs being shown in such international venues as New York, Paris and Tokyo. The photographs, large vividly-coloured photographs of celebrities' penises, erect and flaccid, had seen queues of eager visitors and voyeurs clamouring for admittance. A list of the participating celebrities was on display in the foyer of the modernistic gallery. It was then up to the perplexed viewer to 'put a penis to the person'. However, Claudia Cordelle, the wily doyenne and owner of the gallery, was keeping silent. Nobody, but nobody was ever to know which cock went with which celebrity. Rumours were rife that the whole exhibition was a hoax, that an impressive George Clooney – if it *was* him – was in fact a labourer working on an extension to the Cordelle penthouse in Kensington who have been paid to 'do the honours.' Claudia kept quiet and kept counting, as the customers and the cash kept rolling in. Copies of the original photographs and the cock-teasing list were selling, to quote the owner, 'like cock cakes!'

'A definite "no no" darling,' she would drawl to a frustrated purchaser begging for a clue as to the identity of an appendage that appealed. 'May I suggest you just dream on. See it as I *see* it: a mere two-thousand pounds and a glorious photograph of your fantasy beneath your pillow to finger yourself over? He's worth it!'

The hired limousine drew up slowly in front of the brightly lit gallery. As with her opening of 'Penis Profiles', Claudia had rolled out the – literally – stained carpet; the ubiquitous red carpet being replaced by a severely stained, mottled one – basically beige but stained in dubious beige, grey and yellow whorls and swirls. Two massive doormen who would have made the Chippendales turn a distinctive shade of envious bile green, stood ready to welcome the eager guests. Claudia, who had been looking out for the arrival of her star, pushed her way between the two plastic-covered men wearing identical transparent boiler-style suits, their blurred torsos decorated with swirls and whirls of bright body paint, an impressively bulging thong of gold lame' adding a touch of modesty to each.

'My star! My genius! *Toute Londres* awaits you!' crowed Claudia taking Clytemnestra by the arm. She added dramatically in the loudest stage whisper she could muster, 'They're all salivating, darling, positively *salivating.*' Claudia gave a loud shriek. 'But now you've arrived, change that to masturbating, darling! Positively *masturbating!* They simply *love* the show and those red dots can only indicate my nubile staff working overtime!'

Taking Clytemnestra in one arm and a bemused Ethelred in the other, the tall, soignée woman swept them into the main gallery. 'Ladies and gentlemen,' she sang out, 'meet your star of the evening! Ladies and gentlemen, I give you *Clytemnestra Jones*!'

'Go and slay them!' whispered Ethelred as Clytemnestra was gently pushed forward by Claudia, 'I'll circulate as they masturbate!'

Clytemnestra gave Ethelred a dazzling smile. Lifting the small semen-filled phial from around her neck, she kissed it softly and mouthing, 'Love you.' Turning away, she was immediately caught up in conversation with a well-known politician who guided her over to a large canvas. Jabbing enthusiastically at the painting with an extended forefinger in an almost parody of sexual thrusts, the man listened with rapt attention as Clytemnestra explained the inspiration behind the vivid piece. The canvas, four square metres in size, featured a background reminiscent of a white and grey moonscape with a series of yellow, gold and brown striations running vertically down the picture. 'It's called "Morning Routine Regular,"' announced Clytemnestra in a conspiratorial tone. Taking the awestruck politician by his stubby finger, she pulled him closer. 'To me,' she added putting on a suitably serious expression, 'nature even in its most basic moments is beautiful. We *are* nature. This piece to me is beautiful. How do you start your day, sir? Urinating or defecating? Both are natural to the body and therefore both are beautiful. What you see before you is defecation in its true beauty. To some it may be just a smear of faeces on a piece of toilet paper, but to me, it's a colourful representative of the wonders of our bodily functions. Seen under the wonders of a microscope, I strongly believe myself when I say bowel movement is beautiful and shit sublime!'

'I'll take it!' Gulped the politician. 'Err... you mentioned... urination?'

'That canvas over there,' said Clytemnestra leading him across the gallery and smiling in acknowledgement to the enthusiastic, well heeled and elegant crowd crying their greetings and plaudits. Placing him in front of a similarly sized canvas she explained the concept. 'Early morning urine should be seen as a golden sunrise. The humours of the night collectively known as blood, phlegm, yellow or black bile can also contribute to this golden shower' – the politician, renowned for his lusting after sadistic rent-boys and being pissed over, gave an uncontrollable shudder of delight – 'so I have captured my husband's early morning expulsion by having him create a specimen which I captured in a crystal Baccarat vase. I viewed his glorious, pungent offering through a jeweller's eye glass. Do you approve, sir?'

Another gulp and the obvious swelling of a rapidly growing erection in the man's loosely cut trousers confirmed his approval. 'I'll take it!' he managed to gulp for the second time within a few minutes.

'Wonderful,' breathed Clytemnestra. She beckoned a young man clad in a matching outfit to the doormen's but clutching a clipboard to hide his modesty. 'This gentleman, Mr... err...?'

'Jettison-Jarvis. Marcus Jettison-Jarvis.'

'Oh, Mr. Jettison-Jarvis, I should have known! Only a man of your renowned taste and formidable collection of erotica would home in on what I consider two of my most sublime works!' With a gracious wave Clytemnestra glided towards a beckoning Claudia who was holding court with a group of immaculately groomed elderly gays and their young consorts.

'Darling,' she cooed. 'Come and meet Sir Terence and his friends. They're mad about the triptych you've called "On the Spurt of the Moment". Do come and explain *all*!'

Several hours later and Claudia declared the exhibition a sell out and a 'mega, monstrous success!' From the sale of twenty canvasses the Cordelle Gallery had taken a staggering three-hundred and fifty-thousand pounds. As Clytemnestra was to sleepily murmur later to Ethelred as she lay clasped in his hirsute arms after a suitably frenzied, celebratory fuck, 'Not bad for a load of shit, semen, piss and saliva, was it?'

'No my precious; not bad at all, and talking of semen; Ethelred's ever ready, above average endowment down below, seems ready to make some more, so – if you move over, my darling…'

'Move over? Oh no, *you* move over, my precious one. Forget Ethelred Junior being ready! Mummy wishes to lower herself deliciously and brutally onto his sometimes even bigger and better doppelganger; my very own Vlad the Impaler!'

———————

Over breakfast in a steel-domed room adjacent to the kitchen the two eagerly scoured the following morning papers for any reviews. The most anticipated, those in the likes of The Spectator and The Sunday Times would have to wait.

'Good one here, dearest,' said Ethelred handing over a tabloid. He gave a frown as Trisomy, strapped into her high chair by a large leather belt, suddenly sneezed; a large glob of mucus landing in her orange juice. 'Honestly… at times…' he muttered, giving the scowling child a glare as he dabbed the splattered paper with a handy paper serviette.

'Stop it, dear,' reprimanded Clytemnestra. 'You know we have to take the rough with the smooth.'

'Maybe, but at breakfast I don't expect *that* sort of roughage!'

'Very funny darling.' Clytemnestra leaned across and wiped a growling Trisomy's nose with a black, bordered, paper serviette. '*There*!' she crowed, looking at the scowling child, 'Nasty snotty wotty all gone!' She took the proffered paper with her free hand.

'Uh uh! Not so good.' Ethelred angrily tapped the opened page of another paper, 'Our friend, that little arse-licking piece of crud, Jason Jeremiah. Listen to this. "Clytemnestra Jones claims her work deifies and beautifies the most basic of bodily functions. This Ms. Jones does with aplomb. The so-called *Bacterial Artist* has delivered what can only be described as total load of it!"'

'Little pansy cunt!' muttered Clytemnestra. She looked up at a scowling Ethelred. 'Don't worry, dearest. One day little Jason will get his comeuppance, and it won't be in the usual form of a gigantic dick!'

'Well said, princess precious, well said. *Trisomy*!' Ethelred lurched forward in time to catch the falling child who had mysteriously managed to loosen the belt holding her to the chair. 'Naughty, naughty girl!' he said, gently placing the small figure onto the floor. Giving a cheerful gurgle the little girl shuffled off briskly in the direction of the kitchen and the large conservatory leading off from it.

'Oh shit!' spat Ethelred, rising to his feet, 'She'll be wanting to play with those fucking cacti again!'

'No she won't! Mrs. N? Mrs. N?' called Clytemnestra. 'Can you catch Tris please, she's on the rampage and is heading your way!'

'I've got her, Mrs. Clyte!' came back the disembodied voice. 'Don't worry, you and Mr. Red keep on looking at your papers; Trisomy is about to help me start preparing lunch, aren't we, *dear*?'

'Thank you Mrs. N,' called back Clytemnestra. 'That woman's a gem,' she added to a scowling Ethelred. 'Inadvertently she's my inspiration – or *sin*-spiration as she claims I always say – plus she's always unbelievably patient with Tris.' She looked at her husband. 'However, I do think the time has come...'

'So do I,' cut in Ethelred. 'She needs a fulltime minder and someone who will understand.' He gave a light laugh. 'If you catch my drift... Look at it this way, if Armin Miewes, that German computer engineer who advertised for a victim on a cannibal website and got lucky, could do it, so can we.' Ethelred gave a snigger. 'Not that I'm suggesting we eat our darling daughter. Simply, we need someone who can look after her, understand her and eventually work with us and our future plans.'

'Miewes? He did eat his victim, didn't he? The victim being quite willing about the whole thing?'

'Correct. Some guy called Brandes.' Ethelred couldn't resist a snigger, 'Led to a *brand* new form of cooking!'

'Really dearest!' Clytemnestra couldn't resist a giggle at the ghastly pun. '*Cock au vin* with a difference!'

'Now that was almost as bad as my one!' Ethelred gave Clytemnestra an adoring smile. 'But seriously, we do need someone. The older she gets the more difficult she will become, but our needs are greater than hers.

'I'll put out an advert today. Something subtle but of such subtlety that only a higher intelligence will understand.'

A sudden crash from the kitchen followed by a loud scream of anguish broke into the conversation.

'What the fuck now?' Ethelred pushed back his chair and raced through the steel-lined archway into the gleaming room. 'What happened?'

He looked anxiously across at an ashen-faced Mrs. Norelle who was clutching her arm, a trickle of blood seeping through her fingers.

'She sliced me bleedin' arm, she did! Little b… err naughty, *naughty* girl!' The large woman glared down at the child who stood, feet wide apart, an evil snarl distorting her small mouth; a vicious-looking kitchen knife grasped in her tiny gnarled hand.

'Nasty lady,' growled Trisomy, 'Wants Twisis' cawot.'

'Cawot?'

'She means carrot, Mr. Red.' Mrs. Norelle gave Ethelred an embarrassed look. 'She err… pulled down 'er knickers and was trying to put it up 'er err…' the woman's voice trailed off.

'Oh Christ!' Ethelred knelt down in front of the scowling child. 'Naughty Tris! How often must Daddy Ethelred tell you *not* to put things up your foo foo?' He gave the still trembling woman an anxious look. 'The carrot?'

'Still up there!' gasped the woman, going a deep puce in colour. 'She wouldn't let me near 'er to pull it out. When I tried, that's when she sliced me!'

'Jesus. *Clyte*?' He looked towards the breakfast room.

'What is it?' asked a concerned Clytemnestra making her way quickly through the arched opening.

'It's a carrot this time! Can you? She wouldn't let Mrs. N, and she certainly won't let me!'

'Oh Trisomy!' A gently smiling Clytemnestra knelt slowly in front of the still snarling child. 'Mummy's not going to hurt you but Mummy has to take that nasty cawot out. Cawots are for cooking, *not* for putting up your foo foo!'

'Nice cawot!' growled Trisomy.

'No, naughty cawot!' replied her mother. 'Now, let Mummy take *out* the naughty cawot and then *good* Tris can have *two* chocolate cookies!' Clytemnestra glanced up at Ethelred regarding the defiant child with a frown. 'Red, see to Mrs. N's arm while I deal with this and Bugs "it ain't fucking funny" Bunny here!' With a quicksilver-like movement she pulled the little girl's knickers back down, prior to deftly removing a deeply embedded, seven inch carrot. 'Jesus!' gasped Clytemnestra looking straight into the child's beady, black eyes. 'You're only a little girl, Trisomy. Didn't you hurt yourself?'

Trisomy glared balefully at the offending carrot clutched between Clytemnestra's long, elegant fingers. 'Nice cawot,' she said. 'Twissis' cawot,' and promptly pissed a strong hot jet of urine onto the tiled floor, splashing her aghast mother's feet in the process.

'At least it wasn't Barbie as before,' camped her husband later. 'I was beginning to fear that our daughter was going to turn out to be a raving lesbian with a penchant for large titted blondes!'

———————

Two hours later Ethelred's advert was on the internet in the personal column. '*Discreet private family doctor required – cerebral and caring,*' read the advert, the final sentence containing the three most famous Japanese words of legend. '*Mizaru, kikazaru, iwazaru.*' 'See no evil, hear no evil, speak no evil'.

It was several days before there was any response. To Ethelred's disappointment there had only been the one, but on checking out the background of a certain disgraced Charles Conrad Crosby, M.D. – Ethelred having a computer hacker friend with 'connections' – he knew he had found the answer to his and Clytemnestra's dilemma, and a safeguard to their future ambitions.

To the delight of her parents, the rapport between the stork-like Charles and the monster child was immediate. To their personal satisfaction they found a similar rapport between themselves and the disgraced doctor. Final complaisance was achieved by Charles, when invited to join the couple for supper and an after dinner DVD, had come up with his own unique suggestion for a film. With a smug smile Charles had produced a disc of feature which he claimed he was 'particularly fond of'. The film, 'Grimm Love', based on the real life drama of Ethelred's often referred to hero, Armin Meiwes, saw the sculptor and his wife in a genuine state of shock.

'Charles!' Ethelred had managed to splutter. 'This must be the most fucking coincidence of all time! Armin Meiwes inspired us to look for *you*!"

'Not a fucking coincidence, Red dearest!' laughed Clytemnestra, her voice rising hysterically. 'It's a fucking miracle!'

'And I've been looking for you… and a Trisomy!' replied Charles with a wolverine smile.

———————

It was several weeks later Charles noticed the fine scar of Mrs. Norelle's arm. 'Nasty cut, that,' he commented. 'A childhood scar? I've never seen such immaculate stitching. In fact, you can hardly see any stitch marks; extraordinary.'

Mrs. Norelle looked down at the faint line on her arm. 'Goodness, Doctor Charles, It'd never crossed my mind. Childhood scar? Not at all. It's where little Trisomy cut me a few weeks ago, just before you arrived to join us.'

'But that's impossible,' muttered Charles. 'That's not a new scar. Are you sure the cut isn't on your other arm?'

Humouring the man, the woman gave out an exaggerated sigh before showing him her other arm. 'Seein's believin,' she said, smugly.

Charles took hold of both her arms, examining the two in turn. 'Where did you have this attended to? Which Ac and E? Which Accident and Emergency?'

'This A and E!' Mrs. Norelle gave a laugh. 'It's Mr. Ethelred, a right one with 'is potions and poultices 'e is. 'Ave you seen them 'ydroponic tanks at the end of 'is studio? Grows all sorts of weird plants in them 'e does. It's one of Trisomy's favourite places. Loves playin' among the plants, poor little thing... spends 'ours there with 'er dolls an' mumbling to the plants...' She shook herself out of her reverie. 'All Mr. Red did was to boil up some of them strange leaves an' Bob's yer uncle. My arm was right as rain within a few days.'

'But you must have had some stitches, some clips...?'

'Not one! On me little Donnie's 'ead, I swear it. Mr. Red simply plopped on the poultice with a bandage an' that was that.' Mrs. Norelle gave a chuckle. '*And* 'e got little Tris to 'elp. Proper little nurse she was an' as good as gold.' She gave a sigh. 'So sad really, could 'ave been her vocation but, as you know, with 'er problems...' The sentence was left unfinished.

'Yes, I know, Mrs. N.' said Charles softly. 'A sad, sad tale indeed but look on the bright side, isn't she blessed with Mr. and Mrs. Jones as her mummy and daddy? At least she will be experiencing total love in her allocated space on the Good Lord's earth.'

'God bless her,' whispered the cook in a suitable deferential tone.

'God bless us for having her,' responded Charles in similar vein.

———————

Charles, on his arrival at Bethlem Báthory and during the initial 'grand tour' as Clytemnestra described it, had been particularly impressed by the vast studio complexes created by the owners. Clytemnestra's light, airy studio comprised of the two top floors of a wing to the mansion, the flooring in between having been removed and the walls reinforced to make a vast, cavernous structure of skylights and full height windows. A high tech laboratory for her specimens, slides and various microscopic equipment; a freezer room for her specimens; an office; a shower room; a kitchenette plus a small sitting room-cum-bedroom completed the rest of the complex Clytemnestra was known to spend several days alone in her 'sanctuary' when in a working frenzy over one of her 'bacterial beauties'.

Ethelred's studio on the floor below was a reflection of the above but without the skylights. A large conservatory leading on to a paved terrace housed the special tanks for Ethelred's experimenting with hydroponics. A positive jungle of rare plants and herbs from all over the globe grew here in a luxurious, pampered frenzy. 'No orchids and the obvious for me!' the smug director would boast.

'Meet instead my true friends from the jungles of the Amazon and Africa and the plantations of the Deep South. Allow me – for example – to introduce you to this elegant-looking lady, *Dionaea msucipula,* or to the layman, the Venus Fly Trap. Innocent looking in her pretty colours, isn't she? Looks as if she wouldn't harm a fly!' Ethelred would laugh, before going on to introduce his guests to other carnivorous wonders such as The Body Snatcher and the Scary Ghost Plant. One visitor, on making what he considering a witty quip said, 'Just as well I've a zip in my pants instead of flies!' was greeted by stony silence, Ethelred taking his collection of plants extremely seriously.

The basement of the second studio acted as a hermetically sealed filming unit along with an area marked 'No Entry' and strictly prohibited to all visitors. Only Clytemnestra and Euros Peacock, Ethelred's trusted cameraman, were allowed access to this holiest of holies. The director would loudly claim this no-go area housed his dark room, cutting and editing rooms plus a concrete and steel lined vault where all his treasured and unique films were stored.

'God forbid that anything should happen to Bethelm Báthory, but I can assure you, not even a nuclear bomb will be allowed to destroy Ethelred Jones's works, which I will be leaving for posterity!'

Charles found his time being fully occupied with the daily management of the errant Trisomy. At times the child could be placid, pleasant and – as a frustrated Charles would regularly say to a sympathetic Mrs. Norelle – 'almost child-like,' whereas at other times she could be what he deemed 'a positive monster.' The doctor was also intrigued by the great devotion and patience Ethelred would occasionally show the little girl; a sharp contrast to his irritable snapping at her when in company of the cloistered household. Trisomy was never happier than playing by herself in the confines of Ethelred's special conservatory garden, which Charles had inadvertently dubbed 'Trisomy's Treasure Trove.' Only Ethelred and Trisomy were allowed to tend to the hydroponic tanks, the little girl – under the tender and watchful eye of her father – becoming more and more expert in administering the requisite nutrients for feeding the vast array of rare plants. Charles, on first witnessing Trisomy totally absorbed in her task, was amazed. 'It's as if she's taken on a totally different persona,' he confided once again to the ever patient Mrs. Norelle. 'Why, she even holds long, mumbling conversations with the wretched things!'

'She's a different little girl when alone with Mr. Red, an' I can 'onestly say they 'old quite lengthy, almost sensible conversations together. It's when she decides to behave in 'er usual tantrum-like manner I really feel what she really needs is a good smacking!'

'Not very politically correct, Mrs. N,' said Charles with a laugh.

'Forget all that nonsense,' sniffed the cook. 'When my little Donnie was no more than a sprog, a quick clip around the ear 'ole did wonders. Why, today 'e's what they call a parallelogram!'

'I think you mean paragon, Mrs. N,' added Charles drily, 'unless you gave him a double smack of course!'

'Eh? No need to, one of me whoppers was enough!'

Monday, who happened to overhear this latest observation about Trisomy talking to the plants and disciplining of Donnnie, responded in his deep, rich, chocolaty baritone. 'Nothing wrong with Miss Tris talking to the plants; I talk to my plants around the estate *all* the time!'

'As does the Prince of Wales!' added Mrs. Norelle firmly, determined to have the final word.

'I rest my case,' muttered Charles, holding up his hand placatingly. 'And I wouldn't say no to another *cafe au lait* and a Tris Treat, thank you Mrs. N!' Casting a side long glance at the smiling black giant, the daily questions flooded back into his mind. What is your real story Monday? Who do you see? What do you get up to in your off duty moments? More importantly, who or what do you fuck?

CHAPTER 3

Present Day

'Monday, may I see you for a moment?' Ethelred, standing in the open doorway to his studio conservatory, beckoned to the tall black man who was busy clipping a piece of topiary. The bush, in the form of a huge breast complete with erect nipple, was one of a pair. The two so-called 'works of art' commissioned by her husband, had been duly dubbed 'Clytemnestra One' and 'Clytemnestra Two' by a tongue-in-cheek Ethelred.

In retaliation, 'Ethelred Erect' was the name given to a further topiary spectacular by an equally appreciative Clytemnestra. The tribute, a towering privet growth – 'from privet to private!' as she would laughingly explain – had been dexterously clipped into the shape of a large curved penis and boasted a tall feathery head of unkempt tendrils.

'I can never quite make out whether the waving growth at the top is meant to represent my crumpled, sock-like foreskin or else a rather erratic orgasm!' Ethelred would inform a suitably stunned visitor. Two neatly clipped, verdant green, bulbous bushes on either side of the thick, central form were, in their turn, referred to by his adoring wife as 'Ethelred's usual load of bollocks!' Not to be usurped by Clytemnestra's sense of humour, a high parallel hedge of neatly trimmed yew leading up to a spectacular, towering modern bronze sculpture by the legendary John Farnham, had no alternative but to be named 'Clyte's Cunt' by her worshipful husband. Ethelred's punch line was always the predictable – '*And* furthermore, she boasts the neatest Brazilian compared to any other bush in all of our extensive gardens!'

'What's up?' A smiling Monday, wiping the sweat from his high, handsome brow, stood looking up at Ethelred standing at the top of the steps leading up to the conservatory terrace. 'You got some more film work for me?'

'Actually yes.' The director gave a wry smile, 'And I'm sure it's right up your alley, if you catch my drift.'

Monday gave a mock grimace of disapproval. 'Not a manky-wanky, money-shot and nothing-else again, is it?'

'No Monday. No manky-wanky but some proper hanky-panky!' Ethelred gave a laugh. 'Why, you even get a chance to speak… when your mouth isn't full!'

The black man gave a groan. 'Don't tell me… blow job or munch job?'

'Don't be so picky on a Monday, Monday! Put down those sheers and come and join me in the studio; I was just about to open a bottle of wine.'

'You're on.' Monday propped the sheers up against the retaining wall and made his way up the steps, his muscular thighs and calves flexing and rippling provocatively beneath his snug, cut-off denim shorts. 'Jesus, Monday,' laughed Ethelred. 'Don't let our constipated Charles see you in those. Poor old queen would have a fit!'

'He wishes!' Monday gave a hearty laugh, showing a row of dazzling teeth. He made an obscene circular gesture around his massive crotch. 'And an even bigger fit if I tried to *make* it fit!'

The two sat down opposite each other on a pair of brightly patterned facing sofas set inside the comfortable conversation area. From this vantage point next to one of the tall picture windows, they were able to look out onto the aforesaid topiaries and the avenue of yew. 'My balls have never looked better,' laughed Ethelread, 'Pinot Grigio, OK for you?'

'Whatever.' Monday accepted the beaded wine glass from Ethelred. 'So, this film, tell me all.'

'Whoa! Steady Neddy!' Ethelred gave a light laugh. 'Before I go into details about my major production, I simply have to first get Clyte off my back. She's determined to go ahead with this ridiculous idea of hers. Her "Adonis in Reflection" exhibition will now be accompanied by a video drama documentary – made by yours truly – which will be shown continually alongside the exhibits in a specially built mini-style cinema. The documentary follows the demise of a young man who falls in love with his own image. She plans two major canvasses, one of him when he first sees his reflection and falls in love…'

Monday couldn't resist his quip. 'I thought that was that little faggot Narcissy?' he said with a deep, belly rumble.

'You're absolutely right, of course. It *was* Narcissus. But you know Clytemnestra; she's quite capable of changing even the most revered of Greek mythology to suit her needs.'

'Is it going to be a gay film?'

'Gay? Why should it be gay?

'Well you said *mythology*, unless you've suddenly taken to lisping!'

'Oh, fuck off, Mon, or listen to your director here!'

'I'm all ears.'

'And the sodding rest!' Ethelred poured them each another glass of wine. '*This* is the story my elegant wife plans to paint and which I, in a moment of lust and a mega thrust, promised to do!'

'Red,' reprimanded Monday with another laugh. 'Haven't I told you before, never ever make a promise to a woman in the middle of fucking her. An approaching climax always ends up in career catastrophe. Look what happened to me!'

'Teach you to fuck the boss's wife who'd been shagging another member of the company crew! You promising to marry her when she announced she was pregnant, resulting in her old man having her thrown out. Not only did you lose your job, the kid turned out to be whiter than white, with ginger hair to boot! What happened to all that black power in those mega black balls of yours? Tell me about it!'

The two men laughed out loud, comfortable in each other's company.

'Yeah, and poor, destitute Monday ends up taking freelance work on any available building site until, lo and behold, like in the movies, along comes a randy film director and the aforesaid scaffolder ends up *in* the movies!' The big black man looked fondly at the tall, gently smiling director. 'Does Clyte have any idea?'

'What, that we fucked each other? Oh undoubtably. She would have to be pretty dumb not to notice the spasmodic arse bleed occasionally messing up the hallowed marital sheets. My blood stains, similar to a fucking Rorschach test, completely overshadowing *her* demure monthly contributions!' Ethelred gave a camp snigger. 'Clytemnestra has sometimes fucked me with a dildo strapped to herself to try and see *it* from a man's point of view – a gay man obviously – but never to the extent that I bled.'

'Shit!'

'No: blood!'

The two men laughed companionably once more. 'Getting back to this *bloody* documentary," quipped Ethelred, 'There was a kid the other evening who would have been ideal for her Adonis, but I since talked her out of using him. We now have other plans for the little butt-twitching prick.' He leaned forward and emptied the remainder of the bottle into their glasses. 'Hold on a sec whilst I get us another.' Returning with a second chilled bottle Ethelred topped up their glasses and having taken a hefty sip, continued. 'Clyte's original idea was to paint a portrait of a perfect young man, Adonis, catching his utter, utter perfection again in a reflection. She strongly denies any connection with the aforesaid Narcissy – Narcissy? – Clyte *will* be amused. No, she plans to be filmed creating the face and figure out of the model's own cum which will be painted onto a vast sheet of mirror instead of a de rigueur canvas. The film will incorporate the arrival of the model, the interview, the strip, the self-admiration and the model's frequent wanking off onto the artist's palette. Scenes will be filmed of Clytemnestra applying his *cum* to the mirrored surface and *outlining the model's actual reflection,* but in a magnified form!'

'Double shit!'

Ethelred gave a chuckle. 'I'm never surprised at how a woman can be so easily duped. Determined to stick to the name Adonis, while every bloody cunt will obviously keep questioning as to why she hasn't named the fucker *Narcissus,* I've come up with the perfect solution, if you'll excuse the pun.'

'Slay me!'

'Adonis, poor chap, had a rather unpleasant mother whose behaviour adds a convenient dark side to my documentary and, therefore, the picture. Are you following me?'

'Not really, Red. More of a lost fart in a thunderstorm than blinded by any flash of reckoning.'

'Adonis's poor muddled mum, Myrrha was in fact the daughter of Doni's dad! Myth has it the poor woman was turned into a tree with Adonis ostensibly being born from its trunk!'

'A hunk from a trunk! Or maybe that should be the hunk *with* a trunk?'

'Quite so... God, Mon, at times your wit...'

'I know, I know, becomes almost too much. Rather like something else I possess, *bleeder*!'

'Up yours!'

'Whenever!'

'Getting back to Clytemnestra's latest. I've gone so far as to suggest that because of our subject's murky past – child of incest and all that nonsense – why not do a *darker* portrait? Really *go* for the drama.'

'I'm now beginning to see the light.'

'I thought you would. So, instead of a white Adonis, this perfect young man Oswald our Charles so cleverly went and caught in his evil web, we have a black Adonis. You! And instead of the work being on silver mirror, Clyte now paints it on a *black* mirror; a dark reflection indeed.' He paused for a moment. 'I'll certainly be seeing the lad from the other night, for he fits in perfectly with the new idea as unveiled the other evening. Whereas that is now on hold due to Clyte's insistence it's full steam ahead for Adonis or, putting it bluntly' – Ethelred couldn't resist a snigger – 'full *stream* ahead!'

'Jesus, Red!' laughed Monday. 'Another form of finger painting, perhaps?'

Ethelred waited until their laughter had subsided. 'It's a big canvas, or – to be more accurate – a big mirror, Mon. Life size plus in fact. The bloody thing's to be almost two metres in height. That's a hell of a lot of wanking; several gallons of cum in fact.' He gave another whoop of mirth. 'Fucking hell, Mon, you'll wank your dick away; the mighty Monday monster worn down to a Monday midget!'

'Maybe a case of finding who your real friends are?'

'Spot on, sir! Charles has already agreed to contribute the odd spurt or two in order to help out. He'll do anything when it *comes* to pleasing your err… palette. After all, cum is cum and who's telling? I can assure you, he needed no encouragement in being publicly asked to perform a zillion million wanks into deposits of *your* cum!' Ethelred gave a chuckle. 'Let's face it, it's the nearest thing the poor frustrated old doctor can do instead of wanking over the fantasy himself!'

'And the always ready, Ethelred?'

'Oh, I'll be doing my fair bit. In fact, we'll also get the new kid on the block to add his little input. Windsor and Newton eat your heart out!'

'And the documentary?'

'A no holds barred coverage of the whole concept from wank to bank! However, the only stars of the whole feature will be you, the black Adonis and Clyte the artist. Charles, young Oswald and me squeezing our personal *paint tubes* won't be filmed! Christ, when people talk about you shooting your load, they'll be talking about a fucking shooting range!'

Monday, in between giving Ethelred a hearty high five along with a huge, rumbling belly laugh, barely managed to cough out, 'I can't wait for the private screening before the exhibition proper. The audience will no doubt be glued to their seats!'

'On that appalling *emission* Mon, it's *your* turn to fetch another bottle!'

'And the second mirror? You mentioned two,' Monday continued, their glasses duly replenished.

'To use a favourite gourmet choice of phrase once again – this time Leonardo Da Vinci – poor Adonis, aka you, on his dark journey from perfection through reflection, ends up in what I can only assume is a plagiarism of the Renaissance artist's "Turin Shroud". Yes, Adonis ends in a two fold wrap; wrapped up in a shroud and the *wrapping up* of the film!' Ethelred gave a roar of laughter. 'How's *that* for a combined piece of pure artistic genius *cum* con crap?'

Monday doubled up with more laughter. Pulling himself together, he added with a grin, 'So – from what I gather – this magical film *cum* video by the great Ethelred Jones, sees me firstly being auditioned by Clytemnestra. In the opening scene she will explain – for the benefit of the poor dumb audience – her vision, concept or whatever explanation turns her on.' He gave the amused director a wink. 'Shall I continue?'

'It seems as if I've just been made redundant as director!' laughed Ethelred. 'So, pray, do continue. Tell me the rest of *my* scenario!'

'My pleasure "Mr. Not-Wanted-on-the-Voyage!"' Monday gave a grin of fiendish delight. 'Lights! Camera! Action! With the appropriate welling up *music* – note I said *welling* – the scenes dramatically unfold. My repetitive Oscar winning performance being to wank, pose and come as she paints. It's all there in glorious colour: WPCP. Wank, pose, come, paint! Wank, pose, come, paint!'

'Something like that. But it's not going to be in colour or black and white. I plan to film all the sequences through a blue filter. It's literally' – Ethelred gave a howl of laughter – '*A blue movie!*'

Laughing loudly Monday made a weak attempt to speak.

'And before you utter that fucking word "shit" again, yes, you *have* already come up with the final finish!' Ethelred dissolved into more howls of laughter. 'We've had the blue-tinted opaque *cum* hither look in portrait number one,' he chortled, 'which brings us to the darker shroud and, guess what? Yes, go on Mon, you've already said it! Clytemnestra paints the shroud in…' Here the two reached across to slap each other's hand in another high five.

'*Shit*!' they bellowed in unison.

Wiping the tears from his eyes, Monday eventually managed to confirm his final obligation in front of the camera. 'So, a long zoom shot – or should that be a shoot of my shit chute as I take a massive dump?'

'Right on to the artist's palette, my friend, where your steaming offering will be blended with the finest of linseed oil by my inspired wife and her equally inspired palette knife into a gouache-like paste. The application of this suitably dark combination and the usage of a bronze tinted filter will see your "Turin turd" immortalised across the duplicated canvas – or mirror to be exact. So, there you have it, Monday: you as Clyte's "Adonis in Dark Reflection" and "Adonis in Final Dark Rejection".'

'Bloody hell!'

'At least you didn't say "shit".'

'So it *is* all wanky panky and no proper hanky panky!'

'Patience, Monday man; didn't I say there would be? Let's get this one in the can then *plenty* of hanky panky to follow, I can assure you. Charles, I may add, is "jes rarin' to go" and talking about Charles, any sign of cousin Charlie?'

'He's here tonight.' Monday gave another deep laugh. 'There's a queue of people waiting to meet my cousin of good cheer from Columbia!'

'How's that little sideline going?'

'Can't complain.' Monday lapsed into a camp, American Deep Southern accent. 'I knows I'se black an' a poah slave, Massah Red, but jes' how many of dem Rolex watches can dis poah nigga wear at one times?' He gave an amused Ethelred a broad wink. 'Let's put it this way: Monday is known in certain circles as "Make Day Monday." I may be black, but what I sell is pure, pure white!'

'I wouldn't say no to a toot right now.'

'You a mind reader as well as a fucking genius?' laughed Monday, 'I was about to suggest the same.' He rose to his feet. 'As the big Austrian dude says in all dem Terminator movies – "I'll be back!"'

Ethelred sat for a few moments sipping thoughtfully. 'Jesus Clyte, I know your Adonis works are going to be an international phenomenon, but when we put our heads together over "Tears for Trisomy," the impact will be even greater.' He paused before taking another long sip and saying out loud. 'However, when I open our eventual combined epic, the darkest, sickest epic to end all epics, nobody, but nobody will have seen anything like it.'

'I agree.'

Ethelred spun round in his chair to see the ethereal-looking Clytemnestra smiling down at him. 'Oh, hi dearest! I didn't hear you come in.' he said with a furtive grin.

'I ghosted in just on the tail end of your conversation with Monday.' Clytemnestra gave a light laugh. 'Don't worry, dearest heart, I wasn't eavesdropping. I merely caught the end of the Uncle Remus act and your curious comments about something you're about to do; something obviously unparalleled by mere mankind before!' She picked up the empty wine bottle. 'Mind if I join you for a few moments. I need a break. Another?'

'Why not? And Clyte make it a bottle of the Cristal. And as you may have gathered from my talking out loud, "Adonis in Dark Reflection" and "Adonis in Final Dark Rejection" can begin as soon as you are ready.'

'*You darling man*!' Clytemnestra gave out a wild, ecstatic shriek and flung herself across at a laughing Ethelred, smothering his face with kisses. 'Dear, dear darling man!' she cried again. Kissing him lovingly once more on his aquiline nose, she added mischievously, 'At least I got to kiss your nose before Cousin Charlie did, and, speak of the angel, here he is!'

Later, suitably satiated with several lines of the finest cocaine and the finest champagne, the three happily discussed the planned schedule for the proposed documentary; Clytemnestra in the meanwhile having excused herself to make a quick telephone call.

'I suggest we have a meeting in two – no make that three days time with Euros. Meanwhile, I'll draft out a rough scenario. How long do you think the paintings will take, my love?'

'I have already prepared two canvasses, but, on hearing the mirror idea I've already put several sheets of the black on order; hence my urgent telephone call a few minutes ago. These should be ready for delivery in a few days time. Monday, you'll have to make two special easels to carry the mirrors; none of my standard easels could possibly bear the extra weight of the glass. Once the mirrors are in position, I can see no reason as to why we can't begin straight away.' She smiled at Ethelred and Monday in turn. 'I must say I cannot *wait* to see Monday in all his rampant glory, oiled and expertly lit. Who else will be involved with the filming?' This directed at Ethelred.

'Apart from yourselves, there'll be me, obviously; Euros and Kevin, for cameras and lighting; Pandora for make-up and, if I may suggest it; Oswald the arse-stretch – in between cum contributions – acts as a general dogsbody!'

'Maybe I'll need a fluffer?' quipped Monday with a grin.

'Oh, I'm sure the good doctor would be only too happy to assist you with that little privilege!' said Clytemnestra drily. She gave her husband an arch look. 'Whereas you – my own, very dearest darling – will be far too busy directing your glorious wife as she brings her own special brand of *black* magic to the mirrors!'

'Quite,' agreed Ethelred.

'Take it as already done,' murmured Monday, giving Ethelred a furtive, sideways glance.

'Oh, and don't I just *bloody* well know it!' snickered Clytemnestra, smiling wickedly at the sheepish-looking men. She lifted the dripping bottle from the ice bucket. 'More champagne anyone?'

———

'Oswald?' questioned Ethelred frowning at the smudged print on the crumpled piece of menu. 'Oswald *Argent*?' he repeated, thinking, Oswald *Silver*? I hope to Christ that's your acting name. Whatever, we'll soon change that!

'Speaking,' said a sleepy voice.

'Ethelred Jones, you gave my wife your... err' – Ethelred couldn't resist a small smile – 'business card the other evening at the Golden Phallus awards ceremony.'

'Ohmigod Mr. Jones! Ohmigod!' squawked Oswald into the telephone.

'Not quite – yet – Mr. err Argent.' Ethelred gave a chuckle. 'Oswald, it sounds as if I wakened you. No, don't make excuses. Have you a pen handy? Good. Now, take this number and call me back in half an hour after you've had a cup of coffee or tea and gotten your head together. I need to talk to you about your career!'

'Ohmigod! Ohmigod. Oh fuck! Oh shit! Ohmigod! Yes, Mr. Jones. I've found a pen!'

'*Good* for you! Now take down this number.' In between chuckles Ethelred was asked to repeat the number four times. 'Half an hour, Oswald!'

'Ohmigod!'

———

'Mr. Jones? It's Oswald!'

'Ohmigod Oswald, is that really you?'

'Pardon?'

'The Jones humour Oswald. Right young man, let's not beat about the bush. What are your plans for the day?'

'I've err... not a lot, I was meeting a friend for lunch and then I have to be at Balans at seven.'

'Balans?'

'It's a restaurant in Earls Court. I'm working there as a waiter in between err... consignments.'

'You make yourself sound like a package. Have you a reasonable package, Oswald?'

'Pardon?' The light tenor voice switched to a treble.

'Package, Oswald, package. Dick, cock, prick, penis, schlong, dong, trouser snake! A package!'

'I don't understand...'

'Oswald, you've obviously seen some of my films. While they're not ostensibly porno, they do require a lot of full frontal shots and, as in the one for which I was given the award the other night, a pair of erect penises were required to play a duet on a set of drums! Could you cope with that? You must be aware I'm not exactly into Shakespeare!' Ethelred gave another smile at the whispered 'Ohmigod' quavering over the phone. 'Oswald?'

'I'm here, Mr. Jones.'

'Are you going to answer my question?'

'Err... well, Bryan, my friend, calls me his OTT Oswald...'

'Over the top Oswald?'

'Yes, sir.'

'Well OTT Oswald, how about you and your friend skipping lunch and hopping on a train to Windsor instead? Whereabouts are you in London? Clapham? Even better. You can easily get a train there for Windsor. Check the times and call me back. See if you can get into Windsor around one. I'll have my car take you back to London well in time for your evening shift at Balans.'

'Err... I'll have to check with Bryan... err... Mr. Jones.'

'I think you've got the wrong end of the stick here, OTT Oswald. Bryan or no Bryan, if you *are* serious about a job – *any* job – with me, Ethelred Jones the director; you'll get your butt down here *tout de suite avec* Bryan or Bryan-less. If I haven't heard from you within ten minutes, forget it.' Ethelred slammed the phone down. 'Goddam kids today,' he muttered.

'Want the world but don't want to get off their fucking arses...' He had hardly finished his ranting when the phone went.

'Mr. Jones it's Oswald again. I'll be at Windsor at one o'clock and I'll be Bryan-less!'

'Brilliant!' responded Ethelred. 'See you one-ish!'

'Fucking A!' said Oswald Argent out loud to the drab, dimly lit bedsit.

'Got you!' said Ethelred out loud to the stylish study. 'To quote dear Charles, you've fallen for it – hook, line and blinker – you stupid, arrogant, attention seeking, brown-nosing little cunt!'

CHAPTER 4

'You made it!' A smiling Ethelred waved at the young man who had stepped out of one of the last carriages and stood anxiously surveying the platform. Giving a relieved smile and a camp wave in return, Oswald sashayed his way over to his host.

Christ, thought Ethelred, *you'd even make Quentin Crisp look butch! Just as well, you're only going to be used for a bit part.* 'Oswald!' Greeting his guest with a warm handshake – Ethelred's firm and bony, as opposed to Oswald's limp and damp one – Ethelred uttered the usual inane questions such as 'Pleasant journey? Train crowded?' while guiding the nervous young man out to the car park. 'Great get up,' he added eyeing the skimpy T-shirt, tight designer jeans and obviously designer labelled trainers. 'Very country!' he added drily.

'I wasn't sure what to wear,' murmured Oswald, blushing furiously, 'And I had to hurry to catch my train,' he added defensively.

'You look fine,' Ethelred assured him. 'We're all very informal down here.' Aware of his own apparel, a soft beige suede jacket from Armani, a rust-coloured cashmere roll neck from Joseph, black trousers from Ralph Lauren and the inevitable Gucci loafers, as contradictory to the remark, he added a quick 'We're here,' automatically releasing the door locks to a gleaming silver Mercedes coupe.

'Wow!' said Oswald, his large blue eyes widening. 'What a beauty! Tell me if I'm dreaming but am I about to ride in a Mercedes-Benz SLK, the very latest model? An Edition 10?'

'Well done Oswald, you certainly know your cars. I bought it at the Paris Show earlier this year.' Ethelred looked at the awe-struck young man. 'Care to drive? That's if you have a licence!'

'Care to drive? Mr. Jones, can I? And yes, I do have a licence!'

'I've just asked you if you'd like to! Here,' Ethelred tossed the keys across to Oswald who deftly caught them in his slim hand. 'Hop into the driver's seat. I'll make myself comfortable alongside and give you directions.'

'I've only ever driven my sister's Polo before!'

'Well, Oswald, as they say, there's always a first time and, if I may say so, I think you should start aiming for higher things than a Polo; unless it involves a horse!' Ethelred was unable to hear any reply, Oswald having already turned on the ignition. Intent on revving the engine, he pressed down on the accelerator without first checking to see if the gear lever was in park. With a powerful roar, the Mercedes accelerated backwards, crashing into parked car behind. An ashen-faced Oswald turned to look at Ethelred who sat shaking with laughter as opposed to rage. His laughs – almost covering the sound of tinkling glass from one of the headlights of the unfortunate car behind – causing the young man to dissolve into a series of shakes, followed by a loud wail and violent sobbing.

'Ohmigod! Ohmigod!' wailed Oswald, burying his head in his arms and pressing forward onto the steering wheel. 'Ohmigod!'

'Oswald! Oswald!' Ethelred leaned over and put an arm around the narrow, heaving shoulders. 'It was an accident. Here, look.' He opened the dash compartment. 'I'll simply leave a note and telephone number and ask the owner to ring my accountant who will take care of it. Now come on, stars don't sob, stars *shine*! So – get your act together, I'll only be a sec and then we can set off again; only this time with a little less foot enthusiasm and preferably *not* in reverse!'

Ethelred stepped out of the car in time to see a red-faced man storming towards them. 'What the bloody hell do you think you're doing, that's my car!' roared the tall, heavy figure, his large arms whirling like a pair of demented windmills. 'Oh shit! Ethelred!' The massive man stopped in midstride, his ruddy face breaking into a broad grin. 'I should have known. Only a flash bugger like you would own such a flash car!'

'And good morning to you too, Miles!' laughed Ethelred, holding out his hand. 'Sorry about the mishap, but young Oswald's foot slipped off the brake and onto the accelerator! I was just about to leave a note for the owner. A Peugeot Miles? I would have thought at least a Bentley or

Roller more you!' He turned to a silent Oswald. 'Oswald, meet Sir Miles
Anstruther, our local property mogul and also known as Sir *Midas* Miles
in the world of overseas development! Miles, meet Oswald Silver, a name
about to become a household one!'

Miles gave the young man a cursory nod, giving a double take and
subjecting Oswald to the coldest, most calculating and penetrating of gazes.
Oswald would later claim, when describing the incident to Charles, 'Talk
about homophobic! If looks could have killed, I would have been killed
stone dead. But what a glorious, sadistic shit and what a way to go!'

'Mr. *Silver*?' said Sir Miles Anstruther, his voice tightening as if in
distaste on saying the name. 'Mr. Silver?' he repeated. Muttering a strained
'Err, welcome to Windsor...' the large man gave a bemused Ethelred and
scarlet-faced Oswald a brief, thin smile, before moving briskly back to his
dented car.

Oswald, in an unexpected bout of masochistic fervour, found
himself falling deeply and hopelessly in love.

'Home sweet home,' said Ethelred, having instructed Oswald to
slow down and take a left before stopping in front of the impressive set
of solid, high black painted gates. Pressing a control button on his mobile,
the gates opened silently to show the beginning of a long gently curved
drive bordered by a neatly clipped low yew hedge backed by lush bushes of
brightly flowering rhododendrons. 'Keep it slow, Oswald. We have a family
of peacocks who have a habit of suddenly appearing when least expected.
One evening, Mrs. Norelle, our cook, was press-ganged into recreating an
Elizabethan feast, following the arrival of an overzealous driver behind the
wheels of a Porsche. Two strutting cocks' – Ethelred couldn't suppress a
snigger – 'not bothering, in their complete arrogance, to check the drive
for us lower mortals, ended up – feathers stuck up their arses – as the main
course for dinner!'

On cue, a large bird suddenly appeared from out of a small space in
the box hedge, causing Oswald to jump on the brakes.

'Move you silly cocksucker!' yelled Ethelred, banging the side
of the car door with the flat of his hand. With an indignant harsh cry, the
massive bird gave a leap into the air and scuttle off through the opposite
growth.

'That was Lily,' he explained as they resumed their journey.

'Lily? But he – she's a peacock?'

'After Lily Savage. Our Lily is a proper drag queen. Catch him on the front lawn in the morning and he makes even the most exotic, feathered dancer from the Rio Carnival look as if she's wearing the dregs from Oxfam! Slow down Oswald then stop a few yards ahead. That bend over there allows you a magnificent view of our little spread, our beloved Bethlem Báthory.'

'Omigod!' Pulling up to a stop, Oswald could only gasp at what, unbeknown to him, was about to become his future – albeit temporary – home.

The striking house with its towers, turrets and main facade of faded red brick glowed warmly in the early afternoon sunlight; the immaculate lawns with their crisscrossing of pristine flower beds of white and scarlet blooms, plus the precision positioning of clipped topiary, giving a sense of the vast building nestling on a giant chessboard.

'It's beautiful,' breathed the young man. 'I've never seen anything like it.' He turned excitedly towards a bemused Ethelred. 'It's like a mad Disney-style castle meets the House of Usher!' He waved a thin, elegant hand. 'It's quite, quite *the* most extraordinary piece of architecture I've ever seen.' He gave a gasp of amazement. 'This is your *home*? You actually *live* here?'

'I do – and still did – before coming to meet you!' Ethelred gave a laugh; Oswald's smiling face and keen enthusiasm was catching. 'Let's move on,' he said, 'Park in front of the main steps and come and say "hello" to Clytemnestra and the rest of the team. Clyte's looking forward to seeing you and is delighted you could come down at such short notice. The rest of the team are equally keen to meet you – if not a tad curious – as to who the mysterious young visitor from London might be.'

Oswald pulled the gleaming car to a halt and, making sure he had placed the gear lever in park, looked up toward the massive doorway at the head of an impressive set of stone steps.

'And there she is!' Ethelred waved to the tall, elegant figure materialising wraith – like, from the cool darkness of the house.

'Oswald!' cried Clytemnestra with a welcoming wave, 'You made it! Welcome to Bethlem Báthory!' Without further ado, she skipped nimbly down the steps, her long tanned arms and legs showing off a pale blue Grecian-styled silken shift to perfection. Gold bracelets, a gold headband holding back her raven black hair, and a pair of strappy, high heeled gold Jimmy Choo sandals completed the stunning picture. 'And Red let you drive! Now there's a first! He'd never *dare* let this mere woman sit behind the wheel of his favourite mistress!' Reaching over the side of the driver's door, she gave the bedazzled young man a welcoming kiss on his cheek, engulfing him in a heady exotic scent. Standing back and eyeing him with a twinkling smile she added. 'Why young Oswald, you're even prettier than I remember you, if that were at all possible!'

For the second time within half an hour Oswald felt himself turning a flame red.

'He is, isn't he?' agreed her husband standing alongside the car. 'Come on, young Os, out you get. You can't be allowed to sit and wallow in all this admiration. Too much of it can cause the head to swell.' He gave Clytemnestra a broad wink at the innuendo. 'Drinks on the terrace?'

'As it's such a glorious day, I've asked for lunch to be served in the poolside pavilion so that's where we'll be. Maybe drinks on the terrace later? After a swim?'

'Not possible, I'm afraid.' Ethelred gave Oswald a reassuring smile. 'I promised young Oswald he'd be back in London by six. Boris will drive him back.'

'That wouldn't be Karloff, by any chance?' cut in Oswald with a nervous giggle. Seeing the curious glances of his hosts he began to stammer an explanation. 'I mean, the house is so... so.' He looked desperately from Ethelred to Clytemnestra, 'As I said to err Mr. Jones, a mad Disney castle and err... the House of Usher,' he ended lamely.

'You mean Castle Dracula!' laughed Clytemnestra, taking him by the arm, 'That's what the locals call it, but feel free to call it what you wish. We called it, or call it, Bethlem Báthory.'

Taking Ethelred's arm with her free arm, she began to lead them along the wide terrace adjacent to the house, explaining between bursts of warm throaty laughter, the significance of the name.

Oswald suddenly paused, causing the husband and wife to be jerked back in their stride. 'Oops! Sorry! I didn't mean to cause you both to stumble, but may I tell you what my name for your magical house would be?' Oswald gave a giggle.

'Not at all!' laughed Clytemnestra. 'Do tell us!'

'As long as it's not something on the lines of "Shangri La' or 'Mon Repos,' chipped in Ethelred.

'Weeeel,' here Oswald nervously drew out the word, acutely conscious of the two pairs of eyes sharply scrutinising him. 'If I was to ever own a place as magical, as *compelling* as this, I'd call it... *Capreae*!'

'*Capreae*? You mean Capri?' said Ethelred in a puzzled voice. 'But why Capri? It's a fucking house not an island!'

'Oh but it *is*! Don't you see it?' Oswald waved his long, well-toned arms in an all-embracing gesture. 'The house, your house, is exactly like some exquisite island! Look again. A wonderful fantasy of bricks and mortar set in a landscaped sea of green, white and red!' His enthusiasm getting the better of him, Oswald's voice had risen to an almost high, weird falsetto. 'I could live here like my hero, my doppelganger, my reincarnation, Caligula, the greatest Roman emperor of all time. Caligula, whose glorious, notorious palace of sin was on that very island, Capri, or as I, the original Caligula called it, *Capreae*!'

'I think,' said Ethelred slowly to Clytemnestra, both stunned by Oswald's unpredicted outburst. 'Our luncheon guest has just won himself an Oscar!'

'And *I* think Oswald has just won himself *the* most enormous drink! Look, there's Charles. Charles!' Clytemnestra carolled. 'Our guest has arrived.' She swept across to a tentatively smiling Charles, pulling along Oswald with her. 'Oswald, meet Charles and Charles meet...' Clytemnestra gave a mischievous giggle, 'Caligula!'

'Caligula?'

'A joke, Charles dear, a joke. His real name is Oswald Argent, Red insists on calling him Oswald Silver but Oswald – and quite rightly – secretly harbours the name Caligula and, as life at Bethlem Báthory is all about fantasy, Caligula he shall be." Clytemnestra gave the blushing Oswald a playful smile. 'Now that's settled, yes to one of those delicious Pimms please Charles, but no to *Capreae,* Oswald Caligula! While you're here, *our* island remains Bethlem Báthory and when you get *your* island, *then* you can call it by your chosen name!'

Charles gave a nervous Oswald a sharp look, resulting in Oswald changing from red to a pale grey. Unaware of Clytemnestra, Ethelred and Charles having orchestrated the whole charade, Oswald – firmly believing the meeting was an arrangement set up between Charles and himself – gave the doctor a discreet reassuring nod on accepting the proffered Pimms; the nod not going unnoticed.

A high pitched wail followed by a series of strange squeaks suddenly rent the air. Oswald, thinking for a moment it was one of the infamous peacocks spun round to see, standing in the shadows to one of the vine covered pergolas leading to the poolside pavilion, a small, stooped figure reminiscent of an elderly bald-headed monk.

'Trisomy, darling!' cooed Clytemnestra.

'Come and say hello to Uncle Caligula!' added Ethelred wickedly.

The small figure, after a momentary pause, shuffled out from the shadows. Oswald managed to withhold a shocked gasp. Charles had forewarned him about the little girl's condition but even so, the first sight of Trisomy was worse than he had imagined.

Jesus, he said to himself, *poor little thing. She looks mummified! Old, brown as well as wrinkled. I can't believe she's nine or ten! She looks a sixty year old midget or even a dark old wizened, seventy or even eighty!*

Trisomy slowly shuffled up to the silent man. Giving him a curious, silent up-and-down look, she peered up at Charles through narrowed eyes, her thin, cracked lips parting in a parody of a smile to show her toothless gums. Holding out a tiny gnarled hand, she gently touched Oswald's limp one. 'Hello Unka Caligla!' she gurgled. She turned to her parents, her toothless smile becoming wider. 'Like Nurse Charles,' she said, 'Tris *like* Unka Caligla!'

'*Nurse* Charles?' For the first time Oswald felt himself returning to some normalcy.

'Charles is actually a doctor, but he looks after our little girl for us.' Clytemnestra gave a brave smile. 'Charles has an interesting hobby – taxidermy – and occasionally he allows Tris – Trisomy – to assist him with his work. His little nurse, he calls her and she, in turn, calls him Nurse Charles.'

'Oh,' said Oswald, for want of something to say and not daring to look at Charles. This was something he had not been prepared for. Pulling himself together he surprised the three adults by dropping to his knees and taking the little girl by her emaciated shoulders – he remarked afterwards to Charles that it felt like holding a small, delicate bird – he smiled gently at the drooling child. 'And Unka Caligla likes Trisomy. Would little Trisomy like to kiss Unka Caligla hello?'

To Oswald's horror, Trisomy demonstrated she would.

———

'Nurse Charles?' Oswald gave a peal of laughter as he held the receiver away from his ear in an attempt to stave off the torrent of abuse coming over the wire. 'And lovely to see you too, *nursey*!' He listened for a few moments before answering. 'No. I found them both mad as a pair of March hares but goodness, ooooh so sharp! So on the ball. Trisomy? No problem there, the poor thing – for it *is* a thing! – just needs some TLC. TLC? Tender loving care to the layman but, in her case, read that as *Tread Lightly Charles*! When the shit hits *that* fan, it'll make Pompeii look like a simple puke!'

'Charming! I trust you were driven back to London with no problems "on the voyage"?'

'No, the substitute driver, the magnificent Monday as opposed to the threatened Boris, was charm personified.'

'Ah yes, Ethelred forgot it was Boris's day off, or Boris Karloff as you called him.' Charles gave a snigger. 'Perhaps Boris was having a quiet wank in his coffin!'

'Very funny Charles. In fact, the magnificent Monday man came in for a coffee before heading back.'

'And?' Charles's voice took on a querulous edge.

'And? There were no "ands" about it Charles. God, you can be such an old *queen* at times! King Dong is straight. All your little fantasies should be put back firmly in the closet, Charles, for if anyone else in that household is gay, it's the spectral Ethelred! Rest assured, we'll have no problem with him!'

'Nonsense, he's totally devoted – obsessed even – by Clytemnestra.'

'Don't be too taken in by that siren on the cocks either! I bet there's more to Ms. Clyte than meets the eye. It wouldn't surprise me if Mrs. Jones and Mr. Monday were playing naughties behind Mr. Jones's back! If so, and I strongly believe it to be so, it makes our plan even easier! And the fact that Monday is the biggest, black stud on his personal two Pillars of Hercules also helps!'

Charles swallowed audibly across the static. 'So what's next? What have you arranged with Ethelred?'

'It's a case of, don't call me, I'll call you. He's described what I would be required to do *should* he go ahead with "Adonis in Reflection."'

'*Should?* But I was given to understand that's it definitely on?'

'Calm down, Charlie boy. Of course it's still *on*. Ethelred's simply playing the power game. Unless my shell-likes deceive me, I'm to be official gofer and also contributor to a sperm-bank of sorts! Ethelred asked me if I'd object to wanking into a dish on a twice to thrice times daily to – and I quote him – "enhance a prop!"'

Charles gave a cry of laughter. '"Enhance a prop?" Did he explain exactly what he meant by that?'

'No, but our friend rather enjoys talking in riddles. And as for all those bloody innuendoes... Fuck me!'

Charles made no comment on Oswald's last expletive but quickly explained about his, Ethelred's, Monday's and now Oswald's contribution to Clytemnestra's palette.

'If I may be so bold as to ask,' camped Oswald. 'Just which of her *palettes* are we referring to?'

'Very witty – *Caligla*! I'll speak to you later tomorrow. Have a good evening.' There was a pause. 'Are you calling from work?'

'No, I'm actually in my local having a drink with Bryan – he says "hi."'

'Say "hi" back!'

'Will do. No, after Ethelred called this morning I managed to switch shifts with another guy at work just in case I was late in getting back. Pete, the guy at work, needs the extra loot.' Oswald gave a camp giggle. 'Unlike someone else I know, poor Pete doesn't have a camp old beneficiary who moonlights as a nurse!'

'Fuck off, Oswald!'

'Love you too, Charlie boy. Speak to you *domani*!'

Charles slowly put down the mobile. He smiled over at Clytemnestra and Ethelred sitting opposite him, the three having settled themselves down for a nightcap in the conversation area of the director's studio. 'Bull's-eye! Our little *Caligla* has fallen for it all; hook, line and blinker!'

———

Oswald looked at Bryan lying next to him on top of the crumpled, sweaty, semen-stained sheets of the put-u-up couch. 'Reading between the lines, we're on. I may, just may, be going to be working with the "is he for real?" Ethelred Jones.' He gave his scowling lover a smug smile. 'Charlie didn't say as much – I think he was still sitting with them – but it does look as if it's full scream ahead!'

'It will be a scream from what you tell me about Mandingo who brought you back!' came the sour reply. Bryan gave Oswald's long, thin, flaccid cock a tweak. 'Clever pair you two, aren't you?'

'No, Bryan, clever pair *us,* and don't you ever forget it!' said Oswald giving the stocky, dark-haired young man's thick, cucumber-like cock a reciprocal squeeze.

'I know, I know and I appreciate you saying so, but it was your chance meeting with Charles that led to all this.' Bryan let out a long, pained sigh. 'As it stands, Charles firmly believes it's just you and him and nobody else. To him, I'm simply Bryan – some nondescript friend who's no more than a drone in some downmarket travel agency. In fact, I've never had the pleasure of meeting your mystery man.'

There was an ominous silence. *Shit, here we go again,* thought Oswald looking straight ahead. Bryan's possessiveness was becoming claustrophobic, his mood swings unpredictable and his jealousy over Oswald's strange relationship with Charles, almost reaching levels of paranoia. Swallowing audibly, he said in a low, tight voice. 'Give it time.'

'Time? How much time? How long have you been spinning this guy along?' Bryan pulled his hand angrily away from Oswald's cock which he had been softly stroking as they spoke. 'From what you've been telling me, you're off to live it up; swanning and pouncing around in some fucko's weirdo mansion!" He gave Oswald an irritable look, "But what about me? About us? Only a few minutes ago, it was *us* and now you're telling me to give it time. Well, I've giving *it* enough fucking time.' Bryan pulled himself off the bed and reached for his jockey shorts. 'You can tell your Charles unless your other half can join you, it's a no go situation. Tell him you can't be separated from me!' He looked wildly around the small, untidy studio room 'Tell him that we're even planning a civil ceremony or some such crap, but, whatever you do, I want in!'

'You've just had *in!*' laughed Oswald with a snort, trying to make light of the situation. 'Oh, c'mon Bryan for Chrissake!' He stretched out his arm and patted the jean-clad, sulking Bryan, playfully on his firm buttocks.

'Don't touch me!' Bryan spun round and glared at a startled Oswald. 'Let's face it Oswald. You're crap as an actor, crap as a waiter, crap as a lover so you may as well go and kid yourself that you're *not* crap with your bloody Charles!' He gave a snort. 'Charles!' he repeated with even more derision. 'Someone gives you a fifty quid tip and suggests you join him for a drink after dinner? He then bamboozles you with his tales of a massive pad in the country, plus some bizarre proposal involving blackmail and Christ knows what else, before finally carting you off to some upmarket doss house in Knightsbridge for the night...'

'The Jumeirah Carlton Tower is *not* a doss house and the proposed plans came later, much later!'

'Fuck the time-scale! Besides, anything to do with you and a screw must be a doss house! Look at the shit heap you let me screw you in, for example.' Bryan gestured at the dismal room. 'And this Charles, what's he really up to, eh? All those cheques, the amazing coincidence someone should ring you at work and – out of the blue – suggest some part-time work conveniently helping out with an awards' ceremony dinner held at Grosvenor House? And how come you get an invitation – for it *was* a perverted type of invitation no matter what you may think – to meet those fucking weirdoes, Ethelbed and Clitoris Jones? Think, dummy, think!

'They're *Ethelred* and *Clytemnestra,* if you don't mind. *Madam*!'

'Oh, for Christ's sake, I may as well go and speak to a fucking black traffic warden for all the sense I get out of you! I tell you, Oswald, it's all too good to be true! It's too easy and, as my old mum used to say, there's no such thing as a free lunch!'

'You never had a mum!' spat Oswald spitefully. Fully dressed, he stood glaring defiantly at Bryan who looked as if he had been slapped. 'Nor for that matter, even a legit dad. You don't have any parents, which makes you nothing more than a fucked up bastard,' Oswald hissed. 'An envious, fucked up, *unwanted* bastard!'

'You cunt!' screamed Bryan punching a startled Oswald on the bridge of his nose with a rocket-like fist.

'Ow!' screeched Oswald, clutching his face in his hands and falling backwards against the wall, 'By dose! By dose! You'be boken by dose!'

'Lucky it wasn't your fucking neck!' shouted Bryan, as he stormed out of the front door.

'Fucking tosser!' muttered Oswald peering at his bruised reflection in the small bathroom mirror. He gently touched his red, swollen nose gently. 'Hmm, I don't think it's broken. Bugger it, Bryan. There was no need to punch me quite so hard!'

Moving to the small kitchenette, he reached into the fridge for the one and only ice tray. Wrapping a few cubes in a dishtowel he returned to the studio room; the makeshift ice pack held firmly to his nose. Folding back the bed he slumped down onto it, but not before pouring himself a large vodka to which the remaining few cubes of ice had been added.

'Bloody fuck!' he said out loud to the depressing room. He glared at the shabby wallpaper and the lopsided roller blind, his eyes slowly taking in the scratched dining table and equally forlorn-looking chairs. 'This place *is* a shit heap,' he announced to a drunkenly leaning table lamp alongside him. 'And Bryan is right. If I'm to move on, he's to move on with me!' He picked up his mobile and punched in the familiar number.

'What' came the immediate, surly reply.

'It's me and I'm sorry...'

'Fuck off!'

'*Bryan*! Don't hang up. I'll tell him – *them*. I'll tell Charles it'll require the two of us in *Ethelbed's* package! I'll also tell him the two of us combined make one helluva package!'

There was a long pause. 'You will?'

'Promise; I'll call him in a day or two... no, I'll call *Ethelbed himself* in a day or two and say I'll only consider the deal if it involves you.' There was a pause. 'You're not under contract to the agency, are you?'

'No, they pay me cash. I'm not even on their books.'

'Brilliant. So leave it to me, and Bryan...'

'Yes?'

'I love you!'

'Love you to, OTT!'

———————

The next few days saw Monday hard at work constructing two new, massive, seven-foot-high tripod-style easels, each formed out of stalwart three by three lengths of polished wood with a resting shelf held in support by a series of heavy, polished and lacquered brass angle brackets with similarly finished straps holding the completed supports in a rigid position.

'Beautiful,' complimented Clytemnestra on viewing the two gleaming edifices.

'Magnificent,' agreed Ethelred. 'Why, they both look a piece of fine sculpture; an impressive tracery of line in pyramid or apex form!' He gave his wife a wicked look followed by an equally wicked chuckle. 'Pity to hide them Clyte; they'd make an ideal feature in Tate Modern. "Two to Triangle," perhaps?'

'At times, husband dearest, your jokes can only be credited as none other than pure puerile perfection!'

'So be it.' With a grin Ethelred began to chant, 'Mirrors, mirrors, on the wall, who's the most puerile of us all?'

'Why, Ethelred of course!' cried Clytemnestra and Monday, laughing with delight.

The positioning of the two massive mirror sheets, each backed in black lacquered supportive wooden boards, took the combined strengths of Ethelred, Monday and Charles to lift the shining pair onto the supporting shelves. The three stood back with Clytemnestra to admire the reflective rectangles. "I've made my preliminary sketches and now I cannot wait to start on committing my glorious Adonis to his two most unusual *canvasses,'* murmured Clytemnestra. She smiled at the three men. 'Mr. Director, I'm waiting for you to say "camera, lights, action!" In the meantime, I will require Monday to pose as from next Wednesday. Your gallant contributions, gentlemen, may begin at any time. Suitable beakers are at the ready and all donations will be kept chilled until required.' Clytemnestra gave a broad smile, 'What about a glass or two of champagne to toast what is – without a doubt – the world's most unusual sperm donors' bank!'

Champagne flutes duly procured and filled, the four stood around the two mirrored edifices studying them contemplatively, the three men riveted by what Clytemnestra was planning.

'Houston,' said Ethelred, breaking their reveries, 'we may have a problem!'

'Let me read your lips as you've read my mind,' said his wife quietly. 'You guys are *not* Superman.'

'Well sussed, Clyte! With all the will and all the wanking in the world, dearest – and even with the additional input of young Oswald – we will never be able to supply enough cum to cover those vast areas in any desired shape or form.'

'And that's where your former award winning film comes to the fore, husband dearest!'

'Award winning film? What film? How?'

'"Oswald the Arse Stretch"' Clytemnestra gave the three puzzled faces a grin. 'Don't you see? A substitute sperm to exaggerate or, if you'll excuse the pun, extricate your output! Albumen!'

'Albumen?' questioned Ethelred.

'But of course, egg whites! Genius, my dear Clytemnestra, pure bloody, brilliant, beautiful genius! And you couldn't be accused of cheating!' Charles, his face filled with admiration, turned to a confused Ethelred. 'Because, Red dear friend, sperm is an egg and albumen is the opaque white gunk in an *egg*!'

'And where, if I may as so bold to ask do we find an obliging ostrich?' This from a slightly miffed Ethelred at having had to have such an obvious connotation explained. 'Or do you plan a consignment of happy ostriches being brought over from Oudtshoorn?'

'Really Ethelred, let's not us having *you* doing a Trisomy!' sniped Clytemnestra. 'I've already been Googling madly and, would you believe, there are several ostrich farms here in England? I've gone and downloaded details of one in particular; spoken to them and they are happy to supply eggs by order. Problem solved.' She added drily, 'In fact, boys, apart from several requisite "money shots" of Monday ejaculating onto the actual palette and me doing my first bit of "magi mixing," you two lads are now redundant!'

'Bullshit to that!' laughed Ethelred. 'As director, my input is vital!'

'And my medical input is also vital,' laughed Charles. 'After all, I feel I have a responsibility when it comes to the quality – no, make that *consistency* – of the final glaze!'

'Points – or should that be penises? – noted. Your contributions will we warmly welcomed!' laughed Clytemnestra.

'I'll drink to that!' said Ethelred with a chuckle.

'No you won't!' reprimanded his wife. 'Not unless you fetch another bottle!'

CHAPTER 5

'Seriously Charles, how reliable is this Oswald creature?' The two men were sitting alone while Clytemnestra, having dealt with the initial sketches for the two works, had returned to her studio to add final touches to her preliminary script for the forthcoming documentary. Ethelred planned to go through the rough dialogue copies with her later.

'There's no need for a great deal of dialogue,' he explained, 'I've given you the basic scenario and at the end of the day it's more action than talking. We'll start with a shot of Monday catching your ad on the internet followed by his arrival at your studio. The shots of you sending the email, you at work on your first sketches, then you receiving the reply can all be done in one day. We'll begin shooting day after tomorrow.'

'How reliable…?'

Charles's mind flashed back to the initial conversation between himself, Clytemnestra, Monday and Ethelred, about his latest film offering. The original discussion with Ethelred concerning a suitable candidate for an Adonis figure had taken place a few weeks beforehand. However, with Ethelred's newly planned film, all could seriously change. The earlier conversation had been clear and to the point.

'We need a young man, Charles, very beautiful, vain and obsessed with his personal appearance. I suppose someone gay could be the answer; a gay young man who's a bit fly-by-night, not too bright, works in a mundane job where his presence is immaterial within the great pattern of things!' Ethelred gave a cynical smirk. 'A waiter or part-time tradesman – remember the body beautiful bit – would be ideal. Most gays I've met in that sort of business seem to spend most of their spare time at the gym or else getting pissed, being picked up or picking up!'

'Not quite true, Red.'

'But true enough. So, a young man who won't be missed is what I'm really looking for.'

'Why, is your Adonis going to disappear into the ether?'

'No, not quite the ether, but once Clytemnestra finishes with him, I do have an idea which has been festering in my brilliant mind.'

'Festering?'

'Indeed Charles. Festering, suppurating, formulating… call it what you wish, but it's an idea to cap all previous Ethelred Jones's art formats.' He gave Charles a long, calculating look. 'It also could lead to an interesting – how shall I put it – sideline for you, *doctor*! Do you think you could find such a… putting it tactfully, participant?'

'Easily, simply get one of those gay magazines, QX or such and call up one of the many rent boys who advertise.'

'Do that then Charles. Where can you get such an enlightening tome?'

'I'm in town tomorrow evening; I'll call by the Queen's Head in Chelsea or otherwise, as I'm at Balans in Old Brompton Road later for dinner, I'll pop across the road to the local Clone Zone and pick up QX and a few other magazines from there.'

'Balans?'

'A fun, elegant gay restaurant in Chelsea; it's where I'm dining with an old friend who runs an antique shop in Pimlico Road.'

'Pimlico Road? Poufs alley? Say no more!'

'Maybe Pip knows someone…'

'No way Charles; no way! This is strictly between us. I don't want, in fact I *insist*, no one but no one apart from us will be involved with what I am planning to do!'

Charles raised a placating hand. 'Point taken, my lips are sealed!'

'No, Charles, not sealed, not sealed at all! For it'll be your *non*-sealed lips that help you find our Adonis!'

———————

'Sorry I'm a few minutes late, Pip, but – and you'll never believe this – I simply had to dash across the road to Clone Zone!' Charles smiled down at the dapper, elderly man seated comfortably on one of the small banquettes alongside the bar in the popular restaurant.

Pip looked up from his copy of *The Standard*. *'Clone Zone?* Surely you're a bit old for sex toys Charles?' he said with a grin.

Charles gave a chuckle. 'No time for sex toys, you mean!' He slapped a handful of magazines onto the small table. 'Escorts, Pip! Bona fide escorts, or should that be *boner* fide?'

'Very droll, dear! And before you get carried away with your sage on a page, how about a drink?' Pip glanced up at the handsome, tall, dark haired young waiter smiling patiently down at the two men, Charles having now seated himself opposite his dinner guest.

'What are you having? A Martini?'

'Yes, but mine's gin, you prefer vodka, don't you dear?'

'Yes.' Charles smiled up at the waiter. 'Vodka on the rocks please, with a twist. Thank you err…'

'Willie,' smiled the young man. 'One vodkatini coming up,' he confirmed before turning away to deal with the order. 'On the cocks and with a twist!' he camped as he sashayed off to procure the order.

'No doubt who's Martha to some big butch Arthur with that one!' laughed Pip.

'Bit of the pot calling the kettle beige, dear,' retorted Charles, looking affectionately at the spry little man perched daintily opposite him, reminiscent of a naughty pixie: Pip sporting a blond coif, dapper yellow and blue polka dot tie, pink shirt plus a neat fitting navy blue suit and bold pink, blue, yellow and cream bargello-patterned waistcoat. 'You don't exactly scream Mighty Mouse, more Minnie!'

'Bitch!' hissed Pip, wriggling with delight at the comparison. 'This evening is going to be fun. I adore a dinner with skin and hair flying as both a starter and main course!'

'The vodkatini?'

Charles looked up at the waiter, not Willie but perhaps the most beautiful blond young man Charles had ever seen. 'For me, err and thank you.' said Charles, giving an ingratiating smile, 'Err…?'

'Oswald, sir; I'm your waiter for this evening.' He handed them each a menu. 'Would you like to know tonight's specials now?' He nodded to the specials of the day written up on a blackboard at the far end of the bar, 'Or would you like me to come back?'

Christ! Yes, I'd adore you to come back and get you on your back, legs in the air! thought Charles, saying instead, 'Yes, give us a few moments please. Meanwhile we'll definitely have another two of these before we order. And thank you, *Oswald*!' he added, his voice heavy with innuendo. *Ethelred, dear,* he said to himself, *I've just found your Adonis. Gorgeous, obviously on the make, fairly predictable, part-time I should think – possibly a wannabe actor – possibly a loner and, if the bait of a few spoiling dinners and some very nice cash-in-hand thank yous, along with a few little Gucci and Dolce prezzies are forthcoming, I think we're home and very, very wet!*

'You have that look,' murmured Pip, glancing at Charles from over the top of his Martini glass. 'By the pricking of my thumbs, I think you're thinking young Oswald's buns!' The little man gave a mischievous giggle. 'Am I or am I not a witch?'

'Yes dear, and one of the Miss Macbeth's originals!'

'Touché!' Pip couldn't resist a further giggle. 'However, you do surprise me dear, I would have thought the South African rugger bugger would have been more up your much experienced alley!'

'Rugger bugger?'

'The delicious Andries!' Pip nodded at the massively built, tall, dark, handsome man approaching their table. 'Surely you couldn't have missed him when here before?'

'Nobody could miss *that*!' hissed back Charles. 'I've simply been unlucky!'

'Good evening, gentlemen,' said the beaming man in a deep, clipped South African accent, 'Oswald looking after you?'

'Oh yes,' simpered Pip. 'But only as your understudy!'

'Excuse me?'

'Forgive my friend,' laughed Charles. 'He has a tendency to talk in riddles. Yes, thank you err…?'

'Andries.'

'And where are you from, Andries? I mean, which part of South Africa.'

'Cape Town. Ah, here's Oswald with your drinks. Enjoy your dinner.' With a dazzling smile, the beefy charmer made his way over to greet some new arrivals.

'Another few minutes please, Oswald,' said Charles with a smile. 'And then we'll order.' He gave a camp laugh. 'I take it you're one of the specials of the day?'

'Ohmigod sir!' shrieked Oswald. 'I *wish*!'

'You don't seriously fancy *that*, do you?' said Pip, an incredulous expression on his smooth, Clinque – enhanced face as Oswald glided away.

'Since when have you gone for the prancing pansy? I would have thought the able-bodied Andries more your type?'

'Andries the manager? The meeter and greeter? Andries, in case you mayn't have noticed, you drooling, salivating old queen, is straight with a capital "S". I remember him now from another Balans where I was put in my place firmly on that point.'

'I think I'll have to have a third Martini before I even *glare* at a menu!' pouted Pip. He gave a theatrical sigh, followed by an exaggerated shrug of his narrow shoulders. 'But you still haven't answered my question; why the fascination with the blond Barbie doll?'

'Pip, dear Pip, although I go for the big, butch bears, a change is as good as a rest. Inserting as well as being inserted depends on my mood. Tonight I fancy a bit of insertion!'

'Well, la di da di bloody da!' camped Pip, adding. 'By the way, have you read that little gem by Robin Anderson? No? You don't know what you're missing, dear. It's a *hoot*!'

'Good, I need something to cheer me up in Castle Dracula.' Charles gave a small, theatrical shudder. 'I'll add it to my silk stocking list for baby Jesus' big day.' The shudder was replaced by a high pitched giggle, 'However, in answer to your *penetrating* question, Miss Hemlock, *dear*! I may – depending on how the evening goes – suggest a quiet after closing drink with our frail Justin Bieber lookalike.'

'You wouldn't dare?'

'Watch this space, sweetheart.'

Several hours later and after a fifty pound gratuity, Oswald duly arrived at the Jumeirah Carlton Tower for a 'nightcap' with Charles in his suite. Charles, on Ethelred's insistence, had reserved the opulent space on one of the upper floors. 'Dazzle the shit out of our guinea pig to be!' had been his given instructions. 'And, depending on the malleability of the lad, perhaps not only a discreet envelope to say "thank you" for a night to remember, but an early morning skip in lieu of a jog across the street to Gucci wouldn't go amiss!'

Charles had, as instructed, duly inserted; produced the relevant envelope; escorted Oswald across the elegant Sloane Street to Gucci and ended up treating him to a glamorous lunch at the famous San Lorenzo restaurant in Beauchamp Place. The sight of international socialite Ivana Trump lunching with a group of elegant women capped Oswald's day.

As Charles confirmed later when regaling Ethelred with the night and day's events, 'I have a feeling the chosen Oswald is about to be well and truly bitched. Having been so brilliantly buggered and bedecked, he is now totally bedazzled! In other words, the malleable little cunt is completely and utterly bitched, buggered and *very* bewildered!'

It was to be several weeks after a series of what had become a weekly routine of frantic couplings and wild extravagances before Charles broached the young man about a possible scam, a scam which would see both their fortunes 'go beyond any imaginings,' with the devious doctor planning to mentally seduce Oswald into joining him as his partner in the sure fire scheme. Oswald, a regular visitor to Charles's suite – 'The Sloane Street Shagella' as they both dubbed it – at the luxurious hotel on Cadogan Place, had again joined Charles after his part-time shift at Balans. Charles, lying back against a bank of pillows, an enormous recently-used black, latex dildo glistening on the bedside cabinet alongside him – Oswald's insatiable demands for being "bottom" to Charles's "top" had resulted in a by now acutely disinterested Charles having resorted to a starling variety of oversized sex toys for their weekly dalliances! – smiled inwardly. *Well, Ethelred and Clyte,* he said to himself, *it's now or never! So my dears, here goes!*

He glanced over at the dozing young man stretched out on the king size bed, his legs and arms akimbo on the tousled sheets, his long, limp uncut penis hanging forlornly between his muscular, sunlamp enhanced thighs. He gave a slight smile at the familiar small, tattooed 'His' on Oswald's right ankle; a sheepish Oswald having confessed on an earlier occasion how he and Bryan, when stoned, having had their ankles done. 'Our Samantha Cameron's' he had giggled, referring to the small tattoo which could be seen on the ankle of the British Prime Minister's so-called stylish wife, and referred to by Oswald as 'that frump in a frock.' He had giggled even more when revealing the tattoo on his lover's ankle read 'Hers.'

You are quite, quite glorious young Oswald, Charles said to himself once more. *Such a pity...* 'Oswald, Ossy dear, you awake?'

'Mmmm... just dozing.' Oswald opened one large blue eye. 'Did anyone ever tell you you're a demon with a dildo?'

Charles gave a false laugh, 'Only you, my pet!' he said, giving Oswald's rapidly swelling cock a small tweak. 'Think some pure thoughts for a moment while I get us a glass of champagne. Or would you prefer something else?'

'Champagne would be perfect,' murmured Oswald, opening his other eye and regarding his cock rising determinedly from its nest of soft blond curls. 'Your little friend is becoming wide awake," he giggled. "And what's more he's missing his thick new black friend already. Oh shit!" Oswald added on letting out a soft, burbling fart. 'I think Mr. Dildo's extra coating of KY has just decided to make an exit!' He placed an exploratory hand behind his toned rump. 'Fuck! Make that definite shit as opposed to "oh shit!"'

Charles withheld his grimace at Oswald's crude remark. 'Get up and put on some clothes and join me in the sitting room,' he said somewhat brusquely. 'I have a serious business proposition to put to you!'

'Oh my,' trilled Oswald, 'I do so like it when you get butch, business and brutal, Charlie!' He pointed to his rampant hard on. 'It makes me go all weak at the knees and totally *rigid* with fear elsewhere!'

Charles couldn't help but laugh. 'Silly tosser!' he said affectionately. 'C'mon young Ossy, I really do want to talk to you.' He gave the curious young man a wink and held out one of the courtesy bathrobes. 'Here, I'll get the drinks while you have a quick shower and sluice off Mr. Dildo's deposits. We wouldn't want skid marks on the nice upholstery now, would we?'

'Pity, I was rather looking forward to doing some finger painting!' replied Oswald with a titter.

After a few minutes, Oswald joined Charles sitting on a sofa, a note-pad on the coffee-table in front of him.

'Ah, bathed and even more beautiful,' said Charles, having berated himself for his slight loss of temper earlier. 'Cool it, Charles,' he'd muttered admonishingly. 'No slip ups at this crucial stage, doctor dear; in fact, no slip ups, period!'

'Sorry about the slight temper tantrum back there, my love. But what I'm about to discuss with you is extremely serious.' He gave the puzzled young man a piercing look. 'What do you really think of me Oswald? I mean, seriously think? And I don't mean as a part-time fuck or – God, how I hate the expression – a bit of a soft touch!'

Oswald's expression changed from puzzlement to one of shock. 'Charles,' he gasped. Moving quickly around the table he put his arms around him. 'A bit of a soft touch?' he whispered, 'Are you *insane*? You silly, demented queen, I'm in *love* with you!'

Charles's solemn expression changed to one of bewilderment. 'You are?' he said weakly. 'Oh my darling young man, then it makes what I'm about to say much easier.' He cleared his throat. 'I love you too, Ossy. So much so I'm about to tell you something that, should you decide to do the dirty on me, could see me in a lot of trouble.' Charles paused for added effect. 'You may not know it, but I have a record, a *criminal* record. I was a bona fide surgeon before being struck off the medical register...'

'No!' cried Oswald, his thin hands flying to his face in a parody of Edvard Munch's, 'The Scream'.

Charles couldn't hide a smile. 'It's not *that* dramatic!' he laughed. 'But, if what I am about to tell you was known by anyone else, I'd be in severe trouble again.' He took Oswald by the hand. 'I'll need your help with this, Ossy. Now you've said those three magical words, I know my idea can only be a success. Here, let me get our champagne and I'll explain.' The bottle duly fetched, Charles settled back comfortably onto the sofa. 'First of all, I've got to arrange for you to meet the Joneses, the ridiculous Ethelred and his cunt of a wife, Clytemnestra – or Clit, as I secretly call her. Then there is the daughter, Trisomy, not only a mongoloid but a mongoloid afflicted with an ageing disease.' He gave a disparaging snort. 'And no, before you ask, not even *I* could have made that one up.' Charles took a sip of champagne. 'The poor child's parents plan to make a cartoon film of the pathetic child's brief life. A *cartoon,* would you believe? Clit, who is a bacterial artist; which means she paints using such materials as shit and spit.' He looked at Oswald who sat regarding him with disbelief. 'I joke not; she truly does and makes a fortune. Isn't there an old saying about muck and money?' Charles gave a light laugh. 'But here is the sickest part, mummy is going to be using parts from Trisomy, yes Oswald, body parts of the poor little bitch, to create a series of puppets for the film which daddy is going to produce and direct. Trisomy's hair, what's left of it, will be used on some shrunken, papier mâché head – or more than likely her *actual* head – her nail clippings possibly used as eyelashes! They are going to use parts of their own flesh and blood for a supposed fucking *art* movie! It's the Muppets but with the monster child being the Munster-like child!'

Oswald gave a horrified cry, 'No! No! You can't mean it...?'

'Oh but Ossy darling, I *do* mean it. Also, it's been under some very serious discussion.' Charles lowered his voice conspiratorially. 'Because of my past misdeeds, I've already been offered a substantial fee for my cooperation. I've more or less agreed to assist Red and Clit, and, should you be willing to help me – and I do need your help – this is where we, as a team, as soulmates, come in.' Looking Oswald straight in his wide blue eyes, he added with a hiss. 'We let those two devils, incarnate go so far as to incriminate themselves; then we expose them! I'll need your assistance in gathering all sorts of incriminating evidence, taking photographs and such. Once those sick fucks, the Joneses, are incarcerated for what can only be life sentences, we produce a book – I've even thought of a title, *Trisomy, The Twisted Trimvirate* – and after the book, we sell the film rights of the whole, hideous plot. Better still' – Charles paused before final denouement – 'As nobody will ever know which is the *real* Trisomy, we ourselves then go on to make the cartoon picture that never was!' He added sinisterly, 'But will we or will we not be using the real McCoy?!'

Charles gave an evil chuckle. 'Rather like those mysterious McCaans? Did they or didn't they? Keep funding but you'll never find out!' Charles added his final punch line with relish. 'Is the child the Joneses eventually bury, *really* the real tragic Trisomy? The genuine artefact? Even as a disgraced doctor I am still capable of verifying a death if needs be. Who's to know the aged, wrinkled Progeria – induced corpse isn't in fact the body of a monkey as opposed to that of their precious little girl, a true, sad victim of nature's hideous cruelty?'

'I think I'm going to be sick!'

'No, you're not, Oswald. You are my lover and about to become my partner in both business and crime. Furthermore, we are going to become the most famous – and rich – gay couple on the planet!'

Oswald did not throw up but kissed Charles instead.

'And,' added Charles much later as Oswald lay alongside him with Charles's fist and forearm firmly impaled up his arse, 'there's also talk of the Clit painting a portrait of Adonis *before* the Trisomy debacle. Apparently little Trisomy has to age a little more so, nothing will really start for at least another six months; hence the portrait.' He slowly withdrew part of his arm much to his lover's annoyance.

'Push it back!' whined Oswald. 'Ossy wants Charlie to play pumping pistons again!'

'Christ, I've been so blind!' Charles suddenly cried. 'The fucking answers staring us right in the face. Why, it's you Ossy! *You* can be Adonis!' In his excitement he inadvertently jerked the rest of his fist from Oswald's gaping arsehole, resulting in a loud phut, followed by a series of squelches and long, dribbling wet fart.

'That *hurt*!' grizzled Oswald, biting his lip and crimping up his sphincter muscle. 'But Ossy want's *more*!'

'Later darling,' continued Charles, ignoring the demanding buttocks thrust determinedly against his exposed hand. 'What we have to do is make sure you meet the Joneses. The rest will be a doddle or, in your case young Oswald, a *dil*-doddle!'

Charles's call to Ethelred was succinct. 'The little fruit is right for the fucking! So, Red, full steam ahead with those dinner arrangements and we've got ourselves a bountiful beauty. Clyte has her Adonis, you your star and me my donations! Who said good things don't come in threes?'

True to plan, Oswald was waiting at the Joneses dinner during the awards dinner and approached Ethelred and Clytemnestra as arranged; the introduction leading to an invitation to Bethlem Báthory. Not once did Oswald and Charles let it slip they knew each other or supposedly instigated the initial introduction.

CHAPTER 6

'Where is everybody?'

Ethelred looked up at Charles from a sheaf of papers he was reading. 'Clyte is in her studio preparing for tomorrow's take with Monday. Meanwhile the man in question is presently playing big brother to Trisomy in between clipping Clyte's cunt!'

'A charming scenario!' Charles sat down opposite Ethelred. 'Who's collecting the sacrificial lamb when he arrives tomorrow if Monday's in cahoots with you and Clytemnestra? Boris? Or shall I?'

'Definitely you, if you don't mind, Charles. You meeting him gave you the opportunity to remind the dear lad you and he have never met; apart from his only visit here.' Ethelred gave the doctor one of his famous penetrating stares. 'This Oswald we're staking so much on? I worry about any loose ends, friends and such; people who may just miss him. I know he says he has no contact with his family and apart from a few acquaintances at work, there seems to be only this one friend, a lover perhaps? Most important of all, are you one hundred and *ten* percent sure about our choice? Do you think he's capable of playing along, no questions asked?' He gave Charles a reassuring smile. 'There's still time – if you're having any doubts, Charlie boy – to look around for another waif and definite stray; one of the homeless perhaps?"

'Rest assured Red, our choice could not have been better! The only blot on the landscape' – Charles couldn't avoid a snigger at his indirect reference to Clytemnestra's paintings – 'is, as you say, the friend, Bryan;

Bryan something-Italian-or-other. But as for Oswald, he has *no* idea as to what is in store for him. He seriously thinks the whole matter is a devious scheme innocent old me has dreamed up, a scheme which sees the demise of you and Clyte. But only after the conniving little shit has had his fifteen minutes of fame as a Jones star, albeit a bit player!'

'I like the 'bit player' *bit*!' said Ethelred with a laugh. 'I'll enlighten you on the *bit* later.'

'He's desperate to be part of the Jones magic whether simply as a gofer or even a – and please don't go on about it again, Red – bit player. I really feel his fifteen minutes of fame is all the little sod really cares about! To be quite honest, I don't think he really believes he and I could pull off such a coup involving the two of you.' Charles gave a sly smile, 'Meanwhile, while I don't know *exactly* what devious ploy you're up to, I have a pretty damn good idea.'

Ethelred chose to ignore the dig. 'Maybe this Bryan something-Italian-or-other could – if needs be – be persuaded to join his buddy? I mean, if the Italianate Bryan poses a threat, at least if he's here, he can be dealt with.'

'May I suggest we cross that bridge when we come to it?' Charles gave a laugh. 'I must say Clyte is right when she says you talk in riddles. Talking to you at times is like trying to find one's way out of a maze of double entendres and innuendos!' He glanced at the pile of papers and booklets in front of Ethelred. 'Anything new on the riddling Jones's agenda before we all meet?'

'Actually yes; apart from the exorbitant price of those fucking ostrich eggs,' Ethelred waved the offensive invoice at him, 'there *is* something else which is very, very up your street! Now, where did I put it…? Ah, a little number I ordered for you!' Ethelred gave a laugh. 'No, not that sort of little number, no ill-fitting twin set from a mail order catalogue! Here, take a look at this.' He held out a loosely bound book about half an inch thick. 'It's to do with what I was about to discuss the other night before we got carried away with Clyte's own bloody demands. This could be incorporated with what I want to talk to you all about at our meeting later. With the imminent arrival of Oswald, I would like to get the preliminaries out of the way; keeping everything strictly within the family as it were. Hence the Spanish Inquisition type scenario concerning the lad. I must say I'm now worrying about this Bryan friend but, as you so rightly say, we'll deal with that little matter should the situation arise.' He waggled the book playfully. 'C'mon, take it if you dare!'

Charles leaned across the cluttered desk to take the book from Ethelred. He glanced quickly at the cover. 'The Breakthrough Mammal Taxidermy Manual?' he said, his face breaking into a wicked grin. 'Are you thinking what I'm thinking?'

'I sincerely hope so! An extension of your already practised err... delectations, if I may be so bold! An improvement on those sheep you've been supposedly stuffing as opposed to fucking over the past few weeks in that vice pit of yours!'

'Whoever said bestiality and buggering didn't mix!' quipped Charles. 'My God, at last a chance to have a go with the real McCoy...!'

Ethelred gave the doctor a matching grin before glancing down at his watch, 'Christ! Look at the time!' He looked back at Charles. 'I'd better go and alert Clytemnestra – time becomes immaterial to her when she's working – and if you could get Madam Trisomy away from ogling Monday's crotch so as to leave her with the ever reliable Mrs. N, perhaps you and the magnificent black Mandingo may deign to join us?'

'And why not, Massa Red,' camped Charles affecting the Deep South tones he and Monday continuously adopted, much to the annoyance of the very politically correct Mrs. Norelle. 'Missy Monday and big Massa Charles may jus deign to do dat. Sah!'

'And whilst you're in your "Gone With The Fart" mode, get Missy Monday to make a pitcher or two of dem big, big Martini pitchers!'

'Yassa massa! En in da return can Massa aska da big Monday mon to fucka da doctor?'

'Jesus, you never give up, do you Charlie boy? The only Charlie big Monday is interested in i*s white* powder Charlie!' Ethelred shook his shaggy head in mock disbelief. 'How many times do I have to tell you Man Monday is as straight as the M4 motorway and is shagging Angela Anstruther, our local baronet's rapacious and – so Mon tell me – insatiable wife!'

'Bugger!'

'Unfortunately no!' Ethelred gave a snigger. 'Sadly for you my, friend, I'd say the chance of you ever getting Monday into the sack in order to satisfy your undying lust is bugger all!'

'A disgraced doctor can dream...'

'Dear disgraced doctor, wait until you hear what I have to say to the team. It'll be a case of me, Ethelred the director supreme, winner of the Golden Phallus, giving the doctor a prescription to cure *all* his longings and lustings!'

'Can't you tell me now?'

'What, and put you out of your misery? You seem to have forgotten, my friend, Ethelred Jones – at times – is a bona fide sadist.' Ethelred gave a snort. 'Rather like your namesake, Miz "Charlotte" Manson!'

'Jesus, just because I inadvertently hacked of someone's balls… besides, *you're* the bloody Manson lookalike!' He gave Ethelred a pained look. 'And you *know* I hate it when you and Clyte refer to me as that!'

'Of course we do! That's why we do it! Now, hush, hush sweet *Charlotte*!' Ethelred blew Charles a kiss, 'Go on! Away with you! Off you go and take over from the dear little Trisomy from gawking at Mandingo's dick! And Charles…?'

'Yes, you cruel, uncaring, nonconformist sod?' replied Charles with a grin.

'If you're really desperate, there's always *moi*!'

'Now I *know* you're the most evil sadist of them all. What a *horrendous* fate for anyone! Sadly, my memory serves me only too, too well!'

———

'So?' Clytemnestra looked at the three men sitting comfortably on the deep, upholstered sofas in the conservatory off Ethelred's studio. She lightly toasted each in turn with her Martini glass. 'Spill the sperm, Ethelred dear. We're all ears. Thanks to you finally seeing the light and me now having my moment of glory with "Dark Reflections" – it's your turn. The floor is yours!' She gave her husband a playful smile. 'Really, darling, I don't know what's going on in those black cells in your equally as black, evil brain, but you look more like a cat that's just got a gallon – never mind a saucer – of something slightly more satisfying than mere cream!'

'*Still Life*!'

'Still life?' questioned Clytemnestra raising a perfectly formed eyebrow and shaking her head in mock exasperation. She gave Monday and Charles a wink. 'Still life? Of course there's still life. In a way, the shroud painting involved with "Dark Reflections" can be seen as such a form.'

'Still Life,' repeated Ethelred with a wolverine smile.

'Still life?' Clytemnestra gave a light, irritated laugh. 'Ethelred you can be so maddeningly *obtuse* at times. Kindly explain what you're getting at with this *still life* you keep referring to?' With a theatrical sigh she glanced at Charles and Monday for support. Seeing nothing but their smirks at her obvious irritation she turned back to Ethelred in exasperation. 'You do talk the most unexpurgated shit at times, Ethelred, my sweet! As I've said before; stop talking in *riddles*!'

'I'll say it again. "Still Life" is what I'm talking about and "Still Life" is to be the title of my next major – and I sincerely trust – award winning film.' Ethelred smiled at the three faces staring back at him; Charles and Monday trying to stifle their laughing and Clytemnestra's mouth was beginning to twitch. How they enjoyed teasing 'Herr Director' when he got on his pompous and extremely high horse!

'What are you planning to do, show the exhumation of the Queen Mum and have her doing a Moon Dance with Michael Jackson?' Charles gave a guffaw at his flash of wit.

'Or, better still, have Hitler doing the crematorium cha cha with a line of shaven-headed Jews in striped Bruno-inspired shorts singing "Crema – torium here we come?' This from Clytemnestra.

'Or Idi Amin in drag doing a Shirley Bassey and singing "Bad Niggaaaaaah!?"' boomed Monday, letting out a deep belly laugh at his contribution.

Ethelred shook his head, 'Tut tutting' sadly as he gave the gleeful three a pitiful look. 'So sad, so very, very sad,' he muttered as he stretched forward to pour himself another Martini from the pitcher. 'Right, enough is enough. For all your slanderous, puerile and childish jibes, you actually are being very complimentary by showing an appreciation of how very dark and twisted the Jones mind can be! But now my dears, instead of behaving like spoilt little Trisomys, it's time to be sensible grownups and listen to what Daddy Ethelred is about to say,' the timbre in Ethelred's voice having the desired effect.

With apologetic murmurs the three rearranged themselves accordingly in front of their lord and master – Charles having quickly refilled their glasses – and sat back waiting for him to continue. With his innate directional skill Ethelred had managed to make them aware that what they were about to hear was, in fact, determinedly adult and also very important.

'As I said before, my lovelies, it's to be a major film with a theme which will be of benefit to us all.' He held up three fingers to his left hand. 'One,' he pinched the first finger with the fingers of his right hand. 'You, my dear Clytemnestra, will need a new exhibition to cap your "Reflections" success. Mark my words, your "Dark Reflections" – which I strongly suggest you show as one massive double work along with only the video documentary and no other paintings to detract – will see London's elite thronging to the Claudia Cordelle gallery to see this extraordinary, latest offering.' He bowed his head gallantly in his wife's direction, a mesmerised Clytemnestra hanging onto his every word. 'I therefore suggest, my dear, a further exhibition in the same genre of "Secretions" as a major follow up to this.' His smile broadened. 'Doesn't the title "Corpses, *Coup d'oeil* and Collages" conjure up a whole new universe of never seen before imagery?' He held up his right hand to silence her. 'Two,' he pinched the second finger on his left hand. 'You, Monday, your expertise in creating a suitable ambiance – in other words – getting the models into the mood will see you much, much in demand. Again, your exceptional personal attribute will also have its place – or should that be places? Supply and demand, Monday man. Supply and demand! Think stimulation, masturbation, copulation and even a touch of necrophilia thrown in for your extraordinarily large measure!'

Monday couldn't resist a self-satisfied smirk at the innuendo and compliment, his look becoming slightly puzzled by the last referral.

Ethelred took a deep breath before pinching and wiggling the third finger. 'And finally number three! Now what does – or did – our disgraced doctor supply for which there is always a demand and very little supply?'

'I *knew* it!' yelped Charles, jumping from his seat and giving Ethelred a high five. 'I fucking well *knew* it!'

'Knew *what*?' cried Clytemnestra in frustration. 'You're still talking in ridiculous riddles Ethelred, and I'm *none* the bloody wiser!'

Ethelred paused for a teasing moment before saying in a ghoulish whisper. 'I'm finally going to do it. "Still Life" is going to be an honest to God *snuff* film!'

Clytemnestra and Monday remained thunderstruck whereas Charles kept repeating to nobody in particular. 'I knew it! I just knew it! Bless you Red! Bless you! Bless you! Bless you!'

'A *snuff* film?' whispered Clytemnestra, 'Husband dear, have you gone totally mad? You're talking murder here!'

'No I'm not, Clyte dearest.' Ethelred gave his wife a beatific smile. 'I'm talking about *art*! Art with the biggest capital 'A' you can imagine! You, Clytemnestra Jones, will be the "Still" part of the work. Your imagery of the victim, the corpse, will be, literally, a camera-like "Still" part of the life I film. You Charles, you're the "Life" part of the painting because you, with your contacts, will be selling off various vital, much needed organs to those undercover organ donor organisations.' Ethelred gave a snigger, 'Organ-nisations – geddit? And also think of all the money we all *ged*! As for you, Monday,' said Ethelred, looking pointedly at the eagerly listening man's melon-like bulge. 'Your responsibility will be getting all the models, male and female, into a suitable euphoric state before the final denouement! You'll be able to fuck, enjoy a suck and to perform the wildest, most sadistic and *disgusting* images you have ever imagined; no holds barred!' He gazed piercingly at the large, visibly aroused giant, beads of perspiration appearing on his high black forehead. Taking a slow sip from his glass, Ethelred – well aware that the three opposite were now entirely in his thrall – added softly, 'The way I plan it there will be more than one model required, but I have already selected our first "rehearsal" as it were.'

'Rehearsal?' questioned Clytemnestra.

'Well, Clyte dearest, pray tell me *exactly* what one is supposed to do with a left over, never-even-*scene,* Adonis?' Ethelred gave a small chuckle, 'An Adonis who will be completely redundant after he's made his little deposit! It's so obvious; we use little known, "he won't be missed" Oswald, for a practice run!'

'Ethelred, have you really thought this through? Thought about all the possible *criminal* consequences?' An ashen-faced Clytemnestra sat looking at Ethelred with genuine horror and disbelief.

'Before you condemn what could be the most momentous and prestigious happening in all our lives, Clyte, please hear me out. You haven't heard, as yet my dearest darling, the grand finale to end all grand finales!' He nodded to Charles who stared back at him as if momentarily stunned.

'But of course!' Charles suddenly cried, holding up the book he'd been given earlier. 'I think what Ethelred is trying to say is, after we've had our wicked, wanton ways with Oswald, we – literally – *stuff the snuff*!'

'How long will you be away?' asked Bryan, looking forlornly at his friend across the table in their local Indian restaurant.

'Depends on how long the shoot takes,' said Oswald loftily, having no idea as to what they would be filming, nevermind the title of the venture.

'Oh. Will you miss me?'

'Of course I'll miss you, you idiot.' Oswald gave Bryan a reassuring smile. 'It's only Berkshire, not bloody Bulgaria!' He broke off a piece of his popadom. 'Tell you what, once I've checked out the shooting schedule' – *at least that sounds right,* he said to himself – 'I'll see if I can invite you down for the day. Perhaps you could even stay overnight, that's if you could get away.'

Bryan gave his congealing chicken masala a lethargic stir before looking up at Oswald, his eyes brimming with tears.

'What?' Oswald startled. 'Jesus Bryan, don't do this to me! For fuck's sake, don't start blubbing in the fucking Bengal Star!'

'It's so bloody unfair,' sniffed Bryan. 'Oh shit, Os, I wasn't going to tell you. I didn't want to mess up our last evening together but,' – his voice broke – 'I've been made redundant!'

'*Redundant*? When? Why?'

'Two days ago,' replied Bryan sheepishly. 'I was caught giving Geoff Masters, the manager, a blow job in the Gents!'

'You *what*?' Oswald crumpled up the paper serviette and threw it onto his plate. 'I don't believe you! One moment you swear undying love and the next moment you're *blowing Geoff Masters* in the fucking toilet? Fuck that for starters; I'm out of here!' Pulling a wad of notes – courtesy of Charles – from his pocket, Oswald smacked a twenty down on the Formica topped table. Pulling himself up to his full height he tossed back his blond head before saying dramatically, 'As they say in show business, "Don't call us; we'll call you!" Good *bye*, Bryan!'

'Shit!' Bryan sat looking at the empty chair opposite. 'Shit!' he said again.

'Everything to bestest perfection, sir?' The young Indian waiter stood looking anxiously at the muttering customer.

'Oh, bloody bestest perfection, thank you,' muttered Bryan, 'if you like shit!'

'Sir?'

'Oh, sorry! May I have the bill please? My friend wasn't feeling well – no, no, nothing to do with the food – so I need to go and see if he's alright.'

The bill was produced at lightning speed and paid in the same manner. Bryan had half expected to find Oswald waiting outside for him as was usually the case after one of what appeared to be their ever increasing spats but, to his dismay, the street was empty. 'Fuck!' He kicked out at an empty lager can lying in the gutter. 'That, Oswald Argent, is where you're going to be, sooner than later, mark my words.' Hands placed firmly in his pockets, Bryan made his way to the bus stop. 'Your friend Charles is up to no good and you – you stupid queen – can't see it. Don't be too surprised, my friend, if you find yourself involved in something *very* unpleasant.' He gave a laugh. '*Wannabe Actor Goes AWOL* as a headline in *The Sun* wouldn't surprise me at all!'

———————

Back in his bedsit, Oswald sat looking around the dismal room, the de rigueur vodka and orange juice in his hand. 'Fuck!' He kicked out at the scarred coffee table. 'No, make that a *no* more fuck where you're concerned, bloody Bryan pain in the arse, bloody Eye Tie Scima!' He took a long sip. 'Well, my ex-friend, tomorrow sees this Oswald off to a new life, a new beginning.' He raised his glass. 'Here's to you, Ethelred Jones and here's to you, Charlie boy. What a breakthrough meeting you in Balans that night. But, at the end of the day, let's forget the two of you. You're just the bottom rung of my ladder! I have my sights on other things. Forget being a half-baked star in one of your – let's face it, fuck awful, dismal films, Mr. Jones – this Oswald has bigger fish to fry. Now, take that Miles Anstruther, there's someone I'm definitely planning on *bumping* into again!'

———————

Bryan sat on the bus, deep in thought, staring vaguely at the passing street. *Fuck it!* He thought. *Life is for living and maybe Oswald Argent is for forgetting. Once the stupid cunt's come to his senses, but only then, I may possibly see him again.* He looked at his watch. 'Why the hell not?' he muttered to his reflection in the grimy window. 'The bus literally stops outside.' He gave a small hollow laugh. 'Maybe destiny's brought me here! Infinity, here I come!'

Infinity, a popular late night gay bar situated on the Old Brompton Road in Earl's Court, was – to quote one visitor standing by the crowded bar – 'bursting at the jeans!' Bryan, having purchased himself a large vodka and tonic from the long bar, made his way to the inner sanctum of the club where he stood, surveying the animated, happy crowd. The night was young enough for the usual predatory atmosphere of such late night venues not to have made itself known. People were more intent on enjoying themselves as opposed to entering into serious cruise mode.

'An improvement on the old Bromptons, don't you think?' Bryan gave a startled look to his left from where the question had come. The speaker, a tall, thickset, good-looking, middle-aged, ruddy-faced man, casually dressed in a roll neck sweater, well-tailored tweed jacket plus dark twill trousers, and looking definitely out of place among the Tee-shirted, jean or chino clad young crowd, smiled hesitantly down at the shorter young man.

'Err... I can't really say,' replied Bryan. 'I only came here once or twice when it was Bromptons.' He gave a self-deprecating laugh before adding, 'To be honest, I was usually too pissed to notice!'

'Well,' said the tall man with a smile. 'If I offer you another drink hopefully you won't be too pissed to notice?' He gave an embarrassed laugh. 'Not that I'm suggesting you are... oh, shit! You know what I mean...'

'I'm not pissed; not planning to get pissed and yes, another drink would be great, thanks!' smiled Bryan, 'Vodka tonic.'

'Likewise. Hold on here and I'll be right back. Oh, the name is Miles, by the way.'

'Nice to meet you Miles. I'm Bryan.'

Miles returned with their drinks, which they sipped slowly, eyeing each other warily and making small talk about the other people in the bar. Bryan was delighted to note Miles had a waspish sense of humour behind all the bluster, while Miles, in turn, stood admiring the stocky, well-built and very handsome young man. *Nice bit of a jack-the-lad,* he thought. *Not a bit of rough but not an obvious queen either; either a salesman or something else equally mediocre and safe.*

Bryan's thoughts were running in a similar vein, his mental views being, *the guy's a gent – probably a banker or something in the city. Good looking guy though, big bugger, bet he's got a dick and a half. He gave an inward giggle. Bit of a contrast to you, Os. Big man boy as opposed to a beautiful camp boy!* 'Sorry! I didn't hear you?'

'I was saying,' said Miles, 'if you haven't eaten, I'm famished, and would you care to join me for a bite to eat? It's still early and I'm sure there's a place open near here.'

'Now you mention it, so am I,' replied Bryan, the congealing plate at the Bengal Star already forgotten. He looked at his watch. 'It's just gone ten and there's a great place about five minutes away.'

'Ah,' said Miles, 'Talk about telepathy! You must mean The Troubadour! Great jazz club there as well. I still use the restaurant and was a frequent visitor to the club many years ago! What a good idea. Shall we?'

I was actually thinking Balans, thought Bryan wryly. *But why not The Troubadour? Besides, all those Balans queens will be wondering why I'm there if Oswald isn't working tonight.*

Bryan would inevitably come to Balans at the end of Oswald's evening shift, have a drink and then the two would leave either to return to Oswald's bedsit in Clapham or, on very rare occasions, to Bryan's flat in Fulham. Oswald's flat was the more acceptable due to Bryan having a flatmate who, though not a lover or even ex-lover, drew a line at Bryan having Oswald to stay overnight. To quote Bryan, 'Os and Tim are like a mongoose and a cobra! They can't stand the sight of each other!'

The walk to the Troubadour took less than a few minutes, and Bryan was surprised by the warm greeting given to Miles by the dapper little manager who rushed across the crowded room to greet him, hand outstretched and with a beaming smile; his second surprise coming at the actual greeting. 'Sir Miles,' said the little manager. 'What an honour and a pleasure! Long time no see! You'll be dining?'

'Good evening, Dariusz,' replied Miles. 'Yes, two please, if you can fit us in!' He glanced around the crowded restaurant. 'You're jumping as always.'

'Yes sir, and Sir Miles,' added the diminutive Dariusz conspiratorially, 'we have Prince Harry in the club tonight! He's becoming quite a regular!' He gave another smile. 'Would a table in the Chalet be suitable? It's a bit quieter in there.'

'The Chalet will be fine, thank you Dariusz,' smiled Miles. Motioning Bryan to follow, he made his way in the wake of the manager past the long bar to the small panelled dining room. Having been seated and their drinks ordered – Miles had suggested they went straight on to wine and promptly requested a bottle of *Crozes Ermitage* from the ever smiling manager – he then suggested they both have the Troubadour Rib Eye Steaks, medium rare, with Bernaise sauce and French Fries. 'Do you like garlic?' questioned Miles. 'The mushrooms they serve with the steak are very garlicky, but if you're game, I'm game.' The big man immediately flushed at the implication of his remark. Bryan however, his head spinning, seemed oblivious to the comment but remained looking at the other elegant people sitting and talking animatedly around them. *Sir* Miles? And obviously, from the greeting he had received, well-known to the management and staff. For the first time Bryan became aware of his too tight T-shirt, his scuffed leather jacket and well-worn jeans. *Christ,* he said to himself. *I must look like some fucking rent boy or dumb hustler. This guy must be crazy to bring me here or perhaps this is where he brings all his tricks and they're so used to it, they don't bat an eye.*

'You seem to be well known here, *Miles*!' said Bryan, his cheeks reddening. 'I gather I'm not the first bit of ignorant rough you've dragged in here?'

'Ignorant rough? Dragged? What are you going on about, Bryan?' said Miles looking genuinely concerned. 'Oh,' he added, leaning back against the wooden seat. 'Don't tell me? Simply because Dariusz knows me and because you're not exactly GQ in your getup *and* I ordered for you, do you think anyone, but anyone, is going to take the blindest bit of notice? Come on Bryan, you're bigger than that!'

'Why did you ask me for dinner? Is it in the hope to get laid?' Bryan's earlier, pent up frustration and anger with Oswald coming to the fore.

'Bryan, please!' Miles nodded discreetly at a couple who, having heard the brief exchange, were eyeing them with some alarm.

Bryan, about to shout 'What the fuck are you looking at?' thought better of it, murmuring a quiet, 'Sorry, I didn't mean to be rude...'

'Ah, our wine,' said Miles in a relieved voice. He smiled up at the waiter. 'Thank you Adam, I'm sure it's fine; simply pour it, will you?'

Oh shit, thought Bryan, *now he's embarrassed and probably thinks I'll throw another number if he tastes the wine. Then not only will I look a complete yob but no doubt begin behaving like one!* 'What do you do, Miles?' he asked, changing the subject.

'Me, I'm in overseas real estate amongst other things,' said Miles with a disarming smile. 'And what do you do, Bryan?'

'I was in travel...'

'Was?'

'Well, with the economic climate, people are cutting back and,' Bryan took a deep breath, 'I've just been made redundant.'

Miles looked at the dark, handsome young man in genuine dismay. 'That's tough,' he said. 'Tell me about it, if you want to. No,' he raised his glass. 'Seriously, tell me about it and tell me what you are now planning on doing instead.'

To Bryan's surprise he found himself talking openly to the bluff, kindly man sitting opposite him. A second bottle of wine was ordered plus two steaming plates of steak pie, the original steaks and fries having been overlooked in the heat of Bryan's mini tirade. It was towards the end of their main course Bryan took the plunge. 'I take it you are gay, Miles, otherwise you wouldn't have been in Infinity?' Miles gave an affirmative nod. 'And you have, in a way, picked me up?' Another nod. 'Well, let me tell you why I really lost my job!' Instead of a shocked response at the cause of Bryan's dismissal, Miles gave a great roar of laughter.

'Now that's a dismissal with a difference!' he chortled.

'You're not err... disgusted?'

'My dear young man, why on *Earth* should I be disgusted? Lucky Geoff is all I can say.' Miles leant across the table. 'Tell me Bryan, do you speak any foreign languages?'

'Err… yes, I do. I speak a pretty good Italian – my mother was Italian – and I can also make my way in French.'

'Your mother *was*?'

'She died a few years ago.'

'I'm sorry. And your father?'

'My mother never married. My father, or so I was told, left her while she was pregnant with me. They were, so she says, to be married, but he simply up and disappeared.'

'Sorry again,' Miles gestured for the bill. 'Bryan, two things; and please feel free to answer these as you wish. One, come home and have a nightcap and two, if you'd like to take it further, so would I. It really *is* up to you. I won't be offended if you say no, but I would be disappointed.'

Bryan looked at the gently smiling man. *Christ, he'll probably want more than a blow job, maybe even want to fuck me.* Bryan gave an inward laugh. *Not that I mind being fucked. Bloody Oswald always insisted on being the passive one so I suppose I've gotten used to being the doer as opposed to the being done!* 'You're on, Miles,' he said with a grin. 'Or, should that be *Sir* Miles? I think I've got the message!'

Miles's flat was a grand duplex in London's exclusive Cadogan Square. Having polished off two large cognacs each whilst listening to a selection of light jazz, Miles's passion; the two eventually ended up in a large, heavily curtained four poster bed, which a giggling Bryan was to refer to as a tomb in a room. Miles proved himself to be a considerate and skillful lover. Initially Bryan – blanching at the size of the man's enormous penis – had tried repeatedly and unsuccessfully, to take the swollen, pulsating organ into his widely stretched mouth. Determined as he was, he could barely accommodate the bulbous, purple-coloured head without gagging and spluttering. 'I can't, Miles,' he gasped. 'Jesus, what diameter are you? I've never seen anything like it!'

Miles, who remained lying on his back, his eyes closed, said softly, 'I know, Bryan; I know.' He gave a sad laugh. 'Do you know, at school they used to call me "Miler" Miles because of the size of my cock. In a way it was envy, but while all the other boys were either blowing or buggering each other, all I ever got was a mutual wank. My wife can barely take me completely, so sex with her is, in reality, a thing of the past. We've one daughter and everyday her mother reminds me of how much pain she went through not only with conceiving Sophie, but also in giving birth to her! Some fantastic sex life there!' He gave a hollow laugh. 'According to local gossip, she's screwing a black employee of a near neighbour of ours in the country! Obviously the legend cannot be all that true if he is more easily accommodated than this monster!' He took his enormous, flaccid penis in his large hand and waved it slowly so it lolled from side to side like some gigantic salami. 'Big, my friend – when you're this big – is *not* beautiful; it's a bloody burden!'

'Fuck me, Miles.'

'What?'

'I said fuck me!' Bryan slowly lifted Miles's hand off his massive cock and replaced it with his own. 'I don't know if I'll be able to take you but I'm going to have a bloody good try!'

Slowly and with great deliberation, Bryan applied a heavy coating of KY jelly to Miles's formidable erection. 'Now me, Miles,' whispered Bryan hoarsely. 'Open me up with your fingers first and when you've managed to insert all five, turn them slowly. I'm then going to sit on you and try to lower myself down onto what I can only describe as a rival to the bloody Loch Ness monster!'

The hot, dark interior of the four poster bed, illuminated by only a small picture light above the headboard, was silent except for a few whimpers and sighs as Bryan, his eyes screwed up in pain, his jaw clenched and his lips clamped tightly together, slowly – and with an unbelievable sensation rippling up through his bowels and his stomach – impaled himself onto Miles throbbing, swollen, searing, hot cock.

'Oh my God, Bryan!' gasped Miles. 'Oh my God!'

In between the pain, the thrill and the pure, glorious sensation of being completely and overwhelmingly possessed, Bryan almost burst out laughing with Miles gasping 'Oh my god,' being reminiscent of Oswald's moaning, 'Ohmigod! Ohmigod!' Only on this occasion Bryan – apart from the soft whimpering and the groans – being the almost silent receiver.

───────────

A smiling Miles, seated at the glass-topped breakfast table and clad in a brightly patterned silk dressing gown from Turnbull & Asser, looked across at an equally smiling Bryan, similarly clad in a much-too-large bathrobe loaned by the ever considerate Miles. The two had wakened early and experienced a less painful, energetic and satisfying early morning fuck, both coming twice in a series of shuddering, gasping, grunting, heaving giant orgasms. Bryan, to his amazement – and increasing delight – found the mere thought of Miles's extraordinarily large, pulsating penis entering him again and again – any former pain replaced by a glorious ecstasy – causing him to get an erection at the breakfast table.

Miles, not noticing the effect he was having, stretched out his big hand, taking hold of Bryan's smaller chunky one. 'Thank you Bryan,' said the big man, his eyes crinkling into yet another smile. 'Not only has it been great but *you* are great!'

'You're not so bad yourself,' laughed Bryan, trying to hide his confusion at the compliment and blushing furiously. He looked around the lavish, brightly tiled, state-of-the-art kitchen. 'Some pad you have here, Miles, some kitchen! NASA meets Architectural Digest!'

'You read Architectural Digest?' asked a surprised Miles from where he stood preparing a fresh pot of coffee.

'Because I worked in a travel agency doesn't make me a complete Philistine, Miles,' laughed Bryan. 'Put it down to a secret longing to be an interior designer or, even better still, an architect. But, as the song goes… "To Dream the Impossible Dream" etcetera, etcetera.'

Miles had turned away from the coffee machine and was looking at Bryan thoughtfully. "Any chance you could meet me for lunch today?'

'Today?' Bryan shook his head and made a whooshing sound with his mouth. 'Today you say?' He gave a thoughtful nod. 'Now, today may be difficult Sir Miles. It's a full time occupation being redundant. I'd have to check my diary!' He gave the big man a broad grin, 'Of course I can, Miles, but on one condition.'

'And that is?' Miles looked at him anxiously thinking, *Oh Christ, don't tell me, he's going to ask me for money and here I was hoping he would be different from the rest of the young men I've so unsuccessfully picked up before.*

'We make it around 1:30-ish so that I have time to get back to the flat, have a shower and dress accordingly. I don't think it's exactly right for your image – or mine – Miles, if you are seen out with a bit of scruff rough! Gucci meets grotesque; Dunhill meets the dregs! No, I think two gents about town is a far better scenario.'

'I wasn't going to say anything…' began Miles.

'You don't have to,' laughed Bryan. 'As I said, even ex-travel agents can own a suit, albeit Selfridges best!'

'You're on!' Miles glanced at the chrome wall clock. 'I have to go to the office for an hour or two. My office is in Berkeley Square, so I would suggest we meet somewhere close to it, if that isn't a problem?'

'Berkeley Square is easy, Miles.'

'Come to the office then; here, I'll give you a card.' He rummaged in his dressing gown pocket and pulled out an engraved business card.

'Do you always carry business cards in your dressing gown, Miles?' asked Bryan with a grin.

It was Miles's turn to redden. 'Not always; today is a first. I was rather anticipating – no, make that *hoping* you'd agree to lunch!'

'Well, your wish is granted. Now, if you don't mind, I'll go back to my after midnight rags…'

'After midnight rags?'

'Yes Miles, after midnight rags. This morning you're looking at your Cinderella fella! Only this lucky Cinders woke up *with* his Prince Charming *intacto!*' Bryan added with a quip. 'Though I'm not quite sure if poor Cinders little arse is!'

'Come here and get a hug, you adorable young man!'

'Cinders, if you please!' laughed Bryan throwing his arms around Miles, 'And from now on, *you*, Sir Miles, will be known only to me, Cinders of the now *very* "Opened Sesame," as his big, wicked, buggering baronet with the biggest, buggering bayonet!'

'A fairy *tail* with a happy ending?' laughed Miles.

'Definitely!' chortled Bryan, 'Or an advert in QX Magazine!'

Not only did the two lunch at Bellamy's – an exclusive, up market restaurant in Bruton Mews where the genuine Queen was known to have partaken of a meal or two – but they met again later for dinner. Miles was riveted by the transformation with Bryan. Being honest with himself, he had instantly regretted his suggestion Bryan come to the office prior to their luncheon. Although Mandy, his larger-than-life secretary seemed unshockable, the appearance of a possible rent boy could be the one happening that would shock.

The young man who presented himself at the Berkeley Square office was a very different Bryan to the one met in Infinity. As Miles said later, 'It was Cinderella reversed! I met you before your fairy godmother had waved her magic wand' – his comment resulting in a lewd snigger from Bryan – 'which was dazzling enough, but to see you in all your finery, as if ready to go to the ball? Wow!'

The Bryan standing by the reception desk was a handsome, well-built young man, wearing an immaculate dark grey suit with a light cream shirt and deep blue patterned tie – a blue and ivory paisley design handkerchief in his breast pocket. Even Bryan's dark curly hair looked more designer-tousled than unruly. As Mandy, his personal secretary remarked to Miles on his return from lunch, 'Now there's a young man a girl like me would certainly not mind taking home to meet my mother!'

'Why you wicked, wanton woman, Mandy Mashona! And here I was believing you to be a happily married wife, mother of three grown-up children, and not an impure thought in that lovely head of yours!'

Mandy Mashona, Miles's devoted secretary of several years and a large, buxom, jolly black woman originally from Zimbabwe – 'My Oprah Winfrey,' Miles always claimed. 'She resolves all my problems!' – gave Miles a lewd wink. 'I may be old and I may be a happily married woman, Sir Miles, but Mandy Mashona is not yet *dead*!'

'Seriously Mandy, what did you think of him? You know I run all potential new staff past the Mandy Mashona radar!' Miles had already decided during lunch he was going to offer Bryan a position in the company, the choice of word causing him to smile broadly on his walk back to the office across the Square. 'I'm thinking about the vacancy in our foreign section. Mr. Scima – the name's Italian, like his mother – speaks both French and Italian and I thought of giving him a trial run in the sales section for Sardinia and the hill development in Liguria.'

'I'd be looking into a mortgage right away if that man was going to be my salesman, Sir Miles!' Mandy giggled girlishly, her face breaking into a wide, bright smile. She wiggled her broad hips suggestively. 'He can deliver me a family sized pizza anytime!'

'I take it, *Mrs.* Mashona, that is a yes?'

'Even a *slice* of pizza!' cackled Mandy, sashaying out of Miles's office.

'Well, young Bryan. I'll make the proposition to you over dinner.'

———————

Dinner was at Scalini's, a favourite Italian restaurant of Miles', situated in Chelsea's elegant Walton Street and convenient to the flat in Cadogan Square. It was towards the end of dinner Miles came out his business proposal over the tiramisu. Bryan's acceptance was immediate and the deal duly signed and doubly sealed later in haven of the large four poster bed. Bryan, in a new suit from Harvey Nichols, purchased, on his insistence, via an advance on his wages, began work with Anstruther International the following week.

The young man proved to be an immediate hit with Mandy and all the efficient, lively and fun-loving staff, and his charm and skill when dealing with his first few clients was apparent; Bryan's few years with the travel agency having given him a good grounding. Whether or not the office knew of their relationship was never made obvious by any of Miles' adoring staff. Bryan, to his uttermost delight, found himself totally happy and, for the first time in his life, secure. As he said to Miles one night as they lay in the snug haven of the large four poster bed. 'For the first time in my life, Miles, I feel completely fulfilled, and I'm not only referring to that giant cock that just happens to be inside me!'

CHAPTER 7

'Your friend, Bryan…?' Charles looked across at his passenger.

'Oh, forget *her*!' snorted Oswald. 'Silly cow threw yet another tantrum during supper last night. Her *last* supper, I may add!' He gave another snort. 'Really Charles, talk about possessive. Jesus, Miss Scima would make a rampant Rottweiler appear like a toothless old hag!' Oswald gave a smirk at his bitchy comment. 'The last glimpse I had of madam was her sitting morosely over her chicken masala!'

'So, you've had a fall-out then?'

'Fall out? We'd never even fallen *in*!' Oswald gave a camp flutter of his long, slender hand. 'Put it this way, the Italian job was OK for doing what she was best at: an Italian job. Fabulous in bed' – he gave Charles an anxious glance – 'or so gossip has it!' Back pedalling, he stammered, 'She did make a pass at me *years* ago but I said no, a thousand times no!' He gave Charles's bony thigh a reassuring squeeze, adding coquettishly, 'You *know* I go for the more, erudite scholarly type…' followed by a sibilant, blown kiss. 'Like my lover, the doctor!' he camped, his eyelashes fluttering furiously for extra effect.

Yea, and like the Pope's got a nineteen inch dick, thought Charles, saying instead, 'You really do love me, don't you Oswald? And you are happy about our plan, our commitment?'

'I love you as much as the wide blue yonder!' chirruped Oswald waving at the low grey, leaden sky above. 'As for the commitment, why my darling Charles, your *casa* is my *casa*!'

Fortunately, Charles was saved a reply to this strange comparison by their arrival at the main gates to the house.

'I thought it more diplomatic you were put in one of the guest suites,' Charles reminded Oswald as they drew up to the main steps. 'After all, officially we've only met once before. It'll take some time before we can make our true feelings known.' Now it was his turn to give the startled Oswald's leg a squeeze.

'I quite understand, Charles,' said the young man putting on a suitably soulful expression. 'Not even a sneaky?' he added plaintively.

'No, my darling, not even a sneaky!' laughed Charles thinking, *not even a kissy.*

You're so fucking right, thought Oswald, *not if that big buck black has anything to do with it or that big, butch bugger, whose car I bulldozed first time round! No, Charles, no sneaky, but I'm going have a bloody good try at getting not only Mr. Mandingo, but especially Sir Miles Midas Anstruther up my hallowed alley! Mandingo for a fuck, Miles Anstruther as a future; Lady Oswald Anstruther would suit me just fine!* He couldn't resist a small smile. *Better still, why not Mandingo both as a valet and a substitute fuck when the master of the house – in his busy role as provider – is away earning even more to keep the new, lovely Lady Oswald in even more luxury?*

'Penny for them, Ossy?'

'Oh, they're worth much more than a penny, Charles. Oh look, I do believe the welcoming committee has just arrived!' He gave a groan. 'How sweet, it's mummy with the mummy!'

There was a rasping cry of recognition from Trisomy, who had been told about Oswald's impending arrival. 'Caligla! Caligla!' she croaked, falling to her hands and knees and scuttling, crab-like, down the steps to the car. 'Twisomy kissy Caligla! Twsiomy kiss Caligla hello!'

'Oh shit!' muttered Oswald.

'Make that total shit!' hissed his so-called lover.

'Hello Trisomy!' cooed Oswald camply as he stepped cautiously down from out of the sleek, silver Honda CR-V, used solely by the staff. Going immediately into the loveable mode of his original visit, he too fell on all fours and, pursing his lips, scrunched up his eyes before cooing again. 'Where is Trisomy's kiss for her Unka Caligla?'

With a dry, scraping of her thin, creased lips against his plump, cupid-bow-like ones, Trisomy answered the question.

Jesus! said Charles inwardly, barely able to restrain a shudder of revulsion.

'Isn't he too, too adorable!' cried Clytemnestra. 'Tris, darling,' she continued, stepping forward and helping the little girl back to her feet. 'You must let mummy kiss Unka Oswald as well. It's share and share alike here!'

Oswald visibly paled as Charles visibly winced.

'Oswald, welcome to your new home!' Taking him by the hand she drew him to his feet, kissing him lightly on his burning cheek. 'So kind,' she whispered into his ear. 'So considerate and gentle... really lovely and loving you are!' Clytemnestra kissed Oswald again. 'But look, here's Monday to help you with your suitcase.' She smiled up at the big man who had suddenly appeared by the side of the steps. 'Oswald's in the Easy Rider suite, Monday.' This was interrupted by a self-deprecating giggle, 'As if you wouldn't have guessed, knowing you!' Oswald stood momentarily stunned by the malicious jibe while Clytemnestra blithely continued, 'Mrs. N. and Viola were busy buffing up the bikes in there all yesterday afternoon!' She took Oswald by the arm and began leading him up the steps. 'One of Ethelred's more bizarre decorating ideas. All the guest suites are decorated in a tribute to one of his favourite vintage films. We have a *Wizard of Oz* suite complete with an old cast iron bath with Dorothy's red slippers as feet instead of the usual dreary claw and ball...'

'I didn't realise Dorothy had four feet!' quipped Oswald, making an attempt to 'go with the flow'.

'She didn't!' snapped Clytemnestra. 'But we're obviously strong believers in poetic licence here!'

'Oh,' mumbled the young man, suitably chastened. 'Sorry Clyte, I was just trying to be funny.'

'Of *course* you were!' cried his hostess, giving his arm a squeeze. 'And forgive me for being such a silly moo. It was very, very funny and an even more clever observation!'

Jesus Clyte! It was Charles's turn to scrutinise the woman. *What's gotten into you or – more than likely – not got into you this morning?*

As if reading his mind, Clytemnestra reached out for Charles's. 'PMS,' she whispered. 'But ideal for a quickie I promised one of Claudia's patrons!'

'Claudia? A quickie? I don't quite follow...'

'Claudia of the Claudia Cordelle Gallery. One of her buyers wants something similar to my original "Red Dust Storm" where I used menstrual blood in a swirl effect against a previously prepared yellow phlegm, streaked canvas!' Charles and Oswald visibly blanched at this artistic denouement. 'Now my cycle is doing what a good cycle should be doing I can complete Red Eye Estoril, which is an eye – red of course – bloodshot and staring, painted on an open fan; *very* fan-dango!'

'Why didn't she just say fanny and be done with it!' muttered Oswald.

'I heard that!' shrieked Clytemnestra but with a shriek of laughter this time as opposed to her former indignation. 'Now *that*, young Oswald, was *bloody* funny!'

'I think I need a drink!' said Charles wiping his forehead in a camp, theatrical gesture.

'May I suggest a Bloody Mary?' chortled his hostess.

'At least you didn't offer us a Bullshit!' expounded an increasingly confident Oswald – he was falling in love with Clytemnestra all over again – 'as opposed to a Bullshot!'

'Oh,' said Charles, determined not to be a loser in this war of words. 'Imagine, just imagine if one was offered a large Negroni?'

'You called, sah?' A beaming Monday, having reappeared from depositing Oswald's one and only suitcase in the aforesaid Easy Rider suite, gave the startled doctor a mock salute.

'If only it was at real Negroni one was offered to swallow!' camped Charles.

'Keep your mouth wide open, Charlotte Manson!' quipped Clytemnestra. 'You never know who may want to put a sock or – better still – a *cock* in it!'

'Ah, Oswald, you got here safely!' A beaming Ethelred, arms outstretched, strode across the wide living room in which they were standing. Taking a startled Oswald into his long, thin, sinewy arms, he gave the young guest a firm kiss on the mouth. 'Now *that*,' he said, turning to face the three bemused onlookers, 'now that wasn't a Bloody Mary, a Bullshit nor a Negroni, *that* was pure nectar!' He gave a loud chortle. 'But you buggers can't be boozers unless you're drinking champagne, so who's joining me?'

'Me!' cried Clytemenstra.

'Me!' echoed a grinning Charles.

'Yussah! Anytime!' boomed Monday

'Yes please!' laughed Oswald.

Champagne duly poured and handed round by a smiling Monday; the conversation drifted vaguely into the plans for the coming week's shooting

– Ethelred was being particularly vague with an eagerly enquiring Oswald – when a totally unexpected question cut in among the general murmuring.

'Do you have a big wee wee cawot, Unka Caligla?' croaked Trisomy who, unnoticed, had crept in and joined the group. 'Can Twisomy play with your wee wee cawot, if she's vewy, vewy good?'

'No! Naughty Trisomy knows what happens when she plays with a carrot!' This from an irritated Clytemnestra.

'Yes, I put it up my foo foo and...' began Trisomy, her distorted mouth twisting into a misshapen leer.

'No!' repeated Clytemnestra. 'Before you even begin to say what I think you're about to say, *stop it right now*!' The mummy and the ancient mummy-like child glared momentarily at each other. 'Now go straight along to the kitchen and ask Nanette for one of your cookies. There's a good girl. The grownups want to talk.'

'Cunt!' growled Trisomy as she shuffled off out of the vast room.

'Charming!' said her father. 'Absolutely charming!'

'Our pride and joy,' hissed Clytemnestra.

'Well, I like her!' laughed Monday. 'We get on well together.'

'Best she sticks to carrots as opposed to aubergines!' laughed Charles.

'Talking of which,' said Clytemnestra. 'I see Viola beckoning. Lunch is served.' She smiled again at a bewildered but beaming Oswald. Offering her arm, she added with a smile, 'It's not every day one has the pleasure of the most beautiful young man in Britain to escort one into lunch! Will you do me the honour, kind sir?'

'But of course, madam!' Taking Clytemnestra's proffered arm, Oswald gave Charles a broad wink as they made their way towards the glass and chrome double doors leading to the elegant dining room.

———————

'They weren't here on my first visit.' Oswald pointed to several sheep standing silently on the neatly clipped lawn. The fact four of the seven animals were bright red and only two the traditional white was not commented upon. Clytemnestra, busily pouring the coffee seemed oblivious to the question as did Charles and Monday who were deeply engrossed in conversation. Noticing a further bright red sheep standing at the end of the large terrace – they had moved to the dining terrace after lunch for coffee – Oswald repeated the question to Ethelred who, having excused himself for a few minutes – 'I feel a mighty torrent coming on!' – had returned to the terrace and was now standing alongside him; his arm resting casually around Oswald's shoulders.

'Charles's latest hobby; they're stuffed.' Ethelred replied with a grin. 'I suppose one could say that our Charles, in his spare time, has taken to fucking sheep, a regular country pursuit "oop North" – or so I'm told!'

'Stuffed? You mean as in… well… er *stuffed*?' Oswald's expression was one of incredulity. 'Like in… *stuffed*?'

'I think the word you're looking for young Oswald is taxidermy,' replied Ethelred with a deep chuckle. 'It's a new thing of Charles's. He claims it all started from his impossible insomnia. Instead of counting sheep he found it more fun stuffing them!'

'But where…?'

'From our local abattoir. They're used to Clyte's requests for various animals' organs and when Charles had this brilliant idea of a few colourful sheep grazing on the lawn in front of the terrace – real sheep shit everywhere and would have spoiled the green velvet finish we so covet! – the local *abba* was only too willing to *offal*!' He gave a louder chuckle. 'He must have been working on them during your last visit. He's converted one of the outbuildings into a fine studio.' Ethelred nodded at the silent red sheep standing sentinel on the terrace. 'That one's called Redputin. Red because he's a *commie* cunt, and Putin because Putin's both!'

'Ah,' said Oswald, determined not to be fazed by such an announcement. 'Like Rasputin, you mean.'

'No, *Red* Putin,' replied Ethelred drily. 'There is certainly no *razz* in being a dyed, dead, stuffed sheep I would have thought!'

Oswald gave up, letting out a discreet sigh of relief as Clytemnestra joined them. 'Now, husband dearest, with what bullshit are you now boring our lovely new house guest?' she asked with a smile, putting her arm around Ethelred. Oswald, feeling as if he was about to be trapped – little did he know! – shook himself free from Ethelred's arm resting heavily on his shoulders.

'Ethelred was just explaining about the other red, Redputin,' he replied. Giving a laugh, Oswald pointed nervously at the other four silent red effigies on the immaculate lawn, 'And their names? Red-if-you-dare perhaps?'

'Oh Oswald! Red Adair as in fire fighter?' Oswald nodded weakly, 'That is *so* clever! Isn't that *so clever*, Ethelred darling?' Clytemnestra gave a light, tinkly laugh. 'No, Redputin is special. The two white sheep are named Baa Baa and Black while the other four are called One Skin, Two Skin, Three Skin and Five Skin! We thought it rather insensitive introducing our less enlightened visitors to a bright red, woolly, stuffed sheep called Foreskin!'

'Oh, but of course,' answered Oswald lamely, while thinking, *I could really grow to love this place. They're all fucking barking!* His heart gave a leap of pure, undiluted joy. *Goodbye Clapham, goodbye cuntish Scima, hello Capreae!* Giving his host and hostess a simpering smile, he added coquettishly, 'Perhaps I'd better be called Soswold!'

'Soswold?' This from Ethelred.

'The seventh foreskin,' shrieked their guest. 'S for seven so, Soswold! I take it that Redputin, under all that wool has the sixth?'

'I *told* you he was so clever, didn't I Red?' cried Clyemnestra, her eyes sparkling. Taking Oswald by the arm, she led him briskly across the terrace towards a curious Monday and Charles who – having finished their conversation – were straining to hear what was being said by the other three. 'Mon and Charles,' she cried merrily. 'You simply *must* hear the gems our lovely new guest, our delicious Oswald, has just spurted forth. They're *divine*!' She stopped suddenly as if struck by a thunderbolt. Looking at the smiling young man, she couldn't resist uttering the chilling prediction. 'Oh Oswald, you are *so, so* beautiful!' There followed a moment's silence before Clytemnestra voiced Oswald's death knoll. 'You are such perfection! What a pity *you* couldn't be stuffed for all eternity to enjoy you!'

Oswald, about to reply with some witty riposte, stopped himself in the nick of time. Instead of saying, 'But Charles has already had a start at regularly stuffing me!' he quickly changed this to, 'Now there's a challenge, Charles!'

Charles gave a small, inward sigh of relief. Later, when possible, he managed to give Oswald's arm a light squeeze. 'Keep it up!' Charles whispered. 'You're doing brilliantly. They have no idea!'

It was while they were having a pre-dinner cocktail in Ethelred's conservatory that Oswald was able to ask Ethelred the permanently burning sixty-thousand dollar question. Clytemnestra and Charles meanwhile – having been joined by the exotic Euros Peacock, his partner Thrift, an out of work actor and part-time gofer, Kevin, the second cameraman and Monday – were busily discussing the next week's shoot at the opposite end of the light, airy room.

'Red?' – the shortened form was catching – 'whatever happened about our minor prang a few weeks ago with that guy, Giles-something-or-other, the property dealer?'

'Giles? Oh, you mean Miles, Miles Anstruther.' Ethelred looked momentarily perplexed. 'Do you know I have no idea; no doubt Hennie – Henrietta Moore, our secretary – will have dealt with it. Why?'

'Oh, nothing…' Oswald gave a shrug, 'Just curious. He seemed a nice guy, that's all. Very understanding!'

'Oh, Miles is understanding alright.' Ethelred leant forward and whispered conspiratorially. 'Incredibly understanding; given the fact Man Monday over there is fucking his wife!'

'What?'

'Oh yes, take it from me. Like all those upper class ladies who in the past were fucked endlessly by the likes of that black American entertainer Hutch or the Indian guy Nehru, Lady A cannot get enough of the Monday monster.'

'What does Miles say?'

'Not a lot. He just let's them get on with it. No doubt Miles has some bimbo in town.' Ethelred leant closer. 'Between you and me, the daughter's a bit odd as well, and I wouldn't be at all surprised if, when Lady A is making hay, dear daughter Annabel isn't pitching in there as well!' He gave a lewd chuckle. 'After all, catch Monday in his shorts and you can see he does boast a massive *pitch*-fork!

'Ohmigod… ohmigod!' muttered Oswald in reply.

'You'll meet them all two weeks on Saturday,' added Ethelred. 'Clyte, in one of her many divine moments of madness, decided to have an impromptu dinner to celebrate the conception of Reflections. She's prone to this when she's about to commit herself to a new project; something to do with keeping her mental stimuli stimulated, while the muse is upon her – or some such complete and utter fucking shit!' He gave a laugh. 'She also says it gives Mrs. N and Viola something glamorous to do.' Ethelred gave an evil snort. 'Also, she enjoys having Monday and Viola serving at table. Keep your eyes on Monday and see what Cltye means by her "crotch watch!" Lady A has a very active elbow when Mandingo's serving her. Quite a change, no doubt, to have him serving her while standing!'

'Ohmigod!' Feeling a distinct stirring in his nether regions Oswald – to Ethelred's surprise – suddenly perched himself demurely on a nearby chair.

'You alright, young Oswald?'

'Absolutely fine, thanks Red. I just think it's all the excitement, my arrival, too much wine at lunch and now this absolutely lethal Martini; it's suddenly all caught up with me!'

'Never mind, you can have an early night. Clyte, Charles and self are going to watch some film Clyte's mad keen to see. If you feel like nipping off before we settle down to watch this, feel free. Breakfast is at eight – it's always a family get together and Monday will buzz you a wake-up call at seven. Now, let's see what those three reprobates are up to. Care for another Courvoisier? In fact, why not take one up to your room?'

'Thanks, Ethelred, I think I will.'

Back in the Easy Rider suite, Oswald straddled one of a pair of replica Harley-Davidson *Hydraglide* bikes as seen in the nineteen-sixties. The bikes, positioned as a sculpture feature on either side of a free standing king size bed set in the centre of the vast, black and gold coloured sitting room to the suite, were again shown in vast posters of the bikes as well as posters advertising the legendary film. The silver grey, gold and black fifties swirl-patterned carpet blended perfectly with the black, faux leather walls, gold coloured ceiling and the luxurious wolf fur spread partly turned down to reveal the black bed linen. Black Roman-style blinds covered the windows with dress 'curtains' made out of metal chains.

'Not very different to Clapham,' giggled Oswald, taking a large swig of his brandy. Lifting himself off from the bike, he walked unsteadily to a large grey, gold and black lacquered unit which housed not only a vast television screen but what proved to be a well-stocked bar, complete with ice maker and an appetising array of cocktail snacks. 'In fact, Os my friend,' he slurred between a set of giggles, 'It's *exactly* like Clapham; another sweet, dear, cosy little home from home.' Further conversation was curtailed as Oswald, having set himself down on the edge of the bed – the now empty brandy balloon cautiously set down on the carpet alongside his still shod feet – simply fell back across the fur cover and passed out.

Monday's repeated buzzing several hours later led to no response and it was a startled Oswald who found himself being shaken awake by the grinning black giant.

'Ohmigod!' sighed Oswald, his cock beginning to swell rapidly against his tight, restricting trousers. 'Ohmigod!' he almost shrieked when he realised that Monday was real and not a dream. Clutching his bulging, straining crotch he gave the smiling man a weak, embarrassed smile. 'I must have fallen asleep before I had a chance to get into bed properly,' he muttered sheepishly, his face turning flame red.

'I'll leave you to have a shower and make yourself presentable,' the big man said in his deep baritone. He nodded towards Oswald's now obvious straining erection. 'You're certainly awake now! I'll see you back in the breakfast room in thirty minutes,' the remark being accompanied by a knowing wink.

'Oh *shit*!' groaned Oswald, clutching both his throbbing head and his throbbing crotch. He glanced at his watch. 'Thirty minutes? Why not?' With another groan he lay back on the bed, unzipped his fly and pulled out his now rampant cock. Pulling back his foreskin to reveal an already tumescent head, he proceeded to masturbate furiously, the image of a smiling Monday still fresh in his mind. With a triumphant shriek Oswald ejaculated over himself and part of the spread, much to the disapproval of a silently watching Peter Fonda and Dennis Hopper.

CHAPTER 8

'Right, Euros. We'll do the shot of Monday's arrival at Windsor station tomorrow. The weather promises to be shit which is perfect! I want the big man seen looking bewildered and confused while standing on the platform as the train pulls *out*! If it's pissing down, all the better! Mon, you'll be in a loose rain slicker – I don't want anything of the body beautiful on display just yet! – as Cltye, with large golfing brolly comes up to you and greets you. Next shot will be the CR-V leaving. This shouldn't take too long. We'll cut in shots of BB to suit and then we go straight into Clyte's studio. I'm going to take some shots of the easels, the mirrors and such along with a zoom shot or two into the pristine palette. Next we have the scene where you, Mon and Clyte, discuss the concept. Clyte will then ask you to strip. I will need several salivating shots of you – you'll have oiled yourself beforehand – doing a type of slow strip and definitely cock tease!'

Ethelred went on to give instructions about the first scene of Monday ejaculating onto the palette, then stepping back into a pose as Clyte put the first daubs of his hot, quivering cum offering, onto the mirror. There was to be an initial shot of Monday's ejaculation and the resultant globules hitting the palette. Unbeknown to the viewer, Thrift, with a massive veterinary syringe full of albumen – two dozen ostrich eggs had arrived and been duly stored in one of the large freezer units in Clytemnestra's studio – would contribute to the illusion of a torrential, heavy splattering by jettisoning huge spurts of egg white in accordance with Monday's own, massive ejaculation.

The dollops of the enhanced cum mixture would be mega; huge, trembling, oozing globules of thick, translucent liquid, briskly mixed by Clytemnestra wielding a special paintbrush made up of a thick tufted top created from a combination of pubic hairs. 'I plan to daub and then sweep all of your blended cum into a mixture of swirls, twirls, plus linear stripes and streaks. I feel a brush of pubic hair will be so much more erotic, more in keeping and, well, more *genital*, which is what my mirrored canvasses – my reflective inspirations – will imbue!'

Several previous close-ups of a serious Clytemnestra carefully plucking out the giant's thick, black, curly lustrous crotch hairs with a pair of silver tweezers, led to the unexpected bonus of Monday achieving what could only be described as a massive boner and a diversion from the original script. Not to waste the shot – Clytemnestra having claimed she had plucked enough hairs for the head of her brush – Ethelred immediately instructed Oswald who, in turn, had been watching the whole scenario whilst experiencing a rampant erection, to perform – in his role as gofer-cum-unexpected fluffer – a slow, deep blowjob on the rampant giant. 'I'll work in a fantasy scene somehow,' Ethelred quickly explained as an eager Oswald fell to his knees. 'Euros, a soft filter please – somehow we'll make it look as if it's being viewed through a veil of cum. Leave it to the mighty Ethelred!' Clytemnestra, unfazed, returned to her work on the aforesaid brush as Monday – with a series of gasps and a mighty bellow – came, his vast orgasm causing Oswald to gag furiously. A final, violent, pelvic thrust from the gigantic black man saw Oswald falling backwards onto the floor; a groaning Monday deeply impaled in his throat.

'Jesus!' said Monday, a few seconds later as he sat wiping his sweaty torso, crotch and armpits, an enormous grin on his face. 'Where the fuck did you learn to suck and take a cock like that, Os? It's how I've always imagined being sucked by a fucking *industrial* Hoover would be like!'

Ever conscious of his props, Thrift had been on hand to niftily catch Oswald's own jettisoned load in a glass beaker. 'One for the load!' he shrieked, raising the relevant contribution. Like his own, Monday's, Charles's and any future ejaculations by Oswald or an over-excited Ethelred, the collected cum was carefully stored in a refrigerator by the ever vigilant Thrift, alongside the drained albumen from the ostrich eggs. After several days of seemingly endless rich omelettes made from the leftover ostrich egg yolks, Mrs. Norelle's omelettes – however varied – were put on indefinite hold.

Charles, being privy to the whole scene, stormed off in a jealous rage. Within the matter of a few hours, Oswald – without any planning or effort – had achieved what he had striven unsuccessfully to achieve over the course of two years at Bethlem Báthory. 'Bastard! Little shit bastard,' hissed Charles, glowering at the towering topiary of Ethelred's penis, 'As you are about to find out odious Oswald, hell hath no fury as this *bitch* doctor whose yearned!'

———————

Clytemenstra appeared possessed; the scenes inspired by Monday in all his proud, naked glory, becoming wilder than even she could ever have imagined. One scene of him helping Clytemnestra mix his freshly ejaculated cum onto an already burgeoning of palette of quivering, opaque, jelly-like mounds, included not only the 'money shot' of his jerking, spurting cock as he pumped his massive, black, about-to-burst length, furiously with his large hand, but of Clytemnestra also grabbing hold of the bobbing Monday monster in one hand, and using the vast, purple head to vigorously blend the mixture alongside the equally vigorous brush, held in the other.

'This film is going to have them coming in their seats!' an enthusiastic Ethelred kept assuring her. Meanwhile Clytemnestra kept dabbing, daubing, twirling and swirling while the bit players, off camera, kept masturbating. The spectral figure of Monday's figure gradually took shape; a luminous effigy on its dark, reflective ground. It was some five weeks later before Clytemnestra claimed her first work complete. On viewing the ghost-like portrait Ethelred could only whisper, 'Christ, Clyte. Not only is it exemplary, beautiful and unique, it's the best painting you have ever done and then some!'

'You really like it?' the anxious artist had asked.

'Like it? My darling, having already come over it, I'm now in *orbit* over it!'

Charles and Oswald were equally as generous with obviously genuine praise, and both kept saying how proud they were to be, literally, 'in the portrait itself!' Monday's only comment on seeing the final work was to give Clytemnestra the biggest, possible grin and say, 'Wow! Get a *load* of that!'

Praises and comments abounding the massive, glowing work was duly toasted with several glasses of champagne. In anticipation of the next day's shot which Clytemnestra wittily promised would represent 'a very proud shroud,' an enthusiastic Monday – on Charles's instructions – was invited to eat a hearty dinner, accompanied by several glasses of fresh prune juice as opposed to his usual rum and Coke. 'Ethelred has asked me to ensure your dump tomorrow is not too solid. But then we don't want a torrent of shit either, do we? Remember, Clyte – for the benefit of the camera – has to be seen blending your freshly dumped shit with a thin stream of linseed oil, this being symbolic in its association with a stream of piss!' The vital question as to what time Monday took his regular morning crap had also been taken into serious consideration. Monday, assuring Ethelred, Clytemnestra and Charles his bowels were as regular and as streamlined as Japan's legendary bullet trains, would present himself 'ready to dump' in Clytemnestra's studio at six o'clock the following morning.

Meanwhile, Ethelred, Clytemnestra plus Euros and Kevin would be ready with the relevant cameras to immortalise the scene. Oswald, in his new, proud role as gofer and handling of special effects, was also instructed to be on the 'set' half an hour before Monday's appearance. Having filmed the first sequence using a blue filter, Euros would be switching to amber for the second. For this particular take, Monday would position himself in a squatting position above a thick plate of glass set up on two supporting trestles. Two cameras, the main one operated by Euros, would shoot the black giant from behind, immortalising his glistening, slowly clenching and unclenching buttocks as he defecated. A second camera, held by Kevin lying beneath the glass, would capture the actual emission of the anticipated large, moist turd. A similar scene was to take place the day after where Monday would be seen defecating directly onto the artist's palette.

Monday's two mornings' of perfect, moist but solid enough bowel movements proved to be of the highest professional standards and the shots of his enthusiastic defecating were – to quote a delighted Ethelred – 'straight in the can!' Neatly cut pieces, taken from the squares of pristine cheesecloth Clytemnestra insisted the black giant wipe himself, were carefully placed onto a series of glass slides to be used as additional details for Monday's pictorial shroud. On checking the first slide, Clytemnestra was ecstatic. 'Think tiger's eye, think amber, think molten gold, think striations! In other words, think of a perfect shit!'

The next few days saw Ethelred and Euros deeply involved with the editing of the almost completed documentary. The sound track, a soft salsa beat, was dubbed with an additional voice over by Clytemnestra in which she detailed her inspiration and reiterated her message about the beauty of bodily functions. During the actual filming, it was Clytemnestra alone who spoke with the magnificent, gleaming Monday remaining macho and mute. Sounds of heavy breathing and the relevant gasps were added in afterwards with Euros doing the honours. 'I've always been a frustrated heavy breather,' the grinning cameraman announced. 'And now I'm being paid to do this!'

After ten weeks of dedication, the two works – 'Literally two and a half months since my first stroke and the boys' endless strokes!' – were complete, and Clytemnestra was able to make the first of two forays up to London to show Claudia Cordelle photographs of the two finished mirrored 'canvasses,' and finalise details for her exhibition; the dates having been provisionally booked almost a year in advance. Invitations were to be squares of black glass with the wording printed in gold and opaque white or, to quote Clytemnestra, 'Shit and cum.'

The gallery owner was ecstatic. 'Compared to this, your former show, "Secretions", would appear – in retrospect – more of a drought than the requisite dribble!'

'You really like them?'

'*Like* them? Darling, to top this you'd simply have to top *someone*! And I mean literally!'

Oswald asked if he could join Clytemnestra on the first trip up to London. His growing panic at the end of the filming of the documentary and the gnawing fear this was 'it' as far as his relationship with the Joneses was concerned – a brief stint as a gofer and cum contributor plus one impromptu blow job on a willing Monday! – had been quickly shelved, following a few reassuring few words from an always aware and astute Ethelred. Oswald's proper 'role' would not come to fruition for a month or two but in the meantime, the young man had to be 'kept sweet.'

'Planning something as unique as "Still Life" will take time and every possible danger or mistake must be anticipated, analyzed and resolved before we even consider starting.' Ethelred confided to Clytemnestra, Charles and the two cameramen. 'Our main hurdle, the so-called star, seems to have been overcome and working out quite nicely. Oswald is slowly but surely becoming Mr. Anonymity, and he must be kept in that role. We must all endeavour to make him feel he is still involved, still an integral part of the team.' He had gone on to cement his comments by offering a few words of advice to the so-called star in waiting.

'See the few days spent working on "Reflections" as a mere *taster* of things to come!' he said with a chuckle, "For let me assure you, there's more from where that came from!' Sensing Oswald was neither amused nor fully aware of what he'd said, Ethelred, with all the patience he could muster, continued. 'We won't be starting the actual filming of "Still Life" for several weeks, maybe even several months. There is a tremendous amount of ground work to be attended to. However, rest assured you are now definitely on the payroll and a fully-fledged member of the team. There will certainly be a few bits and pieces you can busy yourself with, perhaps even help Charles with his taxidermy!'

'No thank you!' replied Oswald tartly. 'I can accept helping out with various bits and pieces Ethelred, but taxidermy? Thanks but no thanks! I'll leave that to Charles and his little helper!'

'Little helper?' asked Ethelred feigning innocence.

'Trisomy! Now *she* seems to enjoy playing nurses to Charles's vile hobby! Why, the other day she proudly announced she and Nurse Charles had been stuffing a bloody rabbit!' Glancing at Ethelred, Oswald added slyly, 'What I wouldn't mind doing is helping out with Trisomy when she's *not* stuffing rabbits! Maybe teach her a hobby such as drawing? After all, I did go to art school for a while...'

It was Charles, on one of the few occasions shared with Oswald in the privacy of his suite, who again stressed the importance of a so-called friendship with Trisomy. 'She trusts me and likes me,' he repeated. 'And while I appreciate she's both repellent and grotesque – and that's on a good day! – it's vital you get on her good side; gain her trust Ossy, and keep her sweet. It'll all work to our advantage in the end!'

Charles also expressed the importance of being occupied and helpful. 'See it as if resting between films. Offer to do other odd jobs, though helping out with that ghastly mummified obscenity couldn't be more odd! If needs be, offer to help Monday with some gardening work! Whatever happens, you don't want to find yourself back on a slow train to Clapham!' What Oswald did not realise was all such dialogue had been gone over time and time again between Charles, Clytemnestra and Ethelred.

Having dropped the hint about helping out with Trisomy, Oswald had blithely gone on with the Monday suggestion. 'Perhaps I could also help Monday with some gardening?' Seeing Ethelred's feigned expression of surprise at this second suggestion – Ethelred had almost overdone his surprise at the 'helping with Trisomy' scenario – Oswald continued. 'I've always wanted a garden of my own... to feel nature at my fingertips, to bond with the soil...'

This unexpected bit of theatre – Ethelred having simply expected an offer to help in the garden, not the waxing lyrical – delivered with a suitably but definitely over-the-top wistful expression, did not fool Ethelred one iota. 'More likely he'll be planning to play with Monday's big black hose, and if Monday decides to water him with it, so much the better!' The latter observation made to an amused Clytemnestra soon afterwards.

'Quite,' she replied. 'What the poor little queen doesn't seem to realise is Monday, unless being paid to do the other, is ruler straight. More a case of a hose pipe ban than a fan methinks!'

'Touché!' laughed Ethelred. 'The main thing is we've got him here for as long as it takes, and it couldn't be more fortuitous. He's made a complete break with that so-called boyfriend, and as far as I'm aware, nobody else knows where he is. Furthermore, I shouldn't think anyone is missing him. He's not been out since he's been here and, like so many of his sort, he'll simply fade away.'

'But what a fade out,' commented Clytemnestra drily.

In the weeks following the initial takes, an unprecedented amount of valuable time had been wasted on the completion of the first portrait, due mainly to Clytemnestra having to work on a slippery, glass surface. Whereas the filming had proceeded without a hitch, the in-between stages were proving to be both frustrating and time consuming.

'Why are we waiting? Why are we waiting?' was chanted more than once in a discordant chorus by a bored Euros and Thrift until Ethelred blew his top and told the cameraman and his lover to 'shut the fuck up!' He went on to say Clytemnestra could not, and would not, be rushed and even suggested Euros and Thrift take a two week's break. 'Bugger off to Mykonos or some such tourist shit hole and get your arseholes well and truly serviced!' Two days later the two, having taken his advice, flew off of the notoriously gay Greek island.

Meanwhile Clytemnestra patiently continued with her experimenting and her painting. From the very beginning, the mix of cum and egg white had not proved a happy combination. Due to the slipperiness of the background surface and the even slimier medium, it had been impossible to apply the so-called paint to the shiny surface and expect it to hold. Clytemnestra had, on several occasions, almost been reduced to tears on finding her delicate brush work of the day before had simply slid down the mirror having teasingly stayed in place at the start. The answer could not have been more obvious with the first of the two large mirrors laid flat on the floor. 'I can't have them on a set of trestles,' she explained to a bemused Ethelred. 'I need to *control* my work. It's not like pasting fucking wallpaper, if you must know! In case you may not have noticed, it's a teensy, weensy fucking bit more exacting than that!' With a sigh of relief, Clytemnestra was able to leave the intricate whorls and whirls to dry in their own time. 'I don't want a fucking heap of meringues!' she had said sarcastically when Ethelred came up with the bright suggestion of a heater or a hair dryer to speed up the drying process. 'My portraits are to be opaque, not fucking sand blasted shit!' she growled.

During the drama of what Charles drily dubbed, 'The Aqua Olympics of The Sperms', Oswald found himself spending more and more time with Trisomy and, to his amazement, found the sad little creature to be an attentive pupil. She had been ecstatic, clapping her tiny, wizened claw-like hands in delight when Oswald suggested her beetle collection be assembled into a gleaming collage. To her added delight, Oswald made a rare visit to a picture framer in Windsor where the mounted, duly shellacked board and its beetles had been carefully framed. On Trisomy's insistence, the finished article was to be hung in Oswald's sitting room of the guest suite he had been assigned on arrival all those weeks ago. 'My beetles – like Twisomy – *like* Caligla!' she explained to her equally delighted parents. To everyone's surprise the beetles blended in perfectly with the Easy Rider decor.

'Brilliant, Oswald!' trilled Clytemnestra.

'Fucking A!' cried Ethelred.

Trisomy's foray in depicting some of the more… phallic-looking cacti in the conservatory was not as successful. 'Christ, she makes every spine on a leaf look like an enormous dick!' had been her so-called art teacher's immediate observation.

'Bloody size queen, rather like her teacher!' had been Ethelred's.

Oswald's other plot – his attempt to come to grips with either Monday, Mother Nature or both – proved to be a disaster.

'When I asked the guy to give me a hand with the pruning, he attacked every shrub and bush as if he was a rampant rabbi on fucking speed amongst a sea of hissing foreskins, as opposed to serpents!' Monday camped to a chortling Clytemnestra and Ethelred.

'Very poetic, Monday!' laughed Clytenestra.

'Thank Christ he wasn't let loose on my cock and balls in the topiary garden!' chuckled Ethelred.

'Never mind your cock and balls!' giggled his wife. 'What about my Brazillian?' her comment leading to more laughter.

'As for his skill at weeding. Why, if I let him loose on any of the lawns he'd have the place looking like the fucking Namib Desert in no time!'

'Enough, Monday!' shrieked Clytemnestra. 'Obviously his forte is dealing with fauna as opposed to flora... much better he sticks to his art classes with Tris.'

'Poor Arse Stretch, that's all he really wanted you know, Mon!' This from Ethelred.

'What?'

'His own pretty little arse *stretched*!'

'Oh, piss off Red. You know that's not my scene... but again, there is always that very interesting little question...' Monday gave Ethelred a lewd wink and licked his thick lips lasciviously with his even thicker, moist, pink tongue – 'How much?'

'A tenner?'

'Wow, Red! When do I get to do the dirty deed?'

'How about tonight?

'How about never!'

It was with some reluctance Ethelred and Clytemnestra decided Oswald should be allowed to join Clytemnestra on one of her business visits to Claudia in London.

'If he get's the slightest hint he is, in anyway, a prisoner down here, he'll more than likely do a runner and we don't need that now, do we?' Ethelred said with a grimace. 'No, let him tag along. I can only suggest you simply try and keep him with you at all times, Clyte. Why not give Claudia a call beforehand and see if she can find him a playmate, someone who can give him a tour of some of the neighbouring galleries or shops?'

'That's a bit of a tall order, even for the wily Ms. Cordelle. However, knowing Claudia, she'd probably ring one of those sordid male escort agencies and ask for a so-called male nanny in the guise of George Clooney!'

'The little bugger would enjoy that! No, simply keep him to heel. Say we'll be needing his help in the setting up of another exhibition, help from a managerial point of view. That gay manager of Claudia's can show him the ins and outs – I don't mean that literally! – regarding the gallery office. Show him what is basically required in the preparation of an exhibition and all that sort of shit! Anything which makes him see himself as a vital cog will see the arrogant little bugger buying it – to quote Charles again – hook, line and blinker!'

'You don't like him do you, Red?'

'Like him? I can't wait to snuff, stuff and possibly even dismember the little shit!' Ethelred looked at Clytemnestra, his expression deadly serious. 'While he's quite adamant he's finished with this Bryan creature, one never knows with his sort. Queeny and flighty are never good bedfellows! I suggest you watch the little sod like the proverbial hawk!'

Despite his vow never to contact Bryan, Oswald was determined to do so, his intentions however, being far from honourable. On their arrival at the Cork Street gallery, Oswald had immediately – to Clytemnestra's chagrin – leapt from the Bentley and, shouting back over his shoulder at the startled woman and Boris, the chauffeur he 'had things to do,' and would meet up 'later' at their agreed luncheon venue, headed off in the direction of Bond Street. The ever efficient Clytemnestra, during the journey up to London, had already given details of their planned lunch with Claudia at the elegant Flemings Hotel in Half Moon Street.

Stepping smartly into the nearby Westbury Hotel off Bond Street, Oswald quickly found a public telephone. From there he dialled the familiar number for Bryan's flat on the off chance Bryan would be there. 'What's the bet that the moping, silly queen hasn't found herself a job yet?' he muttered, 'And if madam isn't there, I'll simply leave a message on the answering machine. God forbid, the dreary "I wannabe an actress" flat mate is there enjoying one of her endless "rests" before her major break. Hello?' he said on the phone being promptly answered.

'Timothy Tyburn,' crooned a fruity baritone.

'Hi,' said Oswald breezily, 'Bryan there by any chance?'

'You've got a fuckin' nerve!' came the quick-fire reply, the smooth, rich voice rapidly changing in both timbre and tone, 'And no, you cunt! He's not! He's at work! So fuck off Argent, I'm waiting for an important call from my agent; not from a piece of low life trash like yourself!' The line went dead.

'Charming.' said Oswald, slightly taken aback at the unexpected description of his persona. 'Your agent?' he snickered, 'That, Mistress Tyburn, must be the biggest joke for the biggest jerk of two-thousand-and-thirteen! Your *agent*?' he repeated, 'For fuck's sake, who's she when she's at home? Elizabeth R?' Oswald gave an indignant snigger, accompanied by a shrug of his slim shoulders. 'Fuck you too, you prick, though that in itself would be a first! Dismal, wannabe cunt! Let's face it, your name Tyburn couldn't be more appropriate, for all you do do, you dismal twat, is exactly that, "hang in there!"'

Making his way from the booth, he paused momentarily before sashaying into the stylish Polo Bar. Ordering a double vodka Martini – Ethelred having put him on a generous retainer – he sat back, glowering at the luxurious surroundings for want of something better to do. Nodding a curt 'thank you' to the attractive waitress, he took a large gulp of his drink before muttering to himself. 'So she's gone and gotten herself a job, has she? That was quick! Probably stacking shelves in some suburban Sainsburys. That'd be right up her much used and abused alley.'

This last comment was, in reality, quite unjustified. Oswald, from their first meeting, having been insatiable in his role as the demanding, supposedly, sole recipient to Bryan's energetic eight inches. He took another large sip, his mood darkening. 'Shit! Double shit and fuck!' he said out loud, startling a nearby couple. 'Shit! Shit! Shit!' he repeated out loudly again. 'Fuck, he doesn't even have my number so he can't ring me. But I bet he's tried to find it!'

He paused, seemingly oblivious to the two stunned faces staring at him in some alarm. 'I bet she's been trying to get the Jones's number, though they'd make even ex-directory look open house!' he muttered. Oswald's glower changed to a smirk. 'I know; I'll drop a note!' he continued, his gaze inadvertently focussing on the inoffensive couple who, in turn, were looking at him in growing confusion. Although he wouldn't admit it, Oswald's sole reason for contacting Bryan was not to make amends but to gloat. 'Poor mediocrities,' he murmured, referring to both his ex-lover and flat mate. 'Poor, pathetic bloody never-ever-beens; poor, fucking, pathetic pieces of human flotsam!'

Catching more startled looks from the couple staring open-mouthed at the extraordinary young man talking out loud, Oswald added, 'No, not you two ugly, gawking old things, my ex-lover! I've just thrown her out!' He gave a shrill laugh. Totally carried away and encouraged by the growing angst of his unintentional audience, Oliver leaned forward, saying *sotto voce*, 'Sad old cow's had to take to the streets! Poor thing, she's going to learn the hard way prostitution at her age doesn't pay!'

'Well, *really*!' said the elderly woman. 'Has anyone ever told you that you are a very, very rude young man?'

'Frequently!' replied Oswald. He put on his most winning smile. 'I must apologise if I sounded rude, but I am deeply, deeply distressed. You see, not only is poor Bernadette *old,* she's also had a mastectomy which certainly doesn't help improve her allure! Unless, of course, the old bitch gets lucky and find's a one armed punter!'

'Good *God*!' spluttered the woman's elderly male companion. 'You, young man, ought to be ashamed of yourself!'

'But I'm not, see!' sniped Oswald, waving the payment slip folder in the direction of the waitress. 'In fact, I'm extremely pleased *with* myself. Allow me to introduce myself, Oswald, Oswald Argent, an international porn star who would never do either of you two geriatrics a service.' With a further dazzling smile, he rose to his feet and glided out from the bar, leaving an open-mouthed couple and waitress, the young woman having found a twenty pound note inside the folder left to cover the bill for thirteen pounds including the service charge.

With nothing else to do but kill time until he met up with Clytemnestra and Claudia, Oswald spent the next hour happily window shopping in Bond Street before making his way through Berkeley Square to Curzon Street and on to Flemings. Had Oswald not stopped to look a gleaming Rolls Royce convertible in the window of the Jack Barclay Showrooms, he would have walked straight into Bryan who, at that very moment, was walking along with Miles Anstruther en route to Bellamys for their regular lunch date.

'Bryan, I've got something very important to ask you and I don't want you to answer right away. I want you to think very seriously about it. Take as long as you wish but please hear me out. What I have to say I simply have to get off my chest. It's imperative that I do.'

'Jesus, Miles! You've got me breaking out in a cold sweat.' Bryan glanced round at the busy restaurant. Although he and Miles were seated at their usual table towards the rear of the popular Mayfair establishment, it was quite possible that they could be overheard.

Miles lowered his voice so even Bryan had to strain to hear his next few sentences. 'I'm desperately in love with you Bryan, my dear. I want to spend the rest of my life fully with you; sharing your company and not shying away from the fact that you're my lover.' Miles took a deep breath. Looking directly at the startled young man, Miles said gently, 'Angela has asked me for a divorce. Once this is final I would like you to accept my hand – to marry me – in a civil ceremony.'

Bryan, about to take a sip of Chablis, dropped his glass onto the table where it smashed into several pieces, the wine spreading rapidly across the pristine white table cloth. 'Fuck!' muttered Bryan. 'Apologies!' he added, smiling sheepishly at the waiter who had dashed over to mop up the mess and take away the broken pieces of glass. He and Miles sat in an embarrassed silence as the cloth was replaced and the cutlery repositioned.

The wine steward dutifully poured Bryan a fresh glass and left the two men sitting staring at each other.

'Perhaps I should have sent you an email!' said Miles with a gentle smile, attempting to make light of the situation. 'Sorry, Bryan, I didn't mean for you to get such a shock. I thought, well, I hoped, you were aware of my true feelings for you.'

'Jesus Miles,' replied Bryan softly. 'Don't be so silly! I've been desperate for you to say something like you've just said, but I never went quite so far as to ever dream that you'd go to such extremes.' He felt for the big man's knee under the table cloth. 'Marry you Miles Anstruther? I'd be honoured.'

'Ready to order, gentlemen? We have a delicious steamed turbot as our special today.'

'Oh, Sir Miles and I are definitely off fish as from today,' said Bryan looking up quickly and giving the patient waiter a wicked grin. *Christ, did he happen to overhear what we've just been saying?* 'I'll have the lamb, pink please.'

'Me too,' said a beaming Miles. 'And two glasses of champagne as soon as you can!'

'But what about Angela and Sophie?' Bryan couldn't stop smiling, nor could Miles – Miles having slipped his large hand under the table was holding Bryan's firm, smaller one.

'No problem,' said Miles, his face bursting into an even broader smile. 'Oh, Bryan,' he whispered, 'you've made me the happiest man on the planet.'

'Me too, but cool it Miles, people *are* beginning to stare. Tell me about Angela.'

'Oops, sorry, Bryo,' – Miles's special term of endearment for Bryan when they were in private – 'It's quite strange, actually. I know she's been screwing around with that big buck black who cohabits with those odd Joneses, our not-so-near neighbours in the country, but now there's someone else on the scene apparently, some Texan billionaire, so Lady A has decided to hot foot it off to the land of the oil wells with – and can you believe the guy's name – Derrick!'

'You're having me on!'

'No way, and our saviour's name is even spelt like an oil one!'

'And Sulky Sophie?'

'Oh, it's all arranged. Step-daddy simply loves little Sophie and no doubt she'll soon have her own little Derrick to play gushers with!'

'That, Miles, does not do you justice! But this black man. Has it been going on for some time?'

'Oh, I don't know. They always say the cuckolded husband is always last to know. I'm probably the laughing stock of all of Ascot but who gives a shit. I offered Angela the house down there but she wants out with a capital O and is being quite reasonable about it all.' He took another sip of his champagne, 'Which means she's either highly relieved at the change of scene or, even more so, at getting rid of me. Our lives with each other have become more of a charade than you would believe possible. Poor Angela, perhaps at long last she'll find some sort of happiness with this Derrick.' Miles gave a small sigh. 'The poor woman has never been able to be satisfied by me' – Bryan promptly choked on what was now his third glass of champagne – 'and it's well known she's been screwed by every willing male in the county when hubby's been away earning the spondulicks!' He gave a wry laugh. 'We know Derrick Donoghue the Third has more spondulicks than old Miles, let's hope for Angela's sake he has a standard cock!'

'Well, Sir Miles, let's put it this way – and you know you can always put it *that* way! – I can honestly say that I will be delighted to have Lady A's leftovers!'

'Let me get the bill and to hell with the office this afternoon. Mandy Mashona will just have to take over in her role as dominatrix – a role she relishes!'

Several hours, lying snugly against Miles's massive chest, Bryan was startled by a further startling confession by his sleepy lover. 'When Anglea asked me for a divorce – we were both quite amicable about all this – I told her about you. She wasn't surprised, gave us her blessing and has actually suggested you come down for the weekend.' He gave a low, deep gentle rumble of a laugh. 'She said she cannot wait to meet the new Lady Anstruther, albeit he happens to be a handsome, hunky twenty-something-year-old man!'

'Jesus, Miles...' Bryan gave a wicked giggle and kissed Miles lightly on his right, hairy nipple. 'Imagine the dilemma if I suddenly found myself taking a turn for the worse and decided to go for the daughter instead of her dad!'

'We have a cure for that in the country,' laughed Miles. 'We simply bugger the bastards who go after our young daughters. Once buggered by the likes of me, the daughters are soon forgotten!'

'Hear! Hear!' agreed Bryan with a laugh. 'May I suggest you now take it upon yourself to make sure, one more time, the memory of Jennifer? Jemima? – see, I've already forgotten her name! – is well and truly erased!'

'Eraser now erect!'

―――――――――

'How was London?'

'Fucking awful if you must know!'

'Not able to trace your old paramour?'

'What are you on about?' Oswald glared at an amused Charles who has joined him in Ethelred's conservatory, where he had been sitting having a much needed drink, the trip to London having been a total disaster. Having arrived at the lavishly decorated Flemings Hotel, Oswald had sat sulkily throughout lunch in the exquisite fifties-themed dining room, only half-listening to an avidly chatting Claudia and Clytemnestra. The forthcoming 'Reflections' exhibition well and truly dissected and – to quote the elegant gallery owner – 'put to fabulous, fucking bed!' – the two women began to discuss a topic which fascinated women most: other women! It was the mention of the name Anstruther that saw Oswald jerking out of his torpidity.

'You remember that rather handsome, fabulously rich Texan, Derrick Donoghue the Third or something, who bought up half of my "De Milo on the Pillow' exhibition?' said Claudia to Clytemnestra. 'The exhibition with all those Italianate nymphs and those hirsute, well-hung shepherds getting up to no good with both sheep, the nymphs and some even using their crooks as dildos?'

'My dear Claudia, how could I *ever* forget *dollars* Derrick?' replied Clytemnestra with a chortle. 'For what he paid you, it would have been cheaper for him to by a genuine flock and fly them to the States, a few hirsute shepherds and *Shepherd Market* tart-type nymphs included!'

'Thank Christ he didn't!' Claudia gave a light laugh. 'Well, rumour has it that he's about to import one of your neighbours, the very lovely though very loose – and darling, when I say loose, I mean *loose* – Angela Anstruther! Mrs. Anstruther is apparently married to a man who – or so she claims – boasts the biggest cock since Porfirio Rubirosa! In other words, the biggest dick in Christendom as opposed to Latin-dom!'

'Latin-dom? You've lost me, Claudia...'

'Rubirosa came – again another word to be used loosely – from the Dominican Republic, which makes Christendom not *quite* correct.'

'Let's cut to the quick – no, make that the cock. Miles Anstruther has a cock bigger that Rubirosa's?'

'So I'm told!'

'So, if your coy use of the word "import" implies she's leaving Miles for this Derrick Donoghue, what has *he* got to offer in the projectile stakes? The silly bitch must have a cunt comparable to the Euro Tunnel!' Clytemnestra couldn't resist a lewd snigger. 'Surely you must have heard, darling, the *angelic* Angela has also been fucking our gargantuan man Monday? The whole of Ascot knows about it! We call him our man Friday but, according to Viola, our housemaid, he's also known as Lady A's Wednesday!' She gave an inelegant snort. 'When you meet Angela, you'd genuinely believe butter wouldn't melt in her mouth. She's *so* cool, *so* elegant, so... *so* Grace Kelley, and we all know what *that* one was all about; screwed every prince in Hollywood before she married her frog!'

Oswald sat bolt upright, his eyes glued to the two women.

'Well dear – or should that be *oil* dear?' purred Claudia. 'She's divorcing Miles Anstruther and hot-footing off, daughter et al, to the land where everything is bigger!'

'Wasn't it common knowledge,' crooned Clytemnestra, determined not to be outdone in the gossip stakes, 'Rubirosa boasted a cock the equivalent of a serious pepper grinder? Correct me if I'm wrong, but didn't greedy, ghastly little Truman Capote once describe Rubirosa's cock as "an eleven inch *cafe au lait* sinker as thick as a man's wrist?" Or words to that effect?'

Claudia gave a hoot of mirth and beckoned to a hovering waiter. Pointing at her Cobb Salad she carolled camply, 'May I have a pepper mill, please?' causing the two women to burst out laughing.

'Madam?' asked the young waiter held out the large, dark polished pepper grinder above Clytemnestra's plate.

'Oh, definitely some Rubirosa, thank you!' cried Clytemnestra as she and Claudia collapsed into further shrieks. Oswald, who had ordered a grilled sole, simply glared at the proffered projectile, dismissing the waiter with a wave of his trembling hand.

'They're actually coming to dinner on Saturday,' Clytemnestra managed to splutter in between further giggles and sips of wine. 'Of course we've known about her and Monday for ages. Ethelred is always amused by my so-called "crotch watch." Both he and I count how many times the elegant Lady A gets nudged by Mon's massive, always bulging cock and balls, during the serving of the various intercourses!'

Claudia could not resist an even louder shriek at the atrocious pun. 'Oh Clyte,' she gasped, 'that was too, too dreadful!' She gave another gasp. 'Or should that be dreadlocks?' The screams of mirth from the two at this bon mot causing Oswald to visibly shrink back into the velvet covered dining chair.

'Oh poor darling!' gulped Claudia looking at the embarrassed young man, 'How tactless of us.' She couldn't resist giving Clytemnestra a mischievous glance, 'Particularly if one is perhaps more pepper *pot* than *grinder*?'

Oswald's sibilant, 'Go fuck yourself you ugly cunt!' as he pushed back his chair, stood up and strode angrily from the dining room, was completely drowned by further peals of nigh-on hysterical laughter.

The black mood remained constant for the whole journey back to Ascot. Whether it was a deliberate move on her part or not, Clytemnestra insisted Oswald sit in the passenger seat alongside the silent Boris while she sat in the back of the Bentley with the reading light on. Lunch, without Oswald, had progressed to several cocktails in the glamorous Flemings Cocktail Bar, again without Oswald. Clytemnestra made no comment about his sudden departure but, on her eventual arrival at the waiting car, simply said 'Stay where you are!' as he made a move as if to join her in the back. 'I have important work to do,' she added, 'and I need to spread my papers out.' Switching on the reading lamp in the back, Clytemnestra poured herself a glass of chilled white wine from the small bar set in behind the driver's seat. Oswald, to his chagrin, was not offered a drink. His earlier sentence applied to Claudia, namely 'Go fuck yourself you ugly cunt!' kept flashing across the Oswald's mind as he sat, glaring through the darkened windscreen at the countryside flashing by. *If only,* he kept thinking, *if only...*

The rest of Oswald's afternoon had been spent alternating between joining a patiently waiting Boris for a few desultory chats, or else meandering up and down Half Moon Street, careful not to venture out of sight as he was well aware Clytemnestra's resultant mood following his earlier behaviour, would not be the most affable. The thought she could easily return to Bethlem Báthory without him continuing to cross his mind, Oswald made sure he would be only a few yards from the car when she finally deigned to make herself known.

His mind had also been in turmoil over the intimate revelations concerning Miles Anstruther. The impact of his one and only meeting with the man had never wavered, Oswald being unable as to discern whether the feeling was love, lust or a combination of both. Although in his heart of hearts he pined for love, for Oswald – being Oswald – the difference cock and commitment was a one way street. When it came to the crunch, cock would prevail. The casually dropped information the object of his confusion, plus family, were all due to dine the coming Saturday at Bethlem Báthory, had not proved traumatic. In fact, Oswald was positively ecstatic. 'Fuck a mere pepper grinder! I've been forearmed and never harmed! A divorced straight man? Oh, Sir Miles, not for long if I have anything to do with it. I saw *that look*, albeit for an instant, but I know your sort, Miles Anstruther; a homo on hold if ever there was!' Oswald gave an inward smile. 'Lady Anstruther? Now I wonder what silly, common, definitely on-the-scrap-heap Miss Scima would say, were she ever to find out what had finally happened to her ex? Not only a super star, but a titled one!'

Clytemnestra's only comment came when the silent car drew up in front of the house. 'Claudia Cordelle is not a cunt,' she said sibilantly. 'Unlike you Oswald Argent, Claudia Cordelle has a boyfriend who is quite capable of fucking her. And let me assure you – *arse*-wald – the next time you decide to throw a hissy fit it will be your last. Furthermore, you are not expected to join us at dinner tonight!' Taking up her closed briefcase, Clytemnestra stepped elegantly out from the car, thanked Boris who had been standing at attention having opened the door for her, and made her way briskly up the wide stone steps.

'You're in deep shit, young man,' commented Boris, smiling for the first time since the journey. Like the rest of the household staff, his dislike of the arrogant young wannabe star was growing daily. Leaving a stunned Oswald standing alone in the driveway, the smirking chauffeur drove off in a spurt of gravel towards the garages at the back of the house.

Boris's regaling of the slight altercation between Clytemnestra and Oswald was greeted by the domestic staff with glee.

'Proper little twerp!' sniffed Mrs. Norelle.

'Stuck up little prick!' said Viola.

'Bitchy little bugger!' added Boris with a grin; his accurate observation causing the two women to burst out into a fit of giggles.

'Oh Boris, you are a one!' chortled Mrs. Norelle.

'Somehow I don't the missus would agree with you, Mrs. N!' the chauffeur replied, giving the cook a lecherous wink. 'She doesn't call me 'er bonking Boris for nothing!' his comment leading to more shrieks from the two women.

Monday had also changed his opinion since their first intimate 'get together.' 'Nasty piece of work,' he agreed. 'As far as I'm concerned, he can go and get stuffed!' Well aware of Ethelred's plans for the forthcoming 'Still Life,' Monday's words were more a prediction than wishful thinking.

'Touché,' chortled plump Viola. 'The little shit should get himself well and truly stuffed *in every way possible*!' The young girl's unexpected outburst saw the other three double up with laughter.

'I think,' said a grinning Monday, 'that deserves a drink! I'm for a rum and Coke. Nanette? Boris? Viola?' Having poured himself and Viola a large rum and Coke, Boris a lager and Mrs. Norelle a large schooner of sherry, Monday raised his drink in a camp toast. 'To Oswald, may he be well and truly stuffed in every which way of his choosing!'

'To Oswald!' carolled his beaming companions.

'Happy stuffing!' giggled Nanette Norelle.

'I'll drink to that!' chortled Viola.

'Up yours!' toasted the more pragmatic Boris.

'Ahem!' The clearing of a throat caused the four to spin round to the open doorway leading to the dining room. A grinning Ethelred broke into an even larger grin before saying. 'Walls have ears, dears! Never forget it! Is that a rum and Coke I see before me, Mon? Mind fixing me one as well?' Eyeing the embarrassed group, he smiled reassuringly as Monday prepared his drink and replenished theirs. 'Put it this way,' Ethelred said conspiratorially, 'I realise I made a mistake in inviting the young man here. In the two months he's been around – Christ, how time flies – I've noticed a growing atmosphere of disquiet. I am sure he is unaware of what are, to us anyway, his glaring faults: namely his arrogance and his innate rudeness. However, he is here for a purpose and once he knuckles down to some serious film work – as opposed to simply lolling around doing next to nothing apart from watch daytime television and drink – hopefully things will change.' Noticing Monday's expression of surprise Ethelred added, 'Yes Monday; seriously drink. Don't tell me you haven't noticed the bar in the Easy Rider suite that seems to have developed a major thirst? How many bottles of vodka have you put in their in the past few days, Viola? Three? Four? The little runt is always smashed, but once the purpose for his being here is fulfilled there will be, I promise you, no more Oswald. So, may we all drink to that, please? A toast to Operation EO!'

'Operation EO?' questioned Boris.

'Exit Oswald!' replied Ethelred.

'Exit Oswald? I like it!' laughed Monday in his deep rumble.

———

Two hours later, Clytemnestra, Charles, Ethelred, Monday, Euros and Thrift were all seated in the study having an after dinner drink; the impromptu gathering a result of a few brief telephone calls from Ethelred, who, having sensed the general atmosphere in the kitchen, had gone up to his and Clytemnestra's private sitting room where an atmosphere was even more apparent. Clytemnestra, incandescent with rage, had relayed the Claudia – Oswald saga to her astounded husband.

'It's getting out of hand,' Clytemnestra warned. 'He's already snooping around Charles's studio, despite having claimed taxidermy was not his forte. God knows who he may be calling on his mobile!'

'Right,' said Ethelred, 'now we're away from the likes of Nanette, Boris, Viola and Oswald, *especially* Oswald, there's something I must say, something which has come to a head.' He nodded in the direction of his wife. 'Clyte has been telling me about our so-called little star's behaviour up in town today, behaviour which has been rather fortuitous; fortuitous in that he was instructed not to join us for dinner tonight.' He smiled at Euros and Thrift, who were sitting together on the sofa, quietly holding hands, a look of deepest concentration on both their faces. 'Sorry to have dragged you two up from your cosy cottage, but the opportunity was too good to miss.' Ethelred took a sip of brandy, 'To put it in a nut shell – or a *nutcase* shell! – master Oswald is becoming too much of a loose cannon; something we certainly don't need at this stage of our game.'

He nodded at Charles. 'Charles is ready. Monday, you're OK with what we've discussed and your part in it?' The big black man nodded his affirmation. 'And you Euros, and Thrift?'

'From day one,' the two answered in unison, looking like a contented Tweedle Dum and Tweedle Dee.

'And of course Clyte is probably even more keen on getting started than all of us put together. So, my friends, as they say, "Why are we waiting?" The additional backing has all come through; if you'll forgive the double entendre!' Ethelred gave a laugh. 'And before you ask, yes, it's our usual, stalwart friend who prefers to remain anonymous and still goes by the pseudonym of HG – HG as you know being the initials of HG Wells, the author of "The Invisible Man." Thanks to HG, I suggest a meeting to go through all the preliminaries and arrange a suitable working schedule. I've decided, under the current circumstances, it would be extremely unwise to delay the start any longer.' Ethelred added with a wry chuckle. 'So, dear partners in slime and crime, are we all agreed?'

The five smiling faces said it all.

————————

'I've cleared it with Angela.' Miles smiled up at Bryan who had come into his office with some papers he needed signing. 'If you are still agreeable to meeting the family from the House of Usher, as if it were, you're more than welcome to drive down with me tomorrow afternoon and come back Sunday evening. The other alternative is to take the train down on Saturday to Windsor and I will meet you; which ever you prefer, my darling.' Bryan glanced anxiously towards the closed office door. 'Heavens Bryo, I'm not that indiscreet!' The big man gave a chuckle. 'Mandy's out to lunch and, as you know, mine and hers are the only offices on this floor.'

'Sorry,' muttered Bryan with a sheepish smile. 'It's all happened so quickly… it all seems too good to be true and I simply keep waiting to wake up! I simply can't believe so much has happened in only two months. Talk about a whirlwind career and a hurricane romance!'

'A lot can happen in two months!' chuckled Miles.

'Tell me about it!' laughed Bryan happily, moving around the desk and giving his fiancé a resounding kiss.

CHAPTER 9

'So, what time does this paramour, the paramour to end – or should that be to begin? – all paramours, arrive?'

Miles looked irritably at the soignée blonde woman sitting across the polished dining table from him; her long, pale fingers nervously playing with a fork. Slapping it down, she said sharply, 'Well?'

'*Bryan*, his name is *Bryan*, Angela, and *Bryan* is due at Windsor on the mid-morning train. How many times do I have to tell you that?'

'As often as I wish to ask!'

'Oh for Chrissake!' Miles crumpled up his table napkin and threw it on the table. 'If this is how you are going to be carrying on, I'll simply call the guy and cancel him. He'll more than likely be highly relieved.' He looked at his smirking wife. 'Jesus Ange, it was *your* suggestion we ask him down but, if you're going to absolutely bloody about it the whole weekend, let's forget it.' Miles paused before going for the jugular. 'At least he'll be spared the embarrassment of having to watch you grope that bloody black stud's cock at dinner!'

'Bastard!' The Lady Anstruther gave a shriek as she threw the remaining contents of her wine glass at her husband, who, in the middle of getting to his feet, took the brunt of the liquid square in the chest.

'For Christ's sake, Angela,' muttered Miles. Tut tutting and shaking his handsome head, the big man walked calmly from the room.

'Don't you *dare* walk out on me in the middle of a conversation!' his wife screamed. 'Don't you *dare*!'

'Me walk out on you?' Miles stopping abruptly in the doorway, turned to look back at the attractive, visibly shaking woman, saying, *sotto voce* 'I think, my dear, it's a clear case of *you* walking out on me; firstly with half the county, then the black, buck fuck of the Joneses, and now your – to quote your very self – "richer than Croesus" Texan! So, if you'll excuse me, I'll simply go and cancel the paramour who, yet again and for the zillionth time as, well you know, bears the perfectly legitimate name of Bryan. And yes, he is my lover and yes, again for the zillionth time, I'm marrying him!' Turning away from the startled woman, he strode out, deliberately slamming the large door.

'Shit!' Angela Anstruther stretched across the wide dining table, reaching for her husband's unfinished glass of wine. 'Double shit!' she announced to the room in general, then did a double take as she noticed the silent form standing by the door leading to the hallway to the kitchen. 'Oh, Dodds,' Angela crooned without the slightest sign of embarrassment, 'you can clear away but, before you do so, I'd like some more wine.' She gave a wry smile. 'Tell cook the soufflé was a dream and yes, I'll have coffee served in my private study.' Angela gave a small nod as the solemn, angular, stork-like butler, set down a clean glass and filled it for her.

'Milady,' he said deferentially.

'Any sign of Miss Sophie?'

'She said she'd be back around eleven, milady. I believe Susannah relayed the message.'

'Ah, yes. Susannah…' Angela, looking slightly perplexed, tried to remember if the house maid had or hadn't. 'Now you mention it, I believe she did. Ah yes, Miss Sophie is having supper over at the Johnson's.' Angela took a long sip of wine and automatically held up her glass which was promptly attended to. 'How absolutely fucking lovely for her,' added her ladyship sarcastically.

'If you say so, milady,' agreed the butler. 'I'll see to your ladyship's coffee in the library. Shall we say thirty minutes?' he added and quietly left the room, but not before deferentially placing a new bottle of wine in the silver wine coaster alongside the scowling woman.

'Oh shit!' muttered Angela to the empty room. 'Or perhaps "oh bugger" would be more apt!' She gave a small snigger. 'Oh *shit*!' she repeated. Getting to her feet and grasping her glass plus bottle, Angela made her way elegantly from the dining room, crossing the large, airy hallway and stopping outside a the polished mahogany door of Miles's private study. Banging on the door with the base of the bottle, she called out in a contrite voice, 'Miles? I'm sorry! May I come in?' She paused, waiting for a reply. 'I was completely out of order and being a right, cantankerous old bitch. Of course Bryan must come to stay.' Angela gave a light laugh. 'It may sound bizarre, considering the circumstances, but I suppose, in a tiny way, I'm actually quite jealous! There…' she looked expectantly at the silent door. 'I've said it and…' Any further words were stopped by the door suddenly opening.

'Oh Ange,' said a softly smiling Miles, 'I do so hate it when we bicker and squabble. Of course come in.' He eyed the bottle warily, his eyes showing the first hint of a twinkle. 'But firstly, I need to know, are you planning to drink that or throw it?'

'Oh, I've done with the wine throwing; let's just sit and talk. We're both tense, me with leaving England and you with your new life about to begin.' She walked into the oak panelled study. 'Join me or are you having something else?'

Miles gestured towards the open drinks cabinet set among the bookshelves to one side of the elegant, masculine room. 'I'm having a whisky. Are you sure you wouldn't prefer one to what you've got?'

'No, wine is fine.' She gave a light laugh, 'Poor Dodds, I think he must have walked in on our rather dubious duet and been simply riveted, standing in the dark, listening to that elegant little debacle between the two of us.' Angela gave a further, light, tinkly – though somewhat forced – laugh. 'Obviously he and cook are now having a good old chinwag over a glass of cooking sherry; though I have a feeling cook has taken to crème de menthe with a bit of a vengeance these days!'

Miles gave a wry smile. 'I don't think there's much that could shock doddery old Dodds, even references to black dick!'

'However I do think a gay marriage, particularly a gay marriage involving his own lord and master, could be a first – even for Dodds!' giggled Angela taking a sip of wine. Lowering herself elegantly onto the leather Chesterfield, she looked up at her tall, handsome husband. 'Are you sure you're doing the right thing, Miles? I mean, we've always known about the gay *thing*, but this young man; a civil ceremony et al after what – a period of only two months?' Angela took a further sip, her eyes never leaving her husband. 'Are you one truly hundred per cent sure?'

'I could ask you the same thing about your feelings concerning Derrick.'

'Oh, Derrick's for keeps,' said Angela, switching her attention from Miles and looking thoughtfully at the glowing embers in the fireplace. 'I suppose – in a way – it was this always threatening gay thing of yours that drove me to behaving the way I did.' She held up a tiny hand. 'No, please don't stop me, Miles.' Angela gave a small sigh. 'I've always known about your dalliances, however discreet – and dear Miles, you have been discreet – but still, they have always hurt. Again, I'm at fault in that I wasn't up to much in the sex stakes but, God, Miles, you are so *massive* and try as I could, I simply couldn't bear the pain when we did make love. For love it was at first Miles and then, for me, guilt followed by resentment when you took your affections elsewhere.'

'Jesus, Ange,' said Miles softly, 'why didn't you say all this before? Why didn't you tell me? We could have talked about it – tried to work something out.'

'Miles, dear Miles, look at how many couples we know where one or the other has been gay and, in some cases, the companionship thing has worked but, as with us, we both enjoy sex but sadly not sex with each other. Furthermore, I want more of a commitment in a marriage. I want a *complete* marriage, not a sham. With Derrick it *will* be complete, and I know I'll be, once and for all, truly fulfilled and true to my vows!'

'Does Sophie know about me?' Miles's voice faltered. Angela's 'cruel to be kind' act was beginning to make him feel extremely uncomfortable.

'Oh God, yes!' Angela gave a light, nervous laugh. 'She refers to you behind your back as "Thoroughly Macho Millie!"'

To Angela's immense relief Miles threw back his head and roared with laughter. 'Well it could have been worse, I suppose.' He gave an awkward smile, 'I mean, she could have called me, "Thoroughly Mincing Millie!"'

'Darling Miles,' said Angela with mock severity. 'Nobody, but nobody could ever accuse you of mincing!'

'Well, that's a relief.' Miles took a sip of whisky. 'And she's happy about this move to the States? Really OK about it all?'

'Absolutely. She's already made great friends with Derrick's daughter from his first marriage – they're never off the phone – so I don't think our Sophie should be the cause of any concern.'

'So, you're still happy with Bryan coming down tomorrow?'

'As long as he sticks to the spare room and you to your bedroom, it'll be fine.' Angela gave a dry laugh. 'Contrary to local gossip, Miles, I've never entertained a fuck under the marital roof! After all, I am a bona fide lady!'

'Touché,' laughed her husband as he refilled her wine glass.

Later, as she sat in front of her dressing table brushing her long blonde hair with brisk, efficient strokes, a further glass of wine on the mirrored surface in front, Angela Anstruther stared coldly at her elegant, aristocratic features, a slight smile on her perfect mouth. 'Well, dear' she said to her reflection. 'I can't wait to meet this boy wonder.' Angela made a slight moue. 'God knows what he and Miles get up to! I know I like them big but this mysterious Bryan must have an arsehole that beggars – no, make that *buggers* – belief! Oh Lady A, you're sooo fucking elegant at times!' She made as if to put down her hairbrush but suddenly hesitated. 'Oh, why the fuck not?' Angela muttered. Minutes later the elegant Lady Anstruther was lying inelegantly spread-eagled on the large four poster bed, her hand moving rhythmically as she fucked herself deeply with the much-used, silver handled hair brush. 'Oh yes! Oh yes!' she began to groan from deep in the back of her throat as she felt her orgasm approaching. 'Monday! *Monday*!' she screamed as she came, her free arm thrashing wildly upon the satin counterpane.

Miles, already asleep in his own bedroom suite, missed the animal-like sounds coming from his wife's private rooms. Only Sophie, reeling down the corridor past her mother's door in a hazy, stoned state as she made her way to her own bedroom suite, was privy to the performance. Giving a giggle the teenager couldn't help muttering mischievously to herself, 'Takes two to tango, Mummy dearest! Like mother, like dildo!'

Several minutes later a quiet whimpering was to be heard coming from behind the closed door to her own suite. Not be outdone, the Honourable Sophie Anstruther, proud possessor of a bright pink vibrator bought on a clandestine visit to an Ann Summers sex shop in London's notorious Soho, was soon flailing about on her own counterpane, the aforesaid vibrator deeply inserted and vibrating – to quote the gasping Sophie – 'like a fucking two-stroke piston!' – inside her.

———————

'Welcome to Windsor!' A smiling Miles was there to greet a smiling, but apprehensive Bryan as he stepped off the train. 'Very country and stylish!' he added, noting with approval the neat blazer, open-necked check shirt and neatly pressed twill trousers.

'Will I do?' quipped Bryan nervously, unexpectedly holding out his hand. 'Well, I couldn't really give you a whopping smacker at the station, now, could I?' He later laughed to Miles when in the car.

'You'll do for ever,' smiled his lover. 'Now, come along, the girls cannot wait to meet the mysterious Bryan. To make it a bit easier we're lunching at the Thames View restaurant in the Christopher Wren House Hotel in the town. It's right on the river across from Eton. Break you in gently, if you'll excuse the pun!'

'Whatever lover! If this "breaking in" is as successful as the first, it can only be the start to a case of very happy families!'

'God, I love you Bryo!' Miles gave the young man an affectionate squeeze on his muscular thigh. 'Unbeknown to me until this morning, we're also out for dinner tonight. Angela arranged this some time ago. It's with some rather bizarre neighbours – he's a well-known film director and the wife's an equally well known artist.' Miles, concentrating on the road ahead did not see Bryan's face freeze in apparent horror as he continued blithely. 'He goes by the name of Ethelred Jones and she is Clytemnestra Jones. Ring any bells?'

'Unfortunately, yes,' said Bryan through clenched teeth. 'They're the ones my ex, Oswald – Oswald Argent – is involved with. He's making a film with Jones. In fact, he's living there with them as we speak.' Bryan thumped the dashboard. 'Stop the car! Stop the car!' They both lurched forward against their respective seatbelts as Miles jammed on the brakes to the Jaguar. 'I can't do this, Miles. I'm sorry, but I can't!' He turned his anguished face to the startled man. 'Please Miles, don't argue. If you really love me you'll take me back to the station and I'll go back to London. Make up some excuse – say I wasn't on the train and it's only now you realised that there was a text message from me which you'd overlooked – but please, *please,* take me back to the station!' He looked imploringly at the visibly stunned, silent man. Bryan, beginning to panic, let out a wild, almost feral cry. 'If you don't take me back, I'll simply get out of the car at the hotel and take a taxi – or walk – but this is all wrong, too hideously, hideously wrong!' Tears streaming down his face, he added choking, 'Let's talk when we're both back in town on Monday. But now, please…'

Silently, his lips in a tight line and his face impassive, Miles slowly turned into a nearby street and, having made the relevant manoeuvres, drove even more slowly back to the station. Staring straight ahead through the windscreen, he made no attempt to speak during the short return journey; a distraught Bryan remaining equally as silent. Reluctantly closing the passenger door, the young man's heart literally broke as his lover drove off without looking back.

A desolate, almost tearful Bryan, sat silently in the almost empty carriage as the train sped its way back towards London, the difference between the two journeys, the arrival and now the sudden departure, being paramount.

———————

'Where's your guest?' A curious Angela looked up at her husband as he entered the comfortable sitting room in the hotel. She gave Sophie a knowing look as their daughter, looking up at her father with complete indifference, went back to the open copy of 'Hello' Magazine on her lap.

'Change of plan,' muttered Miles vaguely. He made a half-hearted hand gesture. 'I didn't see his message until I was actually waiting for the train. Some mishap in town and he's had to cancel.' He managed a twisted smile. 'He sends his apologies...'

'Oh *dear*!' chirruped Angela, a bit too brightly, 'How *very* sad. Well, there won't be another time now, will there as Sophs and I are away within a week or so?' She smiled at the hovering waiter. 'You know what?' said the Lady Anstruther, 'I'd rather like a glass of champagne! Or shall we make that a bottle, Miles dear? Cristal perhaps? And Sophie, as she was so good at getting home on time last night, may have a glass as well!'

———————

'Sir Miles Anstruther, LadyAnstruther and the Honourable Miss Sophie Anstruther,' announced Monday sonorously.

Ethelred gave Clytemnestra a brief wink. It always amused the three of them – Monday especially – whenever the Anstruthers came to dinner. Monday, slipping into what he called his 'Jeremiah Jeeves' role, would solemnly serve, hamming it up in his role as the black, buffoon of a butler. 'After all, I do give her ladyship a good servicing in private once a week!' the big black man would casually announce without any hint of embarrassment. 'So, serving her at dinner – and in public – is always an added bonus and turn on!'

'Angela, how heavenly!' cooed Clytemnestra, 'You look lovely as always. And Sophie! I love the top! Miles!' She moved forward stretching up to kiss the big man on his cheek. Clytemnestra smiled brightly at the small group. 'Thank you for your message, Angela. How unfortunate your house guest was unable to make it. It would have been such fun to meet a new face!' She turned back to where a sheepish Oswald was standing behind her. 'But, not to be outdone, we have our very own new face! Oswald, come and meet Angela, Sophie and Miles Anstruther. Forget Monday's Oscar winning performance, we're very informal here!'

'Err... Miles and I have met before,' stammered Oswald.

'We have?' and 'You have?' came simultaneously from a startled Miles and an instantly curious Angela.

'Yes,' said Oswald with a coquettish grin. He looked at a puzzled Ethelred. 'You surely can't have forgotten, Red? My famous – or rather, infamous arrival when I backed into Sir Miles's car!'

'Of course!' laughed Ethelred, 'Quite an initiation to Windsor, if I recall.'

Miles, shook Oswald by his thin hand, saying briskly. 'Nice to see you again, Oswald.' *How could I not have remembered you?* he thought, *You're absolutely ravishing. And if you really are or were Bryan's Oswald, how very remiss of him to let you go! Oh Bryo, dear Bryo, how right you were to take that train back to London. Tonight would have been a total disaster!*

'Miles? Miles?' This from Clytemnestra.

The big man shook himself out of his brief reverie. 'Err... oh yes, champagne would be fine, thank you!' He took a flute from the proffered tray held by the smiling Viola. 'Sorry about that!' He gave Ethelred a wink. 'I hope your star in the making comes up trumps, Ethelred! That little dent has made quite a little dent in your insurance, I should think. Powerful motors those German jobs!'

'Oh, I can assure you Oswald's future is *ensured* as much as I am insured,' laughed Ethelred. 'Now, Miles, tell me all about you latest property scam. Is it true that you're buying up half the Cinque Terre or not?'

Unbeknown to a bemused Ethelred and Clytemnestra, while Monday was entertaining the three of them with the familiar 'crotch watch' routine, Miles Anstruther – to his immense surprise – was having his foot well and truly played with by a stocking-clad foot which could only belong to the blond, boy vamp, sitting opposite, his large blue eyes staring at Miles with undiluted desire. *Jesus,* thought Miles, finding himself developing a formidable erection. *Where the fuck did they find you, you so available little tart, and what the fuck am I going to do about it?*

Dinner over, the group retired to Ethelred's conservatory. Angela and Miles, having both made the relevant mutterings and platitudes concerning the absent Trisomy, had gone on to discuss Clytemnestra's forthcoming exhibition. Ethelred's new film was also briefly mentioned before the conversation turned to other trivialities. At no time was the impending divorce or the departure for America mentioned. The only break in the after dinner conversation occurred when Ethelred and Miles wandered out onto the terrace, each with their brandy balloons and cigars to, as Ethelred mysteriously informed them, 'discuss some business.' The ever attentive Monday, checking all their immediate needs had been taken care of, had momentarily disappeared. Oswald meanwhile, seated himself sulkily in a corner while Sophie sat, bored and distant, alongside her mother on an adjacent sofa.

'Ethelred is determined to invest in this Cinque Terre deal of Miles,' Clytemnestra explained, giving a light laugh. 'He's suddenly gone and gotten himself well and truly bitten by this Mediterranean bug. The dear man no doubt sees me duly ensconced, happy smiling locals around me, as I pose creating large canvasses using local materials such as sand, shells, seaweed, fish scales and perhaps even a scaly local fisherman or two! You name it and I'll be doing it!' She gave a self-deprecating laugh. 'I'm quite sure there's a new Ethelred Jones film lurking in there somewhere!' Clytemnestra added with a chuckle. 'And if you think it's only art, the Cinque Terre is also known for its wines and methinks' – she tapped her nose knowingly – 'a small vineyard or two. Who knows, within a year or two, a totally undrinkable Vino de Joneses may be flooding the market!' This gem was greeted with a high shriek from a highly charged Angela as Monday, having silently returned, inadvertently nudged her arm with his giant erection as he leaned over to refill her champagne flute.

'We're back,' announced Ethelred unnecessarily as he and Miles re-entered the conservatory.

'And Miles, we must go,' announced Angela standing and pulling Sophie up with her. She turned to her hostess, 'A lovely evening and delicious dinner as always, Clytemnestra dear.' Angela gave a brittle smile. 'I can only wish you all the best for your new exhibition. Contrary to the fact the subject has been deliberately avoided all evening, Sophie and I shall be in Texas.' She gave an even tighter smile. 'Miles and I are getting a divorce – as you, and the whole of Ascot and Windsor knows – but, as they say, *ce la vi*!' Angela turned to a startled Oswald who, dismayed by the abrupt departure, was looking at Miles both longingly and rapaciously; looks which had not gone unnoticed by his wife.

'Oswald,' she purred, giving both the young man and her husband a knowing glance, 'How charming to have met you and lots of luck with your future in films.' She gave a predatory smile before glancing again at her stony-faced husband. 'You're a very, very handsome young man, Oswald,' Angela commented. 'No, I stand corrected. Make that a very, very *beautiful* young man.'

With a tinkling laugh she couldn't resist a final barb while looking directly at Miles. 'Why, I'd even go so far as to say a positive male Helen of Troy and quite capable of launching a thousand shits! Goodnight everyone!' With a toss of her coiffed head, Angela swept out followed by her giggling daughter and a red faced Miles.

'*What* a bitch!' cried Ethelred with a hoot of laughter as he fell into a nearby chair.

'Dear me,' tut tutted Clytemnestra, a broad grin on her face, 'We all know what *didn't* get into her tonight!' She added with a shriek, 'Monday? Where are you when you are needed most?'

'Hiding!' came a deep laugh from the shadows alongside the wine cabinet.

'Am I mistaken or didn't she say *shits* instead of *ships*?' grizzled a petulant Oswald, his expression becoming even more soured as the other three burst out into uncontrollable laughter.

———

Later that night, to Charles's dismay, a sulking, irascible Oswald had turned up at his private flat demanding a drink. After denouncing the dinner, the guests and finally his host and hostess, the frustrated young man demanded Charles fist fuck him for what seemed an eternity. Finally satiated and having come into his own cupped hand, Oswald collapsed into an exhausted, whimpering slumber.

Charles, a frown on his face, his hand and part of his forearm still impaled within the lightly snoring Oswald, gave a deep sigh. 'As you say, Red, keep him sweet,' he said to himself. 'But I can tell you here and now, young Oswald, the next time I stick something into you it won't be my fucking fist or a fucking dildo; it'll be a fucking scalpel!'

———

Miles called Bryan's mobile from his mobile. 'Bryo? Please, please pick up. I'm on my way back to town. I'm so sorry, my darling. Please forgive me… oh dear, darling Byro, I love you so very, very much. Call me back on the mobile or at the flat. I should be there within thirty minutes…'

'Miles! Oh Miles! Sorry! Sorry darling but I was half dozing. I'm so glad you're coming back… so very, very glad!'

'Don't get a cab; I'll come and collect you; it's on the way!'

'No need to, darling Miles…'

'You mean…?'

'I mean! Yes, you silly sod, I'm in *our* bed in Cadogan Square! If I wasn't to be actually sleeping *with* you I was making damn sure I'd be sleeping engulfed by your very personal Miles pong! I'm hugging *your* pillow so as to be able to smell *your* hair tonic and I'm wearing *your* dressing gown so I'm smothered in MO, Miles odour but…' and here there was a lewd chuckle, 'I haven't quite come as yet so I'll hold off until the real McCoy gets here!'

CHAPTER 10

A smirking Oswald, not bothering to knock, skipped into Ethelred's small office-cum-study and without being asked to do so, sat down opposite the director. The young man had been delighted to find a memo slipped under his door the morning of the dinner party. The memo had simply read, *Meeting, my study nine o'clock Sunday to discuss preliminaries regarding your role, STILL LIFE. Red.*

'Am I early or simply the first?' Oswald gave a camp giggle. 'You can't say I'm not keen...'

'No. you're not early. In fact, you're several minutes late!' Ethelred gave him a stern look. 'And next time, knock. I could have been having a wank, taking a piss or even a shit!'

'In your office?' camped Oswald, slightly taken aback at Ethelred's brusque greeting.

'Checked the waste bin?' came the withering reply.

Oswald blanched. Ethelred's eccentricities were well known and for all he knew, the man could be serious. 'Err... sorry Red, it's simply I'm somewhat over excited at the thought of the film to end all films actually starting!'

'Good, well then...' Ethelred peered at some sheets of paper on his desk before looking up at Oswald. He handed over a sheet. 'These are the arrangements for the coming week. You will see that there is not much filming scheduled. I want you to get used to feeling unselfconscious in front of the crew and the camera which means, as from ten o'clock today – this is when I have called a general meeting – you will be nude.'

'Nude?'

'Yes, Oswald. Nude. Starkers, bullock naked, bare-arsed, dick on display! In other words, nude! Any objections?'

'Err... no.' Oswald gulped, 'And the rest of the cast? I take it there are others involved?"

'There are, namely Monday; in fact, for your scenes, only Monday. Here, if you read the page I've just handed you, you'll see a general synopsis of your role. The rest of the plot is irrelevant as far as you're concerned. I have two other actors for the remaining scenes where people requiring an actual script are involved. The rest of the film is made up of old news clippings in juxtaposition with material supplied by Clyte and whatever I come up with' – Ethelred couldn't resist a slight snigger – 'including a few donations from Charles.'

Oswald glanced quickly over the double-spaced typing. He looked up, an incredulous expression on his face. 'But I'm only in two scenes!' he squeaked, his face turning white. 'I pose as Rodin's "The Thinker" and then I...' he looked angrily at the piece of paper shaking violently in his hand, 'then I... I give Monday a *blow job?* And that's it?'

'A *blow job*? How very Edith Evans-ish or Miss Prism-ish you sound, Oswald! Yes, a blow job. I've no doubt you've been champing at the bit for a repeat performance of the impromptu one you were asked to give him the other day? Now's your chance. *Plus* you're being both paid and immortalised for the pleasure!'

'But you promised!' shrieked Oswald

'Promised what?' snapped back Ethelred.

'I'd be the star of the film! Not... not...' Oswald's mind scrambled desperately for the appropriate word or words.

'Not a *what?* ' Ethelred's voice was reduced to a quiet, dangerous whisper.

'Not a fucking *insert!*'

'Not a fucking insert?' Ethelred leapt from his chair, towering over both his desk and the cowering young man. 'That's it. Enough shit from you, Mr. Oswald Argent! You're out of here. Clyte was right. I heard all about your little scene at Flemings, and I know about all your clandestine calls to London!' He held up his hand. 'I really suggest you don't interrupt...'

'But I've never telephoned London, ever! Why should I?'

Ethelred, completely aware this was true, was not prepared to let Oswald know otherwise. 'I told you not to interrupt, Oswald, so shut the fuck up! A few facts for you young man. You're not liked here and before you say Trisomy likes you, she's confided to her great friend Charles, and I quote what Charles relayed to me, you touched her *foo foo*!'

'That's an outrageous lie!' screeched Oswald leaping to his feet. 'A wicked, wicked, evil lie! I would never, ever do such a thing. Why, that… that thing! That creature…' Oswald, eyes wide, screamed loudly. 'Who'd ever *want* to touch her? Why, not only is she an abomination, she's fucking grotesque!'

'You're talking about our daughter here!' said Ethelred, his voice deathly quiet, 'And you've just proved a point.' He let the heavy silence linger before saying, even more quietly and in a slow, precise manner. 'I know you never touched her – at least you have shown some minor form of decency where one of us under this roof is concerned – but see my – and to use your little word – *grotesque* – suggestion was a test, Oswald; a test to get you to reveal your true feelings about us and the general set up here. Nobody has taken to you, Oswald. You've been the proverbial house guest from hell since day one of you arrival, so I suggest you go straight up to your room, pack and somehow get yourself back to London. You have nothing to keep you here. No contract. Nothing!' Ethelred sat down. 'Now, if you'll excuse me, I have things to do.' He glanced at the stunned young man. 'And before you ask, the answer is yes. Yes there are plenty of young actors who would be more than grateful to appear in an Ethelred Jones film; even if it only consists of posing as Rodin's thinker – it's pronounced Ro*dan* by the way – and give the mighty Monday a blow job. Now, off you go. And Oswald?' Ethelred looked back up at the ashen-faced young man, 'Don't bother saying goodbye to anyone, especially Clyte. As far as the rest of the household are concerned, you were history the moment of your return from your ill-fated trip to London.'

'Noooooo!' The word came rushing out in an animal-like howl. 'Noooooo!' wailed Oswald, tears streaming down his handsome face. 'Forgive me, Etheldred! Forgive me!' With an agonised groan he fell to his knees, his trembling hands clasped as if in prayer. 'I want to be in your film!' he sobbed. 'Please, please forgive me… I'll change! I'll apologise to everyone… I'll ring Claudia… but please, please let me stay, let me be in your film!'

Ethelred looked at Oswald, having changed from kneeling to lying in fetal position on the floor, and sobbing uncontrollably in-between gasping out a few heart-rending cries of 'please, please.'

'Gotcha!' murmured Ethelred with a twisted smile, 'Gotcha you pathetic, arrogant little prick. Oh young Oswald, are we going to have fun snuffing and stuffing you!'

He stood up and made his way round the desk and, kneeling next to the curled up, sobbing body, touched him gently on the shoulder. 'OK, OK, Oswald, that's quite enough. Pull yourself together,' Giving a deep, long theatrical sigh, Ethelred added, 'I didn't realise how much this really meant to you. Now I see it's your everything, and, from what I have just witnessed, I'd be wrong, hideously wrong not to let you stay…'

It took all of Ethelred's self-control not to burst out laughing at Oswald's lightning-like transformation from grief stricken ingénue to a radiant Madonna-like creature. 'Oh *Red*!' he gasped, 'Oh Red, can I? Can I?'

'Only if you promise to behave,' replied Ethelred, his lips twitching.

'Oh, I'll behave alright,' vowed the star in the making. 'I'll be so well behaved that you won't even know I'm here.'

'That a promise?'

'A promise, Red, a firm promise!'

'See that you stick to it!'

Half an hour later a smiling Oswald sat demurely on the sofa opposite Clytemnestra and Charles. Seated in a couple of chairs alongside him were Euros and Thrift, plus Monday and Charles. If the rest of the group noticed the young man was completely naked, his legs crossed demurely with his long, thin cock tucked discreetly between his long, toned, smooth thighs and only his pale blond bush on show, nobody said a word.

The scene of Oswald perched on a pedestal, elbow on his raised knee and his chin on his fist was filmed by the poolside several days later. Monday and Thrift had set the scene by removing an urn containing a flowering shrub from its plinth. The day had been as forecasted; hazy with a warm, golden touch of sunshine.

'Perfect!' Ethelred commented on several occasions as Euros and Kevin, the second cameraman, checked and rechecked their cameras and a red spotlight required for what Ethelred vaguely described as the 'birthing blood.'

'You will first be shown walking slowly towards the camera through Clyte's cunt,' instructed Ethelred, 'suffused in a warm glow of light with highlights of red playing on your torso' – Oswald had already been instructed to cover himself with baby oil – 'but not your bush which will be having some gold sparkle sprinkled on it. I want your bush proud, bright, soft and golden; likewise your armpits. These are to be shaved but covered in oil and glitter. Before you begin your slow, sensuous, seductive walk through the hedges, you will raise your arms above your head and go into a slow, graceful pirouette. Pausing for a moment, you throw back your head – I want to see your arched neck – Kevin's camera will take an angle shot which will be superimposed on the start of your walk towards the second camera. I want your hips to swing so that we have the benefit of your glorious dick swinging side to side.' Ethelred gave the entranced, wide-eyed Oswald, a beatific smile. 'When you hear the sound track you will find your cock swings in time to an accompaniment of wind chimes!' Oswald gave a squeak of camp delight causing Ethelred's smile to broaden. 'The second camera will gradually increase its distance from you as Euros backs away. The shot will go into soft focus and fade. The next shot, which hopefully we can shoot immediately afterwards, will home into you again as you take up Rodin's immortal pose on the urn.'

'Oh Red,' breathed Oswald. 'I love you! I love *it!* I love you all!' he shrilled, throwing his arms into a wide, embracing gesture. 'Ohmigod! Ohmigod! You're going to make me so, so beautiful!' With tears streaming down his cheeks he rushed across to a laughing Ethelred and, clasping him to his – as yet – non-oiled naked body, smothered the tall man in kisses. A startled Euros and Kevin, the assistant cameraman, were also subjected to similar bursts of Oswald's enthusiastic affection. 'If only Clyte was here to see the birth of this masterpiece,' the star-to-be added in a louder shrill. Turning excitedly towards an openly laughing Ethelred, Oswald tucked his hands beneath his chin and, cocking his head to one side, gave an exaggerated grimace before adding the immortal line, 'I'm ready for my close up, Mr. De Mille!'

Oswald's opening scene required eleven takes before Ethelred claimed he was satisfied. 'Cut and print!' he cried, giving the three a laughing, high five each. An exhausted Oswald, having oiled and re-oiled himself for each take had, time and time again, to wash and blow dry his pubic hairs before reapplying the sprinkling of gold sparkle dust. 'Your bush must glow, a positive golden burning bush!' Ethelred kept demanding. 'I can't have your pubes tangled and sweaty. They're to be like spun golden sugar!'

'That's enough for today,' Ethelred announced as Oswald sank limply onto the plinth. He gave a light laugh. 'We can't have our beautiful Rodin looking rogered, now, can we?' a giggling Euros and Kevin joining in.

'You looked very, very beautiful, Oswald,' said Euros, 'Really lovely. I cannot wait to show you the rushes.'

'Yes, I suppose I did and do.' came the modest reply.

Euros gave Kevin a camp look before turning to Ethelred and rolling his eyes. Unbeknown to Oswald, from that moment on he would to be referred to as 'Did-an-doo.'

'Rhymes with pooh,' Euros explained to a laughing Clytemnestra later.

It was later the same day when, after dinner, Ethelred, Clytemnestra, Charles along with Oswald – the latter, still basking from his day's triumph, happily clutching his fifth glass of celebratory champagne – were sitting discussing the success of the day's shoot, Ethelred, giving the young man a smile, said softly, 'May I see you privately for a minute, young Oswald? I've something to discuss with you.' He nodded towards a quiet corner of the terrace. 'Over there, if you don't mind.'

A giggling Oswald, squeaking coquettishly, 'I don't mind if *you* don't!' stood up tipsily and followed the tall, angular figure into the shadows. Ethelred, having tactfully brought along another bottle of champagne, proceeded to top up Oswald's flute as well as his own. He raised both bottle and glass to the slackly-smiling young man. 'Oswald, I must say I was more than impressed with you today.'

Oswald preened, which, considering his present state of inebriation, was no mean achievement. 'Why, thank you kind shur!' he slurred. 'The pleshure wash mine... all mine...' his sentence curtailed by a slight hiccup.

'As you know,' continued Ethelred, 'I was only going to use you in two scenes, but – having given it some thought and discussed it with Clyte – I've decided we simply must use you in some more!'

Oswald's sobering up was instantaneous. 'More?' he shrilled. 'Ohmigod!' the champagne flute crashing to the paving stones. 'Ohmigod!' he repeated, clutching his face between his hands. 'Oh, Ethelred Jones, I love you, love you, love you!'

'You haven't as yet heard what you'll be involved with,' said Ethelred almost inaudibly. 'Your musings or thoughts when seen sitting a la Rodin's sculpture will now become alive in scenes from your life interspersed with action moments as well as stills. Hence *Still Life*!' He looked candidly at the gaping young man. 'I must say, we had all become so exasperated by your behaviour, I was planning to use one of the other actors who will be joining us later this week but' – Ethelred gave a warm smile – 'after your performance today and your behaviour – you were a real trouper, a real pro! – we've decided you're just the lad for the role!'

'Ohmigod!' To further prove his point as a drama queen supreme, Oswald swooned into Ethelred's thin, muscular arms.

'He's out,' laughed Ethelred, roughly dumping the supine body onto a chaise, 'Dead to the world, to coin a phrase!'

'Little does *she* realise it's almost like a dress rehearsal!' camped Charles. He added sinisterly, 'Oh you silly sleeping beauty! If only you knew what little your so-called glorious future holds!'

———

The next few days were spent shooting scenes involving Clytemnestra at work on a major canvas, her inspiration a mixture of blood and pus duly taken from an accommodating boil which conveniently appeared on the neck of Dick, the part-time handyman. Meanwhile Oswald, still basking in the afterglow of Ethelred's praises, was goodness personified. 'Little blighter even offered to help me peel the potatoes!' a taken aback Mrs. Norelle told an amused Clytemnestra. 'Why, you could 'ave knocked me over with a feather!'

'Knowing Oswald, I'd make that a boa!' had been Clytemnestra's quick riposte and exit line.

'Boa? Whatever does she mean?' said the tut tutting cook. 'Honestly, at times this 'ousehold…'

A holier-than-thou Oswald continued in his saint-like mode, taking upon himself the boring task of helping Trisomy roll bandages in a game instigated by the child. 'Nurse Charles wants me to help him in his animal hospital.' she solemnly informed him.

'Animal hospital?' Oswald's curiosity was paramount. 'What animal hospital?'

'Nurse Charles has a woof woof and two squiwels to make better,' Trisomy went on to explain. 'He opens up their tummies and then puts things inside to bwing them back to life!'

'You mean he *stuffs* them.' acknowledged Oswald. 'It's called taxidermy, Trisomy. It's what Nurse Charles did to the sheep on the lawn. Stuffed them!'

'Monday stuffs Lady 'stwuvver!' announced the little girl. 'I heard daddy telling mummy. Is that the stuffing Nurse Charles does?'

'In a way, yes!' said Oswald, doing his best to stifle his laughter behind a thin, elegant hand.

'Would you like Nurse Charles to stuff *you*?' Trisomy's black, hooded eyes stared up unblinkingly at Oswald from her weathered, wrinkled face, her eyes widening as Oswald gave a muffled shriek and quickly exited the room.

———————

'Charles, can you call into my study within the next half hour or so?'

'No problem, Red. I'll just finish peeling this squirrel's tail and once I've finished adding the preservative to the tail cavity, I'll be right with you.'

Making an incision around the base of the small, dead animal's tail, Charles gently pulled back about two inches of the skin to act as a handle for the skinning. With one smooth movement he then pulled the complete skin off without any need for any further fleshing or thinning of the skin. Shaking a dry preservative into the cavity, Charles made sure that all had been tightly compressed into the sleeve-like unit, leaving a small space at the top. 'Right, Mr. Squirrel,' he muttered, 'you are going to be the proud owner of a very fine, very bushy tail. Now let's go and see what our lord and master wants.'

'You rang, sir?' Charles camped, having knocked lightly on the study door before entering.

'Charles! That was quick! Here, take a seat.' Ethelred pointed to his glass. 'Join me? I'm having a vodka tonic.'

'Sounds perfect and why not?' Charles gave the rangy man a smile as Ethelred made his way over to the drinks cabinet. Adding some ice cubes to a tumbler, he poured in a healthy dollop of vodka with only a splash of the sparkling mix. Handing over the drink, Ethelred returned to his chair. 'Clyte and I have been talking,' he said after a moment of companionable silence as they sipped their drinks. 'And the more we think about it the more exciting it's becoming.' He leaned forward, giving Charles a capricious look. 'We've got the film sorted out: got the accompanying art exhibition and now, why not a series of tableaux made up of actual sets inspired by the scenes from "Still Life?"'

'You mean…?' Charles's voice came out a mere whisper.

'*Exactly*! Your taxidermy now comes into its own! Oh Charles! Charles! Think of the fun you – we – are about to have!' Ethelred gave a laugh. 'You said you were stuffing a squirrel. Why not have a woodland setting with your squirrel holding some nuts – Oswald's *nuts*! Add an inverted naked leg or two and you have your first little tableaux called, perhaps, "A Walk in the Park!"' He gave another laugh. 'Some stuffed birds and perhaps even a bisected figure, a figure literally halved, sitting on a bench reading half a newspaper!' Ethelred's excitement was paramount. 'Why, it could even be titled "A Half Hearted Walk in the Park!" What do you think?'

'What do I think? It's brilliant, Red. Bloody fucking brilliant! The likes of such an exhibition-cum-film premiere would be almost impossible to cap! Furthermore the film could be then shown consecutively during the opening hours of the exhibition.' Charles's voice squeaked with excitement. 'I bet young Oswald has no idea his balls are about to end up in a juggling act with a stuffed squirrel!'

'And his tongue Charles! His tongue.' cried Ethelred, caught up in Charles's enthusiasm, 'Imagine a set piece titled "My tongue in your Cheeks!" made as a further V sign to that film I literally took the piss on?' He gave a roar of laughter, 'A suitable set of buttocks with the little shit's tongue well and truly impaled.'

'And what about a tribute to Joe Orton's "Prick up Your Ears" with his prick stuck to the side of his head? Talk about an ear plug – or hearing aid – with a difference!' This final bon mot caused Charles to literally slide off his chair with laughter.

'Jesus!' A laughing Ethelred, tears streaming down his face, struggled for composure. 'And this, by the way, is why I needed to see you. We are now in urgent need of a willing couple!' On the use of the word willing he burst into more guffaws of laughter with Charles joining in.

'Why wait? I can set about finding our additional stars *tout de suite* – like tomorrow!'

'Tomorrow? You sure about this? It doesn't give you much time.'

'We don't *have* much time and yes, I'm one hundred and ten per cent. I know exactly where to look.'

Ethelred, still looking dubious, slowly nodded. 'Well, if you really say it can be done, that's doubly brilliant,' He gestured to their empty glasses and, picking these up, made his way back to the drinks cabinet. Glancing back over his shoulder at the still giggling doctor, he asked. 'How long will the preparations take?'

'I'll need several weeks. I have to make the fibre glass casts for the main bodies once I've gone and actually skinned them. The skins can be stored in the freezer to prevent drying out, prior to stretching them back over their new bodies, so to speak.' Charles, a thoughtful expression on his face, added with a small smile. 'It'll be quite a challenge to create seated figure literally halved!' He gave a chuckle. 'We'll have to work out later whether we keep the right half or the left!'

'To make him slightly different, he can be left-handed and hold the left-half page from the Daily Mail – suitably stiffened – in his one and only *left* hand!' suggested Ethelred with a mischievous grin.

This time the laughter of the two men was almost uncontrollable. After several minutes Charles was able to continue his dissertations in a more serious and practical manner.

'Other vital procedures such as boiling the skulls, saving musculature and so forth, go hand in hand with the general process. As they are complete strangers, such minor details such as the glass eyes and even the hair – I suggest we use wigs, just as a precaution for you never know – and every little change or disguise will help.' Charles gave a snigger. 'The same applies for boy wonder.'

'Would any of them ever be recognisable?'

'No, I shall make sure of that. Oswald will be dismembered, photographed and what parts of him we *do* use for the taxidermy process will be unrecognisable. Any leftovers will be incinerated. With the others I may even swap ears, add a different shape to the jaw line and so on; but I'll make sure the end products are unique.'

'And how's the helper?'

'Genius, pure genius. I must say Red, you and Clyte certainly came up with the Einstein of ideas with that one! I had a suspicion but when you actually told me! Jesus eat your Yiddisher heart out! As I said, genius; pure, fucking, bloody genius!'

'So, no problems then as far as you can tell?'

'None whatsoever.' Charles took a thoughtful sip of his drink. 'When do you plan to film the actual snuff scene?'

'I should think next week. I plan to keep the cunt kid quiet by taking a few random shots of him dancing in the woods and then there is a mega fuck scene with Monday to be filmed. Monday is not only going to cock fuck him, but foot and fist fuck him as well.'

'Monday fuck him with his *foot*? I take it you're not referring to that massive dick of his this time?' Charles gave an envious laugh.

'No, his actual foot. I zoom into our little thinker and then fade into what the audience will see as his thoughts. A slow zoom shot of a piece of broken marble statuary, followed by Monday's actual bare foot, inspires even more bizarre mental contortions for our insatiable wannabe starlet! I'll then get Euros to film Oswald actually impaling himself on Monday's foot!' Ethelred couldn't resist adding, 'A real toe turner!'

'Tell me about it! This I cannot wait to see.' Charles gave a snort. 'You could almost make another short and call it "Footloose and Very Fancy Free!"' He gave a laughing Ethelred an anxious look. 'I trust one will be able to be on set?'

'Where else? I can assure you our Oswald will simply adore an audience. After all, the little shit *is* the star!'

'And our little shit of a shitty star will relish all that! My God, she'll be up and down on that foot to end all "foots" like a fucking-jack-in-the-box!' Charles gave Ethelred a predatory look imbued with pure evil. 'And then…?'

'The final scene.'

'I can't wait.' Charles swallowed loudly. Giving a dry, harsh laugh he put down his empty glass. 'You've really got me going, Red. Really got me going! Christ!' He glanced at the rampant erection straining against his chinos. 'Talk about a turn on! You'll have them jerking off in the aisles! Forget "Taken at the Flood!" Those fucking aisles will be positively swimming!' Charles glanced at his watch. 'Tell you what, things in the studio can wait so why put off tomorrow's quest when I can set this in motion today? Can you alert Monday and make sure all is ready in case I come back later tonight as opposed to tomorrow?'

'Take it as done.'

'Well, as they say in the theatre, let's "break a leg!"'

'*That*, dear Charles,' replied Ethelred with a grin, 'is your job as from now! Good luck and happy hunting!'

'Thanks.' Charles stood up rather sheepishly, aware of the rampant protrusion sticking out against the light cotton of his trousers. 'Err, sorry about the larky ascending!'

'Come here,' murmured Ethelred. He pointed to his own erection. 'You've now turned *me* on, you sordid old bugger!' He gave a smile as he unzipped himself. 'Care for a mutual wank, doctor dear, or would you like to blow the ever ready Red?'

'I'll blow you first and then you can wank me off, *director* dear.' replied a leering Charles, moving over to the grinning man. 'Like old times.'

he managed to murmur as he bent down. Pushing back Ethelred's heavy foreskin with his lips, Charles greedily took the purplish, swollen glans in his mouth.

'Don't you know it's rude to talk with your mouth full!' admonished Ethelred looking down on the busily bobbing, sparsely covered head. 'Very rude!' he added, taking another large swig of his vodka tonic.

CHAPTER 11

'Anyone sitting here?' Charles indicated to the empty space on the bench alongside the plump young woman and her pleasant-looking companion. He gestured at the busy, noisy pub around them with both hands, one holding a glass, the other a bottle of tonic, his smile pleasant, one eyebrow raised questioningly.

'No… please.' The girl made a token gesture towards the shopping bag alongside her. 'You're more than welcome. Just let me move this shopping…'

'No need, there's stacks of room. Thank you.' Charles edged himself down onto the bench seating.

Leaning back he poured the contents from the bottle into his glass and, raising this in the semblance of a toast, muttered a soft, 'Cheers.'

'Cheers!' replied the couple simultaneously, giving the thin, middle-aged man a warm smile.

Charles gave another smile and nodded down towards the shopping bag. 'Harrods, I see. Impressive place, isn't it?' More a statement than a question.

'It's great!' said the girl enthusiastically. 'I thought we had some great shops in Joburg, but there's nothing to match Harrods!'

'Joburg? You're from South Africa, then?' said Charles in mock surprise, immediately picking up on the flat vowels.

'Yes!' said the young man with an even broader grin. 'It's Hettie's and my first trip. The first thing we did after we'd checked into our hotel was to visit Harrods. Next on the list is Buckingham Palace!'

'Well, you seem to have got your priorities right,' murmured Charles drily. 'Fayed House followed by Buck House? The old sod would be delighted!'

'Excuse me?' This from the young man.

'Sorry, a lame *in house* joke.' Charles gave his most disarming grin. 'We Londoners refer to Buckingham Palace as Buck House and to Harrods, as Fayed House, after the owner, Mohammed Fayed.' Seeing the two blank expressions he further elaborated. 'Mad Mohammed had aspirations to becoming the late Princess Diana's father-in-law; until the Paris debacle.'

'Excuse me?' This time the question came from the puzzled looking girl.

'Too complicated,' laughed Charles. *Hmm*, he thought. *Pretty, but not at all bright, and as for the young guy – humpy, hunky but a bit naive. But they could be the perfect new recruits for our plan, very much so.* He nodded at their empty beer glasses. 'Let me buy you a welcome to London drink. Same again?' He noticed the girl looking enviously at his vodka tonic. 'Or would you prefer something stronger? I'm about to get myself another vodka. How about you?'

Looking uncomfortable, the girl hesitated, but only for a moment, before saying, 'We were only trying the beer because all our friends said we should have an English pint.' She gave a dazzling white smile. 'I wouldn't say no to a gin and orange!'

'I'll have another pint if I may; I rather like this Fosters!' said her companion, 'and no, you stay seated err…'

'Charles, Charles Crosby.' Charles didn't have the heart to say the Fosters was Australian as opposed to English.

'Nice to meet you Charles.' The youth stuck out a beefy arm and stubby, muscular hand, taking hold of Charles's quickly proffered one. 'Dirk, Dirk van Niekerk and this is my fiancé Hettie, Hettie Nell.' Dirk gave a warm smile. 'And as you've guessed, we're from South Africa!'

Charles, still smiling at his two new, instant friends, quickly produced a twenty pound note from his wallet. 'Make Hettie's and mine doubles, please Dirk.' He smiled charmingly at the sweet-faced girl. 'Buying up the likes of Harrods can be thirsty work!'

'That's very generous, Charles,' said the smiling young man with the warm, easy familiarity synonymous with colonials. He took the proffered note without any embarrassment and, giving Hettie a small wink, made his way over to the crowded bar. The brief wink had not gone unnoticed by the alert Charles. *Bull's-eye,* he said to himself. *On the make and stupid with it.*

'So, tell me, Hettie,' he continued, as they waited for Dirk to return with the drinks, 'are you and Dirk travelling alone, with a group or what?'

'Oh no, it's just Dirkie and me.' Hettie gave another dazzling smile. 'We've been travelling around Europe for several months now, having both finished up at varisty last year.'

'Varsity?'

'University. Dirkie had been doing his BS at Wits and I've just completed my secretarial diploma.' She looked at Charles for a long moment and, having decided he looked a sympathetic and caring person, added simply and confidingly, 'We're going to be stuck in London for a bit as we've almost run out of money.' She gave a small laugh. 'You wouldn't know of anyone who wants a part-time secretary and an odd job man, would you? Dirkie's a mean bugger with his hands! He can fix anything!'

'What's this about me being a mean bugger?' A smiling Dirk, having returned with the drinks, placed them carefully on the small table. Charles was quick to note that he was not handed his change but decided to treat it as an oversight for the time being.

'*Ag,* stop it, Dirkie!' squeaked Hettie playfully. 'I was only flattering you! I wasn't being rude, Charles, was I?'

'Not at all!' laughed Charles, playing up to the laughing girl. 'Hettie could not have been more flattering!' There was a brief silence as he and Hettie mixed their drinks and Dirk took several sips of his replenished pint. 'So, in London, somewhat broke and looking for some spare time work,' Charles said contemplatively.

'It's not quite as bad as that,' chipped in Dirk, giving Hettie an annoyed glance before showing an equal flash of splendid teeth.

Christ, they're beautiful, thought Charles. *Our little secretary may be a bit plump but our science graduate is quite a specimen of butch male! By the pricking of my thumbs something for our 'Still Life' comes...* He shook himself out of his reverie. 'Sorry,' Charles said, 'I missed that.'

'I was just saying we've enough for a week or two. We found a small hotel in Earls Court which will do until we can get our act together.' The young man squeezed the young girl's hand affectionately. 'If worse comes to the worst, we have our return tickets so we can take off at any time.'

'Do you have to be back at any specific time?' Charles asked, prior to beginning his careful searching.

'No,' said Hettie. She gave Dirk a warm smile. 'Dirk has no family; he lives with an old aunt, who never knows whether he's there or not, and me,' she gave a slight frown. 'I grew up in a convent and so I have no real family apart from the nuns.' She gave the young man another warm smile. 'Dirkie's my family. We plan to get married as soon as we get back.'

'But that could be this year, next year... whenever?'

'Whenever. Who knows?' Dirk gave Charles another dazzling show of teeth. 'I may spot a job in one of the papers tomorrow. Mad doctor needs a brilliant young graduate scientist!'

'Stranger things have happened,' laughed Charles. He pointed to the empty glasses, 'Same again?'

'Oh shit!' Dirk gave an embarrassed smile. 'Charles, what you must think of me. I forgot to hand back your change.' The young man flushed a deep crimson.

'Well then, it's now your turn!' said Charles with a laugh.

Over the second round Charles lightly explained he worked as a financial advisor to a well-known film director and his equally well known artist wife. He confided he was also a fully qualified doctor but had given up practising following the death of his beloved wife. 'I decided that if modern medicine and I couldn't save her, I would have no more time for it. I felt, and still feel, medicine – please forgive me if I am in any way offensive, Dirk – and science have let me down.'

'That is *so* sad!' whispered Hettie, taking hold of Charles's thin, bony hand in her warm, moist plump one. 'You must have loved your wife, very, very much.' She added, tears were glistening in her widened, dark, brown eyes.

'I'm sorry, too, man.' said Dirk. 'And after that sad story, how could I be offended?' He looked at the girl sitting opposite him. 'Hell, I'd do the same if something happened to Hettie and I couldn't save her.'

Charles, knowing when to draw the line, put on a brave smile. 'Thank you,' he said softly. 'You are both very sweet and very kind.' He made a broader attempt at a smile. 'But what's this? You're here to enjoy yourselves and here I am, suddenly casting a depression on your evening.'

'No, you're not!' cried Hettie. 'You're lovely Charles, really lovely. Isn't he?' she added, looking at Dirk as if for confirmation at her observation.

'You're OK,' smiled the broad young man. 'Take a look at me! You can tell Hettie's never wrong when it comes to judging character!'

'Cheeky bugger!' chortled his girlfriend with delight.

'Hey, that's twice now you've called me a bugger!' laughed her beau. 'You just wait until I get you back to the hotel, Hettie Nell!'

'Well, before you deal with Hettie back at the hotel, why don't the two of you join me for dinner? I was simply going to have a quiet dinner by myself at a restaurant I know and like.' Charles had already decided this would not be a case of 'smash and grab' but more of a wooing. His mind was already made up. These two were ripe for the plucking.

'You don't mind?' Hettie gave a small squeal of delight. 'Nobody's asked us out for ages and ages!'

'Well, that's all about to change.' Charles gave another warm smile. 'Dinner will be fun.' He gestured to the noisy pub. 'How lucky I was to drop by here, quite by accident as well. I really don't know South Kensington at all.'

'Us also!' Dirk gave another flash of perfect teeth. 'Hettie and me popped into the V and A after Harrods and then here, as the place looked quite fun. We liked the name as well, *The Hoop and Toy*. It's also right near the tube station for the District line back to Earls court.'

Charles's mind was racing. Careful, he said to himself, *let's play this one by ear. I won't ask them down to the country tonight – too obvious – they may appear to be incognito but they're not that incognito. As they've already booked into a hotel, better to play along. I'll say I'm staying overnight as I have a business meeting in the morning; see how dinner goes and then suggest we meet up later tomorrow. After some more time spent together I'll suddenly have a brainwave and come up with the bright idea of some part time work with the Joneses, and maybe a few days in the country. They can check out of their hotel and always come back if it doesn't work out.*

'Do you like Italian food?' he asked.

'Like it? We *adore* it!' cried Hettie. 'Even though everyone bangs on about French cooking, nothing can beat *bella Italia*!'

Charles gave a hearty laugh. Hettie's enthusiasm was catching. 'Then, *bella* Hettie, Italian it shall be!' He stood up, 'I feel meeting the two of you almost fortuitous, so, let me spoil the three of us! There's an Italian restaurant I know fairly close by. As I've already said, it's a favourite and one of the best in London.'

'Is it expensive?' questioned Dirk, nervously.

'It is, but you're my guests and it's my treat,' smiled Charles. 'I always eat there alone when I stay over in town. Besides, it's not every day that I get to meet such an attractive couple and I'll be more than delighted to show you off!'

'Charles, you are *such* a charmer!' laughed Hettie. 'No wonder you're now in PR!'

'A real smoothie!' laughed her boyfriend.

'Will you forgive me while I go and err… powder my nose!' said Hettie with a grin.

'Me also,' laughed Dirk. 'Only I shake the snake!' Obviously the three lagers were having an effect.

'Dirkie!' giggled Hettie. 'Don't be so crude! Charles will think we are from the *plaas,* not the city!'

'Plaas?'

'Farm.' Explained Dirk. 'C'mon Hets, don't let's keep Charles waiting.'

Once the two were out of earshot, Charles quickly called the restaurant and was pleased to find there would be a table available within a few minutes – 'It will be a delight to see again, *Signor* Charles,' carolled the singsong receptionist. He then called the Jameirah Carlton Tower Hotel and confirmed his provisional reservation. Charles had begun to appreciate earlier an anonymous 'pick up' was not going to be as easy as anticipated, but talk about a reversal of fortune! Keeping a watchful eye on the door, he made a final call to Ethelred. The phone was answered after a few rings. 'Found the perfect couple,' he confirmed. 'I'm taking them to dinner and I'll be staying over at the usual. It'll be another Oswald exercise.' Charles gave a thin laugh. 'I'll see them again tomorrow, play the two along and judge when best to suggest they come down to the house. Maybe the weekend as they are presently busy sightseeing. Warn Clyte and Co. you will be acquiring a secretary and Monday a further pair of hands to assist him in the garden.' Seeing the couple making their way back to him, he ended with a quick, 'Call you from the hotel.'

Smiling at the young man and woman he asked simply 'Ready?' The two nodded, their faces wreathed in smug, affirmative smiles. 'Good,' said Charles. 'Follow me. As I said, it's about a fifteen minute walk to the restaurant. It's in one of the prettiest streets and there are some fun shops and boutiques to window shop in as we walk by.' He stopped for a moment. 'In fact, it's quite close to your favourite Harrods, Hettie. Just as well it's after closing hours!'

Fifteen minutes later Charles and his two guests were being greeted by Valerio, the magnificently moustached, beaming maitre d' at Scalinis in

Walton Street. With a great deal of arm waving, the three were led over to a table set two tables away from where two men were sitting, heavily engrossed in conversation. Charles gave a slight start on recognising the fellow diner who – throughout the whole of the meal – remained oblivious to the three new arrivals. Quickly regaining his composure Charles pointed to a chair. 'Why don't you sit there, Hettie, in the middle between Dirk and me.' With a smooth movement he sat himself down, his back discreetly turned towards Miles and Bryan.

By an extraordinary coincidence, it was at that very moment that Miles was regaling Bryan with his wife's bitchy parting shot to Oswald at the dinner a few weeks back. Bryan's laugh was loud and genuine. 'You see how right I was *not* to meet the Lady A! Christ knows what exit line she would have used against me! Poor Os, he must have been well and truly pissed off!'

'More likely tsnunamied off, if there's such a word!' laughed Miles in return. 'A grappa?'

'Why not? And then back to watch that DVD I found today.'

'Did anyone ever tell you, you are perfection, Signor Scima?'

'Ditto, Sir Miles.'

'What do you think?' Hettie asked Dirk as the couple, having said a cheerful goodnight to Charles, sat huddled together in a nearly empty carriage of the District Line train rumbling its way to Earls Court.

'He's a walk over, Hets; a piece of cake. The guy's obviously loaded… dinner cost a bomb! I say let's wait and see if he does call us at the hotel tomorrow – good move of yours, giving him our number, Het, and not ask for his.'

'He gave it to me, anyway.'

'Yes, but it's not the same.' Dirk gave a laugh. 'The guy's also gay; couldn't take his eyes off my crotch every time I got up to go to the *kazi*!'

'They fall for that poor student shit every time, don't they?' said the smiling girl. 'If only they knew sweet Hettie and Dirk were really Katie and Johannes Viljoen, a rather clever brother and sister team who – let's face it – are not doing too badly at the fleecing game! A couple or more months and then it's back to sunny SA where we open up our dream guest house in the Transkei. And it's all been so *easy*; as you just said, Dirkie, a piece of cake!' Little did the two realise it was to be the 'piece of cake' of their undoing.

'I suppose I'll have to fuck the old bugger!'

'So? That's a couple of hundred to keep it quiet from your loving fiancé!' Hettie gave a clever imitation of Charles's languid, upper class English drawl. 'Imagine, Charles, just *imagine* what poor Hettie would think if she knew I really preferred fucking *you* to her!'

'You're a real pro, Hettie Katie Viljoen van Niekirk, a real pro!' said Dirk with a grin. 'Not that I'd ever sound like that!'

'Like brother, like sister, Dirk Johannes,' laughed the girl. 'Here's out stop.' She tapped her watch. 'What's your bet? I said we were going sightseeing early.'

'He'll call us at eight.'

Charles rang at eight on the dot.

"Let me," said Hettie, reaching for the phone.

Hearing the two planned to view the changing of the guard at Buckingham Palace, then go on to the National Gallery followed by Hettie saying, 'We also want to have a look at Fortnum and Mason; apparently it's even grander than Harrods!' Charles said smoothly, 'Yes, it's very grand,' while thinking, *Fuck, there goes most of the sodding day.* He added amicably. 'How does the idea of champagne and cupcakes strike you?'

'Champagne I love, but what are cupcakes?'

Charles gave a light laugh. 'Cupcakes are small, cup-shaped cakes filled delicious things like cream, jam and preserves.'

'Sounds good to me Charles! Don't you ever stop?'

'Stop?'

'Well, you take us to the best Italian restaurant last night and now a champagne and cupcake bar? I've never heard of one before!'

'Well wait until you see this place. It's really quite something, quite unique.' Charles gave another laugh. 'Shall we say four o'clock? The bar is in Flemings Hotel, about twenty minutes from Fortnum and Mason. You simply walk up along Piccadilly, past the Ritz towards Hyde Park corner. On the right-hand side you will see a small street called Half Moon Street. The hotel is about halfway up.'

'Champagne and cupcakes!' Hettie relayed the information to Dirk.

'Tell Charles he just gets better and better!' called Dirk, loud enough for Charles to hear.

'See you there.' said Charles, quietly replacing the receiver. He dialled Ethelred. 'Extravagant little shits,' he said without preamble, 'Dinner last night and now champagne and bloody cupcakes at Flemings!'

'Flemings? What time and whereabouts in Flemings?' asked Ethelred with a note of concern in his voice. Charles repeated the time and venue. 'Hold on a sec.' He could hear Ethelred conferring with Clytemnestra in the background before speaking again into the mouthpiece. 'Sorry about that, Charles. I was just checking something with Clyte; Flemings restaurant being Claudia's daily hangout, but Clyte says she's always out by three at the latest, and never uses that particular venue. If, on the rare occasion she does imbibe in a late afternoon cocktail, it's always the downstairs cocktail bar.' There was a pause. 'Are you sure about these two?'

'Was I wrong about Oswald?'

Ethelred gave a wry laugh. 'Say no more. Now, the million dollar question, when?'

'I'll be returning to BB this evening. By then I will have had the brainwave of having spoken to you and surprise, surprise, it just so happens your secretary is away for a couple of weeks, as is Boris. So why not a couple of spare hands on a temporary basis?' Charles gave a chuckle. 'I take it there won't be a problem with Boris and Hennie taking a few weeks sudden leave?'

'No problem. Boris was banging on about visiting his daughter in Spain – Jesus, she and her husband run a burger bar there of all things! – and Hennie won't mind at all. She's used to these sudden banishments in the middle of a film. I think she's quite relieved. Our Hennie, for all her airs and graces is not as broadminded – or sophisticated – as she would like to think she is!'

'Good, that gives us three days to get this all underway. If all goes according to plan, shall I suggest Saturday and four weeks guaranteed employment?'

'Perfect! See you later, and Charles? Well done there in your role as Charles Crosby, aka Carl Akeley!' Ethelred's comparison of Charles with the so-called 'father of taxidermy' was greeted by a pleased chuckle.

'Touché, Kenneth Bianchi!'

'Kenneth Bianchi, the Hillside Strangler? Why him?' asked Ethelred.

'Because in your own imitable way, that's what you'll be doing to Oswald, albeit a different form of choking!'

'My, aren't we a just such a deliciously nasty pair this morning! I can't wait to tell Clyte! See you later, instigator!'

'In a while, director vile!' replied Charles with a laugh.

Ethelred gave a groan. 'That, Charles,' he laughed, 'is *so* fifties!'

Charles called Ethelred from the car on his way back to Ascot. 'We're on.' He gave a chuckle. 'I don't think our two South African students are as naive as they would like me to believe. No, I think our Hettie and Dirk are a pair of tough young cookies. They're obviously on the make. They jumped at the idea of a month in the country and some part time work. The bonus of free board and lodging, plus a nice little lump of cash had them simply salivating – even more so than they did over the cupcakes!' He gave another laugh. 'Miss Hettie should be a bit more discreet when leaving her bag lying about. When the two went off to the loo – they always seem to go together and now I know why – I had a quick rummage through her bag. Eureka! Two joints and a gram or two of coke. He obviously carries a stash with him, hence the regular trips to the loo by the two for a quick snort.' There was another, tight laugh, 'But the piéce de résistance? Miss Hettie is no more a Miss Hettie than I am!' Charles went on briefly to explain what he had also found.

'Naughty Charlie, you really shouldn't be searching ladies' bags as you never know what you may find!" chuckled Ethelred.

'At least I didn't play "finder's keepers!"'

'Clever Charlie. Drive safely. Clyte and I will have a large flute of the bubbly stuff waiting for you!'

Hettie and Dirk had walked into the sumptuous Flemings Hotel a few minutes after four o'clock. A smiling, well-groomed doorman showed them through the lavish, marble tiled reception lobby to the popular Champagne and Cupcake Room. Charles – sitting in a wide, high-backed, lemon coloured damask chair – was heavily ensconced in a paperback. On hearing their cheerful greetings he looked up with a smile. 'You made it!' he said with a delighted smile. He pointed to his champagne flute. 'I have a bottle on ice but I have a confession to make,' he nodded in the direction of an elegant, black lacquered serving unit. 'I couldn't resist them. I've already had three!'

Hettie glanced over to the discreetly lit display of cupcakes laid out on either side of a tall central shelving unit. 'It's amazing! Like a technicolour display of jewels! May I?'

'Absolutely! Simply take a plate and help yourself.' Charles gave another laugh. 'Though I must warn you, Hettie, those cupcakes are like a drug. Once you've had one hit, you'll want another!' Charles, whose suspicions from the night before had been well and truly aroused by the couple's frequent visits to the public rest rooms, noted the brief glance from one to the other. *Ah, my little lovelies,* he mused, *not such innocents abroad after all!*

Flutes filled and a selection of cakes piled onto their plates, the young man and woman settled down opposite their host. After a general discussion of the attractions they had visited, Charles came out with his suggestion. 'An idea has occurred to me,' he said, taking a long sip. 'Ethelred and Clytemnestra may just be the answer to your little problem.' He eyed the two of them thoughtfully. 'What would you say to a month in the country – well, not actually country per se, but outside Ascot near to Windsor? You can visit the castle, the famous race course *and* earn a few pennies for your time and troubles.'

Dirk and Hettie gave a pair of obviously well-rehearsed, startled looks. 'Are you being serious?' asked Dirk, his phony incredulity almost farcical.

'Absolutely. It occurred to me when I was speaking to Ethelred this morning – that's Ethelred Jones, my employer – and he casually mentioned his irritation at Hennie, his secretary taking off for a month as from next week, for some very overdue leave. By sheer coincidence, Boris, the chauffeur-cum-general factotum, will also be away gallivanting. Boris helps Monday, our Man Friday, with odd jobs around the house and garden when he's not actually driving.'

'I have an international licence!' cried Dirk. 'And, as Hettie has already told you, I'm good with my hands!'

'Well, what can I say?' replied Charles, raising both hands in supplication. 'Want to give it a go?'

'Do we just!' This came out as a uniform explosion from the two. Both looked at each other and burst out laughing, as did Charles.

'I take that as a yes, then?'

'A yes, yes, *yes!*' cried Hettie.

'Such enthusiasm,' said Charles, 'simply demands another bottle.' Turning to catch the attention of the waiter, he caught the furtive glance passed between the couple. After a few seconds Hettie stood up and excused herself before making her way to 'the ladies.' A few moments later Dirk excused himself. It was then Charles took the opportunity to check the contents of her handbag. *Interesting, most interesting,* he said to himself, eyeing the two joints and the small cellophane packet. 'Not such paragons after all. And, Miss Hettie and Master Dirk, no doubt your names are not your real names, which makes it even more satisfactory regarding your disappearance. And what's this?' He quickly looked at the passport. 'I was right,' he muttered. 'Not a Hettie but a Catherine *and* a Catherine Viljoen to boot!' It then dawned on him. 'Fiancé my arse; they're fucking brother and sister, and I bet a brother also *fucking* his sister!'

By the time the two returned, eyes sparkling, Charles was sitting once more glancing at his paperback. 'Ah,' he smiled, 'the return of our good Samaritans if not the Prodigals!'

'Good Samaritans?' This from a puzzled Dirk.

'Because of your impending arrival at Bethlem Báthory, you've literally saved the day, or, to put it more accurately, the month!' He pointed at their now empty flutes, 'Some more champagne to toast you new jobs?'

'Why not,' cried Hettie.

'Bottoms up! As you English say,' laughed Dirk.

That too, you pernicious little prick! thought Charles as he smilingly beckoned over the waiter. *And little do you know it's going to be yours!*

Flutes duly replenished and cupcakes restocked, Charles gave details regarding the train the two should catch on the Saturday. 'No, bring *all* your belongings,' he instructed on hearing the couple had previously checked two further suitcases into a locker at Victoria Station. 'Why waste money, particularly if it's a bit tight at the moment. There's stacks of space to store anything you bring; in fact, you'll be able to have your own suite in the staff wing!'

Hettie's eyes widened. 'Our own suite?' she exclaimed.

Jesus, thought Charles, *just as well you two decided to become a con artists as opposed to actors.* Instead, he said charmingly, 'Yes, Hettie, your own suite. There is also a pool, a cinema and a small gym.'

'Shit!' said the two, again in unison, this time in genuine appreciation.

CHAPTER 12

'It gets better,' Ethelred announced to Clytemnestra and Charles as they sat later that evening in his study, each with the de rigueur nightcap alongside them. He nodded at a pad on his lap. 'How do you feel, Clyte, about an additional work, "The Babes in the Woods"?'

'The babes, of course, being…'

'Exactly: our little helpers!' Ethelred smiled at Charles. 'I must say, Charlie boy, you do pick 'em. I can see a bonus coming up. Or in your case, a boner and a bonus.' He gave a chuckle. 'Clyte and I have been talking about this and we think you deserve a week or two away to a destination of your choosing, no expenses spared.' He gave the stunned doctor a lewd smile. 'Knowing your predilection for all things big, black and beautiful; somewhere like Ghana or the Caribbean perhaps?'

'Your two are stars!' exclaimed the blushing man. 'And thank you, I'll most certainly give it some thought. But,' he pointed to Ethelred's notepad, 'Your "Babes in the Woods," what exactly have you in mind?'

'It all goes along with Oswald and his musings. His desire to be ravished – no, make that abused and violated – by the sinister, dark Monday; his desire to relive his childhood memories… here I see an old leather-bound book shot in soft focus, the pages turning slowly and settling on a tale or two. The story of the two children in the woods is not titled per se, but then, nor will the story which is loosely based on Jack and the Beanstalk.'

'Jack and the Beanstalk?' This from a startled Clytemnestra. 'For God's sake, Red, this is meant to be a snuff film, not a bloody film for the benefit of the Brothers Grimm!'

'Don't get me wrong,' laughed her husband. 'This will be *very* grim and, as a director supreme, I take the liberty of extreme artistic licence. Our Jack, in Oswald's sordid, sick little mind, doesn't *plant* the single bean seed, but uses it instead as a suppository; the giant bean stalk growing *inside* him! Talk about a Boy Sprout!' Ethelred gave a whoop of laughter at his joke, 'Think of the painting, Clyte, a young man with tendrils sprouting from almost every orifice; death by plantation as opposed to strangulation!'

'Not only are you quite, quite sick, husband dear, but you are also brilliant. I love it!' Clytemnestra gave him a thoughtful look. 'Can you and Euros *really* achieve all those very special effects?'

'Dearest, you paint your portrait and leave the rest to Euros, your genius of a husband and digital effects.'

'Three, no make that four deaths. Will they be enough?' replied Charles thoughtfully.

'Now, now Charles, we don't want to get too greedy.' Ethelred gave a low laugh. 'It does mean you have one more "actor" to pull out of the hat before we can truly call it a wrap. How long to get these portraits done Clyte? I'll go through the actual scenarios with you in the morning. We have the strangulation of Oswald, the dismemberment of the Babes, followed by the force feeding or – in other words – literal *stuffing* of Jack!' He looked at the smirking doctor. 'That's basically the film and Clyte's accompanying set pieces taken care of. Now, how long for your side, Charles? Namely the time you require for the completion of your "life" sculptures – along with Clyte's exhibition – to be ready in order to coincide with the release of the film?'

'I'll need at least three to four months, if not more.'

Ethelred sat silently for a few moments. 'Clyte?'

'I agree with Charles. But I think even four months is pushing it. And you, Red? How long will you need to get your side of the project together?'

'As I'll be working around the two of you, I think it better to be safe than reckless. Why not give ourselves an overall six months? Top whack, another two making it a grand total of eight? Any additional costs will be no problem as my major investor has just given the company a very decent shot in the arm. Again, the payback from "The Day" is proving to be quite amazing! So all this should see us through despite any hiccups which may or mayn't occur.'

'Sounds good to me,' said Charles. 'But we could have a problem with our cast. Oswald I'm not too worried about – he can be kept away from most of the scenes envisaged – but it's those two scheduled to arrive on Saturday. This does concern me. Do we really want them hanging about for all that length of time? As it is, Hennie and Boris can only be legitimately away for four weeks.'

'That was next on my list and I've already sorted it all out.' Ethelred turned from Charles and back to his wife. 'Clyte, I suggest you begin sketching them as soon as possible. We'll also suggest so-called screen tests along with the original part-time work they were ostensibly coming here for.' He turned to Charles. 'You say they'll be vain enough *and* susceptible enough, to believe my sudden decision to include them in an Ethelred Jones film?'

'Most definitely; and Red, should you suggest not only the extra monies for appearing in your movie, but impress upon them the privilege, why, you'll be home and very dry!'

'Perfect. It's all set then. I'll gear up Euros, Thrift and Monday in the morning. The Babes – l'll refer to them as The Babes from now on – will be here on Saturday. Their final scene will be shot on the Thursday of the following week, at the latest.' Ethelred gave a soft, sardonic laugh. 'Any further scenes will only require their *parts* being present. To have them around for any time beyond a week to ten days, could be asking for trouble.' He added with a grimace, 'We then have to deal with Oswald. He is – after all is said and done – still a major a worry. With these three preliminaries out of the way, we have a bit of a breather. It will also give you, Charles, more free time in which to find our Jack the Sad!'

'How do we explain the two additions to young Oswald?' Again, this came from the ever practical Clytemnestra.

'As I said a few moments ago, I've given all this some considerable thought,' said Ethelred. 'And we don't!'

'Don't? But surely…?' This time it was Charles's turn to speak.

'What upsets any visitor to BB the most? Come on, be honest!'

'Meeting Trisomy.' The answer came from Clytemnestra with no sign of emotion.

'Exactly! And who is doing his best to curry favour through his attentiveness to her? Oswald.' Ethelred gave a small, irritable sigh. 'So,

Trisomy and Oswald must be kept out of sight at all costs. As the old saying goes, "out of sight, out of mind."'

'But how?'

'You, Charles!'

'Me?' Charles's voice came out in a loud squawk.

'Yes, Nurse Charles and nice Caligla are disappearing for a week or so. First of all, you will be going to Paris by Eurostar on Friday, where you will be visiting Euro Disney for a few days. From Paris you will continue on to the house in Provence. Trisomy loves it there and so do you Charles. We then sneak you back for the final day of the filming. Tris and Oswald will remain incognito whereas you reappear and take up any odd chores related to helping on the set.'

'But the two young South Africans? How is my non-presence to be explained?'

Ethelred's look was one of almost disdain. 'You'll simply call them, as already arranged, to confirm they are expected down here on Saturday. However, you have been called away; you have to fly to Berlin to discuss the PR for my latest film at the forthcoming festival or something along those lines. I leave it to your fertile imagination. However, I'll be meeting them and bringing them back to Bethlem Báthory. Straight after you've broken the news, you say you're going to introduce me to them and put me on the phone. My charm will do the rest.'

'It still doesn't seem right to me. It's seems... well it seems so contrived!'

'It *is* contrived, Charles. But, from what you've told me, our gruesome little twosome – and I use the word gruesome deliberately – sound a right avaricious pair! They'll still be down here in a flash, heels smoking!'

'Well, if you really think it will work.' said Charles ponderously.

'Will work? Will work? Of course it'll fucking work. Why shouldn't it?'

'OK then.' Charles gave a resigned sigh. 'Who tells Oswald?'

'You do,' said Ethelred, 'and, if the little cunt gives any trouble, it's still not too late to fire him. After all, a body – and I use the word literally – will simply mean you putting out *more* filthy feelers, Charlie boy! We've got our opening shots which couldn't be better and – if push comes to shove – we use a substitute for the fuck and snuff scenes. With some clever camera work and lighting, nobody would ever be able to tell it isn't our original little star!'

'You certainly have it all worked out, Red, don't you?' said Charles' admiringly, his former anxieties temporarily forgotten.

'As I always say, this Ethelred is Ethelred the Ready.' Ethelred gave a laugh. 'I think it's time to call it a night. I'll see Hennie first thing and get her to organise Paris and speak to either Janine or Pierre at the house in Provence. What's a good time to call your cokeheads?'

'I said I'd be in touch Friday morning. They've got stacks on their agenda, or so they said.'

'Good. And probably fleecing some poor other sods in between!' Ethelred gave the two of one of his most winning smiles, 'Any further questions?'

'I don't think so, not for the moment anyway.' Clytemnestra gave a small frown. Looking deadpan, at her husband, she added casually, 'But how remiss of me, there *is* one other!'

'And that is?'

Clytemnestra gave a mischievous laugh. 'I know it's late but who's to say no to another brandy?'

———————

Oswald's immediate reaction on hearing the instructions from Charles was one of complete shock. 'You, me and that *monster* at Disney World. Tell me you're joking?' he gasped in a strangulated voice. 'Tell me this is your idea for the sickest joke of the twenty-first and all ensuing centuries!'

'Not my idea, Oswald: Ethelred's. And he's never been more serious. We leave Friday morning on Eurostar. It's all arranged.' Charles, giving the incensed young man a steely look, added quietly, 'If I were you, Oswald dear, I'd shut up and simply do as you are told. As far as Ethelred and Clyte are concerned, you're still on some form of probation, filming or no filming.'

'But bloody Trisomy! How can one travel with *her*? What will people *think*?' I mean two adults and *that*! Why, we'd make even the most vile of paedophiles look saint-like!'

'Your answer to your very own question.'

'What? Saint-like? You mean dress her up like a miniature fucking Mother Theresa? Oh, c'mon Charles! Don't be so bloody daft. We'd never get away with it!'

'No you nana, not a nun. What did our little Tris dress up in the other day? The day after you and she had finished watching, "Slum Dog Millionaire?"'

'One of Clyte's pashimas, claiming it was a sari…' A beatific smile appeared on Oswald's face. 'But of course, and didn't she just make *the* most perfect hunched up, little old Indian woman? What is it you called her? Great Auntie Agra or was it Granny Goa?' He gave a laugh.

'Both!' laughed Charles. 'But you topped it all with your name for her!'

'And what was that? I forget my own genius at times!' replied Oswald shaking with mirth, his former angst forgotten.

'Deathica from Delhi!'

'I didn't!'

'You did so!'

'Ohmigod!' Oswald's eyes widened in mischievous delight, 'Aren't I *awful*?'

'Yes, you are and that's why I still adore you. So,' Charles gave the still laughing young man a shrewd look, 'you're quite happy about showing your loyal old ayah, Deathica, and your uncle the delights of Disney World, then?'

'Of course Unka Charles! As for a few days in Provence, can I add any *mort* to my delight?'

'That!' cried Charles, 'is *so* appalling, you deserve punishing!'

Half an hour later, a smug, satiated Oswald, his rear still filled with his favourite dildo, lay alongside a pensive Charles. 'Unka Charles,' whispered Oswald. 'Unka Charles?'

'Uh huh?'

'A euro for them?'

'Oh, they're worth much, much more than a euro, Os!'

'Tell me…'

Charles pulled himself into a sitting position and looked down at the pouting young man. *Christ, I loathe you, you little shit,* he thought, saying out loud, 'Christ, I really do adore you, young Oswald. You do know that, don't you?'

'Yes, Charles, I know.' said Oswald softly, thinking, *Silly old fart! I'll keep up this sick charade for as long as it takes, but once I'm a star you're zilch, Charles Conrad Crosby, fucking zilch! Euros? Think Euro Millions you pathetic, broken-down old queen!*

The next few days saw a veritable whirlwind of activity. Rail passages were booked, the house in France alerted of the impending arrival of Charles, Oswald and Trisomy. Janine and Pierre, the live-in staff, were used to the little girl, and she revelled in their pampering. A bewildered Hennie was set to fly off on a surprise, fully paid four week break on Madeira accompanied by her spinster sister, while Boris, without any fuss, was happy to quietly take himself off to Spain.

Trisomy's delight at visiting Euro Disney was paramount. 'Mickey Finn' she kept gurgling happily.

'No, Tris, Mickey *Mouse*!' Charles kept correcting her. Giving Clytemnestra an amused glance, he couldn't help adding, sotto voce, 'Methinks we have a real little alcoholic in the making here! From cooking sherry to Mickey Finns? Whatever next?'

'Don't even give me a chance to respond to that!' laughed Ethelred, who couldn't help overhearing.

'Pity a Molotov Cocktail's only a bomb and not a drink!' Oswald was heard to mutter, much to Charles's amusement.

When told she was to be an Indian princess for the whole of the Disney World visit – it had been hastily agreed a mere Indian lady would not suffice and, with the word maharanee being too difficult for her to understand, Trisomy would be a princess – the tiny figure had gone into a series of delighted gurgles and drooling. Her delight was further increased by the presentation of a selection of miniature saris which Clytemnestra produced from a case storing a selection of such garments as worn in a former series of portraits depicting a local rich Indian merchant's mistress. Vilma, the elegant Indian woman posing for the paintings, had reluctantly agreed to the traditional form of dress as a form of appeasement on behalf of her doting and very generous lover. 'I can tell you,' she confided laughingly to Clytemnestra at the conclusion of the final sitting, 'after having been condemned to wearing each of these wretched, shitty shroud-like garments for several days, I'm simply going to *exhaust* Prada and Dior!'

The ever capable Clytemnestra had spent a fraught afternoon cutting and hemming the lengths of brightly coloured, embroidered silks, aided and irritated by an excited Trisomy.

'What does she wear in Provence?' camped Oswald. 'Similar getups to those of madcap Marie Antoinette playing pretty peasants at the Petit Trianon?' The latter accompanied by a girlish shriek.

'She likes walking around starkers!' announced Charles evilly.

'Jesus!' gasped Oswald, clutching his throat and gagging theatrically. 'Forget the milk pail, Marie, and fetch me the sick bucket instead!'

'Now now, Oswald!' admonished Charles, 'That isn't nice. You know little Trisomy loves her Caligla. Who knows, when at Disney World, she may even want to share her – and God forbid there is such a thing – her Goofy Hot Dog with you!'

'Now I really *do* need the sick bucket!' Oswald threw open his arms towards the ceiling. 'The sacrifices I must make for my art!' he camped.

If the truth be known, Oswald was in a state of high excitement at the prospect of a break away from Bethlem Báthory. As he and Charles agreed, a continuous supply of Amitripyline would see the child – to quote Charles – 'a sleeping monster as opposed to a rival Sleeping Beauty a la Disney World.'

'She'll be no trouble,' Charles assured the young man. 'In fact, you may be surprised. I sometimes feel she deliberately plays it up with Clyte and Red, as she knows she'll get away with it. But,' he gave a twisted smile, 'when all's said a done, a drugged child is a perfect child!'

'Hear! Hear!' agreed his travelling companion to be.

———————

'All set?' Ethelred nodded. 'Right,' Charles dialled the number for the hotel in Earls Court. After a few rings it was answered by a foreign voice. 'Mister and Miss van Niekerk, please,' said Charles. He glanced at the slip of paper in his hand, 'Room twenty seven.' A look of panic crossed his face. 'What if they're not there?' he whispered. 'They'll be there...' Ethelred started to say when he was silenced by Charles flapping a hand. 'Dirk? Charles! How are the two of you?' He gave a laugh. 'Ah, Hettie said she bet it was me on the phone, did she? Clever girl. Why, were you beginning to have doubts about me calling back?' He listened for a moment. 'No, there's been no change in our arrangement but there is a slight change involving me. No, no, Dirk, hear me out. Of course you're both still expected tomorrow but let me explain and then let me put you on to Ethelred. E-thel-red Jones, the man you will be working with. He's got something even more appetising up his sleeve!'

Dirk, having been introduced by Charles to Ethelred, listened intently to what the man was saying. In between giving affirmative nods and appreciative grunts, he kept grinning at his sister and giving her a series of 'thumbs up signs.' He concluded the conversation by saying, 'That sounds brilliant Ethelred. I'm sorry Charles has to suddenly leave for Berlin, but then – I suppose in your business – there's never a dull moment. *Ja*, Hettie and I look forward to meeting you too. See you tomorrow at Windsor then, just after one o'clock.' There was another pause. 'If that's OK with you? *Ja*, in anticipation of Charles's call we already collected our cases from Victoria yesterday, so we'll be with you lock, stock and barrels!' Dirk gave out a delighted laugh. 'Christ Ethelred, Hettie and me in a film? Who would've believed that? Talk about a stroke of luck! See you tomorrow then. Cheers and err… Ethelred, many thanks, man! Cheers! See you tomorrow!'

'What's this about us being in a film?' A wide-eyed Hettie, bursting with curiosity, could hardly contain herself from giving her brother a hug. Instead, she stood grinning as Dirk danced a little jig around the hotel room floor.

'Oh Hets!' he sang as he pranced. 'This is the big time. A month's pay for the two of us plus extra cash for appearing in some film this Jones guy is making down at his country pad.' Dirk gave a whoop. 'Apparently Charles has never stopped saying what a great looking couple we are, and Mr. Jones just happens to require a young couple for a bit part each in his movie!'

'Yippee!' cried his sister, it being her turn to give a few excited hops around the room. 'Transkei, here we come.' Her breath was squeezed out of her, as Dirk engulfed her in a bear-like hug. The hug became more intimate with his mouth hungrily searching for hers. In between their tongues delving deeply into each other's throats, Dirk managed to gasp. 'Christ, you're hot Hets! Feel me, I'm as hard as a fucking knobkerrie!' Tearing at Hettie's track suit bottoms he jammed his long, thick fingers deeply into her moist, hot wet slit. 'Jesus, he groaned, lifting a slimy-coated finger to his flaring nostrils. 'Jesus!' he groaned again as he pulled down his own bottoms and, with one strong movement, threw his sister onto the bed before plunging his giant, throbbing cock – the reference to a thick, round-ended Zulu warrior's fighting club never more apt – deep into her greedily clenching and unclenching receptive opening.

Hettie, giving a strangulated shriek, began to buck and writhe beneath her furiously humping sibling.

'Transkei, here we come!' gasped a sweating, red-faced Dirk as he and his equally sweating sister, did exactly that.

'Jesus, Het!' The young man lay gasping alongside the heavily breathing girl. 'It just gets better and better, doesn't it?'

'Much, much better!' laughed the girl. She looked fondly at her brother. 'You calling your cock a knobkerrie really turns me on, you know!'

Dirk gave a laugh. 'Well, when we get back to SA why don't I get a proper one and fuck you with it as well?'

'Jesus, Dirk, SA could still be a few months away!'

'Tell you what,' said her brother. 'We've still got until tomorrow. Why not a cruise down that Portobello Road and see what we can find? Who knows what we *cum* across? There're a lot of strange stalls along there, particularly under that flyover bit right at the end.'

Dirk and Hettie never found a knobkerrie but found an outsize boomerang instead. Later that night, sitting facing his sister, Dirk slowly impaled himself on one angle of the boomerang as Hettie impaled herself on the other. With his sister slowly beginning to masturbate him, the two began to rock on the wooden V-shaped piece of wood. Gathering momentum the impaled couple began rocking and grunting until, with wild, animal-like cries they both exploded into a shuddering, shivering, spasmodic orgasm. The brother and sister repeated the rite a further three times before finally collapsing into an exhausted slumber as Saturday dawned.

CHAPTER 13

'Well, what do you think?' Ethelred was sitting in his study with Clytemnestra, the two guests having been shown up to their suite by Monday, where they had been left to unpack and 'make themselves at home' before joining their hosts for lunch.

'Deliciously devious, decadent, obviously on the make plus – and my gut feelings have never let me down – extremely dangerous!'

'Exactly my thoughts,' Ethelred leant forward and topped up their wine glasses. 'I think we film the meeting and greeting scene and then go straight to the finale. It's too dicey otherwise.'

'I agree; the sooner the better. How long will it take to film the first scenario?'

'Let's give them today and tomorrow to settle. I will need you, Clyte, to talk to the girl about some secretarial stuff – dictate a briefing regarding your "Still Life" exhibition for Claudia perhaps? – as well as making a list of things to be done. Suggest she does some filing… that sort of shit.'

'What about the boy?'

'Monday can give him some odd tasks to do in the grounds.' Ethelred gave a small laugh. 'Did you see Master Dirk's expression when Monday stuck out his hand to welcome the two of them? Whoever could have said apartheid still isn't alive and well and living in South Africa? It'll do the little bugger right to be told what to do by a black.'

'What about their denouement? The rape scene with Monday?'

'My dear, they will be so out of it on GHB that it won't matter to them whether Monday's pink, purple or black. However, we must get the take done as soon as possible. After the famous woodland scene with our two innocents asleep – *not* under a pile of leaves but under a carpet of dried cow pats. Which reminds me, I must check with Mon whether there is now an adequate heap ready; he was drying a load in one of the barns. The bodies can be put into cold storage until Charles gets back to *perform* the actual dismemberment followed by the eventual stuffing and mounting of the body parts. The same applies to Oswald but, in his case, we recreate the thinker using – as I've already explained – only Oswald's head and arms. I plan to use Dirk's torso and legs for the rest of the effigy.'

'*Effigy*? Statue, if you don't mind, husband dearest! You make my "Thinker" sound like bloody Guy Fawkes!'

'Whatever, our little Os will be *fawkesd* alright. Talk about a Roman candle, he won't know what's gotten into him by the time me, you, Monday and Charles – especially Charlie boy – have finished with him!'

'And how is Charles's little helper doing?'

'A pro if ever there was one! What a duo of geniuses we have been with that little caper, my darling! Talk about water tight!' Ethelred held his hand theatrically against his ear. 'Ah, methinks our guests approacheth!' He gave Clytemnestra a quick kiss on the cheek. 'This should be fun.' On hearing a timid knock on the door to the study, Ethelred called a cheerful 'Come in!'

A smiling Hettie and Dirk nervously poked their heads around the door. 'Sorry if we've kept you waiting,' said Dirk, 'but the house! This house! Not only is it amazing, but it's massive and we somehow got slightly lost!'

Like hell, you did! thought Ethelred, smiling broadly. *Probably did a quick recce to see how much your benign, out of the blue, new employers are worth!* 'It is a bit confusing at first,' he admitted, his smile broadening. 'But you'll soon get used to it. Drink? Clyte and I were just about to open a bottle of champagne to welcome you here.'

'Champagne! Oh, that would be lovely!' simpered Hettie.

'Fantastic!' agreed her brother.

No doubt their reaction would have been the same had I suggested hemlock, thought Ethelred, deftly uncorking the bottle of Cristal with a satisfying hiss. He handed the standing guests a fizzing flute each. 'Do take a seat.' He pointed to the sofa opposite. 'Lunch is in half an hour, but Clyte and I need to talk to you about something that's suddenly come up.' He took a slow sip. 'As you know, Hettie and Dirk, you've been asked here ostensibly by Charles to help out' – he nodded at the smirking girl – 'you Hettie, with the secretarial side of things whilst Hennie – Clyte's secretary – is away, and you, Dirk, as an odd job man to help out Monday – our "Man Friday" whom you met earlier on arrival.'

Dirk, like his sister, gave a smug nod.

'When we spoke yesterday, I also mentioned a bit part each in my current film which we're partly shooting here and – I didn't mention the second location as it wasn't decided until this morning – on Mauritius.' Ethelred noticed the quick glance between the brother and sister. It was obvious the destination, Mauritius, had struck the right chord, the island being no more than a brief flight from Johannesburg. He gave another smile. 'Because of the time factor and now the new location, *time*, I have to stress – and I daren't mention the additional time involved – is of the utmost importance. Therefore,' Ethelred took a long, teasing sip before adding the breathtaking words, 'would you mind leaving the part-time work for a week or two and concentrate on the filming instead? I'd like to start rehearsals and briefings as soon as possible, like tomorrow! What do you say?'

'What do we say? Why we say, bloody terrific! Don't we Hets?' replied Dirk grinning broadly at his sister.

'Me a film star? I can't wait for all those people back in SA to see me in a film!' cried his sister. She gave a camp giggle. 'Do you think I'll win an Oscar, Mr. Jones?'

'Ethelred please.' Ethelred gave a deep laugh. 'I wouldn't stake your life on it, Hettie, but there's no harm in trying.'

'What's the film?' asked Dirk, still unable to accept the couple's sudden change of fortune; the young man being too worldly wise not to appreciate such opportunities had their price.

'All That Glisters.'

'All That Glisters? What's this glisters?'

'It's a part quote taken from Shakespeare's "The Merchant of Venice", It's when the Prince of Morocco, on opening one of three caskets which he anticipates will contain the heroine, Portia's portrait. The caskets are made of gold, silver and lead and he – avaricious, ambitious fool – automatically goes for the gold, only to find, not a portrait of the aforesaid lady, but a portrait of Death, with the message written in it's hollow eye, "All that glisters is not gold, often you have heard that told," etcetera, etcetera!'

'Oh,' said Dirk, none the bit wiser, 'so why Mauritius?'

'Ah,' said Ethelred, mysteriously, 'for that my young friends, you will have to wait until you see the script. Meanwhile, like most directors, I do not film in sequence so, after a few days preliminary filming here, it's then off to Mauritius. After a few weeks on the island, we return to England but' – he smiled reassuringly at the couple – 'your roles in the film will have been completed so you can return directly to South Africa, after a few days sea and sun.'

Dirk gave an even broader grin. 'You had me worried for a moment err... Ethelred.' He gave a laugh. 'A case of so near and yet so far!'

'Like the film,' agreed the smiling director, 'All That Glisters!' He smiled wryly at a bemused Clytemnestra. 'Shall we go into lunch?'

'"All That Glisters?" Touch of the genius there, my darling!' Clytemnestra gave Ethelred a hug, 'Touch of the fucking, bloody brilliant!'

'Yes, it was rather a good piece of adlibbing, even though I say it myself.' Ethelred gave his wife a grin. 'Thank God for small arseholes!'

'I take it you've used the word "arseholes" in lieu of "mercies!" dearest?'

'But of course.' Ethelred gave Clytemnestra a quick kiss on the cheek. 'Sit a moment?'

The two were taking a quiet walk following a brief and fairly strained lunch with their two guests. Although Ethelred and Clytemnestra had done their best to get the brother and sister – they had not admitted to being anything else but an engaged, about-to-be-married couple – to relax and talk about their various travel experiences in Europe, the conversation had been stilted and basically one-sided, the hosts doing most of the talking.

'So, what do you think?'

Clytemnestra squeezed her husband's hand. 'The sooner the better; let's get the snuff shots done *tout de suite*. Charles can then take over immediately on his return. I take it the boys are all geared to go when given the green light?'

'Euros and Kevin can't wait and Monday, to quote him, is "jes a rarin' to *ram*! Massa Red!"'

'Dear Monday, he never lets one down, does he, in every possible way! If you catch my drift...?'

'Oh, I catch your drift alright, wifey dearest! Don't I always?'

'What do you think?'

'Think?' Dirk gave his sister a piercing look. 'Does shit stink? There's something very strange going on here, Het, and I don't like it! Not for one miniscule, fucking moment.' He gestured at the sumptuous guest suite in which they were both sitting, having returned from lunch. 'Nothing figures! It's too, too easy. Firstly this guy Charles – who just happens to have had to fuck off to Berlin – picks us up. Yes, he *did* pick us up, Hets – and in next to no time we're here, in the middle of bloody nowhere, about to be in a film and so on. You may believe in fairy tales, Hettie, but I don't.' He gave a snort. 'Not only is this house fucking creepy; what about that over-familiar Kaffir, their Man Friday called Monday? It wouldn't surprise me if he's not only the hired bloody help but the hired dick as well!'

'So what do you want to do?'

'Just get the hell out of here. Once it's dark, we're leaving.'

'What about all our stuff?'

'Stuff that!' announced her brother, little realising how close to the truth he was being. 'We've got our passports, out tickets and some travellers cheques, plus the bit of cash Jones gave me after lunch "as a retainer."' His mouth set in a grim line, Dirk continued softly, 'I seriously do think, Hets, it's time to cut our losses and run – the sooner the better.'

'So what about dinner? We're expected.'

'We'll have dinner, say we're tired and call it a day. Once the household's asleep, we get the fuck out of here!'

'It's quite a walk to the station…'

'Who says we're walking. I saw Ethelred put the keys to the Range Rover – or whatever the fuck they call those things nowadays – on a board in the lobby to the kitchen. We simply take the thing and dump it in the long term car park at the airport. I plan for us to be in Joburg by tomorrow night.'

'But the film and all that money…?'

'Forget the film, Hets, let's just get out of here.' He gave his sister a fond smile. 'We'll make our own film back in SA, I promise.'

'But to be in a film by Ethelred Jones!'

'Let's face it, Het. Until this Charles bloke mentioned Jones, we'd never heard of him. Judging from what we viewed on the Web, he's one sad, sicko, sack of shit. Jesus, you just have to look at the titles of some of his films. Christ knows what "All the Glisters" will involve; if that *is* the correct title!'

Hettie gave a nervous laugh. 'Glisters rhymes with blisters!'

'Don't even begin to think about it!' Dirk took her hand. 'Look, trust me on this one. After dinner we're out of here and it's goodbye fucking Batty Battery, or whatever the name of this fucker is!' Making a scary face at his stunned sister, Dirk couldn't resist adding in a sinister, Vincent Price-like theatrical chuckle, 'Unless we're drugged and taken advantage of, after what – in reality – could be our last supper!'

'That isn't funny, Dirkie,' whimpered the young girl. 'Not funny at all.'

'Sorry Hets,' said her brother, giving her a hug. 'I was only trying to lighten things up.' Dirk kissed her lightly on the forehead. 'Don't worry, this time tomorrow we'll be on our flight home.'

———

Sitting quietly in Ethelred's cutting room, Monday gave a grim smile as he listened to the amplified voices coming via the hidden microphones in the young couple's suite. Without hesitation, he punched into the intercom. 'They're nervous and planning a midnight bunk,' he growled in his deep rumble.

'As expected,' came Ethelred's calm reply. 'I sensed something like this may happen. Young Dirk is not as dense as he appears. I'll get onto Euros now. Kevin's away so Thrift will have to assist him. Do you mind doing the scene tonight?'

'As I said earlier, Massa Red, I'se jess a rarin' ta ram!'

'Right, Ram boa constrictor! I'll meet you in ten and help get the final bits and pieces ready on the set.' There was a tactful pause before he put forward the question to end all questions. 'Do you need to take anything? It's going to be a long, long strenuous session.'

'Not that I need it, but I'll take a couple of Bigralis along with one or two of the bad doc's so-called other prolonging pills! I can guarantee you, Massa Red, your big, bad, monster Monday'll have both the length and the strength for whatever you have in mind.' The big black man shook his enormous head as he gave a disbelieving laugh. 'Am I'm *seriously* going to be doing what you've said?'

'Yes, big Monday man, you literally are going to be fucking them to death.'

———

'It's just a simple supper,' announced Clytemnestra cheerfully. 'Mrs. N, the cook, has been given the evening off. She's been inundated with endless dinner parties recently, so Red and I thought a "getting to know each other" supper would be much more fun. We've invited our head cameraman, Euros Peacock and his partner, Thrift, to join us. Kevin, or second camera, sadly is unable to be here, but sends his greetings and is looking forward to meeting you. And Monday, of course, will be joining us! I've decided on a Spanish-themed supper, so I hope you all like tacos, enchiladas and such followed by a delicious almond tart – which I have to confess comes by courtesy of Harrods!' She gave a light laugh. 'But to compensate for my somewhat limited culinary skills, I can assure you Monday will be making the *meanest* margaritas!'

It had been agreed one such jug, its only distinction being the shape of the handle, would contain the margaritas laced with the odourless, colourless gamma-hydroxybutryate; otherwise known as the rape drug or GHB. Once the drug had taken effect, the two young people were to be carried down to the soundproofed basement beneath Ethelred's everyday studio. It was here the snuff scene would be filmed.

Both Dirk and Hettie had caused a momentary panic with their refusal of the margaritas and asking for a de rigueur Coca Cola instead. An unfazed Monday quickly produced a couple of cans and – with his broad back turned to the seated group – duly filled two highball glasses with the Coca Cola and the GHB mix. Ethelred, always 'at the ready,' had anticipated such an occurrence. He later told Clytemnestra, judging from what had been overheard, the couple – already wary and suspicious of anything untoward taking place – would more than likely be avoiding any alcoholic drinks, in order to keep their heads clear so as not to impede their midnight flit. In anticipation of this happening, Monday had made sure a discreet, separate amount of GHB was readily available from one of the many decanters placed on the bar counter.

Carefully avoiding the doctored jug, Monday poured Ethelred and Clytemnestra a large margarita each, before fetching one for himself and settling his large, muscular, musky frame down alongside a startled Hettie. On Ethelred's instructions, Monday had spent an hour on an energetic workout in the small gymnasium prior to meeting the others for drinks. 'I don't want you to shower. I want you as sweaty and as raunchy as you can get,' he'd been told. 'Even take a piss and rub some around your crotch. Again, don't shake your foreskin. I want you all male animal.' Ethelred had gone so far as to add, 'And if you just so happen to take a shit, don't wipe your arse!' It had been agreed Monday would be taking his planned tablets – or pills – during the serving of dinner, giving them enough time to take effect.

Hettie, wrinkling her small nose in disdain while uttering a distinct, '*Ag sis!*' – an Afrikaans slang term used to express extreme disgust – moved uncomfortably away from the large, black man. Without hesitation Monday spread open wide his muscular thighs, squeezing the girl between his massive left thigh and the arm of the sofa. The girl eyed her brother in alarm, her eyes widening even further when, placing his large black hand on her thigh, Monday asked in his deepest, dark rumble, 'So, howsit going, Hettie? Enjoying what you've seen so far?' the innuendo, followed by a deliberate, upward thrust of his bulging crotch, which, due to the thinness of his tracksuit bottoms, left nothing to the imagination.

Monday's giant, salami-like penis, a damp patch visible in the fabric next to the bulbous head, and the bulge of his almost tennis ball-like balls, gave an unexpected twitch, causing even the serene, worldly-wise Clytemnestra to blanch.

'For fuck's sake!' cried Dirk, leaping to his feet, his face suffused with rage. 'What the fuck do you think you're doing, man? That's my fiancé you're fucking feeling up!'

'Whoa!' Monday lifted his large black hand as if burned. 'Sorry, Dirk,' he grunted, 'I was just being friendly. No offense meant. Look, I'll move.' The black giant moved a few inches away from the angry girl, before changing his mind and standing up. 'I think I'd better go and check things in the kitchen,' he mumbled, making a slow, deliberate, swaggering exit his massive cock and balls falling loosely down against his left thigh.

'Jesus, Red!' said Dirk, his eyes blazing. 'Did you see what that... that... that... fucking nig... guy was doing?' he ended lamely. Knowing England and its ridiculous grovelling to political correctness, he thought it best not to use the derogatory "n" word uttermost in his mind.

'Sorry about that, Hettie and Dirk,' said Ethelred smoothly. 'Monday simply gets carried away. He's always treated like one of the family and for some people – like yourselves – it took a bit of getting used to.'

'But to put his hand on Hets' leg and show off his err... bits like he was doing...!'

Ethelred raised a placatory hand. 'Look, I'm sorry, very sorry about the *small* misunderstanding. I can only apologise again on Monday's behalf, and he has also apologised. So *let's* forgive and forget, huh? He more than likely thought he was only being friendly and, knowing Monday, he will be mortified if he thought you were thinking otherwise.' He gave a smile. 'We have several weeks of working together' – Dirk shot his sister a quick glance which was immediately picked up by Ethelred and Clytemnestra – 'so let's be cool about it all.'

Feeling both thoroughly evil and devilish – and knowing the drug would soon be taking effect – Ethelred was about to divulge the several scenes planned where Monday would not only be touching the girl, but kissing and fucking her as well as her brother, but decided against it.

Clytemnestra, knowing what was going on in his cynical mind, gave him a reprimanding look. It was at that moment Euros and Thrift bustled into the room.

'Sorry we're late!' gushed Euros, 'but blame it on that wicked Charles! I couldn't get him off the phone. Apparently the three of them are having a positive *ball* at Euro Disney and Trisomy is stealing the show apparently with some of those ridiculous tourists actually believing she's a living, breathing Indian princess! The Indian princess even went so far as to denounce Mickey as a fraud, claiming he was "more of a man than a mouse" – something which obviously doesn't apply to her two escorts!' Euros trilled with mirth at his own wit while his partner looked on adoringly.

'Charles at Disney World? With an Indian princess? What happened to Berlin? Wha... what's going in...?' Panicking, Dirk tried to rise to his feet, his body beginning to sway and his words to slur. 'Wha's going on...?' he repeated, his eyes swivelling in growing alarm. 'Our drinks... wha di... did you put in our fucking drinks...? With a soft sigh he crashed back down onto the sofa alongside his sister who was sitting, staring vacantly into space.

'Oops!' giggled Euros. 'Was it something I said?'

Monday, who had been timing the demise of the two guests, had no need to be summoned to the study.

'Let's get them downstairs!' instructed Ethelred brusquely. 'I don't want to waste any time. Euros, you and Thrift set the lights and we'll be right behind you. So, my lovely Clyte, are you prepared for the woodland scene to end all woodland scenes?'

'Couldn't be more prepared! The bower and the leaves await!'

'And you Mon? Christ, you don't half pong! Quite a turn on even though I say it myself!'

'Ah, Massa Red, you can no beat da allurin' stink of da noble black man's dishonest sweat and toil!'

'Pity your Lady Anstruther isn't about for some of your good dishonest sweat and toil!' This from a smirking Clytemnestra.

'Isa allus got my udda fren!' said Monday going more Uncle Remus than the legendary figure himself.

'Quite.' Came Cltemnestra's cryptic reply.

Monday, without any further hesitation, picked up the mumbling, restlessly tossing and turning Dirk and followed Ethelred, carrying a comatose Hettie, down to the basement studio in the wake of Clytemnestra and the two assistants.

Clytemnestra, along with Monday, had earlier created the woodland setting for the final 'Babes in the Woods' scenario. An undulating mound made up out of suitably placed blocks of trimmed industrial foam covered with faux lawn, had been formed in the middle of the studio room. A backdrop of trees and bushes encompassed the mound with its scooped-out hollow. Piles of leaves had been artistically placed around the depression. Several polythene sacks containing additional leaves and the dried cow pats were stacked nearby. Monday and Ethelred, aided by Euros, quickly stripped the brother and sister and laid them gently on their backs inside the hollow.

Dirk giving a groan, opened his eyes, his head swivelling wildly. 'Where am I?' he managed to gurgle. 'Whassa going on…?'

'Shhh! You're fine,' whispered Clytemnestra soothingly as she stoked his sweating brow. 'Relax, it's only a game… relax.'

'Hettie! Where's Hettie?'

'Right next to you. Look, let me put her hand on that very splendid cock of yours, Dirk! There you go… now, isn't that nice and familiar?' Clytemnestra glanced at Ethelred. 'We'd better hurry. He's not as out of it as he should be. Monday,' she added mischievously. 'I take it that's *not* a dagger I'm seeing before me?'

'Jesus, Monday!' exclaimed Ethelred hoarsely, following Clytemnestra's glance and eyeing the gigantic erection pressed angrily against the black man's stretched tracksuit bottoms. 'Dagger be damned. It's more like a fucking blunderbuss!' He gave a dry, rasping swallow. 'You're certainly looking all set to cock and roll!'

'You bet I am!' grunted Monday. 'So let's get those camera's rolling!'

'In a minute! In a minute!' scolded Ethelred with a laugh. 'There's a small matter' – another laugh – 'of a G-string and your satyr's horns. Over you go, big man. As before, the lovely Clyte awaits to help you with the horns and hiding your own massive one, but only momentarily. Thrift? Leaves please.'

'Of course,' said the second cameraman, shaking himself from his lustful reverie apropos the rampant Monday. 'But of course. Let there be leaves!' Thrift began to pluck handfuls of leaves from the spare sacks, scattering them over the restless, mumbling couple.

'And as they've ended up in deep shit, some cow pats around their necks, please!' cried Ethelred. 'Leave that!' he instructed, laughing at his unintended pun and pointing at Dirk's partly obscured, lower half. 'Dirk's dildo-like dick sticking out will look great in a zoom! Euros? Thrift? Ready?' The two nodded at the director. 'Monday?' He glanced with approval at his magnificent star. Monday, the effect of both the Bigralis and Viagra, visibly enhanced by a soft white leather posing pouch, even more apparent. 'Everest meets Ethelred and ever ready!' he was to quip later. The man mountain, his body freshly greased with visible smears of duck fat enhanced with a sprinkling of golden glitter, and sporting a pair of twisted horns attached to his head by an inconspicuous, black banding, stood growling and pawing at the floor with his massive foot. 'Jesus!' muttered Ethelred. 'Forget sex on legs! This is a sex machine in overdrive!'

Moving towards the set he turned to face Monday. 'Now, it's exactly as we rehearsed it, but this time, instead of miming the whole thing, this is for *real*!' Ethelred looked at the small, eager to please, and even more eager to begin group. 'Remember, team, there can be no retakes so, my partners in crime and about-to-be makers of murder and mayhem, it's up to you!' He nodded to Clytemnestra who quickly handed the black man a phial of amyl nitrate. As Monday sniffed the phial greedily, Ethelred turned to a poised Euros and Thrift. 'Lights!' he shouted. Immediately the tableau was illuminated by a diffused red and golden glow. 'Cameras! And… action!'

Two nights beforehand, Monday, similarly garbed but without the added embellishments, had been photographed emerging from one of the many decorative clusters of saplings and shrubs scattered around the grounds. This particular grouping of flora had been liberally sprinkled with gold dust and, through the use of a tinted lens and accents of discreetly placed red and gold spotlights, the printed scene had appeared both spiritual and surreal. 'The colours and the effects are brilliant,' breathed an ecstatic Ethelred. 'The setting is the ultimate tortured red sky to Edvard Munch's "The Scream," the scream no doubt caused by the sight of Priapus's – aka Monday's – glistening, glittering, monstrous dick!' He gave a wild laugh. 'Who on earth, apart from Ethelred Jones, film director *extraordinaire*, could come up with a quote the likes of that?'

On the cry of 'Action,' Monday pawed his way forward, grunting, prancing, and tossing back his horned head in a drug induced frenzy. Pausing, he stopped to sniff the air. Rolling his eyes and giving a few loud animal-like grunts, he suddenly became aware of the two sleeping bodies, their heads barely visible above the blanket of leaves; Dirk's visible erection firmly clamped in his sister's leaf-obscured hand. The sweating black giant, completely carried away in his fantasy role, fell onto his all fours and began to furiously sniff and nudge the penis delicacy, his wide nostrils flaring, his lips curling into a snarl.

'That's it, my magnificent Mandingo Prince! Not only are you a legend but a giant, legendary, nightmarish bull hog, rooting for truffles!' cried Ethelred. 'Sniff that Dirkie dick! Snort and snot on it! That's it! That's it!' exploded the director, his eyes gleaming and his own throbbing erection apparent, 'Grunt and growl, you beautiful priapic, hedonistic, hellish, monstrous, bastard you! That's it! Grizzle it and play with it between your teeth! Now, *bite* the fucker! Bite the fucker *off*!' he screamed. 'Bite, you black bastard! Bite!'

With a groan Ethelred orgasmed as Monday, throwing back his head, gave a primeval cry before dropping down and, after viciously gnawing on Dirk's rigid penis, finally bit right through.

'Uncover him! Uncover him!' directed Ethelred, foam and spittle flying from his own snarling mouth. 'And yes! Yes Monday! Keep swinging that cock between your teeth! Now lift the bastard's legs onto your shoulders!' He gestured to the blood jettisoning from the torn stump of what used to be Dirk's cock. 'Lube yourself with his blood! Lube yourself well, my mighty black Adonis and then fuck the hell out of the Afrikaner shit! Two cameras on this Euros and Thrift! I'm then going to get Monday to stuff Dirk's dick down his throat! Talk about self-gratification! I want the fucker filmed choking to death on his own dick!' Ethelred gave a manic laugh. 'Talk about death by self-abuse! What a way to go, huh? Talk about swallowing your own pride!'

It took Dirk several minutes to die during which his struggles, however instinctive and however violent, could not compete with Monday deeply impaled inside him, entering and exiting with a non-stop piston like frenzy. His eyes rolled back inside their sockets, the big man viciously fucked Dirk's mouth with his amputated cock, gradually thrusting deeper and deeper down his throat until it was completely embedded. His eyes bulging and his limbs threshing uselessly – Monday had placed his massive knees on Dirk's arms, his one hand firmly gripping the youth's ankles to his neck as the other vigorously worked the severed penis – Dirk's abused body finally gave a few violent shudders and went limp. With a long sigh Monday withdrew himself, but not before Euros had repositioned his camera so as to get a spectacular shot of Dirk voiding himself in a great, gushing geyser of shit and cum as he was, literally, unplugged.

'Unbelievable…' whispered Ethelred. 'Unbelievable.' He glanced at his stunned crew. Unable to control himself Ethelred simply unzipped himself and openly masturbated, coming onto a spare pile of leaves while Euros openly fucked an obliging Thrift who, hand-held camera completely forgotten, had obligingly dropped onto all fours. As if unaware of the frenzied goings on around her, an unperturbed Clytemnestra, both hands encased in surgical gloves, busily set about gathering blood, cum and shit samples from Dirk's disbanded body. 'Mini bites for my microscope' as she would later laughingly label them.

'Right,' said Ethelred as a groaning Euros gave a final thrust into a similarly sounding Thrift. 'I need some more shots of this babe among the leaves and then he can be put in the freezer.' He eyed Monday who had been busily cleaning his own blood spattered body with a roll of kitchen towelling. 'Still hard, I see!'

'Jesus, Red! I could go on forever,' laughed the big black man, proudly.

'Good,' said his employer, 'because now it's her turn. And this time Monday Man, you drag her from the leaves and throw her face down on that extra large, round mound over there. You bugger her first. Then you fuck her from the front, before choking her with your dick. Oh!' He turned back to the main cameraman who was still sweating profusely. 'Euros, can we hold onto Dirk for a bit longer before you put him in the freezer? I want a scene with Monday fist fucking him but a fist fucking with a difference.'

'And how is that?'

'Because Monday's about to chew off Dirk's right arm just above the elbow and fuck him with it! A final shot of master Dirk with his own arm up his arse and his own cock – that's why I asked for a pair of forceps to be made available – sticking up from out of his mouth. Talk about the ultimate self-abuse!' He gestured to his bemused wife. 'Clyte, can you do the honours with the forceps and get Dirk's cock from out of his throat? Meanwhile, Euros, if you and Thrift are ready; and Monday, when you feel you are, we'll deal with sister dearest.' He looked back at Clyte who, having successfully rescued Dirk's wedged penis, had returned to a nearby desk where she sat busily labelling various slides. 'You OK, dearest?' Ethelred questioned solicitously.

'Never been better,' replied Clytemnestra with a smile. She gave a dry laugh. 'Let's face it darling, you and your ploys. Why, you're even more admirable than the fairy tale about the brave little man who killed seven in one blow!'

'I am?'

'Yes, my darling, Red, you most certainly are!' Clytemnestra gave out a lighter laugh. 'I'm sure you must remember the fairy tale about the valiant little tailor by the deliciously decadent Brothers Grimm? The little tailor who boasted of killing seven in *one* blow, but never admitting they were flies!' Smiling at Ethelred's puzzled expression, she added with a chortle, 'Whereas *you*, director husband to end all director husbands, instead of a mere seven, *you* will be slaying *thousands* with your film – only this time it will be their *own* flies being abused! All thanks to you, despite having to deal *three* blows!'

'Three blows?'

'Yes dearest, three blow jobs!' Clytemnestra raised three main fingers of her right hand. 'Blow Job One, Dirk has already choked on or been choked with his own diddling dick! Two, Hettie – lucky bitch! – is about to choke Monday's massive dick and three, the dreaded Oswald is also going to choke on some unfathomable, mystery dick! Hence, one, two and three blows!'

'What a compendium of irrelevant twaddle you can spout at times, my love!' laughed Ethelred, 'But – as always – so brilliantly and bloody right!' He gave another laugh. 'However, just you lot wait until you see the dick to end all dicks chosen for the dubious privilege of choking our odious, little arse stretch!'

'Massa, yo Monday mon can no damn bigger get!' laughed Monday, protesting loudly. 'Dis ol ding o' mine is jes about all prime tuckered out! He's a burstin' point already and dat's a fact! Or should that be a fucked?'

Ethelred and the group burst out laughing. 'Don't worry, Monday Man, you'll still be filmed fucking our little Oswald, your help being even more vital with the final fuck scene!'

'Which involves *what*, exactly?' asked a trembling Euros.

'That, my dear Euros, would be simply telling. All I can say is even your lenses will weep!'

CHAPTER 14

'God, it's good to be back! Provence was perfection but Disney World? Forget it!' Charles gave Clytemnestra and Ethelred a twisted smile. 'However, Oswald and our little proncess loved it. I must say, Tris came out tops. She was like a tiny whirlwind; a miniature spinning top in a swirl of colours.'

'And our wannabe star?' This from Ethelred.

'A preening, pirouetting pansy if ever! God! I can't even begin to tell you about the swishy tantrums. You may not believe this but I have a strong suspicion our Oswald may be a teeny weeny bit jealous of Trisomy, and a bit too curious. At times I was given to think that our princess was about to be unmasked.' He nodded his thanks as Clytemnestra handed him a large vodka tonic. 'If you want my honest opinion, it's got to be now as opposed to a further week or even a month. Talking of which, how did it *your* answer to Disney World, albeit the world of the Brothers Grimm, go? Tell me this tale of woe has the most gory and *grim*-mest of happy endings?'

'A *perfect* tale of woe with a *perfection* of an ending.' Ethelred gave the doctor a warm smile. 'We'll show you the rushes after dinner.'

'Monday perform OK?'

'OK? Mandingo Man Monday was so OK that Clytemnestra has immortalised him in a new song with catchy phrase for the ever growing Bethlem Báthory book of musical repertoire!'

'And what's that, if I dare to ask?'

'You most certainly can.' Ethelred gave Clytemnestra a wink. 'Clyte, if you wouldn't mind. Music mistress, please!'

With a light laugh Clytemnestra walked gracefully to the red lacquered, baby grand piano standing by the window. 'Apologies to Miss Muff Diving Mary Poppins!' she grinned, sitting herself down on the acrylic stool. With a strong rippling of chords to one of the most popular songs to come from 'The Sound of Music,' Clytemnestra then burst into a flighty light soprano with a rendition of her own unique version to 'Supercalifragilisticexialidocious.'

> *'Superfuckerthrobbingpenisreallysoatrocious*
> *Bet you that the size of it will cause you a thrombosis*
> *Once you take up inside yourself it's rather like osmosis*
> *Superfuckerthrobbingpenisreallysoatrocious!'*

A further set of wild, similar verses followed before Ethelred and Charles, doubled up with laughter and tears streaming from their eyes had to beg her to stop.

'I take it from that super fucking fabulous bit of frivolity, Monday Man did 'em proud?' gasped a spluttering Charles.

'Did 'em proud? As I said, Charlie boy, wait until you see the rushes! Forget our dirty little Donny de Sade. What we have created for "Still Life; makes the mad Marquis look positively angelic!' Ethelred nodded across to Clytemnestra who had rejoined them. 'Don't you agree, Clyte?'

'Red's best work to date, which is saying something.' She raised her glass to the doctor. 'I've got some wonderful new and exciting ideas for the exhibition and I need to talk to you in the morning about planned, accompanying features. I'd like to do this as soon as you've dealt with anything Red needs you seeing to.' She gave the doctor a startled look. 'Good heavens, in the midst of all the excitement of your return, I forgot to ask where Tris and Oswald are? How remiss of this most motherly of mothers!'

'No need to worry. Oswald said he'd see Tris has her bath and gets some supper before tucking her up.'

'Is that wise? I mean you've just said...'

'I know, I know. I've explained the Progeria as best as I can. He helped me bathe her when we were away and now totally accepts the scrub of pubic hairs and the pair of tiny, wrinkled pathetic excuses of budding breasts.'

'Poor Trisomy,' murmured Ethelred pouring himself another drink.

'*Happy* Trisomy,' said Charles. 'She's very excited at helping Unka Charles with his new projects. What with her weird herb garden and now her interest in taxidermy, she's a whole new little person. But, as I've said, also a wise little person.' He leaned forward conspiratorially, 'I joke not when I quote what she said on our way back on Eurostar. Your little Tris whispered in that charming, so endearing guttural gurgle of hers, "Unka Charles" – so much more acceptable than the spasmodic nursey! – "Unka Charles, Caligla bad! Caligla dangerous. Tris doesn't *like* Caligla anymore!" Also note, she's dropped the term Unka. So, Oswald has now been demoted to a mere Caligula as opposed to a favourite uncle. As I just said, my dears, let's make that a sooner as opposed to a later.'

'Right,' said Ethelred, 'We're all agreed on that so I suggest we sort this out in the next few days. Meanwhile Charles, as we had to err… film the end sequences for our epic due to the unreliability of our two South African wannabe stars, we still need a couple for a few more *before* sequences to lead up to the already filmed *after* takes. I need to have the two babe figures seen walking through the woods and we also need the new couple to enable us to fulfil your terms of the contract. I take it you have some sources desperate for donors' donations?'

'I do indeed, especially hearts and kidneys.'

'Fine, so what with Oswald and a final couple, or another stray young man and single girl, we can then call it a wrap.' Ethelred gave a snigger. 'Or should that be a shroud!' He grinned with delight at the loud groans from his two companions. 'I can then work on the editing while you and Clyte complete your pieces for the accompanying exhibition.' He continued. 'If all goes according to plan, we're on to a major winner here. I can see this one making us a small fortune. Not only are *we* going to be in clover but our backers will, I'm sure, be *back* for even more!'

'Very droll Red dearest!' Clytemnestra looked up towards the chrome angled entry to the large room. 'Oswald!' she cried, giving the other two and anxious glance. 'There you are. We were beginning to wonder where you'd got to! But here you are and just in time for a drink before dinner.' Rising to her feet she held out a welcoming hand. 'Charles has been saying how wonderful you've been with darling little Tris. He says you were Peter Pan to her Wendy at Euro Disney, and Clyde to her Bonnie in Provence! It sounded such fun shooting all those fluffy bunny rabbits and innocent birds!'

'Hares, Clyte! Hares!' camped a smiling Oswald, emitting a high pitched, piercing laugh. 'And the birds weren't at all innocent, but nasty, nasty crows!' He gave another shriek as he held out a fey hand for the de rigueur flute of champagne. 'Did anyone ever tell you little Trisomy is one mean Annie Oakley with a catapult?'

Oswald's over-hyped performance throughout dinner saw Ethelred, Charles and Clytemnestra exchanging nervous glances. Dinner over, and after Oswald had excused himself by announcing a 'gossamer girl simply has to get her beauty sleep!' the three agreed any further waiting would be a disaster.

'If I didn't know any better, I'd swear he's on drugs!' reckoned Clytemnestra.

'Oh, but he is!' announced Charles drily. 'Even before we set of for Disney World and Provence I was slipping him hallucinogens. The guy's feet – plus mind – haven't touched terra firma for several weeks! I tell you, that little cock teasing *putto* is now putty in our hands!'

'You old dog, you!' laughed Ethelred. He leaned forward. 'Now, if you get yourself a very large and very stiff drink – you can top me and Clyte up as well, if you wouldn't mind – I'll then divulge what's about to happen to our little star who never was.'

Ten minutes later an ashen-faced Charles looked at a smiling Ethelred and Clytemnestra, his expression one of total disbelief. 'You can't be serious?' he managed to whisper.

'I assure you I've never been more serious.'

'Jesus,' breathed Charles. 'James Herbert, eat your heart out!'

'And the rest!' laughed Ethelred; he Charles a mischievous look. 'Your new little charges can't wait to make your acquaintance!'

'I'm sure.' Charles gave a giggle, 'How many?'

'Three – keeping it all in fairy tale and nursery rhyme mode!'

———————

'Oswald, I want you to take up your "Thinker" pose. This time you will be pondering your fantasy, the magnificent Monday. Monday will then appear as if in a vision, the figure of your fantasy.'

'And my fantasy?' Oswald gave Ethelred an arch look.

'Well, we all know how you fantasise about Monday Man so here's your chance.' He gave Oswald a searching look. 'Tell me Os, given the choice, just *how* – in your wildest of fantasies – would you like to meet or see Monday?'

'I have a choice?'

'If what you have in mind is not too impossible I see no reason why we shouldn't work round this for more err... authenticity. If you're happy it'll show not only in your performance but will lighten up the whole screen.'

'I saw a film once,' said Oswald wistfully, 'a porn film about gladiators called "Spar-up-the-Arse," – Ethelred struggled not to snigger – 'in which this massive black gladiator, naked and armed only with a net, catches this cowering Christian and rapes him repeatedly until he begs for mercy, says he will give up *his* god for the Roman gods, the Emperor Nero and especially for the gladiator, but only if he can remain the gladiator's lover! The gladiator had the gorgeous name of Thrustitdeepinus!"'

'Well, Os, I see no reason as to why we can't re-enact this fantasy for you. The pool terrace can be used as a basis for the Coliseum and we can digitally enhance this with genuine shots for authenticity. I am sure Monday will be only too delighted to be your fantasy gladiator and thrust it deep in *you*!'

Oswald let out a high-pitched shriek. 'Ohmigod! Ohmigod!' he squeaked, 'When?'

'I'll set up a meeting with Monday within a day or two. Maddening thing is I have to spend a few days in Edinburgh regarding next year's festival. On my return I'll run through the scenario with you and the big man; then work out the various angles and details with Euros. We'll also need to spend some time checking out the basic set and, as this will all be filmed as an exterior shot, we are also dependent on the sodding weather. If all goes according to plan, let's go for two weeks as from today which you, Os, should *take* as a good omen. As the proverb so rightly says, "Thursday's child has far to go!"'

'Ohmigod!'

'And another thing young Oswald, there will be no rehearsal. I want you to be well and truly raped for this. No lubricants, nothing! Think Irving Stone's "The Agony and the Ecstasy", the novel about the life of Michelangelo. I want you simply, Oswald, to give an Oswald Oscar winning performance!'

'Ohmigod!'

It'll be more than a mere 'ohmigod,' thought Ethelred looking at the smug, self-satisfied young man. Oh, young Oswald, are you going to rue the day you were chosen by Charles that evening in Balans!

———————

Ethelred was sitting with Charles discussing the replacements for Dirk and Hettie.

'I've been thinking,' said Charles. 'Instead of me finding a lost soul or two in a pub as before, maybe one of those innocuous, anonymous type adverts in one of the gay magazine or papers perhaps?'

'No!' said Ethelred vehemently. 'Firstly, we don't have time and secondly, no matter how clever or subtle one is, there is always the chance of being traced. So, Charles dear, another chance to practise what you are now so perfect at. This time it's better you go for single individuals as opposed to a couple. However, I do need them together for a shot where they're seen walking through the woods, plus one extra when they appear as another of Oswald's muses or fantasies.'

'I'd better get going then,' laughed Charles. He added drily, 'Can anyone tell me why I'm beginning to feel like a reincarnated Jack the Ripper?'

'Spot on Charles, but as yet you've still got your disembowelling and other "Ripper" surgery to perform.' He gave a grin accompanied by a grimace. 'However, I'm sure you'll enjoy that!'

'As much as you will, filming it!' laughed his accomplice.

Charles, on Ethelred's instructions, avoided the Jameirah Carlton Tower for a second time round. 'You don't want to become too noticed,' he warned. 'Those concierges are an inquisitive lot and I am sure you and your dallying with the arse stretch, were duly logged. Better to be a condom than conned!' Instead, at Clytemnestra's suggestion, he booked himself a suite at Flemings Mayfair, the luxurious boutique hotel so often frequented by Claudia Cordelle and now a firm favourite of Clytemnestra's. The suite had been taken as a result of an earlier passing comment made by the worldly-wise gallery owner to Clytemnestra during one of their regular 'get togethers' at the discreet hotel.

'I always put my more important artists in a suite here.' Claudia confided. 'Not only is it brilliantly convenient for access to the gallery, but the suite is one hundred per cent discreet seeing the occupier can use a private entrance to the hotel direct from Clarges Street, without having to go through the main lobby and reception.' She added in a sultry chuckle. 'You could sneak in the likes of Messrs George Clooney or Brad Pitt through there, and nobody would be any the wiser!'

On his arrival the following day at the elegant Georgian building, Charles was able to find a convenient parking bay in Half Moon Street on which the hotel fronted. Carrying his light overnight case he made his way into the stylish mirrored and marbled reception area, where he confirmed his booking for that evening. On making enquiries about parking facilities, he was introduced to the Head Concierge, a man of striking, dark matinee idol looks, who in turn introduced himself as Paul. 'No problem, Mr. Crosby,' said Paul, giving directions for a public car park in nearby South Audley Street. Charles noted how convenient this would be for both collecting the car and someone from the discreet private entrance to the hotel.

'Very smart,' said Charles, not letting on he had visited the hotel before. He nodded appreciatively at the glamorous surroundings. 'I take it that's the main bar,' he added, glancing in the direction of a doorway to what appeared to be an even more glamorous lounge area.

'That,' Paul proudly announced, 'is our very popular Champagne and Cupcake Room. In addition to champagne and other alcoholic beverages, tea and coffee is served in the mornings and afternoons along with a selection of cupcakes. But later on we have what we call our Martini and canapé hour, where canapés are served along with cocktails and drinks. There is also our cocktail bar downstairs.'

'Thank you Paul,' smiled Charles, 'Martinis and canapés sound just my forte!' He glanced at his watch, a simple run-of-the mill type, his usual Rolex having been left back at the house. 'Yes, a vodka Martini and some savoury cakes sound just the ticket.'

'I'll have someone take your case up to your suite on the sixth floor, sir,' smiled back Paul, giving a dazzling smile.

Paul, Paul, whoever you are, like the Martinis and canapés, you too are just my forte! thought Charles with a leer. He looked again at the striking young man dealing briefly with a guest making an enquiry. A young Louis Jordan, if ever there was. He was quick to note the absence of a wedding ring on the concierge's well-manicured left hand. Maybe or maybe not? He could not resist an inward smile at his musings. *But sadly, with this divine, tantalising creature, I somehow think definitely not! Oh well, an old, he bride of many exes and experiences can dream can't he...?*

'Sir?'

'What?' Charles shook himself out of his brief reverie. 'Oh, Paul; yes, my bag… thank you,' replied Charles handing the overnight case to a hovering young page. He nodded at Paul's left hand. 'Not married I see?' The outdated term 'bachelor gay,' being too apparent even for an old roué such as himself.

Completely unfazed, the dazzling Latin-looking charmer gave a cheerful chuckle. 'No sir, but I have a long suffering girlfriend.' To emphasise his point, Paul added, 'Nikki and I have been together for some years now.'

'Ah yes,' said Charles slightly deflated and muttering, 'Ah well, such is life…' Rubbing his hands together he added brightly, 'Right then Paul, let the bacchanal begin! Heavens!' he exclaimed as he walked past the open, massive polished wood and glass panelled door and into the subtly illuminated space. Stopping for a moment he turned to the man alongside him. 'Now this, Paul, this is what I call a hedonist's heaven!' Charles stood looking at the elegant guests either sitting or standing in the opulent room of dark chocolate colourings, lime greens with accents of cream, silver, aubergine and rich reds. The use of elaborate Moroccan mirrors and mirrored enhancements to a pair of massive ceiling lamps, gave the feeling of being swept into a brilliant kaleidoscope. 'God help me if I have more than my usual gallon or two,' He muttered with a grin as he approached the bar.

Several Martinis later, Charles bid the charming barman a cheery 'Good night!' before making his way to his room where he quickly showered and changed. Checking his wallet for credit cards and cash, he returned downstairs and made his way to where his car was parked. Fifteen minutes later, having left the car in the suggested South Audley Street car park, he hailed a taxi. Instructing the cab to drop him off at the Cumberland Hotel on the corner of Edgware Road and Oxford Street, Charles – having paid the driver – walked briskly towards Old Quebec Street and the Quebec pub itself, a celebrated hangout for homosexuals, old and young. Charles had already planned his strategy; one young gay man in the bar who was either rent or at least solo, and later, one lone female who could be easily chatted up in the likes of a Primark or some other anonymous store.

One of Charles's most successful previous 'donors' had been found one evening in the former Primark where Charles, on spotting the lone young shopper carefully inspecting a rack of dresses, had approached her and, apologising and stammering profusely, had asked her if she wouldn't mind help him select a blouse or two for his girlfriend. The girl, only too willing to oblige, had not only helped Charles select two blouses and a bracelet – Viola, the young cleaner back at Bethlem Báthory had been delighted at her unexpected gifts – but readily accepted his offer of a 'thank you' drink in a nearby wine bar. The rest had been business as usual. Charles had helped the unsteady girl – suitably doused with wine subtly laced the de rigueur GHB – to his car conveniently parked in nearby Park Street.

Minutes later she was naked on the dissecting table in his basement cum operating theatre. An hour later a discreet black estate car had driven up to the discreet, nondescript mews house and several sealed containers concerning vital donor parts packed in dry ice, discreetly changed hands. The missing girl – Charles had discovered over the drinks that she was a student from Czechoslovakia working as a part-time au pair whilst supposedly learning English – had literally disappeared. All her clothing, tote bag and personal papers were dutifully incinerated along with the remainder of her body. If anyone had noticed her missing it never made the press.

Due to the earliness of the evening the main bar to the Quebec was virtually empty. Not a good move, was Charles's immediate thought. Maybe a bite somewhere and come back later. He was about to make an about turn and head for the main door when a young man standing at the end of the long bar caught his eye. *Jesus!* thought Charles, doing a double take. For a moment I thought it was the dreaded Dirk reincarnated! His mind racing, Charles quickly assessed the situation. He looks as if he's alone and if he is, it's a prayer made in heaven. This one is a pure doppelganger to our dismal South African. All we need now is to find his so-called fiancé-cum-sister!

Without hesitation, Charles approached the bar where he ordered a large gin and tonic. Standing in a relaxed, nonchalant fashion, he looked casually around the club-like room, his eyes finally resting on the young man the same moment the subject of his planned scrutiny happened to be looking discreetly at *him.* Catching Charles's stare the young man gave a start and went back to staring at the room in general. Without pausing, Charles – with a predatory-like movement – sidled up to where his proposed victim was nervously standing. 'Evening,' said Charles companionably. He nodded at the empty lager glass in the young man's beefy, callused hand. 'Fancy another? I'm Andrew, by the way.'

'Err… that's very kind, Andrew.' The young man's eyelids fluttered nervously. 'But you don't have to… I was just about to leave…'

'I know I don't *have* to,' said Charles with an easy laugh, 'but I'd like to! Same again? Or would you like something stronger?'

'Err… I'll have what you're having, if that's OK?'

'It's more than OK, it's absolutely fine.' Charles turned back to the hovering bar tender. 'Two more large Gordon's with tonic,' he said. 'Ice and lemon?' he asked the young man.

'Err... thanks. Ice and lemon would be great,' came the gruff response.

Maybe we'll get him to say more than 'err', thought Charles, grinning inwardly. He glanced at the young man's hands, now devoid of the glass. A gruff with a touch of the rough! Couldn't be better but could be tricky. He's either playing hard to get or is genuinely nervous. Well, Charles Crosby Conrad, sicko surgeon supreme, you'll just have to wait and see!

Collecting the drinks from the barman Charles made a great show of displaying the wad of notes in his wallet. Ah yes, as I thought, Gruff Rough's little eyes came out momentarily on the proverbial little stalks. I sincerely trust *his* little stalk won't be so little! Having paid for the drinks and collected his change, Charles nodded towards a vacant table and chairs in one of the shadowy corners. With what could only be described as a shambling gait, the young man dutifully followed.

'Right,' said Charles, making himself comfortable, 'Here's to you... I didn't get your name, but then you haven't introduced yourself!' he added lightly.

'Dave, Dave Griggs. Pleased to meet you Andrew. And err... thanks again for the drink.' Dave shifted uncomfortably in his chair.

'Is anything wrong, Dave?' questioned Charles solicitously. 'You don't seem very relaxed.'

'Are you picking me up?' came the blurted reply.

'No,' replied Charles calmly. 'I've simply offered you a drink as you seemed a nice guy. And, as you appeared to be here by yourself, the same as I am, I thought it would be rather pleasant to have someone join me for a drink.' He leaned forward in a confidential manner. 'I'm here in London for a business convention. I've had a long, long tough day of meetings and I have an even tougher one tomorrow morning.' He gave a soft chuckle. 'I've left my business associates back at the hotel. They're obviously planning a night out in some strip joint in Soho; but that's not really my scene.'

'So you *are* gay?'

'Well, this is a well-known gay venue, Dave, so I would have thought it fairly obvious. Why, aren't you?'

The young man gave Charles an agonised expression. 'Andrew,' he said gruffly, looking Charles directly in the eye. 'Andrew,' he repeated even more gruffly. 'Aw, shit, Andrew, I don't really know!'

Charles almost spilled his drink. 'You *don't* know?' he asked, his voice and expression incredulous.

'No, I don't,' said Dave, almost defiantly. He gave Charles an imploring look. 'Look, Andrew,' he said, his face a darkening to a deep crimson. 'You look a nice guy, an understanding guy... someone a person one can talk to.' The young man took a deep breath. 'I *think* I'm gay even though I've a regular girlfriend and all that; but I know one or two guys who are gay and the more I see them together, the more I feel drawn to them.'

'And you've never had a gay experience?' Charles could not believe his luck and could hardly wait to relay the ensuing conversation later to Ethelred and Clytemnestra in his scheduled telephone call.

'No,' said Dave. He gave Charles and anguished look. 'That's why I'm here,' he added hoarsely. 'Steve and Ray – the two gay lads I know – have mentioned this place once or twice. They say all sorts come here, young and old. I don't know if they were trying to get a message across to me but... err... well, here I am.' He took a nervous sip. 'They said lads come here and err... sell their favours.' Dave went an even deeper red, adding, 'When I saw you flashing your wallet like you did back at the bar, I thought that's what you were doing; trying to hire me!'

'Dave! Dave!' laughed Charles. 'That's the last thing that was on my mind.' He gave the visibly relaxing young man a broad smile. 'Look, I need to take a pee. Order another round and let's talk some more.' Charles gave an encouraging smile. 'You're great company, you know!'

'I am?' said Dave with a tremulous smile.

'Yes, even though you may not know it! Look, here's a tenner, take it and get us a round and no, Dave, I'm not trying to hire or rent you for a mere tenner! Go on, off you go, before I piss my pants!'

Charles returned to find Dave back at the table with the replenished drinks. Raising his glass Charles silently toasted the nervously smiling young man before resuming their conversation. 'What do you do, Dave, if you don't mind me asking?'

'I used to work for a landscape gardening contractor before I was made redundant all thanks to this sodding recession and all that crap.' grunted Dave. He looked at Charles despondently. 'I've been odd jobbing for the past few months as I want none of that dole shit. I'm now thinking of maybe joining up or something; anything to get myself going again.' He took another sip. 'And what do you do, Andrew?'

'Me? I'm in public relations,' laughed Charles. 'At present I'm here for a convention concerning the promotion of films various for next year's Berlin Film Festival.'

'Film festival? Sounds very glamorous,' said Dave. He gave a light laugh. 'I once worked on a garden design for a well-known movie actress' – he mentioned a household name – 'who turned out to be a total cow and never paid us our final bill! That's the nearest I even got to that sort of glamour, and you can stuff it as far as I'm concerned!'

'Well, I don't work for any movie stars. I actually work with a highly regarded director which is very, very different.' Charles pointed at their empty glasses. 'Why not get us another round whilst I make a quick phone call. I've had an idea.'

While Dave manoeuvred his way through to the now busy bar Charles quickly took out his mobile. Ethelred answered on the first ring. 'Bull's-eye!' whispered Charles, 'Doppelganger perfection! I'm bringing him down tomorrow. This is too good a chance to miss. You've just got yourself a landscape gardener-cum-boy babe! The girl will have to wait!'

'Double bull's-eye!' came the reply. 'Monday has found the perfect girl, at Tescos in Windsor of all places! She's agreed to a drink with him tomorrow evening at some pub in the old town. To quote Monday Man, "dem eyes were a bogglin' at da Monday monster!"'

'Trust Monday. Listen, can't talk, I'll call you later. Dirk's double is on his way back.'

'Where are you staying?' asked Charles having taking a long sip from his fresh glass.

'Oh, here and there,' replied Dave. 'At the moment I'm in a temporary bed and breakfast in Bayswater.'

'What about your friends, Steve and Ray, can't they put you up?' Charles resisted a snigger at the unintentional innuendo. 'I mean, they must be concerned about you?'

'Oh, I hardly ever see them,' murmured Dave. 'They're too wrapped up in their own world. They own a flower shop in Clapham – that's how I met them – through the business. Besides, I wouldn't want to intrude into their personal lives.'

'Well,' replied Charles, 'as I said to you a few minutes ago before you went to fetch the drinks, I had an idea. I made a quick call to Ethelred, Ethelred Jones, my client, a well-known film director and, as I thought, they're short of help apropos the gardens on their estate. How about having a look, say tomorrow, and – if you feel it may be suitable – give it a try before you do something as rash as joining up and getting yourself blown to bits in Afghanistan or some equally hideous shit hole?'

'What, a job as a landscape gardener?' Dave's face took on an almost ethereal glow.

'Well, not quite a landscape gardener but a gardener. However, I'm sure you would be able to make your own artistic mark!'

'Wow!' The young man's face suddenly clouded over. 'What's the catch?'

'Catch? Why should there be a catch? You're an out of work gardener and my business associate needs a gardener. End of story.'

'Do you live with him?'

'I stay in the same house as him. But Dave, to put your mind at rest, Ethelred is married to a beautiful and quite famous artist, Clytemnestra Jones and, more to the point, they have an enchanting little daughter called Trisomy. Does that answer your question?'

'Err... sorry, Andrew,' Dave gave Charles a sheepish look. 'It just seems too good to be true. Half an hour ago I was feeling depressed and desperate; Jesus, I was even about to join the fucking army! Oh, pardon!' Dave put his large hand to his mouth. 'I didn't mean to swear!'

'I have heard – and do use – the fuck word myself!' laughed Charles. 'So, can I take that as a yes or would you like to think about it over dinner?'

'Dinner?'

'Yes dinner and why not, young Dave? Unless of course you have other plans?'

'Plans? Me? Not fucking likely!'

Charles could not help but be amused; from minding to effing and blinding in one easy lesson. Oh, dear, hunky, handsome but thicko Dave, what a gullible, loveable oaf you're turning out to be. 'So, why not have some dinner? Then, if it's not too late and you've made up your mind we can call Ethelred and Clyte – our private name for Clytemnestra – and let them know. Furthermore, you may as well travel back down to Bethlem Báthory with me tomorrow after my final meeting; unless of course you have some loose ends to tie up?'

'My loose ends are simply a case back at the doss house in Bayswater!'

'Fine. If you do decide to take Ethelred up on his offer, I can collect you and your case from there in the morning. So, getting back to my invitation, dinner or no dinner?'

'Dinner would be great. Err... thank you Andrew. Thank you!'

'My pleasure, smiled Charles thinking, What *is* wrong with the youth of today when it comes to conversational basics? We began with 'ohmigod' Oswald and now we have an 'err' Dave. Christ almighty! Instead, he said, 'What do you feel like eating? Steak? Chinese? Japanese? Indian? You name it!'

'As you're the host, you choose!' came the quick reply.

'Have you ever been to Balans?'

'Balans? No, why is it one of those?'

'By one of those I take it you mean Chinese, Japanese or Indian? No, it's not "one of those" in such terms, but it is one of *those* if by any chance you were implying *gay.*'

'I've never been to a *gay* restaurant before,' snapped Dave, immediately on the defensive.

'Rest assured Dave, all the *gay* restaurants I know boast such mundane necessities such as knives and forks – food even – as well as waiters, wine lists and whatever else any other *straight* restaurant may sport!' replied Charles with a teasing smile.

'Err… sorry,' muttered Dave, his handsome face starting to redden for a second time. 'I didn't mean to be rude.' He looked at Charles directly in the eye. 'Am I expected to let you fuck me for all this… the job and such?' he suddenly blurted out.

'Heavens no,' said Charles smiling sweetly. 'I expect *you* to fuck *me*!'

A momentary flash of terror crossed the young man's face. *Oh shit!* thought Charles, *that's gone and torn it.* The silly bugger is probably now going to hot foot it back to Bayswater and endless penury. 'Joke, Dave,' he said, 'Joke. Now, are we on for dinner or not? We can get a cab outside or else, instead of Balans, we can go somewhere nearby. Do you like Italian food? One of the few nationalities I didn't mention on my gastronomic tour!'

'Italian's great!'

'Terrific.' Charles quickly sussed out Dave's dress, neatly pressed chinos and a compelling, tell-tale bulge, open neck shirt and a light weight, cotton jacket. 'In fact, there are one or two very pleasant Italian restaurants within walking distance. As it's a mild night do you mind a ten to fifteen minute walk down to Mount Street? There's a very good, fun family run Italian there called Serafino. Shall we try that?'

'Sounds great,' said Dave.

Thank Christ we're at least adding 'great' to the repertoire, mused Charles. 'Right then, shall we go? Again, it'll be easy for you to get the underground back to Bayswater,' he added as a reassuring afterthought.

Dinner in the warm, stylish, restaurant proved to be agreeable than Charles had expected. Aided and abetted by several glasses of Pinot Grigio to accompany their starter of Antipasto Di Mare, followed by a bottle of Chianti to wash down a delicious Osso Bucco served with a saffron risotto, Dave had shown himself to be both amusing as well as good natured plus, as Charles was quick to note, also gullible and certainly naive. It was when they were toying with their after dinner Sambucas, Dave dropped his bombshell. Feeling under the table for Charles's bony knee he gave it a tentative squeeze and said with a gulp, 'If you want me to fuck you, Andrew, I'd like to give it a try!'

Charles looked at the earnest young man sitting opposite him. 'You *what*?'

'If you want me to fuck you I'm up for it. I mean… oh shit!' Dave gave Charles's knee another squeeze, 'You know what I mean and yes, Andrew, I'd also like to accept the job offer if it's still on.'

'Dave, Dave,' laughed Charles. 'Let's do things accordingly.' Glancing to ensure he wouldn't be a disturbance to any fellow diners, he took out his mobile. 'It's not too late to call Ethelred and Clyte and tell them the good news. It also gives you a chance to introduce yourself. Hold on a sec… Red, Dave has said yes to your kind offer. Yes, we're just finishing off dinner and then he'll be catching his train back to Bayswater. I'll collect him and his belongings after my early meeting which means we could be down in time for a late lunch. Great. Now say hello to your new landscape gardener!'

'Dave?' Ethelred's deep, friendly rumble came clearly over the phone. 'Trust Charles Andrew' – the use of the two names had been decided earlier so as to cause minimum confusion should there be a slip up on Charles's part – 'to find me a Capability Brown in between promoting my latest movie. The man's a genius.' He gave a warm laugh. 'We look forward to seeing you tomorrow then around lunch time. It'll give you some time to relax and check out your new surroundings. Who knows, you could take an instant dislike to the place and demand we put you on the next train back to London!'

'I doubt it,' laughed Dave, his face filled with excitement. 'I tell you what err… Ethelred, I'm really looking forward to meeting you all and seeing your home. From what Andrew… err… Charles Andrew says…'

'Make it plain, Charles,' interrupted Ethelred. 'It's less confusing.'

'Right, err... from what *Charles* says, it sounds quite a place.'

'Seeing is believing and we'll be seeing you tomorrow,' replied Ethelred with a chuckle. 'Now, a few more words with Charles before you hang up, if I may.'

Charles's brief conversation with Ethelred was comprised of mainly a few grunts and several muttered 'yesses' and 'of courses.' He finally clicked off the mobile and sat smiling at the silent young man. 'You'd better nip off and catch your train then,' Charles said quietly. 'Here,' he took a small note pad plus pen from his jacket pocket. Quickly tearing off a page he wrote down the number of the hotel plus his suite extension. 'Call me first thing and let me have an address from where to collect you. I have a meeting at the Westbury at eight, but should be through by eleven at the latest.' Charles gave another small smile. 'By the time I've checked out and collected the car, I should be with you no later than noon.' He looked at the young man who seemed to have developed a visible attack of the shakes. 'Are you OK?' Charles asked anxiously, the last thing he needed was the young man suddenly being taken ill on him.

'Do you want me to come back with you and fuck you?' Dave whispered hoarsely. 'I'd like to try and also, I'd like to try and kiss you.' Bright red with embarrassment, he stammered. 'That's if you want me to! I can then collect my kit in the morning and either come back to the hotel or else meet you somewhere...'

'Are you sure about this, Dave,' said Charles softly. 'You don't have to, you know. You're under no obligation.'

'But I'd like to err... Andrew.' Dave gave a warm smile, his broad callused hand briefly touching Charles's. 'And, if you don't mind, I'm going to carry on calling you Andrew as it's become something special to me. After all, it was Andrew, not Andrew Charles who picked me up!' he added mischievously.

CHAPTER 15

'Humpy! I'm home!' Bryan gave a chuckle as he edged his way through the heavy front door of the Cadogan Square flat.

'Here, let me help you!' A smiling Miles strode across the marble tiled entrance hall. 'I was just making my way to the kitchen to make a fresh cup of coffee. Your timing couldn't have been better. You look frozen.'

'Tell me about it!' Bryan handed over a series of plastic bags. 'Sexy Rexy and Macho Michael in that open shop of theirs weren't the only cod pieces on ice!' His camp reference to the two cheerful fishmongers at the fishmongers' on Chelsea Green was greeted with an even broader smile by Miles.

'If you weren't a happily married poofter I'd be convinced you have secret – no, make that *open* – lustings after Rexy! After all you do refer to him as the Green's answer to Don Dujardin *sans* moustache but with a rod to end all fishing rods! If you do, let it be known that I have noted Macho Michael's equally attractive, eel-like attribute!'

'You wish!'

'As do you, my dearest! In your wettest of dreams! And just what did the sexy Mr. R and the Macho M offer you today?'

'I've got some fantastic turbot, salmon steaks and a couple of their dressed crab. And before you make a crack about their crabs…!' Bryan waved the bag containing several bottles of wine playfully.

'As if I would!' cut in Miles laughing. 'After all, your *crabs* are *my* crabs! Or perhaps that should be your – forgive my appalling Spanish – "your *cangrejos* are my *cangrejos*!"'

'Filthy sod!'

'That I am! That I am!' Miles glanced at the Rolex on his beefy hand. 'I say let's skip the coffee and settle for a Bloody Mary.'

'A crustacean after my own shell! A Bloody would be great and Miles dearest, don't stint on the vodka. There's a whole lot of thawing needed here.'

'Oh? I have another solution for that!'

'Keep that very obvious solution and its spray gun in your pants, maniacal "my-you've a big one" Sir Miles! I assure you this guy needs *mucho* alcohol as opposed to *el amor* at the moment!'

'Charming!'

'I am, aren't I?' camped Bryan sashaying through to the modernistic kitchen. He placed the rest of the parcels down on the centre island and began busily unpacking the rest of the bags. His hand froze as Miles, clearing his throat, said the dreaded words, 'I've been thinking…'

'Oh Miles,' cut in Bryan, spinning around and looking at his now gently smiling lover. 'I know, and so have I and yes, it's about time I cut the crap and came down to the country.' Bryan took a deep breath. 'I don't think I really could spend another weekend here in London without you. It's selfish and quite, quite unjustified.' He moved around the work top and clasped Miles around the waist. Placing a light kiss on his nose he added, 'Let's go down on Friday – I may as well get used to my role as lady of the manor but…'

'I know, I know, Bryo, no Joneses and no Oswald.'

'Thank you, Miles,' said Bryan quietly. He gave the gently smiling man a mischievous grin. 'Now, to use the much abused old adage, "who do I have to fuck to get a Bloody Mary round here?!"'

———————

Ever since the debacle of Bryan's first attempted visit to The Grove, Mile's country house near Ascot, Bryan had been hesitant at any further suggestions of a repeat performance. Despite the fact Angela and Sophie were now living in hedonistic bliss in Texas and only Miles was in residence, the stigma of the nearby presence of Oswald was still an issue.

'I could bump into him anywhere – as you did – albeit in Windsor, at the train station, wherever.' Bryan, his words spoken from between firmly gritted teeth, had been adamant. 'I simply don't want to see the little shit again.'

Miles had never dared mention Oswald's outrageous flirting at the dinner party given by Ethelred and Clytemnestra prior to Angela and Sophie's departure. His reaction to Oswald's predatory attractiveness had shaken him, and he had no wish to relive the experience. Miles had explained to Bryan his involvement in a business deal with Ethelred, an arrangement which he has passed over lightly. 'The devious bastard had spoken to me initially of buying a property in our Cinque Terre development and in the end *I* ended up a sponsor for his latest film!' Laughing, Miles added drily, 'After all is said and done and contrary to what someone like myself may think, his films are a positive gold mine and I can see myself doubling, if not trebling, my investment.' Giving a further, cynical snort, he could not resist the final denouement. 'The critics seem to worship both his and Clytemnestra's so-called artistic brilliance but – if you want my candid opinion – Ethelred's films are nothing more than sensationalist trash and her work a load of bollocks!'

Miles had dropped the subject of Bryan spending a night or a weekend at The Grove saying to himself, given time, his partner would come round to the idea. Miles and Bryan had gone through the official civil ceremony a few weeks after their initial meeting. Miles had been completely stunned when, one evening as he and Mandy Mashona were checking final details on a major property transaction, the comely black woman said gently, 'Sir Miles, the whole of office staff are in love with your Bryan and we love him even more for the happiness he has brought you! Never ever lose him.' Without a further word she had walked briskly back to her office softly closing the door to his office behind her. Miles had sat staring at the closed door for a full five minutes before buzzing for Mandy once again.

'Yes, Sir Miles?' said the motherly woman, a look of concern on her kindly face. Back in her own office Mandy had found herself fighting off a major panic attack. Had she or had she not gone too far in saying what she just said? Although having known Miles for many years he could quite likely have taken offense at such familiarity.

'How long have you known?' asked Miles, his voice barely audible.

'Oh, from the moment Bryan walked into the office that first day,' said Mandy, her face breaking into a relieved smile. She looked at Miles.

'One of my sons is gay, Sir Miles,' she added softly. 'I only hope one day he finds someone like Bryan or someone like you!'

'We're going to make it legal, Mandy,' said Miles. He looked at the beaming woman. He paused for a moment, deliberating. Suddenly he gave Mandy the most magical of smiles. 'I appreciate I haven't asked him as yet but I am sure, Bryan, like myself, would be honoured if you'd be a witness.'

'Oh Sir Miles!' gasped Mandy. 'That is *such* an honour.' Her dazzling smile became even broader. 'And I have just the hat for such an occasion!' She gave a giggle. 'It's made of pink feathers!'

'Saves Bryan or myself having to wear drag then, doesn't it?' laughed Miles with an accompanying wink. 'I take it that's a yes?'

The news about Miles and Bryan spread through the office like the proverbial wild fire. To both their surprises Mandy immediately set about organising an impromptu, small office party for the following evening where the other genuinely happy members of staff were able to toast and congratulate their lord and master and his about-to-be partner in pink champagne. However, the party had not been a complete surprise – Mandy having to make sure Miles and Bryan were free for the celebration – and Miles, in turn, having booked a celebratory table for all his staff at the Ritz.

'The Ritz! Why Sir Miles, it's been a dream of mine since I could remember!' Mandy cried.

'Well Mandy, as they say, dreams can and do come true!' replied Miles's with a smile.

————

'Here we are.' Miles turned to look at Bryan sitting alongside him in the passenger seat of the Jaguar. He took his left hand off the steering wheel and squeezed Bryan's knee affectionately. 'Hopefully, one day Bryo, we'll both be able to say "Home Sweet Home."'

Bryan gave a nervous smile as the car slowed down before turning left between a pair of elegant white painted pillars, the gates open and welcoming. He looked cautiously at the long gravelled drive bordered by a neatly clipped yew hedge. 'Your first view,' continued Miles in a nervous voice, completely alien to his usual robust tones.

'Miles, it's stunning!' Bryan turned to look at his lover, his face bursting into a smile. 'I had no idea… and a lake!' He turned again to look at the view through the windscreen as Miles slowly brought the car to a halt. 'It's like some magical film setting!' He gestured towards the elegant, white building, partly reflected in the placid blue water of a small lake. Adding to the magic of the sunny mid-morning scene were several white swans gliding lazily on the mirror-like surface, their reflections like white-sailed inverted boats.

Miles gave a relieved laugh. 'If you consider this view spectacular, wait until you see the house from the *front*! The original owner apparently was forced to accept the lake when an old underground stream decided to collapse, thus forming the indentation which inspired what we're looking at today.' Accelerating slowly he continued along the long sweeping drive carrying them past the side of the house and into a wide open gravelled front.

'It get's even better,' murmured an enchanted Bryan, 'if that's even remotely possible.' He turned again to an openly smiling Miles. 'Is this really ours?'

'Yes Bryo, *ours*.' Miles gestured towards the striking three story building with its elegant pillared portico, bordered on either side by a phalanx of tall, sash windows.

'Who was the architect?' questioned Bryan, his face now alight with excitement. 'I mean, Milo, it's just so bloody *perfect*!'

'*Milo*? That's a first and I like it!' Miles gave another laugh. 'You're making me sound very Oscar Wilde-ish!'

'I am?'

'Very "Importance of Being Ernest!" Am I to be Miles in town and Milo in the country?'

'Why not? As long as it doesn't ever stop me from being your Bosie!'

'Touché, my Bosie Bryo!'

'Bosie Byro?' Bryan made an expression of mock horror before gesturing towards the open front door where the tall, stork-like Dodds had suddenly appeared. 'I therefore take it that's your equivalent to Jack Worthing's Merriman, the butler?'

Miles gave an approving look. 'I'm impressed, Byro, very impressed. You certainly know your Wilde.'

'I wasn't the prettiest Gwendolyn Fairfax for nothing in my heady schooldays!' camped Bryan in return.

'Well then, you'd better get your pretty arse moving, *Gwendolyn*, and come and meet the man who will be bringing us breakfast for the next trillion weekends!'

'Oh *Jack*!' replied Bryan with a camp, high-pitched squeak. He gave another laugh. 'Better butch it up for the Merriman lookalike – what is Storky the stork's name by the way?'

'Storky? Oh, I see what you mean. That, my darling Byro, is Dodds.'

'Does Dodds have any inkling I'm his new mistress?'

'I think when he's told to unpack your bag in my rooms he'll quickly get the gist!'

A solemn Dodds greeted Miles with a differential nod. 'This is Mr. Bryan,' said a no nonsense Miles to the elderly retainer. 'He'll be living here at The Grove with me from now on.'

'Very good sir,' said Dodds. Without blinking an eye he held out his hand for Bryan's small case. 'I take it then that Mr. Bryan's case will be taken to your rooms, sir?'

'Exactly Dodds.'

'Thank you, sir.' He gave Bryan a flicker of a smile. 'Welcome to The Grove, sir,' he intoned politely. 'I hope you'll be very happy here.' Turning to Miles he announced. 'I have set out the requested drinks in the morning room, sir. Lunch will be served in half an hour.'

'Thank you Dodds, that sound's perfect.'

'Thank *you*, sir and you too, sir.' Giving another discreet nod of his grey head, the elderly man took his leave.

'You never told me your butler was a raving old queen!' giggled Bryan as he followed Charles into the light, airy morning room. 'Never mind Dobbs, he's pure Hobson!'

'Hobson? Bryo, forgive me but you're starting to confuse this new Milo who's starting to feel the token country bumpkin!' He handed Bryan a glass of wine poured from a bottle nestling in a welcoming ice bucket.

'Hobson, the butler played by John Gielgud in "Arthur." Gielgud was more regal than our own living, breathing ER!'

'Jesus…' muttered Miles, 'Christ knows what you'll come up with when you meet Mrs. Turnbull, the cook.'

'I can't wait… oi! What the hell do you think you're doing?' He cried as a laughing Miles suddenly grabbed him and, smothering his face with kisses carried him back out through the morning room door which he had inadvertently opened during their ensuing conversation. Walking back through the open door, Miles kicked it closed once more before giving Bryan another hug and a resounding kiss. 'There!' he said triumphantly. 'As I couldn't really carry you over the threshold in front of poor old Dodds, I've simply had to make do with the door to the morning room!'

'God, I love you Milo!' laughed Bryan, kissing Miles firmly on the mouth.

'And I love you, my darling Bosie Byro!' laughed Miles.

'Does love mean never having to answer my former question?' asked Bryan archly, loosely adapting the famous line from 'Love Story.'

'What former question?' Miles gave the young man a whimsical smile. 'I didn't think there were any questions to be answered?'

'The name of the architect to our homo heaven, you twit!'

Dobbs, hearing the cries and scuffling sounds from behind the closed door discreetly refrained from knocking. Returning to the kitchen he said sonorously to the intrigued Mrs. Turnbull. 'I wouldn't bother with the soufflé for at least half an hour, Mrs. T. I think Sir Miles and young Mr. Bryan will be otherwise engaged for at least that, if not a few minutes more in addition."

'Well, I don't know. I 'preciate it's the twenty first century an' all that, but at times…' muttered Mrs. Turnbull. Glancing at the eggs and grated cheese waiting to receive her magic touch, she gave the elderly butler an impish smile. 'A gin, whilst we wait, Mr. D?'

'I don't see why not, Mrs. T! You sit down and I'll do the honours.'

With two large gin and tonics in their hands the two sat comfortably at the large kitchen table. Without hesitation the cook asked outright, 'So, this young man, Mr. D? What's your opinion? When I asked that Mrs. Mashona which guest room Mary was to get ready for our visitor, she seemed a bit confused so it was easy to put two and two together!' Mrs. Turnbull gave a giggle, 'Two and two? Oh, aren't I a wicked one, Mr. D?' Taking another sip of her gin she licked her lips before repeating her question, 'Your opinion then on this Mr. Bryan?'

'A perfectly pleasant young man, Mrs. T and I think you'll approve. Nothing like that nasty one your sister has had to put up with at the other house.' Dodds shook his head. 'My, my, but what family shenanigans we've had to put up with at The Grove,' he said. 'First we have her ladyship cavorting here, there and everywhere with that black man and now we have his nibs cavorting with a young man. Heaven knows what Miss Sophie has been getting up to.'

'Oh, no doubt she's been up to no good with that Miss Susannah.' Mrs. Turnbull gave a knowing nod. 'It would round it all up perfectly, wouldn't it. Lady Ansturther with the big black man; Sir Miles behaving like all them lot do, that Lord Montagu and what's the other one? The one with the name like that Christine Keeler's friend? Mandy something-or-other?'

'Mandelson, Peter Mandelson.'

'That's him. They're all doing it. Even getting married.' The large woman gave a gasp. 'You don't think…?'

'Nothing would surprise me, Mrs. T.' Dodds took a sip of gin. 'In fact, not only are they both wearing wedding rings but Sir Miles even carried the young man back *out* of the morning room before carrying him back *in* again! Over the threshold so to speak!'

'Well, I never!' gasped Mrs. Turnbull, fanning herself with her hand. 'I can't *wait* to tell Nanette! There, *she's* got the doctor doing *it* with that dreadful actor, but I think Sir Miles, *married*, caps it all.'

'Shall we attempt the soufflé now, do you think, Mrs. T?'

'Oh, the soufflé can wait,' giggled the comely cook. 'Let them celebrate their homecoming while we have another gin!'

Having duly served the delayed soufflé followed by a delicious Sole Veronique, Mrs. Turnbull was duly summoned to the dining room to meet Bryan.

'Christ Milo, I feel as if I'm about to face the Inquisition!' Bryan whispered as Dodds left to collect the cook.

'So? *Your* opinion then, Mrs. T?' This from Dodds after the two of them had returned to the kitchen.

Mrs. Turnbull's enthusiasm for Bryan almost outshone that of Mandy Mashona. 'He's *lovely*, Mr. D! Positively lovely and my, don't they make a handsome couple!'

Miles was later to murmur into Bryan's ear as they lay cuddled up together in bed later that night, 'I thought you'd like to know Mrs. Turnbull said to me if she was a young girl again, she'd be after you in a flash!' He gave a gentle nibble to Bryan's earlobe. 'Furthermore, she went on to say you're going to bring sparkle back to The Grove – that was the very word she used, "sparkle" – and how right she is, my dearest, darling Byro!'

'Robert Adam! Tell me it's Robert Adam!'

'What?'

'The architect for The Grove! Tell me it's Robert!'

'Ah, I see I've now got a rival after all!'

'I'll have to think about that,' muttered Bryan sleepily. 'Although Robert Adam maybe perfectly proportioned, I don't think he could ever equate to the utterly, *utterly* perfect proportions of the Anstruther cock!'

'Thank God for small mercies!'

'If *that* is a small mercy, Sir Miles, please spare me a bigger one!"

———————

Miles and Bryan returned to London early Sunday evening, both to attend a charity performance organised by a friend of Miles to help the fight against Aids in Africa. The evening event was to feature a black South African pianist by the intriguing name of Stringer Chord. 'I've never heard of him,' Bryan had to confess. 'It's quite a story,' had been Miles's mysterious reply.

Stringer Chord's forte was classical music with a decidedly African inspired makeover, the handsome pianist being accompanied by three young men blowing traditional penny whistles, and a drummer beating out exotic rhythms on a set of hollow logs. Stringer and his group's rendition of 'L'amour,' the famous love song from Bizet's opera, 'Carmen,' a wild, pulsating erotic cacophony of unbelievable sounds received the first of several standing ovations. Desmond, the friend and organiser, had organised an after concert supper at his palatial house in Tregunter Road, a tree lined road of elegant, detached houses in Chelsea. Miles had made an attempt to prepare Bryan for what he was about to see but nothing could have described what he witnessed.

'Christ, Miles,' Bryan said on their return to Cadogan Square. 'Thank God for this sane, stylish but still spectacular place and thank you, God, also for The Grove and its *pure,* pure magic!' Giving his lover a warm hug he could not resist continuing, 'But how on earth does one even begin to describe what could only be a technicolored combination of Bollywood meets The Sun King on acid?'

'One doesn't!' laughed Miles. 'If you're in to gilt, smilt, Jewey Louis, Yiddisher Renaissance, lurex, lamé, velvet, marble and mayhem, you're only starting to see the tip of the iceberg! But Desmond loves it.'

'He obviously does in order to live voluntarily amidst all that grotesque, glittery shittery as opposed to good old fashioned, normal campery!' laughed Bryan. 'Although I wasn't at all surprised by his changing out of his dinner jacket into drag, I do think he should have tried to get his Carmens correct!'

'I totally agree,' laughed Miles, pouring them each a large Courvoisier brandy, 'Somehow Carmen Miranda is not quite the same as Carmen from Seville!'

'Especially when accompanied by penny whistles, bongos and a harp! Where oh where did Desmond find a harpist who could play a harp using a dildo for the plucking?!' Bryan gave a chuckle. 'And where oh where did you ever find Desmond is more of an intriguing question.'

'You'll never believe it, my dearest, through my ex-wife Angela! Desmond's the brother of one of her old school friends.'

'He's obviously loaded.'

'Loaded? Think tankers.' Miles mentioned a giant shipping conglomerate. 'That's Desmond's little lot.'

'And what does his family think of his err…eccentricities? I mean, the house for starters; never mind the half-naked caterers, those parrots in their neon strip cages – bars of coloured neon for Chrissake! – and let's not forget the two chimpanzees in gold trousers with matching boleros and turbans.'

'Hmm…' said Miles thoughtfully, a mischievous glint in his eye. 'Yes, I suppose you could say it is a bit different…!'

'Different? As I said, I think it'll take me several days to come down.' Bryan gave a laugh. 'I take it amidst all that kitsch shit there exists a lover.'

'You met him.'

'I did?'

'Yes, Stringer Chord. All that South African nonsense is a load of bollocks. Stringer, alias Basil, is from Peckham!' Miles gave a laugh. 'Good PR, though, don't you agree!'

'I was certainly fooled.' Bryan gave a laugh. 'And the penny whistle players and the drummer? Don't tell me…'

'Croydon as opposed Peckham!'

'Thank Christ for that. For a moment I thought you were going to say something normal like Soweto and then I really would have been thrown!' Bryan gave Miles a warm smile. 'May I suggest something, Sir Miles?'

'Of course, m'lady.'

'When we come back from the country next weekend, may we simply have supper locally or stay in and watch a DVD?'

'What sort of DVD, my love?'

'Anything that's Hollywood and not Bollywood!'

'Your wish is my command; now how about another nightcap before retiring?'

'I wonder? Do they have nightcaps in Bollywood?'

'More likely nightmares!' replied Miles's drily.

———————

While Miles and Bryan were quietly sipping their brandies and relaxing in each other's company, a totally different scenario had been taking place in Ethelred's study at Bethlem Báthory, where an amused Monday was regaling both Ethelred, Clytemnestra, Charles and a riveted Oswald with the latest kitchen gossip.

'So our Miles has gone and gotten himself a he-bride,' chuckled Ethelred. 'Good for him, is all I can say!'

'And he's actually gone through a civil ceremony with this young man?' questioned a stunned Clytemnestra.

'According to Nanette, Dora or Mrs. Turnbull, her sister who, as you know just happens to be the cook at The Grove, says not only are they sharing the same bedroom but they're both wearing wedding bands! Furthermore' – Monday could barely control a deep, rumbling laugh – 'the passionate groom, namely Sir Miles, was witnessed by the ever vigilant Dobbs *carrying the young man across the threshold to the morning room*!'

Clytemnestra could not restrain herself from uttering a shriek of pure delight. 'I love it, simply love it!' she cried. Looking at Oswald who was sitting alongside Monday on the adjacent sofa, she gave the startled young man a friendly smile, her first genuine smile since their debacle concerning Claudia Cordelle. 'Oswald dear, as an authority on the subject, did your perceptive antennae ever detect a vibration or hint of Miles being gay? Had you any idea?'

Oswald, always one to relish being the centre of attention gave a small preen. 'Well, if you must know, I did get a very strong hint at the station the day of my first visit, when I unfortunately bumped his car but' – he paused dramatically for his final denouement – 'all I can say is the night they were all here for dinner – just before Lady A and the sullen Sophie left for the States – Sir Miles *simply* wouldn't stop playing footsie, footsie with me under the table!'

'Talk about team work!' laughed Ethelred drily.

'Teamwork?' This again from Clytemnestra.

'Teamwork,' repeated Ethelred with a grin. 'Monday being the one half of the team working above the table on the oh so innocent Angela, and Miles working below the table on our equally innocent Oswald!'

The five burst out into of laughter.

'And it's teamwork with a vengeance too, or so I believe. The new Lady Anstruther just happens to be a member – and I use that term deliberately – of Miles's work force. Tut tut, Miles,' he added with another guffaw. 'Don't you know it's unfair to being your work back home with you in the evening.'

More laughter filled the room.

'Have we any idea as to whom this young paragon is?' asked Clytemnestra with a chortle.

'Not really,' smiled Monday. 'All Dora, Nanette's sister was able to divulge is that his name is Bryan – and to quote the usually uninspired Dora Turnbull – he has movie star looks and is a total charmer!'

'Good on Miles,' said Charles with a smile. Giving Clytemnestra a sly glance he couldn't resist adding snidely, 'From what your friend Claudia Cordelle tells you, this Bryan with a Y must be one very accommodating young man!'

Oswald, being privy to the very conversation where this gem had been divulged, couldn't resist a snigger.

'There's no question about it,' laughed Clytemnestra. 'Now we simply have no choice but to have them both to dinner *tout de suite*!' she added with a mischievous smile.

'And I can't wait to see what I've gone and been ditched for!' giggled Oswald. 'Talk about foot loose and *nancy* free!'

'*That*, young Oswald,' laughed Ethelred, 'was really truly awful!' Giving the young man a wide grin he added. 'So awful in fact that I think we all deserve another drink! Monday Man, if you'd do the honours.'

As Monday set about replenishing the glasses Oswald sat inwardly seething. *Fucking parasitic intruder,* he thought. *I saw Miles Anstruther first and now he's come out, I'm homing in! So, Bryan, office slag or whatever your pathetic claim to fame, if I have anything to do with it your days as chatelaine to maison Miles are well and truly numbered.*

To Clytemnestra's chagrin any subsequent invitations to dinner were politely turned down by Miles. 'It's very sweet of you, Clytemnestra,' he said, 'but Bryan and I are not quite ready to throw ourselves to the wolves, so to speak. What he and I will be doing is having a welcome dinner for him here at The Grove in due course.'

Miles, knowing Bryan's total horror at meeting up with Oswald, was determined to keep the two apart for as long as possible. Unbeknown to him and Bryan, while continuing to refuse all dinner invitations to Bethlem Báthory, Oswald had already taken his final curtain call.

CHAPTER 16

'Don't you think it's going to be a bit awkward, Charles's new bit being here and we haven't even shot the snuff scene or worked out exactly what this "Dave the Rave" is going to be filmed doing?' An anxious Euros, sitting across from Ethelred in his study, eyed the director warily. Having worked with Ethelred for many years he had, at times, to firmly rein in his employer when Ethelred began to give out visible signs of becoming over enthusiastic. 'I can see there's no problem with Miss Tesco,' Euros continued. 'Monday can get her along here at the drop of his pants – but this new lad? I'm not very happy about him being around the place; particularly when we're shooting our major scene.'

'The lad will be doing exactly what he's being brought down to do. He's been offered the position of gardener and gardening is what he will be doing until his other services are required.' Ethelred gave the anxious cameraman a reassuring smile. 'Leave the worrying up to me, my friend. Oswald's demise will be filmed on a closed set in the strictest confines of the studio basement, and nobody, but nobody, apart from myself, Monday, Charles – you obviously – plus Kevin, will be on set. Clyte will be working in her studio – Mrs. Norelle will be serving her lunch as on a normal day, and Charles will have made sure Tris will be having a longer than usual lie in. Charles will be on set with his eager – we hope – suitably err… enhanced little friends. Meanwhile the Monday Man, after an initial introductory walk around the grounds, the various gardens and the greenhouses, will have given the new boy a list as long as your arm and sent him off on a day's shopping spree to the garden centre in Reading. Charles assures me the young man is not only desperately keen to be employed, but determined to impress! It'll just be our bad luck and good old Sod's Law he turns out to be a bloody good gardener, and just what Dr Green Fingers ordered!'

'Dr Green Fingers?'

'A joke, Euros dear, simply a little "in" joke. Monday's always banging on saying he needs an extra hand – ha! – albeit this one *is* the answer to Mon's fervent prayer for a Dr Green Fingers or not, he is simply doomed to end up an used, abused, stuffed extra! But let's forget all that, for now he'll be at Dobbies Garden Centre where he will be spending most of his away day. If we begin shooting around nine we should have the whole scenario wrapped up within a couple of hours.' He gave the sceptical Euros a reassuring smile. 'It'll be a piece of cake, Euros, a lovely, very *rich* piece of cake for us all to *stuff* our faces with!'

Ignoring Ethelred's weak attempt at making light of any complications, Euros, an even deeper frown cutting through his usually jovial expression, continued. 'Is it vital that this new face comes down with Charles today?'

'Vital or not, it's a bit late as they are already on their way down from London.'

'Shit!' said Euros.

'No shit!' shot back Ethelred. 'Total shit, if you catch my drift!'

Euros couldn't help but join his employer in an uncontrollable burst of chuckles.

Dave Grigg's arrival at Bethlem Báthory was the complete antithesis to that of Oswald's a few months earlier. Having been subsequently introduced to Mrs. Norelle and Monday, he was shown his quarters, a small but comfortable flat set in an annexe behind the garages. It was here Boris also resided while other members of staff lived away from the property. Dave did not meet Ethelred and Clytemnestra until the day after his arrival, and only briefly; Charles having formally introduced the young man to the two in a short interview which took place in Ethelred's study.

'Err... a bit weird those two,' commented Dave after the stilted meeting. He added quickly. 'Please don't get me wrong, Andrew. The place is great and both Monday and Mrs. Norelle seem very nice.' He gave Charles a warm smile. 'But best of all, I'm here with you! See you after I've tried out the power shower!'

Charles's heart momentarily soared only to come crashing down again. *Oh please, please don't let this develop any further,* he thought sadly.

It would be so unfair if young Dave could have been the answer to my prayers, a genuine young man who actually likes me for myself. Shaking himself out of his reverie, he muttered reprovingly, 'No, the film's the thing and even more important, the vast amount of money I'm about to make. With all my organ donations this will be mega so pull yourself together, Doctor Charles Crosby. There are plenty more fish in the sea even though this one seems to be a particular rare species of *marine* life!'

Mrs. Norelle saw to it the small kitchen had been stocked with what she deemed 'necessities' meaning Dave, on his first evening in residence, was able to cook himself a substantial fry-up comprised of eggs, sausages, tomatoes, baked beans and toast. Cans of lager and a bottle of wine had also been placed in the small fridge. Mrs. Norelle, having taken an immediate liking to the quiet, polite young man, quickly arranged a shopping trip with her and Monday into Windsor the next day after 'your meeting with Mr. and Mrs. Jones.'

'We'll 'ave a proper stockin' up for you, young Dave,' she announced, 'an' furthermore I'll make sure you 'ave one or two cottage pies and some of my special apple crumble to put in the freezer.' Mrs. Norelle showed him the laundry room and the large fridge freezer to the main kitchen. 'It's all 'ere,' she said, 'so 'elp yourself. We can't 'ave a growing lad like you working on an empty stomach, now can we?' She gave the smiling young man a sly wink. 'An' if you sweet talk our Viola, I'm sure you'll suddenly find all your laundry mysteriously taken care of!'

Oswald, having been vaguely informed a new gardener-cum-bit player had arrived at the house immediately went into super star mode. Hearing Dave had been consigned to the staff annexe and would not be joining those living in the main house for any meals, his smugness had been paramount. 'I'll acknowledge him should I meet him in the grounds,' he grandly announced to a disapproving Viola and Mrs. Norelle. Turning to Charles, Oswald added witheringly, 'Perhaps I'll allow you to introduce him to me when I see him on the set. As star of the film one has to remember one's position.'

Charles, pretending to be shocked by his former protégée's behaviour and being reminded as to the importance of Oswald's role in the forthcoming production, had gleefully reported the incident to a bemused Ethelred and Clytemnestra.

'What a cuntish little prick!' snarled Ethelred, his thin lips curling in distaste.

'That, my darling is not only a contradiction, it's a fucking understatement!' said a smirking Clytemnestra.

'Well, if it keeps them apart, so much the better,' growled Ethelred in response.

Although set to fly up to Scotland the next afternoon for meetings regarding the Festival, Ethelred had, to his chagrin and relief, been informed that due to the sudden sickness of one of the key figures, the meeting would have to be postponed until the following week, the week planned for the major filming. His decision was immediate.

'We have no alternative but to bring the whole programme forward by a few days.' he announced to a hastily summonsed Charles. 'Can you also find Monday and get him over here ASAP to co-ordinate what now has no alternative but to be a completely rescheduled programme? I suggest we get the new boy over to Reading day after tomorrow. Then we can sit back and relax for a day or two before we do out final shots with this Dave and the Tesco tart.'

'I'll go and fetch Monday,' said Charles quietly. He stood silently for a moment, as if to say something but, making a visible effort, pulled himself together and strode purposefully from the room.

'Oh dear,' said Clytemnestra, 'are you thinking what I'm thinking?'

'It's fairly obvious, isn't it, Cupid – the silly little cunt – couldn't have chosen a worse time to let fly one of his fucking little arrows, could he?'

'And I think, Red dearest, the little shit's scored a bull's-eye!'

'Fuck!' said Ethelred for want of a better word.

'Well, you've just said it; we can always sit back and relax for a day or two, while darling Dave plays at being Mary, Mary, quite contrary, and poor Charles goes off again and finds yet another gilded youth!'

'Let's cross that bridge when we come to it.'

'I think we're already crossing it and, if I were you Ethelred, my love, I'd tell Unka Charles – without further delay – his boy wonder is *not* going the way of all flesh but will be remaining, wholesome and unscathed, in our bizarre Garden of Eden.' Clytemnestra gave a laugh. 'I predict two happy serpents, once our very bad apple has been well and truly disposed of.' She nodded towards the doorway. 'They're here. Tell you what; I'll lure Monday over to the bar while you have a quick word in Charles's shell-like.' She gave her husband a light push. 'Go on, Mr. Big Director, make someone's day! Make our Charles a happy St Sebastian as he positively bristles with masochistic delight at the thought of all those deep, deep arrows! Make him very, very – even ecstatically – happy!'

'You really think so?'

'Yes, I really think so! Make old Buggeranthos's day!' chortled Clytemnestra; her reference to one of the leading characters in John Wilmot's play, 'Sodom,' causing Ethelred to break into a mischievous smile. Both he and Clytemnestra had given most of the employees at Bethlem Báthory nicknames taken from the notorious play by John Wilmot, the Earl of Rochester, a member of the court of Charles the Second in the seventeenth century. Boris was otherwise known as Bolloxinion, the King of Sodom; Mrs. Norelle as Cuntigatia, his Queen and Viola as Cunticula, a Maid of Honour – or Dishonour – as the two preferred to call her. Monday, being big, black, butch plus more ante bellum and pure nineteenth century, simply remained Mandingo.

'Charles? A quick word while Clyte and Mon mix the inevitable pitcher for us as we have a lot of talking to do…'

'Yes Red?' Charles's looked at his colleague with – as Ethelred would later relate to Clytemnestra – the saddest pair of eyes he had ever seen.

'I've been having second thoughts and young Dave is *not* going to be asked to take part in "Still Life." I and Clyte think it best for you and all of us if he stays on as our regular gardener instead. Monday says he's a born natural and as we already know, his former employers are a company held in the greatest of prestige.' Ethelred gave a quiet smile. 'Mrs. Norelle, Viola and even the brusque Boris are already in love with young Dave.' He added teasingly, 'As perhaps even you, Charles; if only a teensy weensy bit!'

An overwhelmed and relieved Charles burst into tears.

'I only hope we haven't made a dreadful mistake and misjudged this lad,' Ethelred was to say to Clyte as they lay in bed later that night.

'If we've made a mistake you can always splice him – literally – into the film at a later date if necessary,' murmured his wife sleepily.

'Mm… yes, I suppose I could.'

'They have woodchip machines in woods…' muttered Clytemnestra starting to stroke Ethelred's slowly swelling penis.

'Mm,' said her husband, 'And talking of such, why don't I just go and stick this rather large, very hard old log into a certain woodchip machine. That's if you're game.'

'Oh, I'm game alright,' came the soft reply, 'Goodness, what a big log you have Mr. Lumberjack. I could have some difficulty in chipping that.'

'There's only one way to find out, Mrs. Lumberjack!'

'Oh, Mr. Lumberjack, that's not a log, it's a fucking forest!'

'And it's fucking well going to give you the logging of all time, my lovely Mrs. Lumberjack!'

_____

In Dave's small flat a similar scene was taking place.

'How would you like your thank you present Mr. Andrew?'

'And what present would that be, Mr. Dave?'

'Well, as I'm a gardener, Mr. Andrew, I am expert in nurturing…'

'Does nurturing involve digging, Mr. Dave?'

'Oh yes, Mr. Andrew. Both digging *and* furrowing…'

'May I have my present now, please Mr. Dave?'

'I must warn you Mr. Andrew I have a very big, wide spade and an equally big plough…'

Charles, unable to resist the pun, said with a camp giggle, '*Field free!*'

_____

'I can't believe I'm actually saying it for real this time, but yes, yes! I'm ready for my close up, Mr. De Jones!'

'Silly queen,' muttered Ethelred. He added in his normal voice, 'Remember *Norma*, I want you to be particularly fey for this scene as you make your way through the woodland grove.' He pointed to the bank of trees and the familiar mounds where Dirk and Hettie had met their fates. 'Monday, in his satyr-like form, will suddenly appear and this is where you swoon, falling gracefully to your knees. Monday will proceed to grab you by your head and force his cock into your eager mouth. Just remember, I want the best gobble scene on print!'

'My pleasure,' simpered Oswald.

'We then have a frenzied fuck scene where Monday will fuck you first of all with you on your back and legs akimbo, then when you are on all fours. After being well and truly fucked you collapse, satiated, onto one of the mounds where Monday, in a moment of fleeting compassion, offers you a drink from his water bottle, or in this case, a ram's horn. After you lie back gracefully, Monday Man takes out his Pan pipes from a satchel thrown aside earlier. As you lie there, a beatific smile on your face – a zoom shot here,

Oswald – Monday proceeds to play a soothing lullaby-like melody causing you to flutter those false eyelashes of yours as you gracefully fall into a satisfied and fitful slumber.'

'Can Monday play the pipes?'

'That's not a problem, Oswald. Such things are *dubbed*!'

'Oh, and what happens then? Does Monday fuck me again?'

'Monday will not only have been lulling you to sleep, Oswald, he will also be calling some woodland friends. These are all imaginary of course and will be superimposed in the final dream sequence. Meanwhile, you just lie there while Euros and Kevin do their stuff. There will be shots of your naked, supine body taken from various angles, all of which will be edited into a perfect rendition of what must surely be a dream sequence to end all dream sequences!'

'As I said,' camped Oswald, pouting prettily and batting his long, gold tipped, false eyelashes, 'I'm ready for my close *ups,* Mr. De Jones!'

'Good.' Ethelred nodded to Monday who was standing by ready and waiting, his horns attached to his head and his rampant erection bobbing like a large, thick, black divining rod.

'Ohmigod!' croaked Oswald. 'Ohmigod.'

After what Ethelred described as the 'gobble scene' and 'frenzied fuck scene' were deemed a wrap he called for a short break. Stunning Oswald, quite stunning, but I would have those grazes on your knees seen to; they took quite a pounding despite the faux grass!'

'A true star is prepared to suffer for his or her art,' replied Oswald. 'Now if you'll excuse me, I simply *have* to go a replace my lashes. Just as well I'm a firm believer in sneaky Baden Powell's motto when dealing with those little scouts of his, "Be prepared!"'

'Quite,' replied Ethelred for want of something to say.

'Time for the lullaby scene,' announced Euros, half an hour later, 'We're all yours, Red.'

'Thanks Euros,' Ethelred, taking position alongside the cameraman, nodded to Monday kneeling next to a supine Oswald, the ram's horn water bottle in his large hand. 'All set, Monday?' The big man gave a nod. 'Right,' studying the tableau for a moment or two Ethelred said in a tense voice, "Lights, camera and action!'

Monday, holding Oswald's head gently in one giant hand, slowly placed the horn to the young man's mouth. Prior to Euros alerting Ethelred for the final scene, Charles skilfully applied a mixture of mayonnaise and Vaseline to Oswald's lips in order to simulate Monday's cum from the previous blowjob sequence. Fluttering his eyelashes in a manner which would have made the most professional of drag queens feel inferior, Oswald duly swooned back onto the faux grass.

'Give it a few minutes,' instructed Charles. 'Once the sedative's taken effect he'll be ready for more than his bloody close up.' Taking a tube of superglue he quickly brushed the closed eyelashes with a coating of the adhesive. He looked up at a tense Ethelred and Euros from where he was kneeling alongside the stretched-out body, 'You sure about this, Red?' Charles rasped, 'It's going to be more than "pretty grisly," it's going to be bloody horrendous. You certainly will have done it this time, Ethelred. Nothing like this will ever, *ever* be seen again!' He looked down at Oswald who was making whimpering sounds, the sounds becoming more panic-stricken as the young man tried to raise his head and open his eyes, his arms threshing weakly.

'Go, Charles, go!' Ethelred looked at Monday 'The tubes Mon?'

'All ready Massa!' Monday's voice was hoarse and he was visibly sweating.

'Euros?'

'Whenever.'

'Kevin?'

'Likewise!'

The lead up to the final snuff scene would be digitally enhanced showing Monday playing on the pan pipes, cutting into three symbolic mice – in this case three large rabid rats – which Charles had injected seven days earlier with the rabies virus; five to seven days being the requisite incubation period for the virus to be effective. In Pied Piper fashion the rats would be seen following the satyr though the woods and up to the sleeping Oswald. At this stage Oswald's body would have been arranged with him on his back, knees up and legs akimbo. In the viewed film Monday, as the satyr, would play a last instruction on his pipes and then, grasping Oswald's feet, would present a zoom shot of his rectal opening. Previous shots of the rats' twitching snouts, the baring of their razor sharp teeth and their demented red eyes would interjected into the sequence prior and during the final scene of the maddened creatures having no choice but to tunnel their way up the unaware drugged-up Oswald's rectum.

'Rectum? They'll bloody well *kill* him,' snickered Kevin, his cock thickening with excitement as he watched the final preparations.

'Christ, these buggers are wild! Here, Monday, put these on just in case and you Red, stand clear.' Charles handed Monday a pair of thick protective gloves before turning to look at the four members of the team. 'Oops!' Charles exclaimed, removing his own gloves, 'I almost forgot!' Leaning forward he viciously ripped away Oswald's false eyelashes. 'We must have the eyes open for what can only be the little shit's "Day of Reckoning" shot!'

'I was just about to do that,' said Ethelred somewhat petulantly. 'But thank you!'

Charles looked at the cameramen. 'They'll panic within the first few seconds so be ready to film not only the *gut* but also the groin; in fact anywhere on the lower torso!' He gave a hollow laugh. 'Forget John Hurt in "The Alien." This is the real McCoy!' Replacing his thick protective gloves, Charles nodded at Monday who, in his turn, slowly inserted a wide, cardboard tube, liberally greased both inside and out, deep into Oswald's receptive arse. Oswald gave a deep, troubled groan, his body twitching spasmodically.

'A bit more, Mon,' whispered Charles throatily, 'and then I'll put the first of the bastards up him!' Charles reached for the steel cage in which the shrieking, shivering and snarling rats were throwing themselves blindly against the bars. An ashen-faced Ethelred with the two equally ashen-faced cameramen and a silent Monday, watched in fascinated horror as Charles lifted the top flap and reached cautiously into the cage. Grabbing one of the squealing rodents, he deftly pulled it out and promptly squeezed it into the lubricated tube. 'Lighter!' Charles commanded, taking the article from Ethelred's shaking hand. Clicking the lighter he quickly seared what was still visible of the inserted rat causing it to disappear completely up the tube. The two remaining rats were quickly dealt with in the same manner. Once all three had disappeared, Charles without any further hesitation, reached out to a small container attached to the cage and quickly produced a large industrial staple gun. Showing no emotion he stapled closed Oswald's sphincter. 'Just in case one of the bastards has the temerity to try and back out!' he quipped to the stunned foursome. Nodding at Ethelred he added quietly. 'I'd start filming, *now*!'

A hideous scream, causing Euros and Kevin to almost drop their cameras, saw Oswald's body begin to buck and writhe in a whirlwind-like fury. Scream after agonised scream echoed around the soundproof basement room as the panic-stricken, rabid rats, began dementedly trying to gnaw and claw their way out from Oswald's heaving, crunching and scrunching body. With a tearing, ripping sound, the snout of the first rat appeared in a splatter of blood from the vicinity of Oswald's groin. With a loud shrieking the rat finally managed to withdraw itself from the ragged, torn opening, only to find itself being grasped by a pair of ready pincers held by Charles and promptly dropped into a lidded pail filled with hydrochloric acid. As the two remaining rats continued to chew and battle their way out from Oswald's out-of-control twisting, bucking and writhing frame, the young man's hideous screams gradually changed to gurgles as his lungs and throat eventually filled with choking blood. Waving, writhing entrails – Ethelred would later describe these to a gripped Clytemnestra as 'Our perfect, hastily growing bean plants or perhaps Medusa's head of serpents!' – burst out in an explosion of white tendrils and spouting mini jets of gore as if deranged. The 'money shot' to end all 'money shots' was caught by an almost over zealous Euros as Oswald's wide, terror stricken eyes, exploded from out of their sockets.

The scenario lasted for another ten minutes before both rats finally joined their colleague in the pail of deadly acid. It was another half an hour before Charles was able to pronounce Oswald officially dead. Knowing his feelings towards Oswald – and as expected – Charles confirmed what Ethelred and the others suspected.

'Unfortunately for poor Oswald, the tranquiliser I gave him would not have been strong enough to contain much pain. I only administered enough for us to basically put in the tube and insert the first rat!' he confessed with a grin. Giving a giggle, Charles added mischievously. 'He must have suffered *abdomen*-ably!'

The four continued to look at the doctor, each with an expression of fascinated horror.

'I can assure you I'll never fall out with you, however minor the incident.' said Euros grimly.

'Likewise.' said an openly shocked Kevin.

Monday, his hands clutched to his naked groin, stood momentarily, a black and silent statue, before discreetly slipping into the shadows.

Ethelred stood staring at Charles in wonderment. With his face breaking into a rapturous grin he said with a chuckle, 'As you so rightly said, Charlie boy, nothing like this will ever, *ever,* be seen again! Absolutely fan-fucking-fabulously fantastic!' He gave a wild, whooping sound. 'Well done team! Well done you load of fucking geniuses!' Giving another whoop Ethelred added, 'Today we have made cinematic history. Try and beat this you European, American and Japanese wankers. You've got more chance of an Eskimo building an igloo in hell than topping Ethelred Jones!'

'Let's drink to that!' Ethelred spun round at the sound of Monday's voice. Holding a tray containing five brimming goblets he added with a grin. 'It's an Oswald Special.'

'Dare I ask the contents?' quipped Charles.

'Oh, it's pure Oswald,' laughed the big man. 'It should – course – be made up out of bullshit, deceit and vanity, but I thought maybe we'd settle for a mixture of vodka, brandy, champagne and a touch of angostura.' Unbeknown to four, Monday had added a hefty dollop of his own cum to the mix, having ejaculated twice into his cupped glove while witnessing Oswald's death throes.

'Sounds OK to me,' beamed Ethelred. Taking a goblet he turned towards the torn, distorted, bleeding corpse, lying in a tangle on the bloodstained mound. Raising the goblet in a salutatory toast he said, *sotto voce*, 'To you, Oswald Argent. It must be said that was quite a performance.'

Later Charles briskly removed Oswald's legs, arms and head from the virtually ripped apart torso. 'I'll put these in the freezer,' he confirmed to Ethelred. 'I know Clyte has plans for using them within her various tableaus. Once she tells me the parts she plans to use I can then get to work on preparing these.' Giving Ethelred a quiet smile he added. 'And now that little scene has been put to bed and as my dear young Dave should have by returned from his shopping spree… if you'll excuse me…'

'Off you go, Charles and Charles…' – Ethelred gave a matching smile in return – 'Thank you, you did a great job today.'

'I know,' said Charles softly. 'My thank you for giving me back Dave.'

CHAPTER 17

'Charles,' said Ethelred in his no nonsense way, 'If young Dave is to become a permanent feature which, even if it's only been a few days, it's a role he's apparently is well on the way to achieving.' He gave a low chuckle. 'What's so apparent is the fact he does seem to be making you deliriously happy and it's obvious the two of you are smitten!' Ethelred added with a small, tight smile. 'Clyte is delighted with your "Dave the Rave," as are Monday, Mrs. N and certainly Viola, so... perhaps a stay of execution while the infatuation lasts?' The barbed backhander accompanied by a tighter smile. 'But now – and more importantly – the Trisomy test. The young man appears to be very perceptive, but how perceptive?'

'He'll understand when I explain Tris to him,' said Charles, immediately on the defensive.

Ethelred raised a sardonic eyebrow at Charles's aggressive tone. 'Jesus, Charlie boy, keep your foreskin on! Take that as a compliment, not a criticism.'

'Sorry,' said Charles humbly, 'but I'm well aware as to why Dave was originally drafted into being here and I still worry.' He looked anxiously at Ethelred. 'Your remark about a temporary stay of execution...' Charles's voice trailed off.

'Well, put that out of your mind for once and for all,' replied Ethelred briskly. 'Plans are made to be changed!' He gave a small, almost playful smile. 'Another advantage in your favour, your Dave the R – and I don't use the term lightly – has certainly gotten to Clyte. Why, she's even gone so far as to suggest he now joins us for meals.'

'Ohmigod!' said Charles.

The two men, suddenly realising the significance behind Charles's remark, burst into guffaws of laughter. 'In your case, Charles,' laughed Ethelred, 'I am happy to say I couldn't have put it better myself. Young Dave seeing you as some sort of deity and you see him a mix of protégé-cum-lover! Please note the discreet use of the word cum in this connotation!'

'Have I not told you time and time again I love you Ethelred Jones!'

'Touché, Charles Conrad Crosby! So how about a glass of vino before you go and break the good news to your young man?'

'I thought you'd never ask!' camped Charles, a happy grin on his face as he watched Ethelred pour out two glasses.

'To you and young Mr. Griggs!' toasted Ethelred. Raising his glass he added flippantly, 'No doubt this will be a case of the recipient fucking the messenger as well as shooting up inside him?'

'As you've just said Ethelred Jones; touché!'

Dave, on being told of his elevation to role of bona fide house guest plus fulltime gardener was, to Charles's dismay, not at all enthusiastic. 'Jesus, Andrew! I don't even know them and I don't think I need to as yet. Can't we leave it for a month or two so as to give me a chance to really settle in?'

'Ethelred was most adamant Dave, and, if I were you, I'd defer to his wishes.'

'*Defer to his wishes*? Fuck Andrew – or should that be Charles Andrew? Or no, perhaps it's now reached the stage of' – Dave made a half-hearted attempt at mimicking Ethelred's deep, resonant tones – 'I would prefer it if you called Charles, plain Charles, Dave, and forget the Andrew completely!' His face suffused with anger, the young managed to spit out one more damning sentence prior to storming out from Charles's sitting room. 'Forgive me Charles,' he spat. 'But I thought we were living in the *twenty first* century, not fucking medieval England!'

'Oh dear,' Charles gave a wry smile at the silent room. 'It seems young Dave the Rave can also indulge in another sort of rave! Well, we'll simply have to wait and see what happens.' Despite his genuine feelings towards the young man, the doctor was no fool. At the end of the day Charles was a cynic, his prime priority the wellbeing of *numero uno.* 'Tread lightly Dave, dear,' he muttered. 'If push comes to shove, it will be Bethlem Báthory as opposed to love!'

That evening, a smiling Dave took his seat at the main dining table along with Ethelred, Clytemnestra and Charles. Dave's relief at Monday joining them for the desert course was obvious. Sitting comfortably at the end of the long glass topped table, a liquor glass of sparkling Crème de menthe at hand, Clytemnestra – at a discreet nod from her husband – tactfully broached the subject of Trisomy.

'Dave,' she said, smiling kindly at the young man. 'Now you've been welcomed into the family' – she glanced at the other three faces surrounding her – 'I think it's time for you to meet our little girl, Trisomy…'

Dave glanced at her sharply, his surprise obvious. 'Little girl? Trisomy? I don't understand.'

'Yes, Dave, we haven't told you before but we do have a daughter, Trisomy, who sadly is unwell and has been since birth.' Taking a deep breath Clytemnestra added quietly. 'Our baby girl is not only mongoloid but a victim of Progeria.'

'I've hear about children being mongoloid but I have no idea of what Progeria is?' said Dave, completely thrown.

'You explain, please Red, I get too upset.' Clytemnestra dabbed her eyes with the edge of her table napkin, her usually composed face appearing to crumple. Dave looked from her to Ethelred and back to Charles, an expression of growing alarm on his face.

As requested, Ethelred slowly and succinctly explained their daughter's condition, ending up by saying, 'So when you meet her Dave – I'm not sparing any punches – be prepared for a shock. Although our little Trisomy is, deep down, a sweet, loving little girl, she looks like an old woman. To put it bluntly, like an old crone. Be kind and gentle with her and treat her for what – to us – she really is. Please see her and treat her like you would any other happy, normal child.'

Swallowing hard, Dave, while answering yes, he most certainly would, sat thinking, Jesus, Charles, what have you gone and gotten me into? I must either be madly in love with you or simply mad by being here! But one thing's clear, I've certainly gone and landed slap bang inside a fucking mad house!

The next morning Dave was formally introduced to a scowling Trisomy who refused to shake his hand or come out from hiding behind Monday's massive, protective legs. Introductions having been made, Trisomy duly left along with Monday to attend to the plants in what was deemed Ethelred's special greenhouse.

'What gives with this special greenhouse?' Dave was later to ask Charles. 'Monday has shown me over all the rest but not this one.'

'Isn't obvious?' said Charles blithely. 'Our magnificent Monday has dear little Trisomy helping him with his marijuana plants – among other things!' The being latter said with the deepest innuendo. Giving Dave a direct look Charles couldn't help but add, 'Take it from me, Dave, seeing *is* believing!'

'No Charles' replied Dave, the Andrew seemingly forgotten, 'take it from *me*! In little Trisomy's case – as far as I'm concerned – seeing is not believing, seeing is *disbelieving*!'

———————

'Clytemnestra Jones has been on the blower again wanting us to come over to dinner. She also says Ethelred needs to talk to me and would prefer to do this in the privacy of their house as opposed coming up to the London office.' Miles looked over at Bryan, his expression anxious. 'I can't go on putting them off Bryo; after all they do consider themselves friends and – forgive me for mentioning her – Angela and self were regular dinner guests.'

Half expecting a gruff 'Well, I'm not bloody Angela!' Miles was completely unprepared for the reply of 'Well, why not? It had to happen sooner or later.' Giving his lover a brief smile, Bryan added mischievously, 'We can't go on being ostriches for ever, Milo. As you sometimes have to – sadly – pull your cock out of me so must we with the proverbial sand!'

'I couldn't have *put* it more prosaically myself!' guffawed Miles as he moved over to give Bryan a hug. 'She's asked us for this coming Saturday, is that OK with you?' he asked, letting go of Bryan and returning to his desk.

'This Saturday, next Saturday, whatever Saturday; simply let's do the bloody thing and get it over with!' Bryan looked at Miles curiously. 'May I ask why Ethelred Jones particularly wants to see you?'

'Hopefully to tell me how much money I'm about to make from my latest investment with him or, worse, see if I'm prepared to put up more money for one of his shitty works.'

'And are you?'

'Am I what?'

'Prepared to put it up for Ethelred?'

'Fuck off, Bryo! The only one I now put it up for is standing right here in front of me! No, my darling, now I have a certain Bryan Scima-Anstruther in my life, things have completely changed.' He looked up from his desk. 'What would you say to a holiday home in the Cinque Terre? A getaway solely for use by you and me?'

'A house in Italy? Do you really mean it, Milo?'

'Well, as I just seem to be married to a dashing Italian, why not an Italian home to go with him?'

'I love you *Signor* Milo Anstruther!'

'Likewise *Signor* Scima-Anstruther!'

Bryan blew Miles a kiss before adding. 'I take it Oswald will be there?'

'No doubt.' Miles gave a conciliatory look. 'Dearest Bryo, if you'd really prefer it, I can always go by myself... perhaps that really would be the answer.'

'No Milo, one can't go on hiding behind your butch leggings forever!' Bryan gave a small laugh. 'In fact, the mere sight of Ms. Argent's face when she meets the new Lady A will be worth it!'

'Great, I'll confirm with Clyte. She'll be delighted.'

'However, Milo, there is a small catch...'

'There is?'

'*Bella Italia.*'

'What about lovely Italy?'

'When?'

'I was thinking next Wednesday.'

'I love you *Signor* Milo Anstruther!'

'Likewise *Signor* Scima-Anstruther!'

––––––––––

'Miles! At long last and you, you must be the mysterious Bryan we've all been dying to meet!' A smiling Clytemnestra swept across to welcome a beaming Miles and nervously smiling Bryan as Monday – in best butler mode – showed them into the stylish, modernistic sitting room. Reaching up to kiss Miles on his cheek – even though wearing a pair of bright red stilettos to complement her red Yves St Laurent evening dress the big man still towered above her – Clytemnestra turned her attention to her other guest, giving Bryan her most dazzling smile. Meanwhile Bryan, having cast his eyes hurriedly around the room, could only discern three other figures, a tall, confident-looking bearded man whom he immediately assumed to be Ethelred; a tall, thin nervous middle aged man who looked like some college professor, and a sullen young man, who – devastatingly handsome and obviously butch – was certainly *not* his former lover. Bryan gave Miles a quick, puzzled glance, only to be met with a similar reaction from his partner.

Noting the exchange of looks, Clytemnestra quickly took the two by their arms and led them over to the group. 'Ethelred, Charles and Dave, our guests have arrived.' She smiled up at Miles. 'Charles you know but I don't think you've met Dave.' Turning to Bryan she repeated a similar introduction. 'Bryan, this is Ethelred my husband and Charles Crosby, a business associate of ours. And, last but not least, the latest addition to the household, Dave Griggs.'

Miles greeted all three men warmly while Bryan's murmured, 'How d'you dos' were more subdued.

'Now, what would you like to drink, Bryan?' Clytemnestra nodded towards a hovering Viola who, clutching a tray containing two champagne flutes, was looking at Bryan with a dazed expression. 'We're having champagne but there's everything at hand.' She gave a dazzling smile. 'Monday mixes a mean Martini, should that be your poison!'

'Champagne will be fine, thank you,' gulped Bryan, thinking, But where the Christ is Oswald? I thought *he* was the flavour of the moment? More intriguingly, who the *fuck* is this dish? Don't tell me he's screwing the old fart Charles? Or maybe it's the whole lot? The wife, the hubby *and* the old collegiate queen, in between coming up for much needed air? Nothing would surprise me from what I've heard about this little gang!

Miles's thoughts were on a similar parallel but more to the point. Where's the whore and who's the stud?

'I hear you're now a partner is Miles's firm? Congratulations.' Clytemnestra gave another dazzling smile, adding, 'And how do you like The Grove.?'

'Adore it,' replied Bryan, determined not to be intimidated by this wildly attractive but obviously very bitchy woman. *Cruella De Vile, eat your heart out,* he thought. 'Not only do I adore The Grove, I also adore being a partner in Miles's firm but not as much as I adore being his *legal* partner!'

'Oh!' said Clytemnestra, totally unprepared for such directness from the handsome young man. 'By legal partner…?'

'I am sure Miles will tell you officially tonight just as I'm sure you must already have heard that Miles and I went through a civil partnership ceremony some weeks ago.' Bryan gave the momentarily stunned woman a sharp look. 'After all, your cook is our cook's sister and we have been quite open about our relationship with all the staff at The Grove.' He gave Clytemnestra his version of a dazzling smile. 'Miles was quite open and frank with all of them. Either they genuinely accepted our situation or else they could find employment elsewhere.'

'Oh,' said Clytemnestra, 'How interesting. Another champagne?' she added brightly, for want of something to say.

'No thanks, Mrs. Jones, I'm fine. I'll hold on until dinner.' smiled Bryan thinking, I've meet your type before, madam, tough as nails and ruthless to boot.

'Clytemnestra, please!' smiled his hostess. 'After all, I am sure we are going to be friends... I can tell these things. Now, come and talk to Charles. Charles is not only a business partner of Ethelred's – Mr. Jones as you wished to have called him!' – Clytemnestra gave a tinkling laugh at the jibe – 'he also indulges in the strange hobby of taxidermy!' She gave another light laugh, 'Or stuffing dead things to be precise!'

It was Bryan's turn to utter a simple 'Oh.' Quickly regaining his composure he added without thinking. 'I take it Dave Griggs is into taxidermy as well?'

Instead of taking offense, Clytemnestra gave a wild whoop of laughter. 'I just *knew* we were going to get on. For that brilliant riposte I insist you have another glass of fizz. Viola, another glass for Mr. Bryan please!'

'Yes, Mrs. J,' stammered the girl, looking at Bryan with adoring eyes. As she was later to say to Mrs. Norelle in the privacy of the kitchen, 'Why is it all the good looking ones are gay? That friend of Sir Miles's makes Daniel Radcliffe look like a poor copy! He's absolutely, gorgeous Mrs. N. Fucking gorgeous!'

'Viola!' exclaimed the shocked cook. 'Please! Your language! I will *not* have the eff word used in my kitchen!' She clicked her tongue disapprovingly. 'At times it's hard to believe you're engaged to that nice young Clive!'

'Sorry Mrs. N,' said the young girl, breaking into a mischievous grin. 'But that Mr. Bryan is quite lovely. Real knicker fodder!'

'Viola!' exclaimed Mrs. Norelle once more but unable to stifle a laugh, 'Maybe I'll just help you serve the pudding course myself so that I can get a good look at this young, god-like creature!' She gave the giggling girl a smile. 'Even my sister says he's a poppet and that, from her, is praise indeed!'

Poppet? I wouldn't mind if he'd 'pop it' in me at any time! thought Viola, saying instead, 'Oh he is, Mrs. N! A definite poppet!'

It was inevitable Oswald's name would be brought up during the course of dinner. Turning to Ethelred, Miles – in between helping himself to another portion of Beef Wellington from a solemn Monday in his role as butler – asked loudly, 'Whatever happened to that young fellow, the actor? The one who pranged my car? I thought we'd also be seeing him tonight?'

Without hesitation Ethelred smilingly replied, 'Typical young man of his ilk! Oswald – that was the blighter's name – went up to London on one of his regular jaunts, this being a few weeks ago. He goes up – or used to go up – ostensibly to see his agent but I also expect to have a welcome break form the confines of Bethlem Báthory. After two days we get a phone call saying he'd been offered a part in some film being made in Cape Town and such an opportunity was too good to miss.' He gave a chuckle. 'The young blighter was back here for two hours, top whack, simply to pack up his belongings and collect his fees for his brief appearance in my latest! End of Oswald Argent!'

'How was he in the film?' questioned Miles.

'To be kind, adequate but no more!' Ethelred gave a wry laugh. 'Like all the kids today, they think stardom is instantaneous. Most of them don't realise it takes blood and guts!' Ignoring Charles's sudden spluttering into his Chevrey Chambertin, Ethelred took a sip from his own glass before continuing. 'He was rather stunning in his role as a replica of Rodin's "The Thinker" and that was it! All Oswald had to do was pose and look, well... posed! Mr. Argent – to put it bluntly – is simply not cut out to being an actor. I did suggest he try his luck at modelling – he was perfect when sitting still! – but now he's got this Cape Town offer, good luck to him is all I can say.'

Miles shot Bryan a quizzical look, getting a relieved one in return. Turning to Dave he asked. 'Are you also involved in films, Dave?'

'No way!' laughed the young man. 'Gardening is my forte and I can only tell you, having a garden like the one here to work in, is indeed a privilege!'

'A gardener?' cried Miles, 'Why that's great.'

'Not only a gardener but a landscape one to boot!' laughed Ethelred. He nodded towards a smiling Clytemnestra. 'I don't know if you know that muddy piece of woodland we have right on the edge of the grounds, but

Dave is busily turning that into an enchanted forest for Trisomy. Explain your forest, Dave.'

A blushing Dave, his face lighting up with enthusiasm, went on to describe the forest he would be creating. 'I am basing it on that amazing Enchanted Forest, an annual event held near Pitlochry up in Scotland. It is one of the most delightful things I have ever experienced!' Ignoring Charles's wine induced snigger, he continued animatedly. 'I plan to have magical lighting effects plus a plethora of woodland animals, fairies, dragons – you name anything from a child's fairy tale and I'm doing it – and, on the actual night of the event, a fireworks display!'

'Goodness,' was all Miles could say.

'Total!' was Bryan's enthusiastic comment.

'And this is to be ready when?' asked Miles, his composure somewhat regained.

'In about two months. Charles here,' he nodded towards the benignly smiling man, 'has his work cut out! I need several animals for use in the tableaus, so he's going to be fully occupied stuffing rabbits and a few squirrels for me. Meanwhile, we're going to have a unicorn and, thanks to a contact up in the north, some live Bambis – I mean deer – for Trisomy to play with.'

'But this sounds fabulous!' cried Bryan. He looked at the smiling Dave. 'If you need any part time help over the coming weekends, count me in!' Ignoring both Miles's and a suddenly sober Charles's anxious expressions, he added excitedly, 'Now tell me Dave, where the aitch do you find a unicorn?'

'Easy,' laughed Dave. 'I persuaded Mr. and Mrs. Jones to buy Tris a pony and, when Tris visits her very own Enchanted Forest on the evening of her birthday, aforesaid pony, along with an artificial horn and silver bridle, will – hey presto! – become a unicorn!' Unaware of amazed faces surrounding him, Dave ended by saying. 'While the forest will be there for her to visit any time during the day, I do plan this one spectacular evening for her birthday. What with the lighting effects, the dragon breathing fire and a firework display over the miniature lake I'm creating out of the small swamp, it'll be a night to remember!'

'And you're going to do all of this within three months?' asked Miles, looking at the young man with open admiration.

Dave, giving a smiling Bryan a conspiratorial wink, simply said. 'Now I've got an extra pair of hands helping me – even if only part time – I don't see why not?'

'But Dave,' Ethelred looked both at him and back to Clytemnestra. 'I had no idea, I mean, I expected something different when you said an enchanted garden, but... but when was all this dreamt up?' He shook his head in smiling disbelief. 'It's *got* to be in a film.' Looking back at a smiling Dave, an equally smiling Clytemnestra and Charles, he gave a chuckle. 'You three,' he said. 'You've had your heads together over this one haven't you?' Ethelred gave another chuckle. 'Give Red the basics and then let him in on the bigger surprise later.' He concluded by saying 'I wonder who'll get the greater surprise, Trisomy or her father!'

Dave went on to explain he and Clytemnestra had decided Trisomy's tenth birthday party would be an evening to remember, beginning with a barbecue followed by the walk to the woods as the evening became darker. 'Even Boris has been roped into helping with the event,' he laughingly announced. 'While I am turning on the various lights and making sure Tubby – she's the unicorn! – is in position and the deer are also roaming free, Boris will be lighting the sparklers lining the route the guests will be taking. Boris will also be responsible for the lighting the gas jet for Puff, The Magic Dragon and yours truly. After sorting out the animals, lighting effects and all, I will literally be up a tree in order to drop down a couple of dancing fairies! These I will be holding and swinging to and fro and up and down on strings!'

'Genius!' cried Ethelred, 'Pure fucking genius! Monday! 'He gestured to the tall man standing silently in the shadows. 'I think such a potential happening deserves a bottle or two of champagne!'

'Yus suh! Massa suh!' camped Monday before striding off, his taut, massive buttocks shown to perfection in a pair of the tightest, black silk trousers Bryan had ever seen.

Toasting Dave and wishing him all the best for his "Evening in the Enchanted Forest," Ethelred answered the question Bryan had been about to ask. 'We must explain Trisomy to you Bryan, unless Miles already has. Miles?'

Miles shook his head, mouthing a quiet, 'No I haven't.'

Taking a sip of his champagne followed by the gentlest of sighs, Ethelred went on to explain about their daughter. A shocked Bryan sat staring disbelievingly as the solemn-faced man described the resultant effects due to Trisomy's illness. 'I can only be openly honest with you Bryan. Meeting Trisomy will be a shock for you but please, please remember she is a child and, like all children, extremely sensitive and receptive to anyone's reactions. She may feel and see herself as a normal little girl but sadly, she is not.'

After a moment's embarrassed silence Clytemnestra broke in. Smiling softly at her husband, she described the further arrangements for Trisomy's special evening in her own Enchanted Forest. 'I thought we'd have some understanding friends down for the evening. I won't suggest they stay as Bethelm Báthory is, after all, only approximately forty five minutes from London.' The 'understanding friends' were to be Claudia Cordelle, Melanie and Peter Peebles, Ethelred's accountant and his vivacious wife, plus dance studio owners Belinda and Freddie Bartholomew. 'And it goes without saying, Miles and Bryan!'

It was the moment Ethelred saw fit to suggest that he and Miles had 'a little chinwag in private,' the two men leaving Dave, Clytemnestra and Bryan to discuss the planned Enchanted Forest. Charles, at a broad hint from Ethelred, had earlier been escorted off to bed by the always solicitous Monday.

'So, your post mortem, Bryo?'

Bryan and Miles, back at The Grove were sitting comfortably in the comfortable, oak panelled study having a late night brandy.

'Bonkers! The whole bloody lot of them! That Ethelred is a ghoul in stuffed sheep's clothing – did you see those red stuffed sheep on the lawn? – Clytemnestra is Cruella Deville and the Empress Wu rolled into one and as for Charles, why he'd even make Adolf Eichmann look more saintly than the Pope!' Bryan took a sip of his drink. 'What the hell that Dave Griggs character is doing there is beyond me! As for Os, what was *his* problem? Surely he can't have seen anything in the guy apart from a pie in the sky ticket to whatever? After all, it was Charles who lured Ossy away from the ravishing me!' Bryan gave a wry laugh. 'Jesus! Doesn't do a lot for one's self esteem, does it?' He gave a hollow chuckle. 'Again, what's all this about a daughter – "old before her time?" Explain *that* little bombshell!'

'A combination of Mongolism and Progeria is what the poor little mite has been blighted with.'

'Sounds more like an *abomination,* if you ask me!' sniped Bryan.

'*Really*, Bryo! I'm surprised at you! That's quite out character.' Miles gave the young man a cautionary look. 'Whereas I suppose you found young Dave Griggs more *admiration* as opposed to abomination?' the latter being said with a touch of a growing resentment.

'Actually you could say that!' replied Bryan teasingly. 'I can't *wait* to give him a hand in his proposed Enchanted Garden.'

Miles, about to make some derogatory comment but thinking better of it, said. 'It's late and I think we should be getting to bed.'

'Sorry, Milo, that was a bit out of order,' Bryan gave a rueful smile. 'I'd put it down to my relief at not finding that bloody Oswald there. Dave was a total saviour.' He pointed to Miles's empty brandy balloon. 'One small one before we go up?'

'Why not?' smiled Miles, taking hold of Bryan's hand as he reached for the empty glass. 'I love you, Bryo,' he said simply. 'And please never stop loving me in return.'

'You silly old sod! Stop loving you? I married you, didn't I? As far as I am concerned, marriage is for keeps!' Bryan bent down and kissed Miles lightly on the forehead. A few minutes later, having replenished their drinks, he sat down opposite his lover. 'I still can't quite believe that story about Oswald doing a flit like that. I mean, giving up all that opulence and luxury – let's face it, the place and their life style is fairly mind blowing – for the chance of appearing in a film in bloody Cape Town, *South Africa*?' Bryan shook his head disbelievingly, 'It doesn't sound the Oswald I knew. Furthermore, he was supposedly having it off with that Charles character who – to me – is obviously being screwed rotten by what can only be a deluded – or very deviant – Dave! Their relationship – if there is one – is something I find genuinely obscene. Vile in fact! I mean, for Chrissake, the man is more atrophied than even remotely attractive!'

'Perhaps it turns Dave on?' said Miles, trying to lighten the conversation. 'I mean all that business about an Enchanted Forest with frolicking deer and a bloody unicorn. Now that is *very* Freudian!'

'What is? Frigging frolicking deer?'

'No you loveable idiot! A unicorn! Think of that long twisted horn!'

'I'd prefer to think of a long, *throbbing* one instead! So, lover of mine, drink up and – as you said a few minutes ago – let's go to bed.' Bryan gave a sly grin. 'All this talk about unicorns is making me feel… well, quite twisted and *extremely* horny!'

With a laugh Miles held out his hand, 'Bedtime then for you, young man! We've a busy day tomorrow as it's the Windsor Dog Show, just in case you'd forgotten!'

'Forgotten? How could I forget when we're about to get our first child! I can't wait to give birth to a Spaniel!'

'What if it's a Labrador?'

'Depends on who the father is!'

'Well, I am, so it had better be a Labrador!'

'Let's compromise, just in case I may have been playing around and not taken the necessary precautions! Let's settle for a Spaniel *and* a Labrador!'

'You're the mother!'

'Spaniel and Labrador then! End of conception!'

Hand in hand the two made their way up the elegant, curved staircase to their bedroom, any further thoughts regarding Oswald completely forgotten.

CHAPTER 18

'The paintings are a dream and I'm delighted so now, Charles dear, it's time to finalise the accompanying tableaux.' Clytemnestra, a slight frown on her otherwise unblemished forehead, handed the doctor a handwritten list. 'Have you enough body parts to deal with them all?'

Glancing quickly through the list of requirements, Charles nodded approvingly. 'Mm, yes I think so.' He ran his eye over Clytemnestra's requests once more, adding, 'Only one problem – and it's a mega one – we haven't a complete body usable for the "Half-Hearted Walk in The Park" figure.'

'Fuck! Of course, Oswald's middle bit having to be incinerated!" said Clytemnestra irritably, 'Is there no way we can get away with a *false* midriff and attach the arm and the leg? Or better still, what has happened to Dirk?'

'Dirk's already been dissected for the "Broken Toys" tableaux," said Charles. Clearing his throat, he added nervously, 'If you remember it was Dave who was going to be used for the walk, but that's all changed!' He gave Clytemnestra a panic-stricken look. 'Can't we adapt... use the Tesco tart instead?'

'No, it's got to be male and on second thoughts, you're quite right, Charles, it's got to be a whole body!' She couldn't resist a snigger. 'Rather like a side of beef!'

'But I'm sure with skilful grafting I can *reassemble* half a male form! Let me have another look at Dirk. I'm sure I can fit something together! After all he will be clothed.'

'But will he? The mind's racing Charles! It *was* originally going to be the perfect half of a clothed figure, not a melding – if that's the correct word – as you're now suggesting, of assorted body parts! You've gone and got me thinking and the more I *think* about it, he simply *has* to be nude – one pure half of a spectacular *nude* male will be nirvana!' Clytemnestra gave a brittle laugh. 'It'll be quite a turn on for you, dear, having to slice a penis in half, only this time lengthways as opposed to across! You'll then have to face it or edge it with a perfect, flat, lacquered finish! And not only the young man's dick, but the full, remaining half body. Genius Charlie Manson Crosby, pure bloody, fucking genius!'

'It's a tricky one but I know I can present you with a perfect, *clothed* human half!" murmured Charles. 'As I suggested, I can…'

'I have no doubt you could, dear, but only if we use a *complete* male body. An admirer of Miss Mary Shelley and her Frank I am not; which means we now have – as I've already pointed out – a major problem.' Clytemnestra couldn't resist a giggle. 'We're a full man short for our *half* man!'

'I suppose this means another trip up to London,' said Charles ruefully. He gave Clytemnestra an oblique look. 'And you're one hundred per cent sure wouldn't consider reverting to a dressed body, as originally planned?'

'No! Definitely not!' came the sharp reply. 'Besides,' added Clytemnestra after a brief silence, 'I have in fact, left the figure basically unfinished in the painting. I have been in two minds as to dress him or not and you, my dear Charles, have made the decision for me!'

'I'm so glad I spoke.' said Charles sarcastically.

'Pity we can't get hold of half of Miles Anstruther's Bryan!' said Clytemnestra wickedly. 'But somehow I don't think Miles would go for only half a share of his glorious young man!' Unable to resist her final goading of Charles – a favourite pastime of hers – she added teasingly, 'Though I must say from all the not-so-discreet glances between him and your Dave at dinner the other evening, I did think to myself, "When does *this* ravishing begin!"'

'What utter nonsense!' spluttered Charles, 'Why, they're both young men who, at times, must find us older people's company fairly heavy going!'

'Speak for yourself, dear. You know I'm ageless!'

Unlike your daughter! thought Charles bitchily.

'Well, what do you want me to do, Clyte?'

'Do, Charles? Why, talk to Red and if he is agreeable, find us another boy!' Clytemnestra gave Charles a worried look. 'Although I really think we should think seriously about this. After all, we've gotten away with three bodies and they do say good things only come in threes. I wouldn't like to press our luck.' She made a dismissive gesture with a long, pale hand. 'Speak to Ethelred. If he gives you the go ahead then fine. But let's make sure it's our last. There's only so much we can keep on getting away with.'

Charles was on his way to the studio to speak to Ethelred when he was intercepted by Mrs. Norelle.

'Phone call Doctor Charles. It's Sir Miles's Mr. Bryan! He did ask for Dave but when I said Dave was down working on that forest thing of his, he asked if he could speak to you. I was about to ask him to call back later when I heard your footsteps!'

'How very intuitive of you, Mrs. N! I'll take it in the study.'

Making his way to the room Charles's mind was churning. It's beginning! Fucking Clyte is right. There *was* something going on between those two the other night! I could sense it, pissed as I was. Well, we'll soon put a stop to that! Entering the study Charles strode determinedly to the desk and, snatching up the phone, barked 'Charles Crosby!'

'I 'aven't put you through yet, Doctor,' came Mrs. Norelle's voice. "Old on a sec. I'm not quite sure which thingamy to press!'

'I'll press your fucking thingamy, you stupid bitch' muttered the Doctor. After a series of clicking Bryan eventually came though on the line.

'Hello? Charles? It's Bryan! I need to get a message over to Dave. Do you mind passing one on for me? I didn't give it to the woman who answered – the cook I think – as I couldn't remember her name and I didn't want to sound rude!'

'What's the message?' snapped Charles, sounding extremely rude.

'Oh, said Bryan, slightly taken aback by the brusque reply. 'Well I'm returning *Dave's* message. He rang to see if I could help him out with his forest project next weekend. The answer is yes, Saturday would be great and also, would he like to come over to supper Saturday evening?'

'Just him alone?'

'Yes, Charles just him. Alone.' replied Bryan, equally as brusquely. 'I take it he's not completely beholden to the Jones household and is allowed some time off!' A statement not a question.

Why, you sneaky little cunt! thought Charles angrily. *Don't think for one minute I don't know what the two of you are up to! Clyte was right, you two were making overtures with each other the other night. Well, we'll soon put a stop to that, Bryan whoever you are!* Taking a calming breath Charles replied with all the control he could muster. 'Dave's a free spirit and, if he wishes to go out for *supper*, so be it! I'll see he gets your message!' Charles slammed the phone back down onto the receiver. 'Little swarthy shit!' he muttered, stalking back through the house and out to his own workrooms. 'Forget a boy hunt in fucking London, why not do as Clyte suggests.' Still muttering he pulled on a pair of surgical gloves. 'Why not use Anstruther's little shit instead?' Reaching into the freezer Charles carefully pulled out one of Oswald's frozen legs. Carrying it over to the steel dissecting table, he laid it reverently on the cold, shiny surface.

Whatever his mood of the moment Charles was always meticulous in his work, his former fall from grace having taught him a-never-to-be-forgotten lesson. Still muttering he began to stroke the cold limb in a deliberate and sensual manner. As usual he found his erection growing as he started to stroke the full limb, his hands moving faster and faster up and down the solid length. With a groan Charle's ejaculated into his underpants before collapsing onto the frozen limb and blindly kissing it through his tears. 'Why did you all betray me?' he wailed, 'First you and now Dave!' Falling to his knees and throwing back his bald head Charles began to howl, wolf-like, towards the high rafters of the converted barn. After a few more minutes of self-pitying sobs, he slowly drew himself to his feet and, having unzipped himself, wiped his cum soaked pubic hairs and mopped his long foreskin, he made his way slowly towards his desk.

'Oh Clyte,' he groaned. 'If only we could…' Still muttering he continued his diatribe. 'Trust bloody Miles Anstruther to have gone and married the little fucker! No doubt the departure of the first fucking Lady A was a godsend but somehow I don't think he would take the disappearance of the second Lady A in quite the same way!' Charles couldn't resist a snigger. 'Though, given half the chance, I wouldn't have minded getting my hands on as well as *into* that one I must admit! However, as the old saying goes, buggers at times have to be losers!'

Seating himself at his desk, Charles unlocked the top drawer and took out a thick folder plus a calculator. Humming to himself he finally sat back, a satisfied smirk on his long, aquiline face. 'Nice,' he muttered, 'very nice.' Stretching his arms above his head he nodded appreciatively. 'Three sets of kidneys, sadly only two livers – fucking rats! – plus three hearts and three pairs of eyes? Not bad, not bad at all and a nice, tidy little sum towards my Shangri La in the sun.' Humming softly, Charles reached for the phone and punched in the number. On receiving a reply he simply said, 'I will be able to supply you with the additional items within the next ten days. As always, I will arrange a suitable time for collection. There will be two of everything as per the requisites of list one.'

In a brief conversation with Ethelred later, it was agreed one more young man was to be found. Monday's Tesco tease would be invited to Bethlem Báthory for dinner once the 'new star' – as Ethelred billed him – was 'in situ.' Charles was to leave for London the following morning, returning the same evening or, as before, stay overnight. This time Flemings Hotel was overlooked with Charles booking himself into the more anonymous Park Lane Hilton. In all the last minute planning plus discussions with Clytemnestra as to what was more accurately required, Bryan's message to Dave was completely overlooked.

Monday, who had spun the girl from Tesco the tale he was a bodyguard to a film director and his wife, would finally 'succumb' to all her pleadings for an introduction. Vicky Watkins, an avid reader of 'Hello' magazine and a firm follower of 'I'm a Celebrity, Get Me Out Of Here!' – to the extent of an almost religious fervour – would have her wish and meet the famous man and his wife. Monday would also drop the hint that Ethelred was looking for a pretty girl to do a 'walk on' part in his next film. Vicky, her mind filled with the heady aspirations of becoming an instant celebrity herself, could only be ecstatic at the idea.

Monday had also found out that Vicky's parents were living abroad and very rarely contacted or saw their daughter. Not only did the young woman have a small, private income, but her main occupation seemed to be a variety of part time jobs in small bijou fashion boutiques either in Windsor or London where, on occasions, she actually did meet a celebrity. One of the highlights during Vicky's odd jobbing, was to sell a programme to Ivana Trump, the glamorous ex-wife of the billionaire, Donald Trump, at a charity event where Vicky was helping out. From the moment of meeting the smiling, elegant and charming woman, Vicky was determined whatever the cost, one day she too was going to be noticed. It was often commented on by various associates a move from Windsor into London itself would have been far more beneficial, but Vicky remained obvious to their suggestions. As one of her more bitchy acquaintances was overheard to say, 'Snotty little cow. No doubt she remains stuck out there in Windsor with aspirations of casually bumping into the Queen and being asked back to the castle for tea!'

Unbeknown to the acquaintance and others, Vicky' darker side was an insatiable greed for black men, the bigger the better. Her forays up to

London saw her staying in a small incognito bedsit she kept in Camberwell. Here, completely anonymous, she would frequent the various clubs and bars where, with her fair English looks, long blonde hair and slightly fuller figure, she found a never ending source of willing admirers. 'Windsor's my camouflage for Camberwell, my cunt cooler!' She would giggle to herself as another exhausted black stud would stagger from her bedsit into the drabness of Havil Street.

On spotting a confused-looking Monday in a shopping aisle in her local supermarket, she could not believe her eyes. Never, in all her experience, had she ever seen such pure, unadulterated, black macho heaven, and when Monday excused himself and asked for her opinion on whether to buy a tin of pineapple rings as opposed to chunks for a fruit salad, she was hooked. Monday was the first man ever – black or white – to be asked back to her flat in Windsor Old Town. That evening, a painful but smug Vicky Watkins, had waved the genial black giant off into the night with a second date planned for the coming Saturday. 'Let's stay in,' the big black man suggested. 'And instead of breakfast in bed, why not make it dinner as well? I'll do the shopping. I grill a mean steak and, as you've just tasted, I'm great at tossing a salad!'

'Tell me about it!' a smirking Vicky quipped back, visibly wincing at the sharp twinge of pain between her severely chafed labia. 'And as you now know, it's far better if you simply use a whole pineapple!' She had given a throaty laugh. 'Pineapple rings as opposed to *chunks*? I trust you won't be asking such a silly question again, will you?'

––––––––––

Bryan, slightly bemused at not having had a return call from Dave, simply shrugged it off as a fun idea having backfired. 'Obviously the mad house has more sway over the guy than I thought, or perhaps he really *is* into that old fart – and I do mean *in* – and screwing the scrawny arse off the old sod! Well, it takes all sorts and good luck to him!' As Bryan and Miles had decided to make a long weekend of their trip to Italy – they had originally planned a two day midweek visit – the two were literally setting off for the airport to catch their mid-morning flight to Genoa the same time Charles was leaving for London in search of gentleman number three.

Arriving at Genoa's Christopher Columbus International Airport, Miles and Bryan took a taxi into the city where they were dropped off at the elegant Hotel Excelsior conveniently situated opposite Genoa's Principe

Train Station. After treating themselves to a 'Welcome to Italy' drink in the hotel's luxurious Christopher Columbus Bar, they made their way across the square to the station where they boarded the Rapido bound for Rome, stopping at the Ligurian town of Levanto en route. Their luggage comprising of a light shoulder bag each, saw no unnecessary waits or hold ups at check in or customs. 'The train's more convenient than hiring a car or getting someone to meet us in Genoa itself.' Miles explained. 'Marco will meet us at the station and take us from there to the development. We keep a fleet of Fiats at the office so if you feel the urge to flee, flee in a Fiat!'

'And we stay?'

'The company has a house where the two members of staff live and where I keep a permanent set of rooms. There is also a small pool as well as the communal pool.' Miles had smiled. 'If you're thinking Breughel and a happy band of smiling villagers – don't! It's more Casa Vogue than Casa Put-together!'

'And I'm no smiling Breughel peasant!' laughed Bryan. 'I *have* done my homework and I *have* seen the promotion video!'

'I stand corrected!'

'I can't wait to see Dossetto,' smiled Bryan as the streamlined train glided out from the station. 'Imagine my husband being the owner of a complete fourteenth century mountain village; albeit one with a twenty first century face lift!' He gave a laugh. 'I only hope your back holds out!'

'Why only my back?'

'All those wonky stone thresholds you'll be carrying me over!'

'And what about any further marking of our territory?'

'With you, Milo, I'll even submit to an even wonkier stone floor. Just as long as the Mile long missile isn't wonky and I am well and truly marked!'

'Keep talking like that and you'll end up having a pre-run as to whether it's wonky or not!'

'Point taken or – rather – point *not* taken! Look at the scenery Sir Miles... why, I do believe we're heading past Portofino!'

The four days passed quickly. Bryan's initial impact at the beauty of Liguria and in particular, the beginning of the Cinque Terre, was completely overwhelmed by the enchantment and style of the redeveloped village. Nestling among verdant vineyards and silver olive groves, the original village built of local grey stone and stucco plaster, had been further enhanced by the addition of several new houses designed so as to skilfully blend in with the original dwellings. All houses – old and new – boasted modern kitchens, central heating, satellite television and air-conditioning. Where it had been possible – mainly with the new houses – a small pool had been included. For the benefit of the remainder houses, a large communal pool and recreation centre housing a bar restaurant, sauna and shower facilities, plus a company offices had been built The ancient cobbled streets, wending their way through the colourfully pastel coloured houses, gave little hint as to the luxury contained behind the wide, heavy wooden doors.

The complex, once advertised, had seen all the properties bought within a few hours. Buyers were either rich Milanese from the north looking for a coastal holiday home with a difference – a journey to the golden beaches adjacent to the seaside town of Levanto took only quarter of an hour down the well maintained mountain road – or German and English families looking for the same.

'I love it!' Bryan exclaimed, time and time again as he and Miles stood looking at the spectacular view from their bedroom terrace. Turning to a beaming Miles, he could not resist the punch line giving his seal of approval. 'Miles in London,' he laughed, 'Milo in the country and here, in *bella Italia* it simply has to be *Meelo*!'

'You make me sound like a bedtime drink!' came the laughing reply. 'So...?'

On arrival at Levanto station Bryan was introduced to Giles, a smiling young Englishman who, along with another couple, Susie and Simon, were responsible for the sales and general maintenance of the development. A fourth young man, Anthony – and Giles's partner – was the resident architect. Anthony, who was also fluent in Italian, had proved a godsend in handling the endless complications regarding planning regulations and the relevant permissions.

'I thought all the properties were sold?' questioned Bryan on the drive up to the village.

'It's a development, Bryan,' came the reply. 'We have seven new houses under construction and these won't be ready to be marketed until next year.' Giles drew the car to a halt and, at his suggestion the three stepped out to stand by the low parapet at the road side. 'Your first and best view of Dossetto,' he had said, pointing proudly. 'Next time you see it will be from the car park above the village where you will be looking *down* on it before descending into the complex.'

'It's fabulous!' breathed Bryan, looking up and the mellow stone houses basking in the mid-afternoon sunshine. 'Why, it's like a marvellous landscape.' He looked at Miles with an adoring smile. 'If Canaletto had done landscapes, this would have been a major work!'

'Oh, but he did paint landscapes,' Miles assured him. 'Not only should the name Canaletto be synonymous with Venice, he was also responsible for a great many landscapes; particularly in our own England where he was commissioned to paint a great many country houses and their surrounding parks.'

'As they say, you live and learn!' replied Bryan, gazing admiringly at the village nestling in the fold of the hills above them. He looked at Giles and Miles, a puzzled expression on his face. 'You say there are *new* houses in the midst of all that? The whole lot look one hundred per cent authentic to me.'

'As they should,' agreed Miles, 'Like us, a perfect blending of the old and the new.'

Later the following day, Miles led Bryan along to a small olive grove with a breathtaking view over the adjacent villages, vineyards and other olive groves. Perching on a convenient boulder, he patted the stone indicating Bryan should join him.

'What do you think?' he asked, gesturing at the surrounding landscape and the sparkling blue nearby Mediterranean coastline.

'Meelo, what do you expect me to *think*? It's nothing more than utter, utter magic.

'And this rock?'

'*This* rock?'

'Yup! *This* rock on which your lovely, delicious and unbelievably talented bum is now sitting.'

'Like everything else connected with Dossetto, *including* its fantastic, sexy, well-endowed owner, it's utter, utter magic!'

'Good! Because this is where *Casa Bryomeelo* is going to be built!' In-between Bryan's hugs and kisses, Miles managed to gasp, 'The plans for the house are in the sales office for your approval. If you wish any changes made, feel free and please ask Anthony to deal with these for you. And by the way, as we're slightly away from the main village there is also room for our own pool!' Smiling at a stunned Bryan, he added softly. 'I want it to be *perfezione,* in other words, perfection; therefore it must be completely you.' Rising to his feet, Miles held out his hand. 'Let's get back to the office. I have some papers to deal with and you, young man, have a house to build!'

———————

Back in London Charles's first night attempt at finding a replacement Oswald had been a failure. Having, for old times sake, decided to pay a visit to a former favourite pick up haunt of his, the Queen's Head, a gay pub situated off the famous Kings Road in Chelsea, he duly arrived, but not before fortifying himself with a few strong Martinis at another favourite, the Rib Room Bar of the Jameirah Carlton Tower hotel. Standing in the main bar situated at the back of the pub Charles surveyed the busy crowd over the rim of his large gin and tonic. To his chagrin most of the imbibers appeared to be in couples or groups. Bearing in mind Clytemnestra's strict requisites, Charles was looking for a Bryan-like figure – 'more chunky as opposed to thin' – and one with a strong face which, when halved down the middle, would still retain significant details of the nose and the mouth. 'Don't for God's sake get a young man with a thin, aristo nose otherwise it will end up looking like an arrowhead!' she had quipped.

Having finished his drink Charles decided to have one more and then, if no success, he was going to call it a night, a wave of exhaustion suddenly washing over him. The past few days had seen him working diligently at his taxidermy where he spent exhaustive time building the necessary frames to support both Oswald's and Dirk's legs which would to be used in the biggest of the tableaux, 'A Half Hearted Walk in the Park.' The elaborate work of filling the limbs – the feet proving to be the most finicky – plus the stretching of the skin over the preserved and reused muscles, saw him working long into the night; Charles's tireless assistant in helping with the processes being none other than Trisomy. Working alongside Charles, the strange, wizened little figure, showed an equal dedication and surprising skill in helping with any stitching and general cleaning. Charles's continual words of praise were acknowledged through a series of pleased little grunts and toothless smiles. The only time Trisomy left the doctor to himself, was when she returned to help Monday in what Dave had dubbed, 'Dave's Out of Bounds' greenhouse.

'Tomorrow is another day,' murmured Charles, a tired smile crossing his face, a smile tentatively returned from a dark-haired youth slouching against an adjacent wall. *Oh ho,* thought Charles. *A bit dago-ish and surly... mean mouth and probably trouble, but the physique couldn't be better. With a dye job, Bob could very well be your nasty uncle! Heigh ho, we'll give it a go and if nothing's forthcoming – ha! – we'll call it a night.* He smiled back at the young man who, draining his pint glass, slouched over to him. 'You buying?' he said brusquely, in a harsh, guttural northern accent.

'Could be,' answered Charles coquettishly, 'If I knew who I was *buying* for?'

The young man gave Charles a direct, calculating look. 'Name's Paul. Yours?'

'Charles,' said Charles promptly. *No need to give you an alias, paranoid Paul,* he thought. *For if I do get you down to the country it'll be lights out before you know it.* He nodded at the empty pint glass. 'Another of those?'

'Naw, a double rum and Coke will do me.' Paul gave a curt nod and added an almost inaudible gruff, 'Thanks.'

'One large rum and Coke coming up,' said Charles, turning towards the crowded bar

'I'll get it. You?'

'Oh, make it a large gin and go light on the tonic,' smiled Charles. 'And thank *you*!'

The surly young man gave another curt nod, but remained standing expectantly.

'Oh,' murmured Charles, 'Of course.' Reaching for his wallet he pulled out a twenty pound note. Silly me thinking I was being offered a drink. This one's obviously rent with a capital R.

Grabbing the note the young man elbowed his way down to the end of the crowded bar before disappearing into the more intimate, smaller second bar area. After a few minutes it dawned on Charles the young man hadn't gone round to see if service was easier on the other side, but had simply disappeared with his twenty pounds.

'Shit!' said Charles, furious at himself for being so easily duped. 'I must be tired to have let myself be so easily conned. Fuck! Fuck! Fuck! Or – in this case – no fuck!' He gave a wry laugh. 'Home is the Hilton' he yawned and, giving a wan smile at a camp young couple who had been curiously eyeing the scholarly, elderly man talking to himself, Charles edged his way out from the busy pub.

A foul tempered and badly hung over Charles – he had attacked the mini bar in his room with a vengeance on his return the previous night – slowly made his way into Shepherd Market to find a small cafe where he could glare at The Mail and indulge in several much-needed cups of double espresso coffees. It was while sipping from his third cup that he noticed a familiar figure sitting at a table nearby. To his increasing alarm the figure gave a casual wave before getting to his feet and slowly making his way over to where Charles was sitting. Charles meanwhile could only gape, open-mouthed, at the young man.

'I owe you a gin and tonic and furthermore, I'll even pay for your coffees,' said the voice, only slight reminiscent to the one from the night before. 'May I?' Without waiting for a response he pulled out a chair and sat down. Beckoning to the waitress he nodded at Charles's empty cup, 'Hi, Mona! Another of those for the gentleman, please, and I'll have a large latte. Thank you.' Having given the order he gave Charles a dazzling smile. 'Talk about coincidences! Surprised?'

'Surprised? I'm completely overwhelmed!' Charles gave a nervous laugh. 'And what's happened to your accent?'

'Ah, my *oop* north bit! Good, isn't it? By the way I really am Paul, and I apologise for not returning with our drinks plus your change last night. It just so happened I bumped into a colleague from school and we got talking. By the time I got back to where I'd left you, you'd gone.' Paul reached into his jacket and took out a wallet. 'Here.' He handed Charles a crisp twenty pound note. 'I'll do the coffees and, if you're still up to it, let's have a drink in a nearby pub afterwards.'

Charles's mind was sounding alarm bells. Thoughts such as, How did he find me? Is this really a coincidence and, most alarming of all, the word school. Surely he's too old to be at school? He must be in his late teens or early twenties to look like that and sound like he does! And what gives with this eloquent accent? In his confusion Charles overlooked the familiar greeting to the waitress.

'I can see your mind going into overdrive,' laughed Paul. 'This is a regular haunt of mine – hence me knowing Mona – and I'm at drama school.' He gave another laugh. 'Reason I'm here in the Market' – he gave a mischievous grin – 'but not *that* sort of market I hasten to add, is because I have a part time job in a small antique shop nearby. I live in Draycott Place, close to the Queen's Head. Q.E.D!'

'But this is amazing,' gasped Charles, not believing his luck. 'But what's with the surly northern act?'

'We're doing Joe Orton at school and I've got the part of the young man in "Entertaining Mr. Sloane." I'm *doing* Sloane and, being given a bit of a free hand by the director, I've decided to make *my* Mr. Sloane a bit of northern rough!'

'Oh,' said Charles, the wind taken out of his sales. Drama school and a part time job? Too easily missed if he suddenly disappeared! 'And when is the err… production?'

'Oh, there's no production. It's an end of term read through type of thing. In fact, it's this evening and there's a small party afterwards.' Paul gave Charles a smile. 'Why not come along – if you're free that is? Who knows, it may even lead to us buying each other another of these somewhat elusive gins!'

Charles's mind was racing. End of term? Part time job?

'So, what happens after tonight?'

'Oh, I'm taking a few weeks off. School's over for our summer break and Pip – he's the owner of the shop where I do part time – has given me the same time off from work.' Paul gave another dazzling smile. *Christ, it's Tom Cruise, perfectly thick, broken nose for halving and all!* thought Charles. 'I plan to take myself off to Morocco and chill out either in Tangiers or Marrakech, depending on how I find it.'

Knowing it was now or never, Charles took the plunge. 'An aspiring actor?' he mused. 'Do you, by any chance, Paul, know the work of a great director friend of mine, Ethelred Jones?'

'*Do I know the works of Ethelred Jones*?' Paul gave an excited laugh. 'Ethelred Jones is my ultimate hero! Ethelred Jones is the king of kings as far as I'm concerned. Know Ethelred Jones? Why, I'd give my fucking right arm to meet him!'

'I'd love to come to your reading tonight,' purred Charles, like the cat who'd got the cream. 'And now, as we've finished our coffees, let's find that pub and this time I take it you *will* drink the G and T which I am definitely going to buy!'

Over their drinks in the nearby Red Lion – 'a favourite lunch time spot of Pip's and mine" Paul had enthused – Charles was further taken aback by Paul saying. 'You do know I really *was* giving you the eye, last night, don't you?'

'Me? Why I thought…'

'Yea, I know what you thought,' laughed the young man. 'A bit of rough and maybe rent. I was that convincing, huh?'

'Very,' chuckled Charles before repeating Paul's words. 'Really giving me the eye, were you?'

'Yes Charles; *really*!' Paul gave another laugh. 'As a kid I had a terrific crush on my uncle – he's a teacher and the splitting image if you! –

and once he let me make him cum! Hence I've been hooked on the... err, how I shall I put it? The more mature, scholarly type ever since!'

'Oh.' Charles gave a swallow. 'And pray, where is this uncle of yours now?'

'Still teaching,' replied Paul with a chuckle. 'I think when you're a kid, anyone over the age of thirty looks ancient and Dan, my uncle, must have been at least that!' He gave another laugh. 'The glasses gave him the scholarly look and won me over; hence my preference for the more mature!'

Charles gave a cautious smile. 'And I fit the category, do I?'

'Perfectly.' This time the smile was even more dazzling. 'Another G and T?' Paul picked up their empty glasses and was about to turn to make his way back to the bar when he suddenly leaned across to Charles and whispered. 'By the way, Charles, I think you should know while *you* fit the category, *I* prefer to do the *fitting*!'

That evening Charles sat through the enjoyable reading of Joe Orton's masterpiece. At the small party afterwards Paul introduced him to the rest of the actors, the director and a few other students. On several occasions, Charles found himself playing down his association with Ethelred as a result of Paul's continued referral to close relationship with the avant-garde director. He had to admit his amazement at Ethelred's popularity and the high esteem with which he was regarded. At this point Charles had not broached the topic of Paul coming along to Bethlem Báthory and maybe taking part in an Ethelred Jones film. Having already hinted to Ethelred and Clytemnestra in an earlier phone call, 'fingers and everything else crossed I may have found the perfect subject for your half man or man half and any other scene Ethelred may have meanwhile dreamed up," Charles ended by saying, 'He's already planned a solo journey to North Africa which sees a clean break away from London. No one, but no one, is expecting to see him around for several months. And as they say, out of sight, out of mind.'

'Say no more,' replied Ethelred. 'Simply see if you can get him here within the next few days.' Giving a laugh he added. 'After all, you're the one who has to deliver the goods – to be suitably damaged! – for the fucking tableaux!'

Three days later Charles was at Windsor station to welcome the young man and drive him to Bethlem Báthory. Two days earlier he had introduced Paul to Ethelred via a telephone call during which Paul had been closely questioned about his ambitions and experiences. Ethelred confirmed what Charles merely hinted; a small part in his latest film. Paul was warned that it was simply a walk on part but he would have the privilege of his name being in the credits. The ecstatic young man immediately accepted Ethelred's proposals and happily agreed to delay his departure to Morocco 'indefinitely.'

It was arranged Paul would be arriving on the Saturday, the same day Vicky had been invited to dinner.

CHAPTER 19

On his return from Italy, Bryan had made two more attempts to contact Dave but on each occasion, messages left with either Clytemnestra (two), Charles (one) and even a further message left with Ethelred had gone unanswered.

Bryan had shrugged off the slight with a simple, 'Oh well, if that's how they guy wishes to behave, it's no skin off my nose!'

Having caught sight of Dave once in Windsor, the two had exchanged a half-hearted wave which Bryan took as a large sign saying 'Do Not Disturb.'

'I cannot understand the guy,' he couldn't resist saying to Miles. 'Christ Milo, I was only offering to help out and, to be quite honest, I really do – or did – think that he would have welcomed a break from all those other weirdoes over at that Munster-like compound!'

'I'd forget about it,' agreed Miles. 'What goes on behind those closed doors at Castle Dracula is probably left well alone.'

'I suppose he really *is* that strange Charles's lover?' remarked Bryan, a bemused expression on his face. 'Christ, talk about chalk and cheese!'

'Perhaps that's what they say about us!' laughed Miles.

'Bullshit!' had been the succinct response followed by a warm chuckle. 'What they *do* say is what a handsome couple those Anstruthers are!'

Meanwhile, work on the plans for the house at Dossetto – Bryan, much to Anthony's chagrin had decided to scrap all the original suggestions and start again from scratch – was taking up a great deal of time as was the sales campaign for a new development in London's Docklands. Bryan had never been happier or busier. The addition of both a Labrador and a Spaniel pup to the household – a golden Labrador Bryan promptly named *Dongigiovanni,* meaning 'lady-killer' in Italian and a golden spaniel promptly named *Spavaldo* or 'cocky' – were also proving to be a time consumer.

Miles had laughingly accepted the names without question but did venture as to why these in particular.

'Easy!' had been Bryan's laughing reply. 'Dongi – because like you, Milo, he's going be just that; a real lady-killer! And Spavi – because like yours truly – he's going to be a cocky little shit!'

'And,' added Miles with another laugh, 'You cannot beat a cocky lady-killer!'

'Absolutely; *Daddy*!'

Bryan could hardly wait for 'the boys' to be taken on their first visit to Dossetto. 'Once they're house-trained, which means they'll also be flight trained, they can start earning their air miles,' he quipped. 'I mean, they simply have to do something to earn their keep! As Mrs. Turnbull quite rightly says, they eat enough to feed an army!'

'I know we're constantly yodelling "Walkies! Walkies!" to the pooches, here in England,' laughed Bryan, 'But how do you call out "Walkies! Walkies!" in Italian? *Andiamo? Andiamo*?'

'Why not stick to good old English Walkies! Walkies!?" came Miles's laughing reply.

Miles was quite happy to let any further invitations to Bethlem Báthory take second place. His attempt at a reciprocal dinner invitation to Ethelred, Clytemnestra, Charles and Dave had been politely declined due to work pressures involved with the film and the forthcoming exhibitions. Miles tentatively suggested perhaps Charles and Dave would be free, but was firmly told their input was 'invaluable' and nobody could be spared. Clytemnestra was, however, able to confirm dates for the November premiere of 'Still Life' – of course, they would be invited – to be shown concurrently with Clytemnestra's art exhibition and tableaux 'inspired by the film and my art!'

Trisomy's 'Enchanted Garden' had now been renamed 'A Christmas Fantasy' and the opening scheduled to take place on Christmas Eve. Clytemnestra had given a hint Dave promised 'a fairy grotto to end all grottos,' Christmas reindeer, a friendly Christmas dragon and more.

'A polite way of telling us to mind our own business or, in other words, fuck off until required!' said Bryan in response to the information. Deep down he was still hurt at Dave's slight, but the young man was soon forgotten in the whirlwind of work and the Italian involvement. Bryan's only other comment concerned the date of November the Fifth for the premiere and exhibition. 'Reminds me of the old childhood rhyme,' he said laughingly to Miles. 'Remember, remember, the fifth of November, gunpowder, treason and plot is Guy Fawkes Day. Maybe the whole fucking thing will blow up in their smug faces!'

'Now, Now Bryo,' came the laughing reply. 'In your heart of hearts you don't mean that. Why, deep down you simply love *all* at Bethlem Báthory.'

'I don't know about *all* at the Batty, but from what you've told me about the poor little daughter, she's the one we should feel sorry for.'

'I wouldn't if I were you,' said Miles dryly. 'Miss Trisomy is not as docile or as helpless as she makes out to be. There's a very nasty little being hidden in there but, with parents like that, she had no alternative but to be a problem; despite being mongoloid and suffering from Progeria.'

'Still, it's not the poor little sod's fault, is it? She simply got the short end of the stick.'

'Your right,' agreed Miles. 'And my comments were quite uncalled for. Poor little thing really did get the end of a very short stick indeed.'

Over at nearby Bethlem Báthory 'The poor little thing' in question was, at the very same moment, busily helping Charles with the stretching a portion of Oswald's skin back onto his strengthened and rebuilt leg. 'Fun!' the little girl acknowledged with a drooling toothless grin as she handed Charles a pair of requested forceps.

'Wait until we do the heads and pop in the glass eyes, Tris! That's *really* fun!' remarked her tutor. 'I'll even let you choose the colours!'

'Gug!' came the dribbled response.

———————

'How are you going to explain the arrival of this new young man to Dave?' Clytemnestra, sitting across from Ethelred at the breakfast table, gave her husband a quizzical look.

'I've already said I have two student actors visiting us with the possibility of doing some future work for me.' Ethelred gave a reassuring smile. 'I can assure you there will be no questions asked. Dave is so involved with his fucking Christmas fantasy, nothing else seems to matter.' He took a sip of coffee. 'I must say he's proving his weight in gold judging from the way he's tackled all the exhausting and exacting jobs Monday's given him. But it's this Christmas treat for Tris that's really got him going. He's totally involved.'

'I'm worried about him and Trisomy!'

Ethelred raised a quizzical eyebrow. 'Now what on *earth* induced you to make such ludicrous comment?'

'It's the way he keeps studying her!'

'What, you think he's not only gay but a paedophile to boot?'

'Don't be so fucking ridiculous, Red! Of course he's not a paedophile and that isn't at all funny! No, there's more to it than just casual looks... there's an intensity I don't like and, if you want my honest opinion, I don't trust.' Clytemnestra gave Ethelred an unwavering look. 'Go back to our original plan. Use *him* for the seated figure and forget about this new one.'

'But what about Charles?'

'Fuck Charles! It's obviously what this new one has done and let's face it, Charles Crosby is *not* the most loyal of souls. Take it from me, if this Paul is a possible new paramour as opposed to Dave the Rave, then let him be!' Clytemnestra paused to take took another delicate sip of her coffee. 'We both know what rules Charles's mind far, far more firmly than a rampant dick up his arse! I don't have to spell it out for you but I will. Charles's mind, heart and *arse* can be always swayed by good old fashioned m-o-n-e-y! Plus he's a fickle old queen to boot, and an affair of the heart to him is no more than a fleeting fancy! He's already hinted on several occasions, Dave the Rave could almost be – if not already – out of *Fave*!'

'That, my darling was quite the most dreadful attempt at Poet Laureate I've ever heard!'

'Mark my words Red, money talks and money sways. Offer the randy old sod sufficient for a swap over, and Dave's your halved figure. Or, to put it more correctly, *my* sitting figure.'

'What about the garden?'

'What about the garden?'

'Trisomy will be very upset.'

'Trisomy needn't be upset at all.' Clytemnestra gave a hollow laugh. 'I am sure Euros and Thrift must have a tame, gay gardener who can take over. Nobody will be any the wiser.' She refilled their cups, adding quietly. 'As soon as we're finished breakfast, I suggest you make the call.

Besides,' – Clytemnestra gave a saccharine-sweet smile – 'Dave's nose is simply *perfect* for splitting!'

Ethelred gave a grin. 'Why is it I can never stop telling you what a glorious, unmitigated, venomous bitch you can be at times, and the more I see of this side to you, the more I adore and worship you?'

'Because, like me, husband dear, you have similar characteristics and the adoration and worshipping is a two way exercise.' Clytemnestra gave a dazzling smile. 'Now, filled with adoration and worship, off you go and find a new landscape gardener whilst I go a set dear Charles on a new not-at-all straight or narrow tangent!'

———

'May I come in?' Clytemnestra stood smiling in the doorway to the converted barn. She waved to Trisomy who sat mixing a bowl of resin, her small, already wrinkled face even more wrinkled and contorted with deep concentration. The little girl waved with her wizened free hand and gave her mother a vacuous, toothless grin. Resisting a shudder of revulsion, Clytemnestra managed to say sweetly. 'My, how busy you are Tris and my, doesn't it look as if you and Unka Charles are having fun!' Giving another vague wave at the child who had now gone back to her mixing, she nodded towards the door leading to Charles's office. 'A few words dear.'

'Now? I'm rather busy at the minute…'

'So am I and yes, now, Charles, if you don't mind…' The veiled threat hung heavily in the formaldehyde and resin scented air.

'Yes Clyte, of course. Let me have a quick word with Tris and I'll be right with you.' He gestured towards the office.

'Thank you. And Charles dear…'

'Yes?'

'Try and not be too long whispering sweet nothings, will you?'

'Cunt!' muttered Charles.

'I heard that!' chirruped Clytemnestra. 'You're slipping, dear. Last time you muttered sweet nothings about me at least I was a "contaminated cunt!"'

Clytemnestra spared no punches. Bringing up the 'countless' messages left from Bryan she went on to infer Dave's unexpected Saturday trips to the garden centre were obviously a cover up for more clandestine meetings or, as a last resort, telephone calls to Bryan. 'And have you checked his mobiles for any calls out?' she'd added, glowering at the elderly, ashen-faced man. Clytemnestra went on to stress the intensity of Bryan's relationship with Miles, Miles's immense wealth and going so far as to say Miles had confided in Ethelred he had already made a generous settlement on the young man, but a settlement with the strictest rulings.

'Dave Griggs may try, but rest assured, Bryan Scima-Anstruther *is* not going to be giving all that up for anyone or anything whereas you, Charles are simply being cuckolded and made a laughing stock! There's a simple term for the likes of Dave Griggs. He's a cock teaser! He's hoodwinked you into what is nothing less than a temporary life of Riley, while setting his sights on pastures new! If he doesn't succeed with this Bryan character, someone else will be along and, let's face it Charles, someone richer and younger than you!'

'Scima? Did you say Scima?' Charles's face having gone from ashen white to chalk white.

'Yes, Scima-Anstruther.'

'Oh my God!' Charles pressed his clenched fists to his jaw. 'Oh my God,' he croaked again.

'Charles! What is it?' Clytemnestra, a look of genuine alarm on her face, stared anxiously as Charles collapsed onto nearby chair. Getting no response she gave an exasperated sigh, 'For Christ's sake Charles! Cut the fucking Judy Garland! I was only trying to warn you... to spare you the eventual heart ache.'

'He's on to us!'

'Who's on to us? What the fuck are you whimpering about?'

'That Bryan, Bryan Scima. Scima. Bryan Scima was the name of... is... My God, Clyte! He's Oswald's *ex*!'

'Nonsense! It's merely a coincidence! Pull yourself together!' Clytemnestra strode briskly to the cupboard where Charles kept his drinks. Pouring him a large, straight whisky she said brusquely, 'Here, swallow this!'

'He's on to us, I knew it was too good to be true... Something was bound to happen sooner or later' moaned Charles, holding out the tumbler for a refill.

'Now you listen to me,' said Clytemnestra firmly as she handed him another whisky, 'If Bryan *is* the former lover, partner, whatever of Oswald, that's the past. Oswald made a clean break from all that when he came here to Bethlem Báthory. We know there has been no contact *whatsover* between the two of them and the mere fact he is now involved with Miles is simply one of those extraordinary happenings. Miles told Ethelred he met him in a gay bar, for God's sake; the two didn't know each other from Adam. Miles even went so far as to explain this was the reason why Bryan was so adamant about not visiting us. Furthermore, although I kept inviting them I knew it was to no avail. The news that Oswald had gone to South Africa hasn't altered the situation either! Furthermore, both Red and I were immediately conscious of Miles's own awareness regarding the attraction between his lover and your latest paramour when – on hearing Oswald was no longer here – they eventually *did* come over!' Clytemnestra's sarcastic usage of the word latest was not lost on Charles. 'Miles was not at all amused, I can tell you! The premiere and the exhibition, along with all the work entailed, have given both sides the excuse not to pursue this so-called attraction further. However' – Clytemnestra paused, before adding triumphantly – 'it seems your Dave is not as discreet or as devoted as you would wish to believe.'

Charles, with all his paranoia and previous misgivings regarding Dave rushing to the fore, drew himself upright and looking the cool, calculating woman directly in the eye, announced dramatically. 'You're so right and I've been so blind! There is only one decision to be taken. As *She* so rightly says, "Duty first, self second!"' Clytemnestra, unprepared for Charles's use of The Queen of England's famous quote, almost choked in her attempt to stifle her laughter.

'David was to be our original figure so David it shall be,' continued Charles, a beatific expression on his cadaverous face. 'There can be no turning back!' Voice harsh with the emotions of a woman scorned, he added in the most chilling tone he could muster. 'We have no alternative but to cancel this Paul!'

'Charles! Charles' Are you sure? I mean, Dave may have his faults but he did – I mean – has made you happy whilst being here!' cried Clytemnestra, wringing her hands. Barely able conceal her look of pure victory, she added the final nail in Dave's coffin. 'I mean, think again; think deeply and sincerely about what you're suggesting. Are you *really* prepared to sacrifice Dave for this Paul?' She gave Charles a small, whimsical smile. 'Let's be honest doctor dear, Dave's *loss* can only be to your gain! No doubt about that!' She paused, allowing her words of dripped venom to sink in. A few seconds later Clytemnestra – her smile broadening – added teasingly. 'Ah, Charles, dear Charles, I know that look only too well! Do I or do I *not* detect a case of someone else having already stepped into a dead man's shoes?'

Charles reciprocated both the smile and the question with a slight smirk. 'As I've already said, my dear Clyte, you're right as always. Why save Dave when there's an even dishier way to misbehave? Let's see this Paul; Paul Gunn to give him his full name. After all, I'm sure Ethelred will come up with something suitable for him for whatever end he *scenes* fit!' He gave a giggle at this bon mot. 'Maybe eventually we can also expect Mr. Gunn as next in line for some fun!'

'Even as a rival to Guy Ritchie perhaps? Maybe Red's next Golden Phallus award could be for the aptly named 'Shock, Cock and a Giant Smoking Barrel!'

———

'What time are you collecting your Tesco tease?' A leering Ethelred glanced up from the breakfast table at Monday, busily buttering a piece of toast.

'Six. I said I'd collect her then. She's suggested a drink in her favourite haunt, which means we should be back here by about eight.'

'A drink in her favourite haunt? A public place?' Taking a bit of a risk, aren't you? After all the two of you as a couple *are* a bit conspicuous! For fuck's sake, Monday Man, you'll be as obvious as a black prick on a snowman!' Ethelred shook his head. 'No, no way Mon, I really don't think you should be seen out in public together; people *will* remember. Bring her straight back here, no questions asked.'

'You're the boss.' grunted Monday. 'Is she going to stay?'

'We'll have to see,' interrupted Clytemnestra. She gave her husband a cautionary look. 'Red and I are getting a bit worried about the number of *actors* we're using. We plan to play this one by ear.'

'And what about Charles's new bit due later this morning?'

'There again, we think perhaps just using him and letting him go; to spread the word as it were. Yes, he was approached to be in an Ethelred Jones film; yes, he did visit Bethlem Báthory and yes, that is why he's there getting happily stoned in the medina in Marrakech! Spread the word, Paul Gunn, spread the word.' Clytemnestra helped herself to another cup of coffee. 'Same applies to the Tesco tease, let her spread the word about us if necessary, but for moment – in case there *should* be a change of plan this evening – you best keep incognito.' She gave Monday a broad smile. 'If we feel she should be returned to her womb in Windsor, we'll simply resort to your old slogan, Monday of "Fetch 'em, feed 'em, fuck 'em an' forget them!"'

Monday gave a deep, rumbling laugh, 'Sounds OK by me!'

'And talking of fellow conspirators,' chortled Clytemnestra looking up from the table, 'Good morning Charles, sleep well?'

'As well as can be expected.' Charles gave a grimace. 'Where's Dave?'

'Dave the Rave was up and about hours ago,' chipped in Monday. 'When I came down to start getting breakfast together, he was on his way out to work on that forest fetish of his!' He nodded at the row of keys on the far wall. 'You'll have to take one of the Bentleys today Charlie boy. Young Dave's already taken the keys for the CRV as he's over at that garden centre later.'

Avoiding Charles's eyes, Ethelred said mischievously to nobody in particular, 'Another trip to the garden centre? These Saturday forays are becoming a regular pattern in Dave's weekends, don't you think?'

'Perhaps there's more to the garden centre than meets the *eye!*' teased Clytemnestra, enjoying Charles's discomfort, 'More the *apple* as in the Garden of Eden, perhaps?'

'Very funny, Clyte,' said Charles, glowering at the smiling woman. 'I'm surprised you didn't suggest a tantalising serpent instead!'

'Spikey! Charlie! Spikey!' laughed Clytemnestra. 'I was only teasing, darling!' She handed over an earthenware pot to the glowering man as he began to viciously butter a piece of toast. 'Honey? To sweeten your mood?'

'Oh fuck off, Clyte!' Charles, his face suffused with fury, sprang to his feet knocking over his chair in the process. Muttering 'I don't fucking well need this...' he stormed out from the breakfast room.

'Was it something I said?' asked Clytemnestra with a tinkling laugh. Clearing her throat she added cryptically, 'Joking apart I see danger signs, Red, lots and lots of danger signs. Our Charles is getting a bit too edgy these days and we all know what happens to edgy old queens like him, don't we?'

'They go completely over the edge!' laughed her husband.

'Exactly,' said Clytemnestra. 'And when they do, best it's a long drop!'

'Or their swan song!' quipped her husband.

'Get you later, incinerator!' chuckled Monday, his big hands slapping the table top in a parody of a rapper beat.

'I *love* it!' cried Clytemnestra and Ethelred in unison. The three beaming faces repeated, in almost child-like glee. 'Get you later, incinerator!

Get you later incinerator!' with Ethelred capping the chorus with an, 'In a while, *geronto*-phile!'

Giving an extra shriek, Clytemnestra dropped her coffee cup.

––––––––––

'Welcome to Windsor! Your carriage awaits you!'

'What? No bunting? No cheering loyal subjects? Why, my popularity must be slipping!' A beaming Paul gave an equally beaming Charles a warm hug. Looking round the neat, tidy station he nodded in appreciation. 'Nice, very nice and smell that country air! Delicious?'

'I think you'll find that "country air" is a touch of Hermes Equipage!' said Charles with a laugh. 'Here,' he reached for one of the three small bags Paul had heaved off from the train, 'let me help you with those!'

'No need!' laughed the young man. 'I'm a strapping lad as you can see! Lead on to aforesaid carriage Macduff!'

Laughing, Charles led the buoyant young man over towards the parked Bentley, Paul momentarily stopping and giving out a low whistle. 'Jesus, Charles, isn't that a Bentley Mulsanne?'

'It is indeed! You seem to know your cars – or should that be your Bentleys? – young man.' Charles gave another laugh. 'This is Clyte's – I mean Clytemnestra's – little runabout. Madam Clyte also has – at her disposal – the use of Boris, a very dour chauffeur and general dogsbody, but today you have to make do with yours truly! Red – or Ethelred – runs a grossly OTT Mercedes which not even God is allowed to touch!'

'Well, if you're going to have a two family car...'

'Oh, there're more, a Honda CRV and then a simple Ford estate for emergencies! The CRV is in use otherwise, I'm afraid, it would have been that instead of the iron horse here.'

'At least I won't have to be incognito in a mere Ford!'

'Would we do that to you? Ethelred's new star!'

If Paul's reaction at travelling in such an exotic car had been enthusiastic, his excitement at his first glimpse of Bethlem Báthory glowing in all its red brick and turreted splendour in the mid-morning sun, was twofold. 'Jesus wept, Charles! Is this for fucking *real*?'

'Very much so,' said Charles, a delighted smile on his long, aquiline face. 'And just wait until you see the interior. Outside it's pure Victorian Gothic while inside it even makes Phillipe Starck look outmoded!'

Looking at Charles, his eyes shining, all Paul could say was, 'Marrakech my friend, you have found yourself with some competition here!'

'Come and meet your hosts!' laughed a delighted Charles, thinking, Oh Dave, what a silly, silly young man you are. *This* young stud is going to be everything you should have been!

Ethelred and Clytemnestra greeted Paul with welcoming smiles and the inevitable glass of champagne. A beaming Viola – her heart had done an immediate loop the loop for here was another Bryan but a Bryan ten times more delectable that Sir Miles's one! – served the drinks while blushing and dimpling prettily at the bemused young man. Paul, used to the harmless flirtations with girls at drama school, gave the young girl a conspiratorial wink when accepting his flute. 'Lovely,' he said, in his deep voice, the word rich in innuendo, 'Absolutely lovely!'

'Oh my, Mrs. N,' Viola was to confide to the cook when back in the kitchen. 'This one's a real corker! He *can't* be one of them!'

'Take my word for it,' said the worldly-wise Mrs. Norelle. 'All them sort are. Look at that Rock Hudson for example. Poor Doris Day!'

Not aware as to whom the cook was referring to, Viola simply replied. 'Well, Jude Law isn't, that's a cert! He's got girls *and* kids everywhere!'

'Well, he's an exception then!' sniffed Mrs. Norelle. 'Unlike that Dr. Kildare!' she added triumphantly to the bewildered girl.

'Monday, our major domo, will show you up to your rooms in a few minutes.' smiled Clytemnestra. 'We've put you in "The Easy Rider" suite. Very macho and butch! Rather apt I think, looking at you, Paul!' She gave another light laugh. 'Don't you agree, Red darling?'

'Absolutely, Clyte!' He smiled warmly at the handsome young man. 'Charles has an impeccable eye. You'll be perfect for the scenes I have in mind!' He gave the anxiously hovering Charles a wink, causing Charles's shoulders to visibly sag with relief.

'Really, Mr. Jones?'

'Ethelred and Clytemnestra, please! And yes, *really*, Paul. You're perfect! Ah, and here's the other main member of the household, our major homo, big man Monday!'

Paul gave Charles a quick look at the words 'major homo' but received no acknowledgement of the glance. *Maybe I misheard him,* thought Paul. *But Christ, if that Monday guy's gay; talk about gay pride!*

'Hi there,' greeted Monday in a deep, dark rumble. 'Shall I show you to your rooms now so we can all relax over our drinks before lunch?'

Did he say *we* all relax over drinks before lunch? I thought he was staff? If Paul was taken aback at the laxity and obvious familiarity within the household, he gave no indication. *Oh well,* he thought, *from all I've seen so far, why am I surprised? After all, this is Ethelred Jones I'm actually standing in front of and we're already on first name terms!*

Lunch, served in the bright, airy dining room – EM Pei meets Richard Rogers meets Norman Foster over soufflé and poached salmon along with a crisp dry Sauvignon Blanc, laughed Paul to himself – was light-hearted with Ethelred keeping the diners in fits of laughter with his anecdotes about the famous and the not-so-famous. A grossly fat actor, recently in the news for an indiscretion in a public lavatory and who Ethelred cruelly described as a 'never-been even has-been panto queen' caused more mirth than anyone else.

'I met the guy once!' cried Paul, 'At a party given by some pompous old pouf gallery owner in Ennismore Gardens. I particularly remember him as he attempted to do a strip tease and was bundled out by the host's lover and a couple of the lover's rough friends *before* the obviously, very deflated, little *prick* tease!' He gave a loud laugh. 'It was all strip, certainly no tease and the poor sod was left standing in the street starkers, with one of the roughs refusing to hand back his clothes until he lay on the pavement kicking his legs, waving his arms and pretending he was a crying baby!'

'Did he get his clothes back?' cried Clytemnestra between chortles of mirth.

'Yes, but only after the lover and the two heavies had pissed on them!'

'Jesus!' muttered Monday.

'Delicious!' whispered Charles. He gave Ethelred a furtive glance, receiving a quietly mouthed 'Bull's-eye!' in return. Paul, for all his warmth and bonhomie had inadvertently let slip a glimpse of another side to the charming character he so readily presented.

'We have another guest for dinner this evening,' Clytemnestra informed Paul as they stood to leave the table, 'A friend of Monday's, a Vicky Watson. Apparently she's a stunner!' She gave a light laugh. 'What with you, Paul, Dave – whom you've yet to meet *should* he deign to return from either the garden centre or his enchanted forest – and Vicky, this, without doubt this will be the prettiest table in Ascot tonight?'

'Enchanted forest? What's that all about?'

'Well, it was to be a forest but now, due to a complication or two' – Clytemnestra gave a wry laugh – 'it's now to be a Christmas Fantasy. Dave is being very secretive about it and while it was initially a case of simply having to wait and see, it's now perhaps a case of wait and perhaps not see!'

Looking directly at Charles she added, 'There is a slight problem in that Dave may now have to leave before the work is completed but, thanks to our ever resourceful Charles, Trisomy's Christmas Fantasy will still be finished on time for it's gala night!'

'Trisomy?' This again from Paul.

'Our little girl, Paul.' Clytemnestra's large, dark eyes suddenly filled with tears, 'Our very, very brave little girl.' Pausing for dramatic effect she added quietly, 'You'll meet her in due course when she's ready. She's extremely sensitive to strangers so please don't take any delay in the introduction as personal.'

'No, of course not,' murmured Paul, looking furtively at Charles. *Now what?* he thought. *You never mentioned a child, old man. Doubtless I'm about to meet some precocious tap-dancing Shirley Temple-lookalike shrieking. 'On the Good Ship Fucking Lollipop!'*

'Would you like to play at little Bo Peep?' announced Clytemnestra skittishly, the earlier tears seemingly forgotten.

'Bo *Peep*?' Paul's voice took on a higher register.

'Not literally, dear!' laughed his hostess. 'But we do have a flock of rather unique sheep on the terrace lawn. Come and have a look!'

Taking Paul by the hand she led him out onto the terrace. 'There!' she said, pointing at the six silent red figures and the two white. Laughingly she named each of the sheep for him.

'Clytemnestra!' yelped Paul. 'I love you, Ethelred, Charles, Monday, Bethlem Báthory, the about-to-be-met Trisomy and most of all, the glorious fact that I'm actually *here*!' Grasping the smiling woman in a warm hug, he gave her a large, wet kiss on her cheek. 'Thank you!' he cried, 'Thank you! It's more than anyone could wish for. It's the Wizard of Oz come true!'

CHAPTER 20

'Do you have a family?' The question from Vicky sitting alongside him in the CRV took Monday by surprise.

'Err… no.' Monday gave a self-conscious laugh. 'I suppose you could say Bethlem Báthory is my family. The Jones practically took me in when I was down and out and I've been there ever since.'

'Oh,' Vicky sat silently for a moment before turning once again and looking at the dark, handsome profile. 'Mine live abroad but, surprise, surprise, Daddy dearest is here next week regarding some investments of his which need looking into.' She stared back out through the windscreen. 'I always find it so awkward having to play the doting daughter on such occasions.'

'Will you be seeing him?'

'Oh yes, duty calls etcetera, etcetera and, of course, there is also that little matter called my allowance!' She turned again and gave a grin. 'A very *important* little matter if you can excuse such a contradiction of words. We're having dinner on Tuesday.'

Shit, thought Monday, *just what we don't need. If she's dining with Daddy on Tuesday that certainly puts the kibosh on any fucking plan for tonight!* He said in his deep, rumbling baritone, 'That sound's nice, seeing your daddy.'

'More of a pain,' giggled Vicky, 'but, as they say' – and here she put her hand across Monday's massive thigh and with a vice-like grip squeezed his cock – 'there's no gain without pain and that monster of yours certainly causes the most glorious pain!'

'Jesus!' bellowed Monday, the sudden, searing agony in his crotch causing him to jerk the steering wheel, causing the powerful vehicle to swerve violently across the narrow road. 'Careful, you stupid cunt!' he yelled, 'We could've had an accident!'

'*What* did you call me?'

'Sorry,' mumbled Monday, 'That was out of order!'

'You're damn right it is!' snapped the girl, surprising Monday with her venom. 'Nobody, but *nobody* calls me a stupid cunt.' Narrowing her eyes she hissed the most derogatory comment of them all. 'Particularly an uppity nigger!'

Monday, slamming on the brakes, slewed the CRV to an abrupt halt. 'And nobody, but nobody calls me a *nigger*!' he roared. Balling his large, ham-like left hand into a huge fist, he slammed it brutally against the startled girl's face. With a large cracking sound, her right cheek collapsed inwards, the cheekbone completely smashed. With a soft whimper Vicky slumped down into the seat, blood streaming from her nose and parted lips, her eyes rolled back inside their sockets.

'Oh *shit!*' exploded Monday, 'Oh Jesus fucking bloody *shit!*' Glancing into the rear view mirror to check that the road behind was clear, he pulled out from the grass verge where the car had ended up, and slowly made his way along the empty road, his mind racing. Monday glanced down at the slumped figure alongside him. 'Fucking, stupid bitch!' he muttered. 'Guess you won't be meeting daddy dearest after all.'

Reaching for his mobile he pressed Ethelred's private number. 'Massa!' he said on hearing Ethelred's cautious, 'Mon?'

'Massa,' he repeated simply. 'Grade A fuck up boss, I'm driving straight to the side door of Charles's workrooms.' Monday clicked off knowing Ethelred would have immediately understood the seriousness of situation.

'What happened?' Ethelred, along with Charles, was waiting for him when he drew up in the CRV, the headlights blacked out.

'Silly bitch hit a nerve and I hit her.' Monday gave a shrug of his massive shoulders. 'Sorry, Red, but she err… made me see just that. Red!'

'Very funny, big man.' Ethelred looked at Charles who was busily examining the unconscious girl. 'How bad?'

'Not good,' muttered Charles. 'That must have been a hell of a punch, big man! Not only have you smashed her cheek but you've broken her jaw.' He looked up at the two men. 'I can patch her up but there'll be a hell of a lot explaining to do.'

It only took Ethelred a split second to make his decision. 'Stick her in the freezer. Or better still, Charles, a change in plan. I'll come up with some excuse as to why you're not at dinner this evening. Meanwhile, you get in touch with your people and see what they need. Anything left over, incinerate. You, Monday, clean up the seat and take the car back to Windsor. Call the house from there on the landline and say you've been stood up and will be not be back for dinner. Say you're off to get pissed in a pub and see if you can find yourself an alternative piece of crumpet! Now go! I'll explain all to Clyte.'

'I'll need some help.' This from a frowning Charles.

'So? Let Ethelred the *always* ready give you some help!'

––––––––––

'I'm so sorry Paul but your welcome dinner party seems to be somewhat depleted,' said a smiling Clytemnestra as the young man entered the main sitting room. 'Poor Charles has been called away for an impromptu meeting with one of Red's associates who has a stopover at Heathrow. The unexpected meeting is taking place at the Heathrow Hilton.' She gave a light laugh. 'As they say, "There's no business like show business" and Dickie – one of Red's Hollywood cronies – is known for these sudden "on the spot" assignations. Dear Dickie,' she mused, 'he really can be such an inconsiderate *dick* at times!' She looked towards the doorway. 'Yes, Viola?'

'It's Monday, Mrs. J. He says he needs a quick word.'

'Now what?' Excusing herself Clytemnestra left to take the call leaving a blushing Viola to stand staring at Paul.

'Hello again,' smiled Paul.

'Oh, pardon me,' stammered Viola. She glanced wildly round the large, airy room, her eyes settling on the open bar unit. 'May I get you a drink? I think Mrs. J was about to offer you some champagne but there's everything else, if you would like something else.' She gave a small smile. 'Monday usually does the drinks, but he's gone over to Windsor to collect the other guest.'

'No, he hasn't! I mean, no, there's no other guest,' interrupted Clytemnestra striding back into the room. She gave a grin. 'Poor Monday, he's been stood up!' The grin increased as did the twinkle in her eyes. 'God knows what this'll do to his ego! Our Monday Man sees himself as quite a

Casanova so this will certainly be a first.' She gave another light laugh and turning to Paul, added, 'I think I jumped the gun when I said our dinner party was somewhat depleted. It's now wholly depleted.' She gave another laugh. 'But then, Paul, what could be nicer than the three of us really getting to know each other? A glass of champagne? I've already opened a bottle.'

'Champagne would be great.' smiled the young man, thinking, Three of us? But of course, I've still to meet the daughter at an appropriate time but then I thought there was another person about, namely the gardener working on this Christmas Fantasy? Oh well, I'll simply have to wait and see. Taking the proffered flute from Clytemnestra he gave his most charming smile. 'Thank you, err, Clyte. And cheers!'

'Cheers to you too, and once again, welcome!'

Paul stood looking at his hostess admiringly. Clytemnestra, in her pale turquoise silk trouser suit with matching plaited silk head band, simply summed up the phrase 'A million dollars.' *No, make that ten million,* thought Paul, smiling inwardly.

As Paul stood enjoying his champagne looking forward to the evening, a smiling Charles stood studying the studying the naked body of the about-to-be dissected Vicky Watson while Dave Griggs's naked corpse lay, as yet untouched, inside a nearby freezer drawer.

———————

Dave's proposed journey to Dobbies Garden Centre near Windsor had never taken place. The young man, about to clamber into the CRV and drive away, was stopped by Charles who, on the pretence of 'having something interesting to show you' had lured Dave into his private workrooms. A grim faced Charles quickly approached a worktop shrouded in a white sheet and with a brusque 'What do you think?' whipped aside the cover to display a pair of muscular, perfectly preserved masculine legs.

'Shit!' was all Dave managed to squawk before the hypodermic syringe was plunged deeply into his neck. Being told to stand alongside a shadowy worktop prior to the unveiling, Dave failed to see the small figure standing silently on the counter top. With a delighted gurgle, Trisomy, on receiving a discreet nod from Charles's, simply plunged the needle deeply into the unsuspecting Dave's neck. The movement was made with sinister precision. Trisomy – under Charles's eagle eye – having been practising the use of a hypodermic on a much pierced melon.

With a soft choking sigh Dave fell heavily to the floor. 'Bigger than melon!' chortled Trisomy.

'And a perfect melon to boot!' sniggered Charles. 'Well done Tris, we'll make a little Florrie, Nightmare on Elm Street, out of you yet!'

Taking hold of the small figure he gently lifted her from the worktop and set her down alongside the unconscious Dave. 'Now, help me undress him,' Charles instructed, 'and then go and fetch Monday, like a good little gargoyle!'

Humming softly to herself Trisomy slipped off Dave's loafers and socks while Charles pulled off his T-shirt. Unbuckling the young man's jeans, he pulled the belt free from the loops before unzipping the fly. Aided by a panting Trisomy they managed to pull the jeans down Dave's muscular thighs and over his naked feet. All that was left were a pair of Calvin Klein briefs which Charles, after a moment's hesitation, quickly pulled down to expose the springy, brown crotch hair, the thick, flaccid penis and a pair of bulbous balls.

'Cock!' said Trisomy, prodding Dave's cock. 'Balls!' she added, prodded the sac. 'Big!' She observed with a giggle. 'Like needle melon!' she added with a chortle which ended in her choking briefly on a dribble.

'Yes, Tris, very big,' sighed Charles. *And that cock could certainly get bigger!* He thought lewdly. 'Now, what's this called?' Charles prodded at Dave's upper thigh.

'Thig!' said Trisomy proudly.

'No, dear, nasty little horrific one; thigh as in why. And this?'

'Karf!'

'Almost right, it's his calf!' He gave the little girl a pat on her bald head. 'Well done, Tris. Obviously our little anatomy lesson with Oswald's leftovers wasn't wasted.' Charles pointed to Dave's face. 'And this?'

'Nose!'

'Yes, so it is, Trisomy and guess what, you are going to help Unka Charles do some magic here and make one nose into two!'

'Gug!' gurgled Trisomy.

'And gug to you too, dear! Now, off you go and get Monday, I simply can't lift this dear man myself.' Charles couldn't resist a giggle. 'And to think of the times I allowed him to hump away on top of me! I'm surprised *this* delicate creature wasn't squashed!' He looked at Trisomy's retreating, shuffling figure. 'So, as the old saying goes "As one door closes, another opens!" Only, in this case it's more a case of 'As one cock goes another cock enters!"'

Charles's immediate plans were to deal with removing the requisite organs from Vicky as soon as possible; hence the excuse for missing dinner. A quick telephone call after Monday's unexpected delivery of the unconscious girl had seen Charles setting about to remove the donor parts during the earlier part of the evening, collection of these having been arranged for around midnight.

With regard to the sudden disappearance of Dave, the general story given to Mrs. Norelle, Boris and Viola was Monday, at the last minute, had been asked to drop Dave off at Windsor station. A situation involving a 'former business matter' had deemed it necessary for Dave to travel up to London where, it being a Saturday, he was planning to stay over for the weekend and maybe even a few extra days. A supposed telephone call would later be referred to where – much to both Ethelred's and Clytemnestra's annoyance – Dave would simply announce that he would not be returning to Bethlem Báthory.

––––––––––

'Very Dame Julie!' quipped Ethelred looking around the dining table.

'Oh?' questioned an amused Clytemnestra, her eyes sparkling, 'And why the Dame of Dire, dear?'

'Simple, dearest. As it's Paul and Paul alone with us, it really *is* a case of "Getting to Know You!"'

'Deborah, dear! Not jarring Julie. Miss "I'd love to blow Yul" Kerr in "The King and I."'

'Whatever!' Ethelred gave a resonant laugh. 'Welcome to Bethlem Báthory Paul. I trust your stay here, however brief or long, will be advantageous for you!'

'Thank you err... Red! And thank you too, Clyte.' Paul, slightly confused by the husband and wife banter but with a broad smile on his handsome face and his eyes shining, raised his wine glass in a toast to his hosts. 'To Bethlem Báthory and err... to all who rail in her!' he ended lamely.

'What a fun, original toast!' tinkled Clytemnestra, 'To all who rail in her? I like it! To all who rail in her!' she repeated, raising her own glass to Paul and her husband.

'To all who rail in her!' chorused Paul and Ethelred.

––––––––––

Later that evening, Paul, a large brandy in his hand, found himself seated on the wide window sill to the sitting room of his small flat, gazing out over the moonlit parkland and the shadowy buildings adjacent to the back part of the house. After dinner he had joined his hosts in the private viewing room where they had watched one of the recently released films now playing in a major London cinema. When Ethelred had suggested they all 'go to the cinema' Paul had not quite known what to expect. His delight at the choice of the film was further increased by Clytemnestra insisting on serving cartons of piping hot popcorn along with polystyrene cups filled with iced Coca Cola generously laced with rum. 'The *only* way to go to the cinema!' Ethelred drawled.

Exactly, thought Paul. *Especially if you have your own twenty-seater private cinema, a small kitchenette for snacks and a small bar to boot! Well, Paul Gunn,* he said to himself, taking a long, thoughtful sip. *I'm not quite sure what's going on here but it's certainly not quite kosher! People who never appear when expected but simply disappear instead?* Speaking out loud, he continued, 'A mystery daughter who is either Shirley fucking "Good Ship Lollipop" Temple or Linda fucking frightening Blair from "The Exorcist"?' And last, but not least a host and hostess whom I feel could give even Frank and Rosemary West a run for their money. While they don't have the misfortune to boast the looks of the F and R' – Paul gave a slightly drunken giggle – 'but the good fortune to have the looks of R and S, namely Rhett and Scarlett; there is something very definitely not quite right.' He took another long sip of his drink.

'Yes, Frank and Rosemary are evil but these two are more than that. Mr. and Mrs. Jones? Why, to me they are positively satanic, almost malignant and therefore not very nice! What's more, beneath all the charm they positively *simmer* with sadism and also – I bet – a touch of masochism! I swear, if Clytemnestra had had her way, she would have preferred a head band of thorns as opposed to fabric!'

Paul was just about to get up from the sill and pour himself a final nightcap when he was alerted by the soft hum of a car's engine. Straining his eyes he was just able to make the form of vehicle making its way slowly across the shadowy courtyard to Charles's workrooms. It was then he realised that earlier he had noticed lights on inside the building, albeit when Charles was supposedly away attending his meeting at the Heathrow Hilton. Thinking for a moment the car in question was the return of the mysterious Monday, he still couldn't make out why the car's headlights were turned off. As it drew up alongside the large door to Charles's workrooms, Paul realised the arriving motor was neither the CRV nor an estate car, but a black painted van. Within seconds of the van drawing up, the door to the building was pulled open and within the light spilling forth, Paul was able to make out the tall, thin form of Charles, and a massive, bulky black man who could only be the missing Monday. Two other figures in turn quickly stepped out of the van and were handed a succession of various shaped pails by the two men. Within what could only have been a brief few minutes, the van with the collected items had purred its way silently back away from the house.

'"Curiouser and curiouser," to quote little Malice in Wonderland,' muttered Paul. 'What *have* you been up to here Charles, when you were supposed to be elsewhere? And you too, Monday Man? Weren't you supposed to be drowning your sorrows in merry old Windsor?' Glancing at his watch and noting the lateness of the hour, he gave a dismissive shrug, 'Probably got back while we were watching the film. But then, what gives with the night visitors and the buckets? As I've already said, "curiouser and curiouser!"' Paul gave a giggle, 'Maybe some strange type of takeaway! But, as I've said before, nothing, but nothing at this bloody bizarre Báthory would surprise me! Now let's see what Charles has to say for himself should he decide to come over here for a "Welcome to BB" fuck!'

Stripping off his clothes Paul made his way into the bathroom where, having brushed his teeth and taken a long, hearty, noisy piss, he collapsed into the large bed where, having lain for a few minutes staring at the motorcycles and other movie paraphernalia, he drifted into a deep, alcohol induced sleep.

The buzzing of the intercom along jerked Paul awake from a dream in which he was being chased by Shirley Temple who in turn was being chased by Linda Blair. Both little girls were carrying pails and waving branches of thorns. As fast as Paul tried to run, the two little horrors managed to remain hot on his tail. Momentarily bewildered by the dark and unfamiliar surroundings, the young man grasped frantically for the buzzing instrument. Finally managing to hold the receiver to his ear he managed to croak a strangulated 'hello.'

'Morning, Paul!' came Charles's cheery voice. 'Wakey! Wakey! Breakfast in half an hour! See you then. You know where the breakfast room is, it's just off the kitchen.' Charles hung up.

'Shit!' Sitting up, Paul scratched his head, let out a long, loud, satisfying fart and lay back with a sigh. Idly playing with his semi erect cock he ended up having an energetic wank, his flat stomach splattered with jet after jet of hot cum. 'See what you missed, Charlie boy!' he laughed. 'That could have all gone *up* you!'

Twenty minutes later, having showered, shaved and changed into a pair of chinos, a T-shirt and a pair of loafers, he was being greeted by a dour Mrs. Norelle and a simpering Viola. A beaming Charles smiled up from where he was seated at the breakfast table. Of his hosts and the ever mysterious Monday there was no sign.

'Good morning again!' smiled Charles. 'Sorry I wasn't able to join you all for dinner last night.' He gave a slight grimace. 'Dear Dickie didn't let me leave until well after two this morning, so I didn't want to disturb the sleeping beauty on his first night here!' Charles gave a chuckle. 'But that's not to say he won't be disturbed from tonight onwards!'

'Two this morning? That's late,' responded Paul, reaching for a piece of toast. 'Come to think of it, I seem to remember hearing a car coming round to the back of the house at about that time.'

If he had expected some sort of reaction from Charles's to his comment, Paul was disappointed. 'Must have been Monday coming back from Windsor. Pass the honey like a good boy, would you?' said Charles with an unassuming smile. 'Red wants to see you in his studio after breakfast. He said elevenish so this gives you plenty of time to attack the Sunday papers.' Charles gave a giggle. 'I always start with The Sun and then work my way downwards. The Mirror is next, then the News and finally, that tome of tedium, The Times! Any of these interest you?' He gestured to the neatly folded pile on the table.

'I'll settle for The Mail.'

'I'll also be settling for *that* – namely a certain delicious young *male* I see before me – later!' chortled Charles.

'Which, as you know from your past reading experience, has a very adequate and very thick Sunday supplement to go along with the aforesaid male!' quipped Paul, a mischievous grin appearing on his face.

'Oh, I'm so glad you're here!' cried Charles. 'Clyte is always right!' Giving Paul a sly look he added conspiratorially, 'I'll explain later! Now, *silenzio* young man! I must return to the confessions of this gay cab driver with a penchant for Sumo wrestlers!'

'You're having me on!'

'Would I ever! Now read your nice Mail on Sunday and leave me to the lusts of cabbie Colin and his Japanese paramour, *Orochi,* which in plain Queen's English translates as "big snake!"'

'Now you *are* having me on!'

'No way. *Orochi* – according to this totally reliable paper – when translated means what I've just said, "big snake." In fact, if the name is anything to go by, cabbie Colin's lover boasts eight serpents' heads and eight serpents' tails on a dragon-like body.'

'Jesus! A fist only has five so-called serpents! Imagine a high eight as opposed to a high five!'

'Do you err... do you enjoy fisting?' asked Charles, swallowing hard and blinking at the grinning young man.

'I'm not known as Gouging Gunn, for nothing!' retorted Paul, giving a stunned Charles a broad wink and a lewd smile. 'Now read your paper like a good old queen; who knows what sort of cab fare I may have to reach up into your very own personal pocket for later!'

'Ohmigod!' With a startled cry Charles knocked over his coffee cup. 'Oh shit!' he added.

'That too, I expect!' snorted Paul.

'Unka Charles?'

Charles spun round in his chair to face the small figure standing in the doorway. 'Good morning, Tris!' he carolled, giving Paul a cautionary glance. 'You couldn't have timed it better, dear. Come and meet a nice new friend. Come and say hello to Paul.'

Paul watched with a growing sense of revulsion as the small, stooped figure shuffled its way across the tiled floor and over to where he sat. Watching the small, black eyes in their hollow sockets eyeing him warily, he was suddenly overcome with an all-consuming feeling of compassion. Instead of drawing himself away he leant forward in his chair and slowly holding out his hand, smilingly said in a soft, kind voice, 'Why, hello there Trisomy. How nice to meet you at long last. I have heard so much about you!' He glanced at the small roll of fabric in the little girl's hand. 'And what's that you're holding?'

Staring up at the kindly smiling young man Trisomy gave a small toothless smile in return. Turning her lizard-like head towards Charles she softly growled. 'Nice unka!' Turning back to Paul she handed him the neat roll of fabric. 'Pwesent fwom Twis to nice unka!' she said.

Charles, a look of growing horror on his face lunged forward to grab the roll but not before the little girl hand managed to place it in Paul's open palm. To his added horror Charles saw the fabric slowly unfurl to reveal a dainty finger. 'Cut it off when Unka Charles busy with other toy's cock,' she rasped. 'You like?'

Paul, who was regarding the amputated finger nestling on the piece of fabric in his hand with growing disbelief barely heard Charles's reprimanding words. 'Naughty, *naughty* Tris! You know Mummy Clyte will be very cross is she finds out you've been cutting up one of her shop mannequins again! Now, give the finger to me and I'll take it back to her studio before she starts to work!'

With a sleight of hand that would have made any conjurer envious, Charles whisked both fabric and finger from out from Paul's hand and, jumping to his feet, leant down towards the little girl. Taking her by her tiny, claw-like hand he whispered. 'Better still, why don't you come along with Unka Charles and help him fix it back on before Mummy has a chance to see us doing this! Then she'll never know and it'll be *our* secret!'

Without giving Paul a further glance. the ashen-faced doctor led the shuffling child from the room.

'A mannequin? Not fucking likely! That, unless my balls haven't dropped, was a fucking finger, Charles Crosby! A fucking female's finger.' Looking wildly round the gleaming, modern setting, Paul found himself repeatedly muttering, 'Just what the fuck is going on here and just what the fuck have I gone and gotten myself into?'

CHAPTER 21

Bryan looked at the unfamiliar writing on the cheap brown envelope. 'Someone must think I'm a cheapskate,' he smiled, glancing up at Miles who was deeply engrossed across the table in The Times. 'Not only a brown envelope but a second class stamp to boot!'

'Never judge a book – or envelope – by its cover,' murmured Miles with a slight smile, 'Could be fiver from some long lost aunt or even a tenner!'

'I have no long lost aunts,' laughed Bryan. He lent down at stroked Dongi, the golden Labrador's head, 'only this happy family.' He unfolded the cheap page of lined paper. 'That's odd,' he muttered, looking back up at his lover. 'It's from Dave, the gardener at Bethlem Báthory. What on earth can he want?' Bryan gave a sardonic laugh. 'He's left it a bit late if he now wants some help with his sodding forest. You should return your phone calls, my friend. Not ignore them.' Without giving the note a further glance Bryan put it back on the pile of already opened post, a sudden sixth cautioning him the contents, if at all indiscreet and blithely read out loud, could be upsetting for Miles. It was only later that a burning curiosity would induce Bryan to return to the note and its contents.

'Did you ever see that young man again?' The sudden question from Miles took Bryan by complete surprise.

'No,' he replied firmly, giving his partner a reassuring smile. 'Apart from leaving several messages for him to call me about some help with his project, I've not had time… as you well know, Sir Miles!'

'Only asking,' smiled Miles placatingly, 'Only asking.' Abruptly folding up his paper he quickly stood and excused himself by saying, 'I need to make a phone call. I'll catch you later.' He smiled back at Bryan. 'What time did you say we were due at the Sargents?'

'I didn't, but they're expecting us around noon.'

'Great.' With that the large man strode briskly from the dining room.

'Now what was *that* all about, Dongi?' Bryan smiled down at the dog sprawled-out on the floor alongside the table. Dongi, raising his head half-heartedly, thumped his tail lazily in reply to the question. 'And while talking to you, where's you soul mate, young Spavi? No doubt making Spaniel eyes at Mrs. Turnbull for another biscuit or two!'

At the mention of the word biscuit, the Labrador's tail began to wag more enthusiastically. With a great deal of panting and some effort, he pulled himself up onto his feet and without giving his master a second glance, trotted happily from the room towards the kitchen.

'So much for loyalty,' muttered Bryan, 'and talking about so-called loyalty, let's see what *exactly* Dave the non-rave has to say.' Without further ado Bryan, retrieved the page from the pile of correspondence alongside him. After a cursory glance at the contents, Bryan froze in his chair.

Dear Bryan, he read. *I don't know why you haven't answered my various telephone messages – I have left at least six for you – but then, perhaps because of Miles, you thought it better not to. I am sorry if you feel this way because I was hoping we would become friends. I don't want to cause undue alarm but, on receiving this letter, I would ask you to call me around seven one evening and as soon as possible please. If you are told I am out, do not accept this and insist I come to the phone or else you will come over. Make an excuse like saying you have something for me that can only be delivered personally. To put it quite bluntly Bryan, I am shit scared. Strange things continue to happen here and I really do not wish to be part of the scene any longer. I am in two minds about staying on to finish up my work on this Christmas forest for the daughter. Do not be fooled for one moment by this so-called child. She is not what she seems to be and I will explain more to you when we meet. Again, there is something very wrong about all this so-called filming that has been going on at the house. Furthermore, there also seems to be a quick turnover of bit players. One guy seems to have simply vanished into thin air. Please call me as I do need to speak to you, sooner than later. Yours, Dave. PS: Please do not discuss the contents of this letter with Miles. I will explain this to you as well.*

On checking the date at the top of the letter he saw that it had been written on the Thursday of the previous week which meant it had been lying unopened for a further eight days, the day now being the following Saturday.

Bryan's first reaction was to do what he had been asked specifically not to do and that was to read the letter to Miles but, having read through it again, he slowly refolded the sheet of paper and put it away in his hip pocket. Making his way to the kitchen he went straight to the telephone. Having checked the Bethlem Báthory number with Mrs. Turnbull – the cook was forever speaking to her sister at the other house – Bryan punched in the relevant digits. After a few cursory rings the phone was answered. 'Clyte? Bryan, Bryan Scima-Anstruther' – Bryan couldn't help a slight smile at his introduction – 'May I speak to Dave please? It's important.'

There was a moment's pause before Clytemnestra answered coolly. 'You could if he was here, but I'm afraid *Dave* is no longer an employee at Bethlem Báthory.'

'No longer an employee? What do you mean?'

'Exactly what I've just said. He no longer works here. Now, if you'll excuse me, Bryan, I must go as I have a client with me.' The phone went dead.

Bryan stood looking at the receiver in his hand before replacing it slowly back on its cradle. Deep in thought he vaguely clicked his fingers at the two dogs and, taking a coat and scarf from one of the hooks in the back hallway off the kitchen, he let himself out into the crisp autumn morning air. After strolling around the lake and having laconically thrown a few sticks for the dogs, Bryan slowly made his way back to the house. Oh well, he said to himself, sorry about that Dave but, if you've gone ahead and left as you said you most probably would; end of story. Half an hour later, Bryan threw the letter onto the fire in Miles's study; Dave and his fears soon forgotten.

Among the other post with the envelope addressed specifically to Miles, was a heavily embossed invitation on thick cream card with a double border of black and red for the combined November ECJ Fifth Film Premiere and Art Exhibition. 'Either very tongue in cheek or else blatantly ignorant,' Miles commented sardonically on seeing the relevant initials ECJ on the card. 'And, godammit, Bryo, they've gone and spelt your name incorrectly; something I could take as a deliberate slight!'

'Not to worry,' replied Bryan nonchalantly. 'It's the combined black and red band that intrigues me; almost funereal and bloody at the same time!'

'Typical Red and Clyte,' replied Miles with a chuckle, 'At least the card is clean. One of Clyte's previous invitations smelt suspiciously of piss!'

'Your're joking?'

'I joke not. The theme of that particular exhibition comprised of – if I remember correctly – paintings made by our dear Clyte showing different styles of lavatories around the world. The paintings ranged from grass huts in Africa to holes in the ground in India, and even a section of the Ganges titled "Golden Garbage."'

'Tell me you *are* pulling my plonker!'

'Yes, I am, actually,' laughed Miles. 'You should see your face!'

'And the exhibition is where?'

'Some exhibition centre in north London. What do you say?'

'Why, we most graciously accept!' Bryan gave a small laugh. 'How could this Bryan with an I and an A instead of a Y, possibly refuse? Besides' he gave a camp laugh. 'Who knows? The new Lady A may – at long last – even get his photograph in Tatler! Besides, due to us being away again in Italy we did miss Clytemnestra's Reflections exhibition, so it's only right we go.'

The "Reflections" exhibition, held at the ubiquitous at the Claudia Cordelle Gallery has received rave reviews with the two 'Cum and See Men in Reflection" – as the glossy black flyers inside the programmes proclaimed the two portraits to represent– being sold at an exorbitant price to a mysterious American buyer. Later investigations had seen a gleeful Claudia informing an equally gleeful Clytemnestra the mystery buyer was none other than the new wife of Texan oil billionaire, Derrick Donoghue the Third. 'Proves there must be something in the old saying,' Claudia said laughingly in a phone call to her friend. 'As with the former Angela Ansturther, once you've been with a black, you'll *never* look back!'

'I love you Bryo Scima-Anstruther!'

'Likewise Sir Milo! Likewise!'

———————

'What do you think?' Charles, a scowling Trisomy standing alongside, looked expectantly across at Clytemnestra.

'They're beautiful, Charles, really beautiful!'

'Thank you, Clyte.' Charles glanced down at the little figure next to him. 'And thanks to Tris as well. She's been ever so helpful!' He gave a laugh. 'I've gone as far to dub her Florrie Formaldehyde due to her formidable skill at preserving bits and pieces!' Charles reached for a perfectly preserved hand. 'Usually the most beautifully preserved skin can appear waxen, but look at this, as smooth as a baby's bottom!'

'Whatever turns you on, Charles,' replied Clytemnestra with a grin, 'But these legs! Oswald, oh Oswald, if you could see yourself now!'

She stared thoughtfully at the pair of legs, each leg mounted separately on a gravel covered plinth. The legs, both upside down with the thighs firmly pinned to the bases, had been slightly bent at the knees to give the impression of being in motion. Charles, on Clytemnestra's instructions, had kept the feet bare so the toes and soles were visible. 'I plan to paint an eye on the sole of each foot,' Clytemnestra explained to Ethelred earlier when discussing the setting. 'The eye emphasising the comment "watch your step" as the loathsome Oswald-that-was cruises the park!'

'How on earth will people be expected to get that bit of symbolism?' came the laughing response.

'It's all covered in the catalogue with an analysis as to the meaning of my tableau.'

'Have you asked Albert?' came the quick riposte.

'Albert? Who's Albert?'

'Einstein, dear! No fucking run-of-the-mill pleb will ever get that one.'

'Oh, fuck off, Red!'

'Now *that* my dear any run-of-the-mill pleb *would* understand!'

Glaring furiously at her grinning husband for a few seconds, Clytemnestra burst out laughing. 'You're so *fucking* right, as always, dearest! "Fuck Off" it shall be! Much more suitable than, "Watch your Step!"'

'Shorter too!' Ethelred quipped, 'The words – not the steps!'

Leaning forward to examine each of the two upturned feet, Clytemnestra gave a small nod of satisfaction. 'Perfect, Charles, absolutely perfect. I plan to inscribe the words in red edged in black. These two colours will be the only accent colours used in the whole group of tableaus. Everything else will be white apart from the natural flesh tones. Items such as Dave's hair – head and pubic – will all be bleached the purest white.' She gave a sigh. 'God, I really do have my work cut out!' She looked back at Charles who, like herself, had given a light snigger at the unintended pun. 'And talking about Dave, where *is* our seated figure?'

Charles pointed to a high covered form adjacent to another steel dissecting table. 'The mount is ready for the final musculature and then we'll begin stretching the skin over this within the next day or two. Give us three days and then you'll be able to see most of your half-hearted young man.'

Charles gave a chuckle. 'Tris has had a great time with some of the leftovers!' The chuckle gave way to a camp giggle. 'She's made the most marvellous "Malice in Wonderland" type caterpillar from the half cock I let her have, while making a lollipop out of the remaining testicle, stick and all!'

'You're sick, Charles Conrad Crosby! Completely and utterly depraved! Poor Trisomy, whatever next?'

Charles lowered his voice conspiratorially even though Trisomy had wandered away from the two. 'You're not meant to know this, but she's gone and made you a special fruit bowl from part of Oswald's pelvis. The *bowl* had been painted a bright yellow and speckled with red. More pus-lookalike than Picasso, but that's artistic licence for you!'

'Jesus,' muttered Clytemnestra.

'No. Trisomy,' laughed Charles. 'Oh, and Clyte, Tris, in her selection of the one and only eye, has settled for a green one. Maybe you can use that in the catalogue. Something like the old proverb, "The grass is greener" perhaps?'

'You can almost go and do what your two *sole* mates are about to do, Charles. Fuck off!' came the laughing response. 'But not before the half-hearted Dave is well and truly signed, sealed and delivered!' She gave another laugh. 'And a definite no to the green eye; I want a red eye and that is *not* meant to be funny, so no bright remarks about my choice being *flighty,* if you don't mind!'

'Would I?'

'Again, Charlie Brown, fuck off! Would I indeed?'

'Joking apart, Clyte, how do I create a red eye?'

'Think lollipop!'

'Lollipop?'

'Yes, lollipop. What bits of Dirk's have we got left over in the freezer, if any?'

'Genius, Clyte as always. Most bits have been used for the scattered toys setting, but his balls are still bagged up, so to speak.'

'There's your answer, then! A red lacquered testicle will be perfect!'

'Take it as done! Furthermore, it'll fit perfectly into the eye socket!'

'Gives a whole new meaning to the word *eyeball*, doesn't it, Charles?' chortled Clytemnestra before turning and making her way elegantly towards the main door.

'Clyte! Hold on a second. There's something you should know, something which may or may not be a problem.' Quickly Charles went on to explain the incident involving Hettie's solitary finger being inadvertently given by Trisomy to Paul.

'Jesus!' A stunned Clytemnestra stared at Charles, her face filled with genuine alarm. 'Do you think he bought the story about it coming from a shop mannequin?' she blurted out.

'Yes and no,' replied Charles cautiously. 'I think the poor lad was even more stunned than I was! Again, I don't think he got a really good look at it. Furthermore, it has been preserved so there was no blood or any such give away.' Giving Clytemnestra a reassuring look even though he himself was not at all convinced by his comments, he added, 'It really *did* look like a plaster finger and, as he wasn't expecting a real one, why should he doubt it?'

'Well let's hope for all our sakes you're right.' Clytemnestra gave Charles a worried look. 'Give me five minutes to present our lord and master with this little Hiroshima! I'll see you back at the house. In Red's study.'

'Leave it,' had been Ethelred's instant reaction to the disclosures. 'The lad's bright but not that bright. And, as you so rightly say Charles, in no way was he expecting to see a genuine finger!' After a moment's pause his face lit up with a crafty smile. 'Clyte dear, you still have a couple of shop mannequins lying about, don't you?'

'Yes, there are two left over from my "Hand Job" exhibition.'

'Perfect. There's our solution to the problem! Lucky Paul is going to get yet another tiny gift from his latest adoring little fan. Tantalising Trisomy is going to secretly approach Paul with a second finger, similarly wrapped and hand – ha! – said finger over as a further welcome present! Only this time it will be a plaster finger!'

'Did I ever tell you, you were a genius, husband devious?'

'Endlessly Clyte, my love, enldessly! Now, chop, chop! – oh dear, did I really say that? – go find our dear little daughter and literally "give her the finger!"'

———

The following morning found Paul, seated in the kitchen at the small staff breakfast bar, a morning paper on the counter in front of him along with a solo cup of coffee which was forever being topped up by the ever vigilant Viola. After her initial good morning greeting and a few stilted sentences the young girl eventually returned to the chore of preparing a pile of vegetables, leaving Paul once again concentrate on the sports section.

'Unka Pau! Unka Paul!'

Discerning several soft snuffling sounds coming from behind, followed by the child's cries, Paul swung round on his stool, looking nervously down at the small, humped figure beadily eyeing him and giving him what appeared to be a fierce scowl. 'Oh, hello Trisomy,' he said, forcing a smile. 'What have you been up to?' He nervously eyed the roll of fabric she was holding. 'Not another err... little present, is it!'

'Yes!' croaked the tiny figure proudly.

'Oh shit!' murmured Charles, taking the roll from her, his hand shaking violently. 'Oh shit!' he cried again as the folded fabric opened and a finger fell with a clatter onto the tiled floor.

'Trisomy!' This from a startled Viola who, staring wide-eyed down at the fallen object, began to laugh! 'Oh naughty, *naughty* Tris!' she cried, 'Oh, naughty! Naughty girl!' Still laughing, the young woman bent down, scooping up the plaster finger in her own plump ones. 'That was a wicked, wicked trick to play on Unka Paul and me! Why, you nearly gave us both a heart attack!' She held out the false finger to an ashen-faced Paul. 'Like parents like daughter!' she laughed. 'Only Ethelred and Clytemnestra's own flesh and blood could ever dream up doing something quite like that!'

'Pwesent' repeated the tiny figure before giving a still shocked Paul and a beaming Viola a toothless, dribbling smile. After a moment's pause, she made an abrupt about turn, before shuffling her way back out of the kitchen.

'Is it really a false finger?' whispered a still disbelieving Paul.

'Totally. She must have gotten it from one of those shop figures in Mrs. J's studio. Well I never! Wicked Trisomy! What *ever* will you think up next!'

'God, that's twice now she's fooled me with that trick,' laughed Paul, visibly relieved. He gave Viola a sly smile. 'I think this deserves a drink, don't you? Shock and all that!'

'There's some brandy in the cupboard next to you.'

'With junior miss playing pranks like that on all the unsuspecting guests, I would have thought bottles of brandy as de rigueur throughout this whole bloody house!'

Viola stood alongside the again seated Paul, sipping her brandy nervously. 'God help me if either Mrs. N, Boris or Monday catches me having a drink with you!' she whispered, looking anxiously at the several arched openings leading into the kitchen, 'Or Charles, for that matter. Right bunch of weirdoes they all are.'

'Which brings me to the question, Viola; why do *you* work here?' Paul gave a small laugh. 'Don't get me wrong but you seem to me to be so, so... well so bloody *normal*!'

'Two things; money and the chance of meeting Ethelred Jones. I once had ambitions about being an actress and when I heard there was a vacancy at the illustrious House of Jones, I jumped at the chance. I saw it as an opportunity of being "discovered" as it were, by the legendary man himself. After all, Lana Turner was discovered in a milk bar; Swabbs – to be exact – on Sunset Boulevard!"

'Lana who?'

'Oh, never mind. Simply some old Hollywood star! But somehow this didn't happen and I'm still waiting to be discovered,' Viola gave a self-deprecating laugh, glancing down at her ample figure. 'Obviously there's only one Bridget Jones and please, Mr. Paul, don't ask me who Bridget Jones is!' She gave another laugh. 'So, my "being found" is now well and truly on the back burner. I have met one or two fairly big stars down here but I don't, and never will, hold a candle to any them. Despite their eccentricities, I find I enjoy working with Mr. and Mrs. Jones.' The young woman flushed slightly. 'Also, one gets to meet nice young men like yourself, even though you are all mostly gay! Oh shit!' Viola put her hand to her mouth. 'Please forgive me Mr. Paul! I didn't mean it to come out like that! I meant no offence!'

'No offence taken, Viola!" Paul gave a soothing laugh. 'Do you have a boyfriend?'

'Oh yes, Clive. His family have a hardware store in Windsor.' She gave a mischievous chuckle. 'I'm always teasing him about the good-looking young men I keep meeting up here at Castle Dracula. Get's right to him at times, it does! Keeps him on his toes too!'

'Well, all I can say is that your Clive should consider himself a very lucky young man! Furthermore, he ought to marry you as soon as possible before Count Dracula or one of his gang get hold of you!'

'Oh, we're already engaged,' giggled Viola coyly. 'We're getting married next summer.'

'Now that bit of news deserves another brandy and I can assure you, I won't be telling.'

Still giggling, the young woman held out her glass for a small refill. 'You're so like Dave,' she smiled. 'It's so sad you didn't get a chance to meet him.' She took a dainty sip. 'Dave was such a nice young man, unlike that dreadful Oswald. Now he wasn't only *gay* but, as Boris described him, a hideous, evil screaming queen!'

'Well, I must say it's a great comfort to hear I don't fit into the same category as Oswald! But tell me more about Dave. He suddenly left didn't he? Several days ago in fact?'

'Yes, last Saturday to be exact; he day you arrived. He was supposed to go over to the garden centre as he usually does – or did – most Saturdays, but suddenly decided to up and leave. Oswald virtually did the same thing. Here one day and gone the next. Most strange, but then most show business people seem to be – well – strange!' Viola gave Paul a small smile. 'That's why I'm secretly glad I decided to give it all up and settle down with Clive.'

'As I said before, Clive's a lucky guy and I think what the two of you are doing is great!'

'Thank you, Mr. Paul.'

'Paul, please Viola. I insist. I'm Paul, not mister Paul.'

'Thank you err… Paul!' Viola gave a warm, gentle smile. 'You are *so* like Sir Miles's Mr. Bryan. You should meet him. Poor Dave thought they would become friends, but Mr. Bryan never contacted him again after the one time they met here at a dinner party. At one stage Dave was hoping Mr. Bryan would be giving him a hand with that new forest he was working on, but nothing came of it… oh shit! Someone's coming!'

Quick as a flash Viola disappeared, brandy glass in hand, through to one of the pantries.

'Ah, there you are!' said Charles walking briskly into the kitchen. 'We've all been wondering where you were! Join us for a drink before lunch? Say in an hour in Red's study?'

'I'd be delighted to!'

'And Paul, I shouldn't be telling you this, but you may be treading the boards sooner than you expected which will enable you to set off for Marrakech within the next few days!'

'Really?'

'Yes, Really.'

An earlier meeting between Ethelred, Clytemnestra and Charles had seen the demise of Paul quickly resolved. 'I'll film him doing a few scenes involving him walking through the yew walk, surveying the topiary; plus his arrival and departure from Windsor station. He'll simply be told he'll be spliced into a new film I have in mind and leave it at that.'

'Won't it seem a bit strange? No co-stars?'

'Ah, but there will be!'

'Oh?'

'You're forgetting Viola!'

'What's Viola got to do with it?' This from Clytemnestra.

'She's always had aspirations about being an actress and, as she's now changed her mind and will be leaving us next year to marry some buffoon whose parents own that shop in Windsor, why not give her a small part as a farewell gift? No, don't look so worried, the two of you! All I'm going to suggest is we have her step onto the train in Paul's departure scene; a touch of "Brief Encounter."'

'If you insist, husband dear, but I don't see this gesture of yours serving any purpose?'

'I'm not thinking purpose, dear, I'm thinking alibi. It adds strength to Paul's *testi*-mony – unfortunate choice of word – him being employed as a *boner* fide actor at Bethlem Báthory.!'

'Very subtle, Red!'

'Why thank you Charles and now, can you take over as director and direct our little Trisomy, finger and all, in the direction of the kitchen and about-to-be convinced Paul!'

'Your wish, as always, is my command.'

———————

Viola's reaction to Ethelred's suggestion was as expected; the young woman was ecstatic. 'Me, a walk on part in your next film Mr. J?' she cried, 'But that's fantastic. Wait until I tell Clive! Imagine his expression when he hears he's marrying a movie star!'

'Furthermore, you'll be in a scene with Paul.'

'Now that *will* get tongues wagging.' Viola gave a tinkly laugh. 'I'm sure Mr. Paul's going to be a super star one day, and I'll be able to tease our kids by showing them what a sacrifice their mum made by marrying their dad and having them instead! Will I be able to get a copy of the film on a CD, Mr. J?' she asked anxiously.

'I'll make sure you'll have at least six copies, Viola!' laughed Ethelred.

'Great, that'll be one for each of the brood!' came the laughing reply.

CHAPTER 22

It took Paul only a day to make his decision. 'No way was that first finger a piece of fucking plaster!' he said out loud in the privacy of the Easy Rider suite. Fortunately for Paul, as with all other guest suites at Bethlem Báthory, this one was also bugged but, due to its present occupancy of one, no transcripts of any conversations were being recorded. 'That first finger was the real McCoy!' He'd further gone on to say to one of the silent motor cycles. 'Plus this story about those two lads suddenly disappearing also doesn't hold any water. Charles is no more a PR person than I am, and as for that daughter? Now that *is* a joke. This whole bloody place is more a horror film than a home, and I've gone and landed myself right in the middle of it!' Having seated himself once again on the window sill, he sat looking contemplatively at the verdant parkland surrounding the vast house. 'Neighbours!' he suddenly said out loud again. 'This Bryan character; I wonder whether *he* knows or suspects anything? Maybe this Dave bloke could have said something before he too so conveniently disappeared!' Paul gave a grim smile. 'Well, Gunn, there's only one way to find out!'

Taking Viola into his confidence he asked for the telephone number to The Grove. 'I'm curious to meet my double!' he'd laughed. 'Maybe the three of us can even go out for a drink one evening and really get your Clive up and running!' Giggling, Viola happily recited the number.

'Good morning. Is it possible to speak to er... Mr. Bryan, please?'

'Mr. Bryan is up in London, sir. May I take a message?'

'Is it err… possible to speak to him in London? It's more a business call than personal.'

'Of course sir, please hold while I get you the office number.' After a few moments the voice came on again, giving the Berkeley Square number.

Thanking the woman who he thought could only be Mrs. Norelle's sister, the gossipy Mrs. Turnbull, Paul dialled the number. 'Anstruther Associates!' came the prompt reply.

'Good morning. May I possibly speak to err…' Paul, to his horror realised he had no idea of Bryan's surname. 'Err… Mr. Bryan?'

'Of course, sir! Whom may I say is calling?'

'Paul, Paul Gunn. A friend of Dave's from Bethlem Báthory!' Paul couldn't help giving himself a silent high five at this sudden flash of inspiration.

'One minute, please, Mr. Paul. A friend of Dave's at Bethlem Báthory!' Paul could not help but notice the slight camp in the receptionist's voice.

'Mr. Gunn?' The voice, deep and resonant, sounded both courteous and cautious.

'Mr. Bryan?'

'Bryan Scima-Anatruther speaking. How may I help you Mr. Gunn? Please forgive me, your name is not at all familiar, but I understand you're a friend of Dave's, the gardener at Bethlem Báthory?'

'Well, not really, Mr. Scima-Antruther; see it more of a curiosity seeker than a friend!'

'Curiosity seeker? Sorry, Mr. Gunn, I'm a bit confused here?'

'Mr. Scima-Anstruther – oh shit! May I call you Bryan and rather than try to give any details over the phone, is there a chance we can meet?'

'Has something happened to Dave?' The disembodied voice had suddenly taken on an anxious tone.

'Well, I don't know if something has actually happened to him, but he's gone and suddenly disappeared. I was expecting to meet him but never did.'

'To meet him? Are you calling from Bethlem Báthory?'

'Yes. I'm calling from my room. Is this a problem?'

'Have you a mobile?'

'I have.'

'Get off this line, pronto! Also get out of the house and call me back from the privacy of the grounds as soon as you can!' Bryan hung up.

'Well, well, Mr. *Scima-Anstruher*! Nice to talk to you too!' Picking up his mobile and taking his duffel coat from the cupboard, Paul made his way down to the kitchen and out of the house. Once in the main topiary garden he punched in Bryan's number. This time he was put through immediately.

'Paul,' came the warm voice. 'I'm so glad you've called back. Our brief conversation has me very worried. Can you explain a bit more about Dave's so-called disappearance, and then I'll explain why you've now got me concerned?'

'You sound like a guy I can speak to quite openly,' said Paul, relieved at the genuine tone he was hearing.

'Please do,' said Bryan. He added grimly. 'And I think what you're about to tell me is going to make me kick myself for being such a bloody, arrogant idiot!'

With some relief Paul explained the sudden departures of the two young men plus the strange incident concerning the two fingers.

'Whoa!' came Bryan's reply. 'Maybe they *were* dummy fingers! After all, you didn't expect the girl to literally "give you the finger!" did you?'

'Put that way, no!' said Paul, unable to hold back a laugh. 'But it *is* all a bit strange don't you think?'

Bryan went on to tell Paul about Dave's note. 'Reading between the lines Dave was planning to do a bunk anyway. More than likely he's back in London and happily gardening away as we speak.'

'Maybe; but what about this Oswald character.'

'Paul, this Oswald character as you put it, is – I can assure you – another story!' Bryan gave a warm laugh. 'Look, what I suggest is you keep a low profile, do this so-called bit of filming work if you must and then get the hell out of there. Though, on second thoughts I really do think we could be making a big pile of shit out of a little one!'

'Maybe you're right.' Paul gave a sigh. 'Tell you what, I'll do these few scenes for Ethelred, collect the loot and hot foot it back to town. After all is said and done, a few days work with the mighty Ethelred Jones will look most impressive on my CV!'

'When do you think you'll be back in London then?'

'Thursday at the latest. We're filming my Oscar winning scene on Windsor station tomorrow. I walk the walk in the topiary garden where I'm actually calling you from, later today.'

'What will you be doing in London?'

'I'll check into a hostel and then take off for Morocco as soon as I've sorted out a ticket. I plan to chill out for a few weeks in Marrakech.'

'Sounds great.' There was a moment's silence before Bryan said impulsively, 'Look Paul, I don't know you from Adam but, instead of staying in some godforsaken hostel, come and stay in Cadogan Square. We've got a spare room.'

'Jesus! Do you really mean that? Why, that would be great.'

'Call me later – here, take my mobile number – and I can give the address and such. And Paul, keep this under your hat, would you? I don't think it wise for the cast of castle Dracula to know any more than essentially necessary! Speak to you this evening perhaps?' The phone went dead.

———————

Ethelred showed no surprise at Paul's change in plan. 'We thought you'd be staying a bit longer but I can understand the lure of Marrakech plus the odd spiff or twelve! Anyway, let's do these scenes while the weather holds. Autumn is always so unpredictable.'

A relieved Paul was pleased to note that apart from Ethelred, Euros and Kevin, Clytemnestra, both Charles and the dreaded Trisomy seemed to have done a vanishing act. He was also informed Mrs. Norelle would be serving him the remainder of his meals in the kitchen. 'With the projects in hand there won't be any small talk, only tedious work stuff so you're better out of it with a magazine or a book!' Ethelred explained.

It was then Paul, more anxious than ever to be leaving Bethlem Báthory, came up with his previously thought out, exit line. 'Why don't I, when instead of simply acting as if I'm about to get on the train and depart from Windsor, I actually *do*?' he suggested to Ethelred.

'Why not?' replied Ethelred, giving Paul a sharp look. 'Only we'll have to have someone put your luggage in another part of the train while we're filming you clambering on. Can't have you looking like an escaping refugee now, can we?' If Paul had hoped to detect any innuendo in Ethelred's passing remark, he was greeted instead by an inscrutable smile.

Paul called Bryan later from the privacy of the terrace lawn. 'A change in plan, Bryan.' he announced, 'and I hope it won't be putting you out but any chance I can come and stay tomorrow night as opposed to Thursday?'

'But of course!' came the reply. 'Miles, my other half is up in Scotland until Friday, so if you don't mind being incarcerated alone with me, that's absolutely fine.' Bryan gave a soft laugh. 'What time do you think you'll get here?'

'Well, we're completely restricted by the departure of the trains so, depending on the daylight, I should think round about six.'

'Brilliant. Tell you what, why not take the circle line from Victoria and meet me in Sloane Square. There's a terrific restaurant bar just along from the station, The Botanist. They make a mean Martini! I'll meet you there. Simply look out for the most handsome guy sitting solo at the bar!'

'You're on and Bryan… thanks!'

'Don't mention it. See you at around six then. Bye!'

A smiling Paul clicked off his phone. 'According to Viola all I do is look for my doppelganger perched over a Martini glass,' he said laughingly to the topiary representing Ethelred's cock, 'Shouldn't be a problem sussing out the most handsome guy in to room!'

———————

'You made it!'

'Bryan, good to meet you and thanks for all you're doing and already done so far!' Paul gave a laugh. 'According to Viola, the maid back at Bethlem B, we could be twins! All I can say is if I look like you, it's quite a compliment!'

'Touché! That Viola must have perfect taste as well as being a seeker of perfection!'

Paul gave a hearty laugh, warming instantly towards the smiling young man. Jesus, he was thinking, aren't you a dish and isn't this Miles character the lucky one?!

Bryan, staring back at Paul was thinking along similar lines with the exception of his final thought. If it wasn't for Miles, he was thinking, I wouldn't have any hesitation in asking this one to join me in a fuck! Instead – and feeling an immediate pang of remorse at so disloyal a thought – he quickly said, 'Maybe a Martini to celebrate our good looks or something else?'

'I'll join you in one of those but preferably with vodka.'

'Like me!' Bryan ordered the drink for Paul and another one for himself. Waiting until the two drinks had been placed in front of them he toasted Paul with a smile and a nod. 'Right, 'he said, 'still thrown by the two fingers? Or have you reconciled yourself to the fact they were dummy fingers after all?'

Paul took a sip of drink before turning back to Bryan, a sheepish expression on his handsome face. 'As you said, I think I really did overreact somewhat. I didn't expect to see a finger in the kid's hand and once I actually took hold of this, second time round, it was false alright!' He took another sip. 'If I'm to be completely honest with you, I think it was more of a case of the whole lot; the house, its owners, plus – in retrospect, Charles – which finally got me. I tell you, Bryan, the combination of the inhabitants, plus the place with its Gothic exterior and way out interior, I found more spooky than had the whole house been a crumbling heap of derelict rooms, with a cast Hammer House of Horror-lookalikes.'

'Tell me about it. I was only there once for dinner, and that was quite enough. Did you meet the black guy, Monday?'

Paul shook his head. 'No, he seemed to steer clear of me.'

'Bloody giant he is and, if you ask me, more than a mere odd job man if you catch my drift!' Looking Paul directly in the eye Bryan couldn't help adding. 'Plus he was fucking the former Lady Anstruther before I came along!'

'Jesus! I'm sorry…'

'Why should you be sorry? Miles and the dreaded Angela had been contemplating a divorce for some time and it just so happened some convenient Texan billionaire chanced to enter the rampant Lady A's life. So, instead of black dick she's gone for a black derrick instead!' Bryan gave a laugh. 'Not that the new lover-now-husband's black, his *name* is Derrick and he's in oil, the colour of which just happens to be black!'

'All's well in oil well!' quipped Paul.

Bryan let out a hoot of laughter. 'Now *that* my friend, deserves another Martini!'

Several drinks later the two young men staggered out into Sloane Square where Bryan immediately hailed a taxi. 'We're actually only five minutes walk from here,' he explained as they clambered into the cab, 'but I don't think the two of us could manage your clobber, even though it's only a case and a bag. We'll drop this off, have a drink and then head off somewhere for a bite to eat. If you like Italian there's a great place round the corner from us in Walton Street.'

On arrival at the flat Bryan let them into the large, elegant hall where, dropping the piece of luggage he was carrying, he clasped and equally clasping Paul into his arms. They never made it to Scalini's for dinner.

———

'Morning Paul, I've brought us a tray with two mugs of coffee, some cream and sugar! I didn't know if you wanted it black.'

'Err… good morning.' A tousled Paul smiled shyly up at a smiling Bryan, resplendent in a brightly silk dressing gown. 'Black with a splash of cream would be great, No sugar, thanks.' He looked furtively round the luxurious bedroom with its cream coloured walls, bright chintz curtains and two comfortable matching armchairs.

'Don't worry, you *are* in the spare room, so no guilty DNA samples for Miles to find!' Bryan gave a light, self-conscious laugh. 'Would you believe me Paul if I told you that you are the first guy I've been with since the advent of Miles?'

'Yes Bryan. I would and I do.' Paul held out his hand. 'Come here and say a proper good morning to your grateful guest!'

———————

Bryan and Paul sat cosily at the glass topped table in the kitchen, two mugs of steaming coffee having replaced the earlier two which had been allowed to get cold. 'Well, Mr. Gunn,' said Bryan reaching for his companion's hand. 'We seem to have gotten ourselves into a bit of a situation here.'

'Yes, Mr. Scima – *nota bene* no Anstruther! – I think we have!' Paul pulled Bryan's hand up to his lips and kissed it gently. 'I think, Mr. Scima, Mr. Gunn oughtn't to stay on but get to that airport and Marrakech as soon as possible!'

'Must you, Mr. Gunn? We do have another day and a night left in which to try and make not only dinner tonight, but even lunch today!'

'Oh, shit, Bryan. Why did this have to happen now? Why did I have to ring you? Why couldn't I just have buggered off to Morocco and never met you?'

'I wish I could say the same but Paul, let's face it. I've been thanking my lucky stars since I left you sleeping this morning to go and make the coffee, you *did* call me!' Bryan lifted both their hands to his lips. 'I wouldn't have missed last night and this morning for anything!'

'Me neither. Jesus Bryan, as they say, quite a fuck up!'

'With you and the fuck part the most fabulous fuck up of all time! Now this other part of the fabulous fuck up must get his act together, and head for the office. Make yourself at home and let us meet for lunch. We have a lot to discuss.' Bryan got up from his seat and moved over to a worktop where he scrawled a quick address onto a notepad. 'Here,' he said tearing off a sheet of paper and handing it to Paul. 'Let's meet here for lunch and have a serious talk. Somehow I think we're more than a one night stand, Paul, and you've got me worried.' Leaning forward Bryan handed him the piece of a paper and kissed him lightly on the forehead. 'See you later, and I've left a set of keys for front door on the hall console table,' he whispered, before turning and making his way quickly out of the kitchen.

Bryan had suggested the two meet at Balans Restaurant in Soho's Old Compton Street. Paul, having visited the premises for Air Maroc in Regent Street and made his reservation for a flight to Marrakech the following day, made his way slowly along Brewer Street before finally arriving at the restaurant, only to find Bryan already waiting, the de rigueur Martini placed in front of him.

'Hi!' A beaming Bryan stood up in greeting and kissed a startled Paul resoundingly on the lips.

'Jesus! Bryan!' cried the embarrassed young man, forcibly pushing him away. 'What the fuck do you think you're doing? We're in a public *restaurant* for fuck's sake!'

Unrepentant, a smiling Bryan simply gave a shrug, replying, 'This is Balans, it's a well-known gay restaurant and nobody gives a damn as to whether I kiss you or not!'

'Still,' said Paul uncomfortably glancing around the glossy, dimly lit interior. 'I'm not one for such openness. I may be gay but I don't believe in being an out and out *gay* gay, if you catch my drift.'

'I think I just have,' said Bryan quietly as he sat down again on the banquette seat. He nodded as a smiling waiter suddenly materialised and placed a Martini glass down on the table. 'I took the liberty of ordering you a Martini and telling them to bring it over as soon as my guest arrived. I trust you don't find *that* too much of a gay thing!' he added defensively.

Paul looked at the glowering young man opposite in surprise. Whoa, he said to himself, his mind racing. Here we go, the guilt trip and what the hell would Miles say should he ever find out. Instead he simply lifted the glass in a silent toast and took a sip. The two sat in a strained silence before Paul spoke. 'What's up? Regretting last night, Bryan? Don't. Simply treat it as a one night stand. We both were a bit pissed and simply fucked, that's all! Our conversation this morning can be seen more as guilt than the genuine article, so let's leave it at that. Let's order lunch and talk about it over dinner this evening.' He gave a wry laugh. 'I'm booked to fly tomorrow anyway, so

I think maybe we can keep out hands off each other and behave in a civilised manner!'

Instead of defending the mutual attractions and actions of the previous night, Paul was dismayed by Bryan's obvious relief. 'I like you Paul, I like you a lot and I would like us to become friends, maybe even part time lovers, but that's as far as it goes. That's what the kiss was for when you arrived.'

'Friends? Part time lovers? Jesus, Bryan, it's either one or the other, it can't be both! It's Miles, isn't it?'

'Yes, it is.' Bryan looked nervously at the agitated young man opposite. 'We've even gone through a civil partnership ceremony…'

'Ah,' said Paul icily. 'I see a replay of a certain scenario here. The new Lady Anstruther simply has to keep up the tradition of a lover on the side, while husband *slaves* away at the business!' He gave a snort. 'Only difference is I'm not black!'

'That is *so* unfair!' bellowed Bryan, this reaction causing a few fellow diners to turn and stare 'You've got it *so* wrong! Jesus, Paul, we're much more than a one night stand! We're both in agreement about that!'

'I know, I know,' said Paul placatingly, glancing around at several sniggering couples engrossed in watching the unfolding scenario. 'Can we discuss this later please and not here.' he whispered.

'Oh, fuck off!' A red-faced Bryan crumpled up his paper serviette and, throwing it down on the table, stormed out of the restaurant. To Paul's added embarrassment one table of very obvious queens gave a loud round of applause at the departing figure, followed by shrieks of 'Get you, girl!' and 'Not so butch after all, eh, butch?'

An equally red-faced Paul quickly finished his drink and, leaving a ten pound note on the table, got up and strode out the restaurant, his formidable glare at the aforesaid queens ensuring a silent exit.

That evening, a subdued Bryan, having tried several times to call Paul on his mobile but without success, returned to Cadogan Square, half expecting to find that Paul had already left. It was with a combination of disappointment and relief when he found the front door simply on the latch and both the keys and a brief note lying on the hall console.

Dear Bryan, he read, *I'm sorry but I feel it best not to see you again tonight. We both know it would only lead to further complications and unhappiness. You have simply come into my life like the proverbial bolt of*

*lightning, but it's obviously too late for anything to come from this. (I keep
using that word come!)* – Bryan, tears welling up in his eyes, could only give
a small smile and mutter, 'You silly, beautiful bugger!' – *so I've decided to
use a hostel after all and will be flying off to Morocco in the morning. Have
a happy life, dear Bryan. I would have loved to have been you lover, but a
fulltime lover and one for life. I really did find my Waterloo with you, albeit
too late. All my love. Paul.*

'Oh fuck! Fuck! Fuck!' sobbed Bryan as he slid down against the
wall alongside the console table. 'Why, oh why, did what happened to you
have to happen to me but only *after* meeting Miles. Viola was right, you *are*
my doppelganger, my soul mate and I've gone and lost you forever!'

After several minutes he dried his tears and made his way slowly
through to the large sitting room where, taking some ice cubes from the ice
maker in the drinks cupboard, he poured himself a healthy tumbler of neat
vodka. In his heart of hearts he kept waiting for the front door intercom to
buzz, or his mobile to ring – he'd tried Paul's own mobile several times,
only to receive a recorded request for a message to be left but leaving none
in return – while accepting the fact this was not and would never be going
to happen.

A wild dash to the airport the next morning was also contemplated,
but again full information regarding Paul's flight was not known and Bryan
was well aware that Paul may even have gone so far as to change airlines.
Several vodkas later, a drunken but more rational Bryan agreed what had
occurred, was for the best. In a fit of tearful remorse he sorrowfully –
wallowing both in self-indulgence and self-pity – begged the absent Miles
for forgiveness over his misdemeanour. Doni, Skavi and the house in the
Cinque Terre were also asked for their forgiveness regarding his 'fucking
one night stand!' the irony of the last request being overlooked in-between
the resulting flood of fresh tears.

———

The following night, Paul, sitting having a glass of wine in the
Medina found himself approached by a laconic, elderly and obviously very
rich American living in a conglomerate of converted houses within the old
town. Several more glasses of wine lead to on to an invitation to dinner and,
on hearing Paul had checked into some dubious youth hostel, an invitation
to spend the night. Paul, delighted by the elderly man's waspish humour and

obvious zest for life, found himself falling under his spell. Not only did he 'pooh pooh' Paul's so-called latest dalliance, but told him to 'get your act together.'

'Take someone like me,' the smiling man had said over their after dinner liqueurs. 'I woke up today and said to myself, maybe today's *my* day – or week – or year and look, here *you are!*'

Two days later Paul had taken up residence in the man's exotic home.

––––––––––

'So much for true love,' he'd muttered to the starlit sky while standing on the terrace on his first night in residence – his host snoring nasally in the large bedroom behind. 'Bryan, oh Bryo – without knowing it he had casually slipped into using Miles's special name for his lover – what a total fucking mess. There you are in England with your lover, and here I am in Marrakech with someone I suppose I could easily get used to! I never saw The Grove but I did get an idea of your lifestyle from Cadogan Square. However, my friend, you should see this little place. *Maison* Godfrey Goulding Junior – although in his sixties! – would give even the most over-the-top Hollywood set designer a run for his marble and lattice! Think Barbara Hutton on crystal meth and you'll still only have a faint whiff of how lavish *this* little pad is!' He gave a small smile. 'Now that's one in the eye for you Viola, I bet *you* have no idea as to who Barbara Hutton was. Or even Woolworth's for that matter, seeing that's also defunct!'

A soft, petulant cry of 'Paulie? Paulie? Where are you?' caused Paul to give the sparkling constellations the finger before breaking into a small smile and calling back softly, 'Paulie's coming Goddie and when I say I'm coming, I'm coming back to bed and *cumming* again and again inside you!'

'Oh goody, *goody*!' came the soft, giggly reply. 'Gorgeous Goddie would like that.' followed by another coy giggle. 'Gorgeous Goddie *loves* Paulie Waulie's big peenie weenie when it does spouty wouty!'

Paul couldn't resist a hissed 'Shit!' before making his way back into the gauze-draped and mirror-tiled bedroom. *Well, as they say, there's no gain if you complain,* he thought, breaking into a small smile as he approached the shadowy figure. And let's face it GG, your Paulie Waulie sees no reason for complaining. No reason at all! I think I'm going to *enjoy* being here whether it be for another day, a week or maybe even a year!

CHAPTER 23

'Well, tonight's the night!' A smiling Ethelred smiled at his wife sitting alongside him in the Bentley as the luxurious motor cruised silently towards the exhibition hall, set in a former food packaging house in the sprawling northern section of London named Islington. He squeezed Clytemnestra's hand. 'Happy?' he asked. 'Happy with what we left a few hours ago.'

'Very,' said his wife emphatically. 'Though I must say I nearly had a purple, fucking fit when part of the lighting circuit went up in sparks! Literally!' Clytemnestra gave a small laugh. 'But all's well that end's well, so the evening should be a great, great success my darling!' She leaned her elegantly, coiffed head against the leather headrest, 'First the showing of the film and then the walk through the exhibition and the tableaus – what an evening for the Jones, dearest. Do you think our star studded guest list has any idea as to what is in store for them?'

'Hardly. The PR and subsequent press coverage has been so subtle and appetite whetting, the poor dears are positively salivating at the mysteries about to unfold.' Ethelred lent forward. Delving into the seat pocket in front of him he pulled out a thin, square velvet box. 'A thank you present, my dear Clyte, for your genius and your being you!'

'Red!' purred Clytemnestra. 'You shouldn't have! Being Mrs. Ethelred Jones is thanks enough!'

With excited fingers she unclasped the box to reveal a sparkling diamond bracelet. 'No phials of cum for you tonight, my dearest.' smiled

Ethelred. 'You'll be having the real McCoy later! They say diamonds are forever so here you are; Clyte and Red forever!' Taking her hand he gave it another squeeze. 'In fact, as we have time, why not try it on now?'

'I plan to!' She gave her husband a mischievous grin. 'Just what are you up to, husband dear? I know that look.'

'So, have a look!' In one swift movement Ethelred unzipped his trousers, showing he was wearing no underwear and thus exposing his long, thick cock. 'His and hers,' he whispered nodding down to the thickening length, the heavy folded foreskin beginning to slide back slowly over the club-like head.

'I *love* it! I *love* it!' With a shriek of delight Clytemnestra slipped the sparkling bracelet over her thin, elegant hand and onto her wrist. Dropping her hand down alongside her husband's erect cock she gave a sharp intake of breath. 'Twins!' she whispered, 'A perfect match!' With a soft cooing of delight she leant down and kissed the matching diamond cock ring tightly embracing the brace of Ethelred's formidable length.

'Make me come!' Ethelred gasped, 'Make me come and I'll show you the ultimate party trick!'

Ignoring the stoic Boris in the driver's seat, staring directly ahead, Clytemnestra began to pump Ethelred's cock with a well-practised expertise.

'We're about five minutes away, Mrs. J,' murmured Boris, his eyes still firmly fixed on the busy street ahead.

'Thank you Boris.' Clytemnestra began pumping away with a renewed vigour and, feeling the start of Ethelred's orgasm, bent down, taking his violent, spasmodic cock in her mouth as he began came in a series of thick, hot spurts. Having greedily swallowed Ethelred's salty offering, Clytemnestra sat up and felt inside her small, bejewelled evening bag for her compact and lipstick, skilfully reapplying the bright red gloss to her smeared lips, as the ever tactful Boris pulled the car to a halt, a discreet distance yards away from the exhibition hall.

'One minute, Boris,' instructed Ethelred. Giving Clytemnestra a quick kiss on the cheek he murmured the words. 'Now we swap!' With a quick sleight of his hand he slid the cock ring down his still saliva-covered cock and held it out to a grinning Clytemnestra who, in turn, removed her own bracelet and slid it back over his now softening length. 'May I?' he said holding his wife's hand.

'But of course!' Clytemnestra replied as Ethelred slid his former slimy cock ring over her hand and onto her wrist.

'Just as well my wife has such a delicate hand and wrist!' Ethelred purred.

'Just as well my husband has such a huge cock!' came the purring reply, 'Imagine if I had ended up with a mere ring as a thank you present!'

'May I now proceed Mr. and Mrs. Jones?' asked the calm voice.

'Of course you may, Boris!' giggled Clytemnestra, 'We wouldn't want to be late for the *main* show of the evening, now would we?'

'Absolutely *not*, Mrs. J,' came the crisp reply.

Several photographers along with a few curious bystanders stood lining the roped-off black, red edged, carpeted steps, leading up to the massive, wide open doors to the towering warehouse incorporating the Invictus Gallery. Boris drew up alongside the carpet whereupon two doormen, both dressed in black trousers with red Nehru-styled jackets were waiting to open the doors. 'Perfectly timed, Boris!' remarked Ethelred with a sly wink, nodding in the direction of the cars beginning to pull behind them, 'Almost as if they were waiting in the wings.'

Yes, and waiting for this performance to start, thought the dour chauffeur. *Just wait until I tell Nanette about the latest performance so blatantly – and noisily! – carried out by our lord and master and the mistress on the back seat of the Bentley!*

A smiling Victor Invictus, a portly, short little man of about fifty, dressed in what Clytemnestra wickedly described as 'a very odd boiler suit on an extremely old boiler,' and his equally smiling partner, a pumped up Chippendale look-a-like who – to the sly amusement of their so-called friends and acquaintances – had named himself Kochno, after the lover of Diaghilev, the founder of The Ballets Russes. 'But why Kochno and what's Diaghilev to do with it?' the young man would be constantly asked. 'Because my Victor is to art what Diaghilev was to the ballet,' he would respond with a self-satisfied smirk, 'An inspiration and a genius!' The final gilding of the lily would be the final denouement. 'He also has the most impeccable and exquisite taste, hence *me* in his life!'

In reality Kochno's legitimate name was Sidney Brim, an ex-rent boy from Falmouth, who had been picked up by Victor one night in a salubrious gay bar in Vauxhall. Having satisfyingly beaten up and fisted Victor during a never-to-be-forgotten weekend, Sidney had been duly ensconced as a definite member of the Invictus household. Several years on, a constantly bruised and sometimes limping Victor still claimed as never being happier. Kochno's impressive collection of rings, Rolexes, designer gear and a never ending succession of flashy cars only went to show – as Clytemnestra dryly observed – 'The proof of that pudding is in the beating!'

Kochno's endless visits to a 'facial and body enhancer' in Brazil were again almost as legendary as his life story.

'Clytemnestra! A divnity in red. Let me guess? Dolce? Prada? Yves?' The rotund little man, clasping her hands in his plump, ringed ones, pursed his equally plump, slightly rouged lips. 'No! No! Don't tell me… *Donna*! It must be Donna!'

'Spot on Victor dearest!' laughed Clytemnestra, air kissing the elderly man above his rouged, apple-like cheeks. 'And Kochno!' she cried, 'Don't you look good enough to swallow!'

'Thenk you, Clytemnessssstra!' hissed Kohno sibilantly through his latest, surgically enhanced lips.

It's a cupid's bow to make the most cherubic of cherubs feel let down and rush off to the nearest botox doctor for immediate resuscitative work! thought Clytemnestra, vaguely air kissing a heavily powdered cheek.

'You isss so kind!' Kochno's idea of a Russian accent was equally as startling as his waxed and artificially sculpted face. 'Eethel!' he went on to say to a grinning Ethelred standing behind his wife. 'As always you look so pees elegant!'

'Why, thank you Kochno! Coming from you that is indeed a piss-taking compliment!'

'Pliss? After all thees years Eengleesh still confuses!'

'I'm sure it does,' agreed Ethelred. 'Now, if you'll excuse us, we have a show to oversee!'

'Cunt!' muttered Kochno to the departing figures, 'Fucking poncey arsehole. Piss off yourself! Who the fuck do you think *you* are Ethelred, bloody Jones?' he added in a pure Cornish burr. With an angry shrug he turned to follow the three into the already crowded lobby of the exhibition hall. A ripple of applause began as Ethelred and Clytemnestra made their through the parting throng, the applause swelling to a loud crescendo amidst cries of 'Welcome! Good Evening! Can't wait' and 'Good luck!'

Having led his two guests onto a podium set up at the end of the vast entry lobby, Victor raised a plump hand for silence. Eyeing the well dressed, excited crowd he began to speak in a shrill, camp voice. 'Ladies and gentlemen,' he trilled, 'It is not often one is blessed, but I am fortunate to be able to stand up here in front of you this evening and say that tonight we are *all* blessed, blessed by the fact that we have the privilege of being with two of the greatest artists this country has produced this century. Ladies and gentlemen, it is with the greatest of pleasure I give you the king of the film genre and the queen of the canvas, Ethelred and Clytemnestra Jones!'

Further applause and excited cries of 'Hear! Hear!' greeted Victor's introduction as the straight-faced guests of honour, not daring to look at each other, kept smiling stoically ahead.

'Tonight we begin with the first ever showing of Ethelred Jones's film, "Still Life," which will be followed by a walk-through an exhibition of Clytemnestra Jones's paintings, some of which have been inspired by her husband's film. Finally there is the ultimate three dimensional experience of actually *walking* through several scenes from the film as well as the works of art. Ladies and gentlemen, our ushers are ready to show you to your seats in our specially constructed cinema for the evening. After the showing you will then be led to the gallery and on to the tableau room. Later, a delicious champagne buffet will be served in the Sky Gallery to celebrate tonight's event. Thank you ladies and gentlemen and enjoy the experience of a life time. And once again, please welcome Ethelred and Clytemnestra Jones!'

A flushed Victor, taking both Ethelred and Clytemnestra by the arm, proudly led them down from the podium and into the cinema tent which had been set up inside the vast, main exhibition hall.

'Just look at their faces?' giggled Clytemnestra, nudging an equally giggling Victor. 'See, they've first of all looked inside the catalogue and having read that they are "Experiencing the Sperm Experience" now realise they are actually sitting inside what appears to be a giant condom!' She turned to her husband. 'Genius dearest, pure genius; only you could come up with the idea of the audience sitting inside a giant, plastic, condom lookalike tent for the viewing of "Still Life!"'

'Well dearest, as the programme duly informs one, we all began life as a happy sperm and sometimes one of those jolly little sperms gets held back! Yet another interpretation of the film's title!'

'Genius! Bloody genius Ethelred!' came a cry from one audience member suddenly putting two and two together. 'Ladies and gents!' he went on to bellow with glee. 'We're actually *sitting* inside a fucking – err, excuse me – inside a giant condom! Read your programmes!'

More laughter and cries of, 'What fun! Such imagination! So original!' and 'Such genius!' kept spewing forth from the highly charged and excited crowd, the cries only abating as the lights dimmed and the film began.

'You've got to give it to the two of them,' whispered Miles who was seated alongside Bryan a few rows behind Ethelred and Clytemnestra – they

had managed a vague wave at the couple as they were taking their seats –
'they certainly know how to put up a show.'

'Tell me about it,' said Bryan with a snort. 'Christ, if this is what a
poor cock feels like in a condom, no wonder riding bare back is preferable!'

'As well we know!' whispered his lover. Squeezing Bryan's
muscular thigh, he added quietly, 'Enjoy the film. I promise you, knowing
Red, we won't be let down!'

A stunned silence greeted the end of the hour long film. After a few
embarrassed coughs, a few claps were heard which grew only slightly in
volume. Eventual muted cries of, 'Bravo! Bravo,' began to echo through the
plastic confines of the tent, more out of politeness than genuine enthusiasm.

'I'm going to be ill!' and the more genteel 'disgusting!' were
interspersed with 'well, it's certainly different' and the more occasional 'I
think it's what they call a snuff film!'

'What do you think?' Ethelred whispered to Clytemnestra as they
stood up to follow a silent and perplexed-looking Victor through to the doors
leading to Clytemnestra's own exhibition.

'Red darling, it's your best ever. It is *so* repellent; *so* fucking odious
and such, such pure fucking *genius* and I have never, ever been more proud
of you!' Clytemnestra made a tiny gesture at the silent crowd following in
their wake. 'The critics will love it while the hoi polloi will try to understand
it and then, not to be out of vogue by those "in the know", will claim it your
best ever! This will *slay* them in the States and it won't be hara-kiri they'll
be practicing in Japan, it'll be *hurry queue-ie* to see the film!

'Did I ever tell you I love you, Clytemnestra Jones?'

'That does happen to have a familiar *ring* to it, Ethelred Jones!'

The reaction to Clytemnestra's painted depictions of several violent
scenes taken from what had just been seen on the cinema screen was on a
par with that to the film. Comments such as, 'brilliant technique,' 'wonderful
colour tones' and 'so realistic,' couldn't override the fact the invited audience
had been well and truly shocked. However, still to be seen were the much
hyped tableaus of 'A Half Hearted Walk in the Park' and 'Broken Toys,'
both of which had been described as being 'wholly independent' from the
film and its associated paintings.

'Christ knows what the tableau room holds for us?' muttered Bryan.
'Jesus, Miles. How on *earth* did they manage some of those scenes? I know
Ethelred's a genius with his digital and special effects, plus the fact Euros
Peacock has won endless awards, but that scene with the rats? Christ!'

'What about that Monday's dick?' commented Miles sourly. 'I can't see why Angela ever complained about mine being too large having seen the size of that bloody anaconda of his! Let's face it, mine's a mere earthworm compared to that!'

'That, Miles Anstruther, is total bullshit!' Bryan gave his lover a nudge. 'Special effects Miles, special effects! Digitally enhanced remember?'

'I'll make sure *you* remember when we get back home!' came the laughing reply.

Having glanced at a few minor settings, including 'The Thinker,' taken from the paintings, Miles and Bryan were finally able to make their way through the thronging, silent viewers to the pièce de résistance of the evening, 'A Half Hearted Walk in the Park.' While the two had expressed amazement at the skill and quality of the other exhibits, especially 'Broken Toys' – a patch of white faux grass containing a scattering of abandoned limbs including an oversized broken doll, her one dismembered leg clad in a white sock and wearing a black, buttoned, strapped patent leather shoe; a boy's arm holding a cricket bat and finally a clown's head impaled on a giant twisted stick of barley sugar – they were completely unprepared for the next tableau.

'Jesus!' muttered Bryan.

'Good God!' murmured Miles.

'Oh, I can't look! Simply can't look!' cried a startled woman before dissolving into a fearful whimpering and having to be led away by her indignant husband whose mutterings of 'Perverts!' and 'Disgusting!' were soon to acquire a substantial following.

Clytemnestra, aided and abetted by Charles and Monday, had duly set up a small paved walk way of white painted bricks edging onto a white faux grass knoll. Positioned to one side of the tableaux was a red park bench on which sat a perfectly halved, naked male figure. The figure, with its pure, almost waxen flesh tones boasted half a head of luxuriant white hair which cascaded down to its one shoulder. Similarly, the pubic hair, adjacent to and partly above the halved penis, was also a dazzling white. The penis, perfectly sliced from top to bottom to leave one half intact, still displayed a perfectly halved foreskin and half exposed glans. The viewable half glans had been finished in a bright red to match the one and only similarly red coloured eyeball; an added touch of whimsy being the toenails to the one foot, three of which had been painted red and two black. 'Rather like those fucking sheep!' Bryan was heard to mutter.

'How on *earth* did she do that?' asked a mystified Miles, to no-one in particular. 'You've got to give it to her; the woman's a bloody genius!' He looked across as Bryan who was studying the upside down pair of legs, a look of pure and utter horror on his face. 'Byro? Byro? Are you alright?'

'Just get me out of here, Milo,' gasped Bryan. 'Please, just get me out of here! I think I'm about to be sick!'

The mere fact that Bryan had used the term 'Milo' as opposed to the more formal, public Miles, proved to Miles just how serious the situation is. Grasping a retching Bryan by the shoulders he propelled him furiously through the crowd, shouting 'Make way, please! Make way! This is an emergency!' Half-carrying the young man down the main steps, he managed to get him to a shadowy corner outside the building whereupon Bryan was violently ill. Holding the shuddering, shivering young man in his arms, Miles whispered consolingly. 'There, there, Bryo, I've got you! You're safe now,' amidst other endearments of 'I love you Bryo,' and the more anxious, 'What is it? What happened in there? Darling, dear Bryo, please tell me!'

'Oswald!' Bryan finally managed to gasp before violently retching again. 'Oswald!'

'What do you mean, Oswald?' asked a bewildered Miles.

'Those legs! Those upside down legs!' Bryan's voice rose to a strained almost screeching sound. 'They're Oswald's!'

'What do you mean they're Oswald's?' asked Miles, his voice incredulous.

'They're his! They're his!' sobbed Bryan. 'Oh Miles, Oswald never left that bloody house; they killed him. Those legs!' Bryan let out an almost feral-like cry. 'Our tattoos! One of those legs in there has the *His* of the *His* and *Hers* tattoos we had done when we were together! The leg! The fucking leg has *His* tattooed on its ankle! Remember, I still have *Hers* tattooed on mine!'

'Christ!' muttered Miles, 'So, at last the shit *does* hit the fan.' He put a comforting arm around his still shivering lover. 'Come on, young man, I'm taking you straight home. I think we have a lot of talking to do.'

Miles raced through the lighter traffic and within a silent forty minutes they were back at Cadogan Square. Bryan had remained curled up on the passenger seat throughout the journey, his eyes staring vacantly at the rapidly passing streets, as if he was in a trance. During one stage of the tense ride Miles had seriously considered taking Bryan to the nearest Accident and Emergency unit but common sense prevailed. I'll get him home, he said to himself, and try and talk him through this. Shit, Clyte! How could you have been so fucking irresponsible? How could you have overlooked such a glaring error? He glanced down at the silent figure next to him. 'Bryan?' He gave the young man a gentle nudge. '*Bryan*!' Seeing he was to get no further response he tapped a number into the speaker phone. On receiving instructions to leave a message, Miles simply said. 'He knows.'

CHAPTER 24

Ethelred had noticed Miles's departure with an obviously distressed Bryan, with a feeling of foreboding. Excusing himself from a group of supposed well-wishers – Ethelred was well aware of a growing hostility towards him and even Clytemnestra from the usually effusive crowd – he quickly made his way to the privacy of a nearby corridor where, pulling out his mobile, he saw there was a message waiting. On hearing the two words, 'He knows,' Ethelred stood frozen for a few seconds before he replied. Miles answered after a few rings. 'Red, we've just got back and I'm about to deal with it.'

On hearing Ethelred's stunned 'Are you sure?' Miles continued. 'Oh, I'm sure alright. Apparently a tattoo on the little sod's ankle was overlooked. A *love* token for Chrissake!' Miles gave a small laugh. 'All *I* noticed was the wording on the soles of the feet! Pity Bryan didn't do just that!' He gave a sigh. 'You'd better get back to your reception, Red, before you're missed. Call me later on your way back to the house.' Miles hung up and, taking a deep breath, walked back into the study where Bryan was seated on the sofa, a large, untouched brandy on the coffee table in front of him.

'Bryo,' said Miles firmly, picking up his own drink and seating himself alongside the silent figure. 'Bryan!' he said more loudly, and almost angrily. 'Bryan, for God's sake pull yourself together! Here, take a sip of this.' Picking up Bryan's drink he held it to the young man's lips. With a wild cry Bryan hit Miles's hand away from his mouth, causing the drink to spill down the front of Mile's dinner jacket. 'Don't you *dare* touch me!' Bryan growled, his eyes blazing. 'I *heard* what you said in the fucking car, Miles! I heard you fucking say *He knows*!' he yelled. 'Just *what* do I know, Miles? Huh? Tell me? Just *what* do I fucking well know? That you all killed Oswald?' The last sentence came out in a combination of a screech and a scream.

'For fuck's sake! Enough is enough!' hissed Miles, slapping Bryan sharply across the face, not once but twice. 'Not only keep you fucking voice down but pull yourself together!' he hissed again, his usual rich, warm baritone venomous and chilling. 'Pull yourself together, sit up straight and listen to me.'

'I don't want to and I don't have to listen to you!' spat out Bryan, glaring at Miles while holding his furiously stinging cheek. 'You fucking murderer!' he added with a snarl.

This time it wasn't a slap but several solid punches to the face, followed by a painful left deep into Bryan's solar plexus which followed this latest tirade. 'Yes! Not only will you listen to me but you're also going to behave yourself. So, instead of acting like some hysterical drama queen, take a sip of your brandy, and *listen.*'

A subdued Bryan, holding his throbbing stomach with one hand and the brandy glass with the other, sat glaring at the stranger sitting calmly alongside him. 'Who are you,' he finally managed to whisper, unable to bring himself to keep looking at the cold, calculating eyes staring so intently and so cruelly into his. 'You're not Milo,' he added almost inaudibly.

'Oh, I'm Milo alright,' smiled Miles, saying sardonically, 'Only, a side of Milo which, until tonight, you hadn't met.' He took a sip of his own brandy. 'Oh Bryo, dear Bryo, what a total fuck up with the sixty thousand dollar question being, of course, what happens now?' He leant back against the comfortable sofa and, staring directly ahead asked simply. 'Do you love me, Bryo?'

The question caught Bryan completely by surprise. '*What?*' He cried, his eyes widening. 'After what you've just insinuated you can still sit there and ask me *do I love you*?'

'Well, do you?'

Bryan looked at Miles, his face a picture of utter misery and confusion. 'I don't know, Milo,' he whispered. 'I really, truly don't now know.'

'Well, I truly love *you,*' came the response. 'God, I really do, Byro, so let me try and explain.' Miles nodded at their empty glasses. 'This may take some time. Would you like another brandy or shall we have a bottle of champagne.' He placed his hand gently on Bryan's knee. 'I'm sorry I hit you, Bryan, and I swear it will never happen again. But I was frightened, frightened of what you were about to do to me and even more frightened what you may try to do to yourself! I love you, my darling, and please, please never forget it.'

'Oh Milo!' said Bryan giving a large, heart-rending sob. 'Tell me it's going to be alright! Tell me nothing's going to change!' With a cry he flung himself into Miles's arms, sobbing heavily against his brandy soaked chest.

'There. There.' murmured Miles soothingly. 'There, there. Everything's going to be alright. That I promise!'

Several minutes later, Miles, his wet jacket and shirt replaced by a sweater and Bryan in a dressing gown, the two were again settled on the sofa in the study. 'Right,' said Miles. 'I'm sparing you no punches, Bryo. What I'm about to tell you is extremely serious, completely confidential and if word ever got out, there would be the most dire consequences for all concerned. This includes me, Bryo, and to be quite honest, I am putting my complete trust in your love and loyalty with what I'm about to say.' Miles paused to take a sip of champagne. 'For some time now Ethelred has always wanted to make a snuff film' – Bryan gave a loud gasp – 'and what we saw tonight was indeed just that, a snuff film. There were no special effects; those so-called innocents in the so-called wood were actually killed by Monday and yes, those rats were real and *did* eat their way out of that boy.' Miles thought it best not to mention that the screaming victim had been Oswald. 'Oswald got wind of what was going on, and threatened Ethelred with blackmail by saying he would be going to the police. Oswald, as you know, could behave irrationally at times, so it was considered the only way to prevent any unpleasantness was for Oswald to quietly disappear.'

'Did he...?'

'No Bryo,' Miles assured him softly. 'He didn't suffer; he didn't suffer at all.' Miles took another sip. 'He was simply put to sleep.' He looked at the stupefied expression on his partner's face. 'And that's the truth, Bryo.' He gave a sigh. 'Ethelred found a letter addressed to you in Oswald's belongings. The letter made no mention of the film but simply said that he, Oswald, was – to quote – "about to make a mint" and then went on to say you would be sick with envy when you saw what you had missed.' Miles gave Bryan an uncomfortable look. 'His last written words to you, my darling, were "May you rot in your mundane misery, you pathetic, nothing queen.

God, even cancer would give you the widest, possible berth!'" Miles looked at Bryan who sat sorrowfully eyeing him, the tears streaming down his cheeks. 'Sorry Bryo, I never wanted to tell you this. When Ethelred showed me the letter I insisted he burned it. I never wanted you to experience such hatred from a so-called friend and former lover!'

Miles took the sobbing young man gently by the hand. 'The boy and the girl used for the snuff scenes were a couple of druggies, derelicts, the scum of society, and no good to anyone. They won't ever be missed. Now Ethelred has achieved what he wanted to do and again, Bryan, yes, I helped him. As you know I have helped finance several of his films and this "Still Life" was no exception. Those so-called business talks about Red investing in the Cinque Terre were simply a ruse. The less the likes of Mandy in the office and others knew about the real financial transactions going on between Red and myself, the better. Commissions were paid into our company and in turn, duly paid out. Ethelred has made me a lot of money over the past few years and anything I invested with him, has paid for itself ten times over. You may not think it at the moment, but with "Still Life" and its companion exhibitions, we stand to make millions.' Miles played his trump card. 'In my agreement with Ethelred regarding "Still Life," you stand to receive five million pounds sterling which will be paid into an account already set up for you in Switzerland. You are, in fact, Byro, at this very moment of time, a millionaire in your own right.' He added softly. 'I was planning to surprise you with this err... little windfall but not quite like this.'

Bryan looked up at Miles, blinking through his drying tears. 'You've done all that for me?' he whispered.

'Yes, Bryo, for you, Now, from what I can see the subject is closed. Forget what you saw tonight and let us simply get on with our lives.' Miles topped up their champagne flutes. 'There, you see I *told* you champagne would be a good idea! To us Bryo. To us, to The Grove, to Dossetto, Dongi and Skavi and again, to Ethelred and Clyte who – if you only but knew it – think you the greatest thing on two legs!'

If Miles's last remark was unintentional, the remark did not go unheeded by Bryan. Toasting their future with a weak smile, inwardly he was seething and filled with a repulsion of such magnitude, he almost snapped the stem of the champagne flute. 'To us, Milo,' he managed to say, giving Miles a weak smile.

After a subdued breakfast the two drove in their separate cars to Berkeley Square where they parked in their permanent spaces in a nearby car park. 'Bellamy's one o'clock?' said Miles with a smile as they strode past the elegant bandstand set in the centre of the legendary square.

'Great.' said Bryan, his face breaking into a typical Bryan grin. 'Catch you there. I've got one or two things to deal with regarding *Bella Italia* and then I want to pop in to Sotheby's to view one or two items on next week's sale. Say good morning to the lovely Mandy for me.'

'Will do.' The two stood silently in the lift until the third floor when Bryan stepped out. Giving Miles a quick peck on the cheek he headed for his office while Miles took the lift up to the top floor. Waiting for a few moments, Bryan made his way down the main stairs and back out into Berkeley Square. Hailing a cab he clambered into it saying to the driver, 'Invicta Gallery, Islington, just near the Green.'

———

'Red, Miles.' Miles nodded his thanks to the steaming cup of coffee handed to him by a smiling Mandy Mashona Making a camp, shooing motion at the giggling woman while pointing to the phone and mouthing 'My other lover!' he waved her out of his office.

'Miles!' Ethelred's anxious voice came echoing over the static. 'How did it go?'

'Like a wet dream,' laughed Miles, 'slightly messy, the tears I mean, but apart from that, he swallowed the story about Oswald's gentle demise and especially the letter, hook line and sinker! Your genius of invention never fails to astound me! Any former feelings or loyalty regarding the whoring little shit have been well and truly scuppered. But, fuck it, Red! The tattoo? How on *earth* did Charles and Clyte miss the fucking thing?'

'Just one of those bloody unfortunate things,' murmured Ethelred. He gave a hollow laugh. 'You should have seen the reaction from Clyte when I told her what had happened. Poor Charles is probably still recovering!'

'And the leg?'

'"Operation Blemish" duly completed. A bit of latex and body paint and aforesaid tattoo committed to the ether! But getting back to Bryan?'

'The thought of his lover being had up as an accomplice concerning the murder of *two* completely irrelevant derelicts who were druggies to boot, plus the added bait of a cool five million in a Swiss bank account, seem to have done wonders in creating a watertight case of complete and utter amnesia!'

'Where is he now?'

'In his office. Why?'

'Just curious.'

'I do love him, you know.'

'I know that, Miles. I only hope the love is reciprocal.' Ethelred hung up.

———————

Bryan walked past the empty cinema – he had been informed at the entrance kiosk the two showings for later that day had been sold out, as were the showings for the next three weeks – but the current video room, painting and tableau exhibitions were open. Ignoring the paintings, Bryan made his way determinedly though to the tableau room. Quickly examining the incriminating leg, he gave a grim smile on noting every sign of the tattoo had now been obliterated. The formidable guide ropes to the tableau made it impossible to reach across in an attempt to try rubbing the newly covered spot where the tattoo should have been. Turning from the posed legs, Bryan turned his attention to the naked, half-figure of the seated man.

Checking to make sure he was unobserved, Bryan – reaching for his mobile – took several shots of the figure, concentrating on the head. His mission complete, Bryan left the hall and made his way to the Underground, bound for Green Park Station. Several minutes later he was back in his office, the whole exercise having taken less than an hour. Bryan had just removed his jacket and sat himself down at his desk, a few scribbled sketches of the Italian house in front of him, when Miles, unannounced, walked in. 'Ah, there you are!' he said rather fatuously.

'Why, where else would I be?' laughed Bryan. 'The Square's no good for cruising at this time of the day!'

'Touché! I know we said lunch at one but Maddy Behar has just called. She and Robin are here from Monte for a few days and – to quote the poor thing – holed up at Claridges. She's asked us for a drink at noon. I said yes, but couldn't vouch for you as you were planning some treasure hunt at Sotheby's.'

'I adore Maddy. Sotheby's can wait but she certainly can't!'

'Right! I'll call by at about five to twelve?'

'See you then, Miles.' Bryan blew a soft kiss. 'Love you Miles Anstruther!'

'Love you too, Bryan *Scima*-Anstruther!'

Giving Miles time to take the lift and get back into his office Bryan, downloaded his mobile into his computer. Seconds later several print-offs of the seated figure were lying on his desk. Zooming into one frame Bryan enlarged the face of the half figure and printed several in turn. Taking up a black felt tipped pen, he carefully superimposed shorter black hair onto the half face. Darkening the bleached eyebrow he sat back to admire his handy work. 'Yes! Yes! It may have only been once but that's more-or-less how I remember the hair!' Reaching into one of the drawers to his desk, he pulled out a small hand mirror which he kept, along with a comb. Placing the mirror down alongside the newly embellished half face, he looked at the full image. 'Well, Mr. Mystery Man,' he said out loud, 'That clinches it! I certainly think I know who you are, but I need someone to doubly confirm this. If I'm not mistaken, and I'm pretty sure I'm not, it's going to be both a horror and pleasure to meet you again Dave, for Mr. "Still Life" is, as far as I'm concerned, you!'

Bryan sat back in his chair and stared thoughtfully at the empty desk top. But who would recognize and confirm this *was* indeed Dave? Bryan realised while *he* was convinced it was the young man from the dinner party, it had been some time ago and possibly his mind was *willing* him to recognise the sculpture as the departed gardener. Who? Who? He pondered. There must be a way, there must be someone? Bryan, racking his brains furiously, sat staring at the window at the autumnal trees viewable in the Square. I can't really ring the house and ask Ethelred or Clytemnestra the name of his former employees. Shit! Shit! Shit! He now sat tapping a pencil against the blotter on his desk. 'The maid!' he suddenly cried out loud. 'That's it. The lovely Viola! She'll know! She's sure to know but the question is how does one get in touch with her?'

'Ready?'

'Oh Miles! Yes, sorry I was just talking to myself.'

'First signs Bryo! First signs!'

'Not quite Miles. C'mon. Let's go and flirt outrageously with the glamorous and very rich Mrs. Behar!'

Later that afternoon Bryan left the office on the pretext of doing some late afternoon shopping at Chelsea Green. 'Rex said he was getting in some lobsters so I thought a couple of those this evening and a DVD?' he said to Miles on leaving Bellamy's restaurant, 'Any preference for a movie?'

'As long as its smooch and yuck making, no!'

'Good, I'll see if I can get out *Mama Mia* from the library. I know it's old hat but the songs are great and we can dance around the kitchen with our lobsters!'

'Sounds like a pure lobster tail to me!'

'*That*, Miles Anstruther, was truly pathetic! See you back at the flat!'

Prior to visiting Rex and Michael at the fishmongers on Chelsea Green, Bryan made a detour to Snappy Snaps in the nearby Kings Road. He had the left half of the doctored face to be professional enhanced into an inverted image, and attached to the original to make a full face. Once this had been done, Bryan had made several copies of the full face. 'Handsome bugger, weren't you?' he said to the unsmiling portrait as he grimly put the new pictures into a large envelope. Meanwhile, the solution to the problem regarding a meeting Viola had been easily resolved. During the course of the ensuing weekend, Bryan, as planned, duly brought up the subject of Bethlem Báthory and the forthcoming Enchanted Forest evening.

'How's all that coming along?' he asked Mrs. Turnbull, the cook, while getting himself a glass of milk from the fridge. Mrs. Turnbull who was well-known to use the smallest of excuses to stop what she was doing to exchange in exchange for a bit of gossip, paused in the middle of peeling a potato and said, 'Strange you should ask about that, Mr. Bryan; that Dave who was there, suddenly up and leavin' like he did! Mrs. Norelle, my sister, tells me that they now 'ave some la di da firm down from London finishing it off. Costing a small fortune I hear an' they're *still* behind schedule! They've even 'ad to rope in some local help. That Viola's fiancé for example, 'e's even giving a hand!'

'Viola's fiancé?'

'Yes, that Clive. Lovely lad he is! They'll make a lovely couple.' Mrs. Turnbull's voice took on a wistful note. 'So young and so in love; makes one warm all over.'

More concerned about meeting the lovely young couple as to Mrs. Turnbull's feelings, Bryan asked as nonchalantly as he could. 'Is this Clive a gardener then?'

'Oh good 'eavens no! 'Is family own the best 'ardware store in Windsor, just off the 'Igh Street. Make a pretty penny they do!' She gave a laugh. 'That Viola! When she's not working at the big 'ouse she's always giving a 'elpin' 'and at the shop. Wednesday's always 'er day off and you can bet your bottom dollar you'll find 'er there making eyes at her Clive and vice versa!'

'Thanks for the milk, Mrs. T. You're a real Miss Marple or Jessica Fletcher!' laughed Bryan, leaving the startled woman to return to her potatoes.

The following Wednesday Bryan, on the pretext of spending the day at the sales – he had told Miles he would be visiting both Sotheby's in Bond Street and possibly Bonhams in Lots Road – caught the mid-morning train to Windsor. Fifteen minutes after his arrival Bryan was browsing in the aforesaid hardware shop.

'Mr. Bryan?' A smiling Viola appeared at his elbow. 'I thought it was you!'

'It's Olivia, isn't it?' said Bryan smiling back at the girl, who flushed with pleasure at being recognised by one of her heroes.

'No, but good try though!' She gave a giggle. 'It's *Viola*! And what brings you to Windsor and to our shop in the middle of the week, if I may ask?'

'You may indeed. Thing is, I was supposed to meet someone at the Christopher Wren House hotel for a mid-morning appointment, but that's now been cancelled. On walking past the shop – I had no idea it was yours, by the way! – I remembered we need a pair of secateurs for London; so here I am!'

'Oh, well let me help.' She turned towards a shelf, only to be interrupted by a handsome young man who called out a cheery, 'Good morning, sir!' as he entered the shop carrying a pile of boxes. 'Gloves Vil,' he cried, 'Stacks and stacks of gloves as ordered by that lot at Castle Dracula!'

'Oh!' said Viola, going an even deeper pink. 'Clive, this is Mr. Bryan, Sir Miles's err… friend. He needs a pair of secateurs!'

'Ah, the lucky man!' chuckled Bryan. On noting the puzzled expressions on the young couple's faces, he added mischievously. 'Mrs. Turnbull has told me all about the two of you!' he laughed. 'There are no secrets between The Grove and Bethlem Báthory, what with those two sisters never off the phone!' He gave another, broader smile. 'Congratulations, by the way!'

While the two were giggling and murmuring their 'thank yous,' Bryan gave a quick glance at his watch and, as if inspired, said. 'I know it's probably totally out of the question, but as my meeting is no longer and I have some time before my train back to London, may I treat you both to a celebratory drink apropos your forthcoming wedding?'

'Why, that would be great!' laughed Clive before Viola could get a word in. 'I'll just tell Mum! Do her good to earn some of her extravagant keep for once!'

Within minutes the three were happily seated in a nearby pub, Viola daringly ordering a glass wine while Clive ordered a pint for himself and a large vodka tonic for Bryan. Bryan, having asked Clive if he wouldn't mind getting their order – 'I can see you're well-known here!' – while tactfully handing over a twenty pound, sat himself down next to the smiling girl. 'Viola,' he said, 'do you mind if I ask you to try and solve a small riddle for me?'

'Of course not, that's if I can,' said the young girl, still smiling.

'You remember Dave, the gardener?'

'Oh yes, lovely young man. Sad he suddenly had to leave like that.'

'I only met him the once, at dinner. But maybe *you* can tell me.' Bryan took the now skilfully enhanced photograph from out of his briefcase. 'This is someone who recently sent in his pic to us hoping for some work as a model in one of our promotion videos. It's not a very good photo but I could have sworn it was Dave, only this guy has given his name as Denzil; unless, of course, that's his professional name.'

'Dave a model and calling himself Denzil? Well I never! He did have the looks though, and I kept telling him he should be doing something with himself, other than gardening!' Viola gave a small conspiratorial giggle. 'Don't tell Clive, but I saw him once with his shirt off. Just like one of those sexy jeans advert, he was!' With a mischievous smile she laid the photograph down on the small drinks table, reaching up to collect her drink from the beaming Clive.

'You mean that *is* Dave?'

'Oh yes,' said Viola taking a dainty sip, 'Pity about the dye job. Dave the rave had really *gorgeous* blond hair!'

CHAPTER 25

'Good morning! Consortium Travel. How may I help you?'

'Good morning. Geoff Masters, please?'

'Whom may I say is calling?'

'Bryan err… Bryan Anstruther.'

'Hold on, please Mr. Anstruther.' There was a moment's pause before the call was put through.

'Masters!'

'Geoff, it's Bryan, Bryan Scima!'

'Jesus Bryan! How the devil are you?' the question being followed by a warm laugh. 'What are you up to? You wicked, wicked young man!'

'Well, avoiding blowing the boss for starters!'

'Unfortunate boss, he doesn't know what he's missing!' Geoff's voice took on a more sober tone. 'Jesus, Bryan. I'm sorry about all that. I would have been in touch but you seemed to disappear.

'Like someone else, I know,' muttered Bryan.

'Sorry?'

'Just talking to myself Geoff; see it as a new habit in-between blow jobs!'

'Unfortunate again – talking to yourself as opposed to giving blow jobs.' Geoff gave a lewd chuckle. 'You were bloody good!'

'I need some info Geoff.'

'Oh oh, not blackmail time, is it?'

'Hardly, Geoff, seeing the whole office seemed to know about our indiscretion!' Bryan gave a hollow laugh. 'No, I need to contact that lawyer friend of yours; the one who hit the headlines year before last with that trial involving the minister and his attempt to have his wife murdered. It was a pretty good defence but your guy won, and the wife is now living the life of Riley in Palm Beach while wicked hubby is learning to make baskets!'

'Why, planning to have *your* husband murdered this time? I take it you're the wife?'

Bryan burst out laughing. For all his faults Geoff Masters was a loveable rogue. 'Consider it one of the great tragedies in your life, you never got to know whether I was a top or a bottom!' he quipped.

'A mere travel agency manager can dream, can't he?' Geoff gave another laugh. 'In answer to your question his name is Richard, Richard Hawkins. If you hold on a mo I'll get you his number.' There was a sound of papers being shuffled, interspersed with several 'Fucks,' before he returned to the phone. 'Here you are and, Bryan, talking about coincidences, I'm meeting Rich for a drink later. Care to join us?'

'Sorry, no can do, Geoff. However, I do need to talk to Richard Hawkins, so I'll do that right away. I take it he *is* the best when it's something particularly unsavoury?'

'The best!' There was another pause before Geoff asked in a curious tone, 'Are you in some sort of trouble Bryan? Problem is, Rich has them queuing and he's bloody, bloody expense.'

'And I, Geoff, just happen to be bloody, bloody rich but I don't think this will be costing me a penny! Thanks for the number. Cheers!' Before Geoff could say another word Bryan hung up.

———————

'Richard Hawkins Associates.'

'Good morning. My name is Bryan Scima. It's imperative I see Mr. Hawkins today!'

———————

A grim-faced Ethelred turned towards Clytemnestra who lay looking sleepily at him. 'That was Victor,' he whispered. 'The police have just raided the gallery, seized a copy of the film and absconded with most of the tableau exhibits!'

'*What*?' With a piercing shriek, Clytemnestra sat bolt upright, her eyes filled with terror. 'What do you mean the police have *raided the gallery*? How can they? On whose authority?'

'That's what I mean to find out.' Throwing aside the duvet Ethelred pulled his lean, naked body from the bed and, reaching for his dressing gown lying on a nearby chair, pulled it on while tying the belt in a deceptively calm manner. 'I'm going down to my study,' he said, striding towards the door. 'Get Charles to join us there. *Now*!'

A scowling Ethelred sat glaring at an ashen-faced Charles and a pale-faced Clytemnestra. 'I've just spoken to Victor again. It's almost impossible to get any sense out of him as the fucking queen was completely incoherent. *What* I have managed to glean from the gibbering cunt is there's been an official complaint about the contents of the film and – I quote – "the disturbing elements regarding some the tableaus."' He let out a roar, causing the two to jump. 'I've never *heard* such bullshit! This is two thousand and thirteen for fuck's sake! Not the fucking Dark Ages!'

'I can understand them seizing the film but why the components to the tableaus?' questioned Clytemnestra. 'Oh my God,' she whispered, 'Oh my God!'

'Exactly,' snarled her husband. 'A movie can be explained, special effects and all that crap! But those figures? Jesus fucking sodding Christ! If they are even remotely examined we're up shit's creek with a capital, fucking neon lit S!' He looked at Clytemnestra. 'Get a few things together. I'll get our passports and sort out some cash. We can get the early Eurostar to Paris. Charles, you stay here and, should the police pay us a visit – which they will – as far as you know we're abroad indefinitely. Say we're on a recce in Germany or somewhere. Anywhere! Give us a day or two and we'll be in touch.'

'Where *are* you going?'

'At the moment, Charlie boy, I have no idea. All I do know is that we're out of here!'

'What do I tell the others?'

'Tell them nothing Charles. Let them face the consequences. They – like you – knew exactly what they were getting into!' Turning to Clytemnestra who had remained seated, he gave a roar. 'For fuck's sake move your fucking butt Clyte! Unless you're planning on spending the rest of your days in Holloway, or some other equally luxurious venue!'

'What about *me*?' wailed Charles.

'Yes, what about you, Charles?' hissed Ethelred dismissively. Giving the cowering doctor a disgusted look, he turned and strode from the room.

———

'Do you really have to go to Italy today?' A puzzled Miles stood looking as Bryan zipped up the small shoulder bag.

'*Non ti preoccupare*! Do not worry, my love. It's only that *Signorina* Antonia is throwing one of her hissy fits over something to do with the new pool complex. Poor Giles, how he copes with that neurotic cow at times completely baffles me!'

'Maybe the *Signorina* has a mega *pene*?'

'Well, even if her *pene* was as big as that fucking Tower of Pisa, it still wouldn't be enough as far as I'm concerned!'

'I'll see you for dinner tomorrow then?'

'You're on and this time, the Rib Room, not Scalinis! After the *Signorina* and her *pene* the thought of an Italian restaurant and the other *penne* would be too much!'

'Love you, Bryan Scima-Anstruher!'

'Love you too, Miles.' Giving the big, buff man a long, cold stare, Bryan walked out from the flat.

'Jesus, now what was that all about?' muttered Miles as he reached absentmindedly for the ringing phone. 'Miles Anstruther,' he barked.

'Miles? Charles, Charles Crosby from Bathlem Báthory. I think there's something you should know.'

Several minutes later a stunned Miles was still seated by the phone. 'You fucking little Judas!' he hissed at the silent room, 'You fucking, poisonous, two-faced little bastard!'

Picking up the telephone he dialled the office in Dossetto. 'Giles? Good morning, Miles. I've had a bit of a domestic panic with one of the dogs here. Stupid Savi has gone and got himself run over by a delivery van of all things! Could you ask Bryan to call me when he arrives? The dog's alright but you know Bryan, if he wasn't told *immediately* about one of his precious babies being involved in an accident, he'll go ape shit and there's only so much a guy can afford from Tiffany's!' Miles gave a self-deprecating laugh. 'What? What do you mean he's not expected? But he told me Anthony had some problems with the pool complex. Anthony's in *Florence with his* mother? I see. Obviously I've got it wrong. Sorry to disturb you, err… Giles.' Miles slowly put the phone down, his face dark with fury. 'Miles Anstruther,' he growled, 'I think you'd better call your lawyer. As for you, Bryan Scima you'd better be praying to God – for your own sake – I don't ever fucking find you! No matter *what* happens, I'll make bloody sure I do, and if you thought what happened to your Oswald was bad, you haven't seen anything yet!'

———————

Within days the scandal surrounding Ethelred and Clytemnestra Jones had become worldwide news. Sightings of the couple came from as far afield as Australia and even Namibia. Charles, along with Monday, had been duly arrested on charges of murder, accomplices to murder and perverting the course of justice. Ghoulish disclosures about the genuine body parts as used in the exhibition, plus the confirmation that the death scenes in the film 'Still Life' had *not* been staged, led to a tsunami of black market sales of the DVD from a copy of film made by the wily Kochno.

Perhaps the most shocking disclosure of all was the exposé of Trisomy; Ethelred and Clytemnestra's brilliantly fabricated, and acted out story of their 'little girl,' turning out to be one of the greatest scams of the decade.

Trisomy, it was discovered, was in fact Patricia Metelé, an elderly West Indian voodooist, befriended and brought to England by Ethelred and Clytemnestra after their honeymoon spent touring the various islands of the Caribbean. Her skills at playacting had been paramount, as had her skills in helping Charles, which had been genuine. A typical example of her skill in the use of magical potions or pastes created from various plants had been evident by only slightest of scarring on Mrs. Norelle's arm, after the voodooist had deliberately cut this in an experiment.

Monday's story was more accurate. However, his penchant for hallucinatory drugs had been skilfully manipulated by both Trisomy – aka Patricia Metelé – and Charles. Monday eventually began to believe he actually *was* Priapus, the 'God of Lust and Fertility' and, according to a wistful and wishful Charles, Monday like Priapus, did boast 'a huge and constantly erect phallus!'

What Charles had never disclosed was his total horror on discovering Monday – his muse and ultimate fantasy – being given regular blow jobs by a rapacious Patricia Metelé in the privacy of their 'special' greenhouse. Having thought that Monday had been taking advantage of a child when the recipient of his mega organ was, in reality, a willing sixty five year old woman, Charles's original feelings had slowly changed from wistful and wishful to one of revulsion. This had increased on witnessing another incident in which he had found a grunting, heaving, sweating, panting and bug-eyed Monday, fucking the corpse of Hettie Van Niekerk before she had been dismembered.

Miles considered himself lucky. Strongly denying any knowledge as to what his so-called legitimate investments with Ethelred's film company construed – he had, in all good faith, invested in several of the director's films before – and due to the lack of evidence, any actions against him were subsequently dismissed. To Miles's surprise his involvement in the 'scandal of the decade' saw his business going from strength to strength. Flushed with new successes, Miles only chagrin was in his thwarted attempts to buy Bethlem Báthory with an eye to turning it into a theme park.

'You watch me,' he would tell Peter and Melanie Peebles who, after the scandal, had made sure they reinstated their relationship with the now much sought after 'celebrity baronet.' 'You watch me,' he would say. 'One day I'll get possession of that place and I promise you, the Chamber of Horrors at Madam Tussauds will be a mere Piss Pot of Horrors to what I'll be able to give the public!'

Of Ethelred and Clytemnestra there was no sign. Unlike their victims, Hettie, Dirk, Oswald and Dave who had – in their own bizarre ways – never quite disappeared, the director and his wife literally vanished.

Bryan, on departure from the flat in Cadogan Square that fateful morning, had made his was directly to Heathrow and taken the first available flight to Marrakech. Having spent several days prior to in the company of Richard Hawkins and a battery of police officers, Bryan had been permitted to leave the country, but was on call to return should his presence be required.

'Maybe you're not even in bloody Marrakech, Paul,' he kept muttering to himself during the course of the flight, thankful the seat next to him was empty so he could indulge in his romantic fantasies and musings without any strange glances or interruptions of attempted conversation. As a buffer against any disappointments at not finding his ultimate goal, Bryan had already made a reservation at the luxurious five star La Mamounia Hotel. 'In for a penny, in for a pound,' he said on reserving a suite. Within hours of Miles's confirmation of the Swiss account and the relevant number, Bryan had in turn contacted the bank. A London representative had met up with the young man, and happily agreed to a transfer of a substantial amount to a further account immediately set up in Monaco. 'The two-faced, conniving, bastard can try and claim his money back, but I doubt if he'll stand a chance,' Bryan told Richard Hawkins. 'But whatever happens, with what I've stashed away in Monaco, I'm set for life!'

Having checked into his luxurious suite, Bryan had taken a long, scented bath and having dressed, made his way along to one of the hotel's five glamorous bars. Unbeknown to Miles, Bryan had sent a packed suitcase to the hotel two days ahead of his arrival. Though expecting five star treatment, Bryan was delighted to find his case unpacked and his clothes put away. Clad in a cream, light weight silk jacket, pale blue shirt and dark trousers, he looked the epitome of style and success as he made his way the first of the exotic five hotel bars. Ordering a champagne cocktail he cast a cursory eye around the other guests, before settling on an elegant group seated on a series of low stools in a shadowy corner.

'No, it can't be! I can't go on having such good luck but I *swear* that's Paul!' Bryan's prolonged staring was soon picked up by a tall, thin white-haired man who, on catching Bryan's stare, returned this with a bold, imperious look, before registering a double take, and excitedly tapping the young man sitting with his back to Bryan. Paul turned his head briefly to catch a look at the person causing such consternation. To Bryan's relief Paul's face lit up with a biggest, warmest, most genuine smile Bryan had ever seen.

'I don't *believe* it!' came the cry. 'Bryo! Bryan Scima. What the *H* are you doing here in Marrakech!?'

Leaping to his feet he rushed over to Bryan, clasping him in a warm hug. 'God, I don't believe this!' he whispered into Bryan's ear. 'You're here, you're actually here!' Stepping back, still holding Bryan in his long, strong arms, Paul whispered. 'I love you, Scima! I've loved you since that first Martini in The Botanist and this time, Miles or no Miles, I'm not letting you go! Oh my God!' Looking aghast at Bryan, Paul managed to utter. 'But of course, he's here with you!'

'No Paul,' said Bryan, laughing and his eyes streaming with tears of happiness. 'No, I'm here, for *you!*'

'Ahem!'

Bryan looked away from Bryan's sparkling eyes to the elderly man standing alongside them.

'I take it you know each other?' the white-haired man said drily. 'Maybe you'll introduce me to your friend, Paulie, and maybe he'd care to join us for a drink?'

'Oh, Goddie! Forgive me.' Turning back to a silent Bryan Paul said proudly, 'Goddie, this is Bryo, the guy I've never stopped talking about!'

'That God for small mercies – or in your case Bryo – for delicious mercies!' chortled Godfrey, 'Now you're here in the flesh, perhaps I can have some peace and get back to finishing a book I'm working on.' He gave Bryan a warm smile. 'Now, come along, come and meet some new friends. I take it you're planning to stay in Marrakech for some time?

Dinner over, Godfrey and his two other guests made their excuses, finally leaving the two young men sitting together in the bar to 'have a night cap and catch up' as he tactfully put it.

'Is it alright, you staying on here with me?' Bryan had asked as he watched the three leaving the bar.

'Why, have you something else planned for this evening?' asked Paul mischievously.

'Of course not, but I thought you and err... Goddie, were... you know, an item?'

'Oh, we're an item alright,' laughed Paul, 'Goddie's pure magic. A totally eccentric old goat who – for some strange reason known to countless others! – adores and worships me, but gives me a free rein. As long as I play peeny weenys and the occasional spouty woutys, it's fine! *Maison Godfrey* is now my home and Goddie is one in a million. For all his camp and theatrics he's a well-known authority on contemporary Moroccan art, and is currently researching a book on two selected artists.'

'I didn't realise there was such a thing?'

'As what?'

'Contemporary Moroccan art!'

'Don't be such a Phillistine, Byro! There are some brilliant modern Moroccan artists around. When we get to the house tomorrow, I'll get Goddie to give you a guided tour of some of his favourites. You'll probably still be there this time next week!'

'What do you mean by when *we* get to the house tomorrow?'

'Well, you don't think I'm turning down a first, do you? I've never as yet – hopefully up until now – ever been fucked in La Mamounia!'

'Well, as they say, there's always a first time so... shall we?'

After three days – 'It took me only two!' Paul would keep reminding him – Bryan was invited by Godfrey to take up residence in the house.

Bryan found himself transported into what he could only describe as pure Paradise. Not only did his relationship with Paul go from strength to strength, but their relationship was eagerly encouraged by Godfrey. While

Godfrey's first tentative suggestion to a threesome had been greeted by Bryan with some alarm, it soon became a regular weekly event, Godfrey wallowing and swallowing in delight with his – to quote the smiling, elderly man – 'two Ganymedes!' his reference being to the most beautiful young man in Greek mythology.

'Your *Zeus* is our command!' had been Bryan's instant riposte at Godfrey's mythological observation.

'Oh my!' the old man had sighed. 'That was brilliant, Bryo, quite, quite brilliant. Zeus spoken in lieu of wish! Quite, quite enchanting. I now know I'm going to love you two boys until the day I die!'

Paul had been both shocked and appalled over the events surrounding Bethlem Báthory. However, he showed no surprise at the exposé of Trisomy. 'I spotted that from the moment I inadvertently met her and given the finger.' He had given a sharp laugh at his jest. 'I'll explain that little gem later. In retrospect it was all so bloody obvious, if only one had simply had the nous to put two and two together!'

'Well, as the saying goes, all's well that ends well, and I can see us slumming it here for many years ahead!'

Godfrey had insisted on making both young men the beneficiaries of his will. 'There's a nice little Fabergé egg tucked away – not literally but I hate the word *nest*! – and the houses are yours' he would repeatedly say. 'As long as I know my Ganymedes are secure, then I'm happy.'

Bryan and Paul would endlessly remind themselves of their good fortune, the security of Marrakech plus the several millions in Monaco simply sitting there are earning interest.

It was several months later that Godfrey, on his way to meet friends at his favourite La Mamounia, had collapsed and died of a severe stroke in the street outside the front door of the house. A saddened Paul and Bryan had watched the old man being cremated in a simple, low-key private ceremony. The irony was not missed by Bryan when Paul insisted on carrying him over the threshold to the house following the cremation ceremony.

———

'I thought I'd go up to the Medina and get a few magazines!' Bryan, clad in a pair of loose cotton slacks and an intricately embroidered shirt that had been a favourite of Godfrey's, gave Paul a dazzling smile, his blue eyes sparking from within his dark tan.

'God, you look beautiful!' sighed Paul. 'If it's true we're doubles, I may even have to have a wank imagining I'm doing it with you!'

'Perfect!' laughed Bryan. He looked down at the paper covered desk. 'How's it going?'

'Slowly, very slowly but fascinating.' Paul tapped a brightly coloured illustration with his finger. 'When Goddie started explaining the ins and outs of these modern Moroccan artists I didn't, for one second, imagine I'd ever get hooked and now look at me, taking over – in a very, very limited fashion – of where the maestro left off!' He gave a small laugh. 'Stick around Byro. I should have this finished by twenty-twenty!'

'I certainly trust it'll be before then!' Bryan gave a laugh, ruffling Paul's thick, black glossy hair. 'Lunch at the usual? One o'clock?'

'See you there!'

'Don't be late!'

'On my cock's honour!'

Bryan, a copy of a two day old Herald Tribune spread over most of the small table in front of him, sat sipping an iced local beer. He was just about to turn a page when a shadow fell across the paper.

'Hello Byro,' said a familiar, deep voice. 'Remember me? In fact, remember us?'

His face paling beneath his tan Bryan, looked up to see Miles, Ethelred and Clytemnestra smiling down at him.

'Surprise! Surprise!' cooed Clytemnestra.

'Lights! Camera! Action!' smirked Ethelred.

'Walkies! Walkies!' suggested Miles.

The mysterious disappearance of the young Englishman from his table outside a small street cafe close to the Medina was soon forgotten. The waiter, when questioned had said yes, Monsieur Bryan had been there – he and Paul were well-known and favourite customers of the small restaurant – but had suddenly left with three friends, two men and a woman. On being questioned as to how the waiter knew they were friends, the man replied simply, 'because each of the men had him by an arm.' The fact that the bill had been left unpaid had not caused any concern as Monsieur Bryan 'had been expecting Monsieur Paul.'

Paul was to live on in Morocco, later to become, no doubt, another eccentric recluse. The four people seen by the waiter leaving the Medina, were never seen again. However, Bryan's money, transferred from Monaco to Morocco into a joint account, remains untouched with Paul a firm believer that one day his true love will return.

———————

News of the continuing success of the new, sensational Argentinian film director, Eduardo El Greco, and his stunning, socialite wife, the artist Dolores Del Moreno, never reached the sheltered environs of Marrakech; nor did the continuing success of a new, luxury residential golf complex, *Naturaleza Muerta* – Spanish for *Still Life* – the brain-child of an Englishman, Bertrand 'Lucky' Lawrence, and financed by El Greco.

The End

ABOUT THE AUTHOR

ROBIN ANDERSON is an internationally known interior designer and author. Born in Scotland he was brought up in the former Southern Rhodesia (now Zimbabwe) and South Africa. Before attending Rhodes University (the Oxford of South Africa!), he hosted his own radio programme in Rhodesia ("The Golden Voice of Teenage Half Hour!") and worked as a cub reporter on the Bulawayo Chronicle in his Gap Year.

Leaving South Africa he spent the early Sixties working with interior design companies in Paris and London before setting up his own London-based company in 1970. Although interior design was his main interest, the designer never stopped writing. Nowadays he a popular guest lecturer with venues ranging from private literary evenings and luncheons plus being invited as a guest speaker at The South Bank, Royal Festival Hall, London.

His first novel REGINA published in 1998 (now updated, "up-bitched" and available on AMAZON Kindle) gives a salacious look "behind the scenes" of the glamorous, but bitchy world, competitive world of interior design. This was followed by a ten year "fallow" period when, due to an accident on a building site in 2007, ROBIN found himself hospitalised for several months. "I wasn't at all ill," he recounts, "but pretty smashed up and apart from my arms and upper torso, was in a plaster cast. It was out of pure frustration I wrote RED SNAPPER, a dark-humoured, *chiller thriller.*"

Since publishing RED SNAPPER – including this and REGINA – the author has published twenty one novels to date plus three volumes of short stories (THIRTEEN TALES OF TEXTUAL AROUSAL, Volumes 1, 2 and 3) and three children's books under the name of ROBERT ANDERSON.

ROBIN is a strong believer in the protection of endangered species and in 1959 took part in the international event, *"Operation Noah,"* which saw the rescue of hundreds of wild animals from the rising waters of the Kariba Dam, built across the mighty Zambezi River in the north-western part of Zimbabwe.

In contrast to the above, he also helped with the salvaging of precious works and manuscripts in Florence, Italy, during the mid-Sixties when the River Arno burst its banks and flooded the ancient city.

An inveterate traveller – a factor which becomes apparent from the varied settings for his novels – such places such as The Amazon, The Yucatan, Borneo, Myanmar, China, Russia, Japan, Sri Lanka, Egypt, Israel, Morocco, Kenya, Australia, Mauritius, North and South America, Canada , Central Europe; most of the Mediterranean countries and last but not least, the Caribbean Islands, have all been visited. ROBIN has walked the Inca Trail in Peru; climbed Mount Kinabalu in Borneo and made a "disastrous attempt" at climbing Kilimanjaro – "Whereby *hangs* another tale!"

In between his travels ROBIN lives in a spectacular apartment in London's exclusive Chelsea. He also maintains a small hideaway in a fourteenth century village in Italy set high in the spectacular Cinque Terre, overlooking the Mediterranean, east of Portofino.

"Have vivid imagination, will write and will travel!" is his mantra.

www.robinanderson-author.com